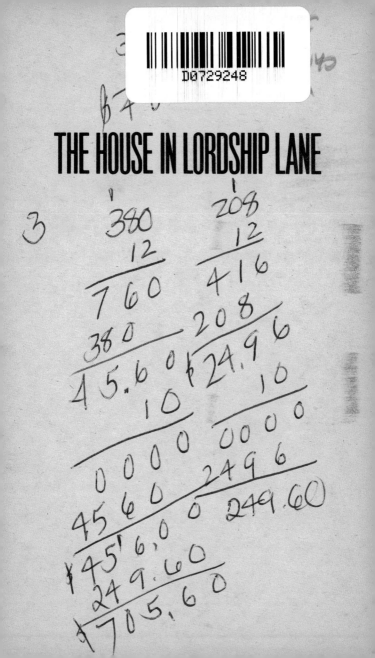

THE HOUSE IN LORDSHIP LANE

Books by A.E.W. Mason
Published by Carroll & Graf

They Wouldn't be Chessmen
The Prisoner in the Opal
At the Villa Rose
The House of the Arrow

THE HOUSE IN LORDSHIP LANE

A. E. W. Mason

Carroll & Graf Publishers, Inc.
New York

Copyright © 1946 by A.E.W. Mason

First Carroll & Graf edition 1985

Carroll & Graf Publishers, Inc.
260 Fifth Avenue
New York, NY 10001

ISBN: 0-88184-140-4

Manufactured in the United States of America

CONTENTS

CONTENTS

Chapter 1

MR. RICARDO IN BRITTANY

MR. RICARDO sat on an iron chair at an iron table outside a Bar and drank with his coffee a sweet and heady liqueur. Yet he was exhilarated. " Nobody would believe it," he said with a little giggle. But it was Brittany and summer time. " Browsing with Browning in Brittany," he alliterated wittily, " and so far I have been fortunate enough not to meet James Lee's wife." Mr. Ricardo was quite alone. He had sent his luggage home from Aix and with his suit-case, his fine big Rolls-Royce and his chauffeur was making a roundabout tour through Brittany to Cherbourg; whence by a transatlantic liner what was to him a preferable entry to England could be achieved. But the car had lurched and something had broken. For three days he must stay in this little town with the uncommon name. But his liner wasn't due at Cherbourg for four days—and it was Brittany and summer time.

Moreover, this drowsy little square of Lezardrieux, with the raised terrace at which he sat, the three sides of shops and houses and the empty fourth, where a steep cliff of sand and bushes dropped to the pool of the Lezardrieux river, made a sharp appeal to him. It was operatic. Below the brow of the hill, he could almost hear the conductor tap with his baton for attention. That boy in the bright red shirt strolling across the square might at any moment burst into song. But it would only have made an anti-climax if he had. For the stout, middle-aged woman who had waddled out from the Bar with a big letter in her hand was now at Mr. Ricardo's elbow.

" You gave my estaminet as your address at Lezard-rieux, sir ? "

" I telegraphed it," Mr. Ricardo agreed. " I had not yet found a lodging in the town."

" Then this letter is for you, perhaps. There is another English gentleman. . . ."

" Captain Mordaunt. Yes. He owns the small yacht in the Pool. Perhaps if you would let me see the letter, I could tell you for which of us it comes."

For the woman, in her desire that so unusual an occurrence as a letter should not miscarry, was clasping it tightly to her bosom. As she showed the face of it, Mr. Ricardo recognised the hand which had written it.

" It's for me," he cried with a little whoop of excitement. He snatched the envelope from her reluctant hand and tore it open. He read :

My dear friend,

I accuse the reception of your invitation . . ., and sat back, reflecting with toleration, " Yes, he would accuse something—it's his nature to—and I have no doubt that he has signed his name like a peer of England." He turned to the back of the letter. There it was. " *Hanaud* "—just " Hanaud "—the name of terror.

" Really, really," Mr. Ricardo said to himself and the smile of amusement passed from his lips.

After all, it was a year since he had invited Chief Inspector Hanaud of the Paris Sûreté to spend a holiday in Grosvenor Square. Hanaud could have accused the reception of his letter a year ago. But he had not accused it. He had kept it on the chance that he might want to accuse it at a later time. And the time had come.

" But I don't know," said Mr. Ricardo indignantly, as he turned to the lady of the estaminet. " It is Madame Rollard, is it not ? "

It certainly was Madame Rollard, as she assured him. But Mr. Ricardo was not thinking of Madame Rollard. He hit the offending letter with his knuckles.

" These are not manners."

" No ? "

" No."

" I do not keep a lodging house."

" No ? "

" Definitely no."

Madame Rollard shook her head as though she had fathomed his troubles, and at each shake her body wobbled like a jelly.

" I must consider," said Mr. Ricardo truculently.

" Yes, yes," said Madame. " There must be thought, and no doubt Calvados to encourage it " ; and she waddled back to her bar.

Over his second Calvados, Mr. Ricardo read the rest of Hanaud's letter, and one sentence in it dispersed all his irritation : " *Besides the holiday, there is a little thing I have to do, a little perplexity I have to make clear, in which I shall ask for your help*." The letter fluttered down upon Mr. Ricardo's knees, and he drew in a breath and his face lost ten years of its age. Those little perplexities ! Didn't he know them ? He would be insulted, ridiculed, outraged, baffled, humiliated, used. Yet there would be thrills, excitements, perils. Life would become once more a topaz instead of a turquoise. He would be helping to track great criminals to their doom. He and Hanaud, or, more probably, Hanaud and he.

Mr. Ricardo turned again to the letter ; and in a few moments sprang to his feet. Hanaud would travel by the Channel steamer to Dover to-morrow. He would reach London by five, Grosvenor Square by five-thirty. But here was Ricardo, marooned in Lezardrieux. He rushed to the Post Office and sent off a telegram to his housekeeper. If only he were volatile enough to travel on that same beam! There was a midnight ship from Havre, but he couldn't reach Havre. He came back into the square. Oh, he couldn't sit in that iron chair by that iron table for two more days and, frankly, however much enthusiasm for Brittany might have hidden the truth from him at the beginning, he did not like Calvados. In despair he walked to the edge of the square and looked down into the pool. There were fishing boats drawn up on the beach, fishing boats afloat at anchor, and amongst them—yes, undoubtedly—a small ketch yacht. The water in the pool was so deep that the ketch was moored close enough under the hill to escape a careless eye. But to Mr. Ricardo's envious gaze, the lustrous black paint of its sides, its white deck and burnished brass were as explicit as a dictionary.

" If I only owned it," cried Mr. Ricardo, noting, to be sure, how calm was the air and the sky how cloudless.

And lo! there was a stir upon the deck. The ketch was slowly beginning to swing her bows towards the sea. Three men clambered from the fo'c'sle, removed the covers from the sails and the wheel and pulled the dinghy in to the starboard side.

Mr. Ricardo looked over his shoulder and saw Captain Mordaunt walking across the square to the path which slanted down the sand cliff to the beach.

" Captain Mordaunt," he said, stepping to his side. Mr. Ricardo remembered him as a retired Captain of Grenadiers who passed from cocktail party to cocktail party but had no intimates ; a man dissatisfied, jealous, with a grudge against the world. But there was no sign of discontent about him now. His face had smoothed out, there was a smile upon his lips, a friendliness in his manner.

" Yes, Mr. Ricardo."

Ricardo looked down at the river. A hand was sculling the dinghy towards the beach.

"That is your ketch."

Mordaunt nodded his head.

"*Agamemnon*," he said with a laugh. "There was a time when trawler-owners fancied high-sounding names. I didn't change it when I bought her. But I added a bathroom."

"Very convenient," said Mr. Ricardo primly.

"Inevitable," returned Captain Mordaunt. "Agamemnon without a bathroom? He would be alive now."

Mr. Ricardo, whose acquaintance with the classics was limited, felt it prudent to titter. He added:

"You are crossing to England?"

Captain Mordaunt became wary. He looked at the sky; he looked at Mr. Ricardo.

"You would like a passage?"

"Yes."

Captain Mordaunt nodded his head.

"Well," he argued thoughtfully, "I have a spare cabin and the boat's sound and the weather looks good. But it's the fourth week in August and one can't count on it, and if it should come on to blow, these little ketches bounce about a bit, and we're very close to the water of course . . ."

Mr. Ricardo raised a deprecating hand.

"I am something of a yachtsman, too," he said with a smile; comrade to comrade, as it were.

Indeed, several times Mr. Ricardo had sailed out of and back into Brightlingsea harbour on the Dutch barge of a friend, and once, on a smooth clear day of June, he had made the ocean voyage from Ryde to Weymouth, but when he said that he was a yachtsman, he was undoubtedly exaggerating. Mordaunt rather obviously doubted but accepted it.

"All right," he said. "I can give you half an hour."

He looked at his watch. " At three the dinghy will be waiting for you."

" Thank you," and Mr. Ricardo hurried away to his lodging with a great show of pleasure.

But the pleasure was evaporating. Had he not, after all, been in a needless hurry ? Who was Hanaud that he could not be left to investigate by himself for a day ? There was no doubt he had been hasty. That was certainly a very small *Agamemnon* swinging round in the Pool, as Agamemnons go. Mr. Ricardo had a suspicion that Captain Mordaunt might have acquired greater merit if, instead of cramming a bathroom into this very small *Agamemnon*, he had bought a bigger *Agamemnon* with a bathroom in it already.

" Half an hour, Mr. Ricardo," had said Captain Mordaunt.

" Half an hour," Mr. Ricardo had repeated.

He gave instructions and money to his chauffeur, packed his suit-case, and was waiting on the beach when the nose of the dinghy grounded upon it.

Chapter 2

MEERSCHAUM

THE ketch, with her propeller turning, slipped down the ten miles of the Lezardrieux river between the buoys and the lighthouses, turned eastwards at the mouth to avoid the sunken slabs, and wriggled out into the open sea. A steady wind was blowing on her beam. The engine was switched off, the sails hoisted, the log run out, and the course laid for the Start. The land sank out of sight.

Captain Mordaunt followed Mr. Ricardo down to the spare cabin in the stern of the ketch.

"We will dine early, if you don't mind. There are only four of us all told, the skipper, the mate, the steward and myself, and at night we want two on deck when we are crossing the Channel, even if the night's fine. I can, by the way, lend you a thick coat and a yachting cap."

The first sign of any change came, indeed, when they were eating their dinner, side by side on the cushioned lounge in the little saloon. The ketch rose and dipped suddenly with a thud, as if it had met some unexpected swell of the sea and, a few moments later, the sheets of the mainsail rattled on the deck as the great wing of canvas was drawn in. Mordaunt looked up at the tell-tale compass fixed above his head.

"The wind has shifted to the north," he said.

The yachtsman of the quiet waters looked anxiously at his host. "Is that"—he searched for a word—"awkward?" he asked, hoping that the tremor was unnoticeable in his voice. After all, they were a very long way from the land.

Mordaunt shrugged his shoulders.

"Prolongs our passage. A cigar?" He reached for a box behind on the shelf. "Try those dates in brandy! We'll have some coffee," and he rang the hand-bell.

But whilst they drank their coffee, the movement of the ketch increased. To Mr. Ricardo she seemed now to hop forward and come down with a noisy crunch. Mordaunt smiled.

"There's some wind somewhere ahead of us," he said. "Let's go up and see. You had better put that thick coat on."

When they stepped from the tiny deck-house on to the deck, Mr. Ricardo was disturbed.

"Glary," said Hamlin the skipper at the wheel;

glary it certainly was. The sun was sinking in the west, a plate without effulgence, a plate as yellow as an old spade guinea. The kindness had all died out of the sky and, when the sun had gone, there were left a livid glare, a cold sea and this little ship alone in the midst of it.

Mordaunt looked up at the topsail.

"We might carry on until we get the weather news," he said. For these were the days before the Second War, when Broadcasting House flung out her warnings and good tidings to all the ships on the near seas.

By nine o'clock night was closing in. Mr. Ricardo was seated in a corner of the deckhouse. Mordaunt leaned over a small receiver mounted on a revolving pedestal. Hamlin's big figure blocked the doorway as he bent to listen ; and suddenly, startlingly, a new voice spoke clearly out of the darkness at their elbows, giving them the weather report :

"A deep depression over Ireland is moving rapidly to the south-east. There will be a gale in the Channel to-night."

"As a rule, that gives us half an hour," said Hamlin.

He and Mordaunt were out of the deck-cabin in an instant, leaving Ricardo almost sick with indignation against the radiant cheerful voice which had announced the direful news.

"Doesn't he know we're out here in a cockle-shell ? " he exclaimed. "He's going home to have supper—a nice hot supper in a nice hot room—on land ! And we're here, drowned men practically."

But there was activity enough upon the deck. A storm jib was set, the topsail taken down and folded away with the big jib in the locker, the main and mizzen sails were reefed, and the sidelights burning brightly lifted on their shelves. The ship was snug and her crew clothed in oilskins and high boots.

Mr. Ricardo stood in the doorway of the cabin looking forward over its roof. The ketch still rose and dipped upon the unbroken swell, but ahead in the darkness lines of white ran out to right and left on the crests of waves with extraordinary speed.

"Here it comes," said Mordaunt. He raised his hand to the mizzen rigging on the port side. Hamlin, the skipper, was at the wheel, lifting the boat gently up to the wind. Mordaunt grinned at Ricardo.

"I should go down and get into your bunk whilst you can," he cried.

Mr. Ricardo shook his head. That was quite unthinkable.

"I'll stay in the deckhouse for a little," he said, and then more bravely, "This is a new experience for me."

He crouched on the divan in the deckhouse with a foot against the rail-guard of the companion, and a few moments afterwards the gale broke upon them like an army. A wave smote the ketch so that it shuddered. Its crest leaped gaily over the port bow and ran in streams along the deck, whilst the bulk of it roared away to leeward from under the keel in an angry tumble of white fire.

"Disappointed, that's what it was," Mr. Ricardo began, but he could not go on.

For all about them was noise, noise unbelievable and yet combined into an awful harmony. The waves hammered and roared; the wind shrilled through the rigging like a Sabbath of lost souls; the planks groaned and clamoured that not for one moment longer could they cling together; and, above all other sounds, the topping-lift thrashed the belly of the mainsail with the crack of a hundred pistols.

Ricardo was terrified into a hopeless acquiescence.

"It can't go on," he said to himself as he clutched at anything which was clutchable in the deck-cabin. "That's all. It can't go on."

But it did go on, hour after hour, until Mr. Ricardo actually dozed and then woke to an incident very pleasant but quite incredible. Mordaunt was at the helm, the skipper by the port rigging, when Mordaunt held the ship up to meet a more passionately venomous wave than any which had gone before. The two men bent their heads as the brine cut their faces like a whiplash.

"That was a nasty one," cried the skipper.

"A beast!" answered Mordaunt; and then, to Ricardo's stupefaction, they laughed, not with the wry laughter of the defeated, but heartily, enjoyably.

"Well, perhaps, after all . . ." thought Ricardo. He was glad that he had not taken Mordaunt's advice and retired to his bunk. He would have been ice-cold with terror. He couldn't say that it was warm up here in the deckhouse, but it was friendly, and near to people who could laugh at the right moment. Again Mr. Ricardo dozed and woke; and now the mate was at the wheel whilst Mordaunt stood on one side unclenching his frozen fingers and Hamlin upon the other. Suddenly they all looked up and, as they looked, a ghostly twilight was diffused about the world. Mr. Ricardo was in the mood to believe that here at last was the Day of Judgement, so unillumined was the light, so pallid the faces lifted to it. But the mate broke the solemnity of the moment by asserting "'Tis the dawning," and after both men had stared at him in admiration of his optimism, the laughter and the raillery were renewed. The mate was the incorrigible consoler. Somewhere, high up, beyond apprehension, and almost beyond faith, a full moon was riding in a blue sky and some sliver of it radiance slipped through. Mr. Ricardo clambered through the doorway and looked forward over its roof, clinging with both hands. As far as the eyes could reach, great black seas, like mountains, raced after each other in a riot of foam, whilst above his head the swaying topmast seemed on the point of scraping and snapping against a roof of grey cement, so solid and so low was the canopy of cloud. But whilst he watched the chink closed up again and once more there was no light but the white fire of the waves and the more friendly gleam of the binnacle lamp.

Mr. Ricardo scrambled back to his corner in the deck-house. He pulled up the cushion behind him so that his head rested more comfortably upon it.

" After all, we're still afloat," he reflected. " I have not been seasick "—this he put down less to his panic than to his quality as a yachtsman—" and those three men, though they are unalarmed, are watchful."

They were more than ever watchful now, it seemed. For more and more often he heard the man in the bows sing out :

" Light ahead, sir."

And more and more often the answer from the man at the wheel :

" Right ! "

For they were crossing now the crown of the great trunk road which flows from Ushant to the Port of London.

To the sound of those cries Mr. Ricardo fell asleep, and was only awakened by someone shaking him by the shoulder. Mordaunt was leaning over him.

" We can see the light at Start Point," he said.

The motion of the ship had diminished, the noise had lost its terror, they were feeling the protection of the land, the gale was dying. Again Mr. Ricardo stood at the cabin door and looked forward. All was darkness, but in a few seconds he saw, as at the end of a long black iron tube, a faint glimmer which broadened out to the likeness of a beautiful incandescent moth and shrivelled again into nothing. Mordaunt, at his side, began to count :

" One, two, three . . ."

He counted up to twenty, and the light shone again.

" Yes, Start Point," said Mordaunt. " But, of course, we're a long way from it yet."

Mr. Ricardo stayed thereafter at the deckhouse door, and so was a witness of the incident which made that night more than ever memorable to him and perplexed the forgotten Hanaud for so long.

A big ancient rusty iron steamer came lumbering up from the west across the bows of *Agamemnon*, but yawing as she came, as if she had not made up her mind whether to run ashore on the long ledge of Start Point or strike away for the French coast.

" Look out, sir ! " cried Hamlin, the skipper, sharply to Mordaunt at the wheel. " She's a dago with the cabin-boy in command and all the rest of 'em asleep."

It was that spectral hour between night and dawn when all is magnified and yards are miles. Mordaunt held his ketch up until he had shaken what wind there was out of her sails ; and it was lucky that he did, for his bowsprit hardly scraped clear of the iron monster's side.

" There ! I told you, didn't I ? " cried Hamlin, and he pointed to where a light shone on the name upon a buoy. " A dago ! "

All could read the name. *El Rey*. But they had hardly time to read it. For a cry, like a wail, was borne to them urgently upon the breeze.

Men who sail in little boats are accustomed to see in the dark of the night and bad weather light on land, where there is no land, and to hear voices from the sea, where no men are drowning—so accustomed that they do not speak of them lest they should be thought to talk foolishly. So now Mordaunt and his crew looked each to the other, hesitating whether they should seem to have heard. But the cry reached them again, weaker, yet nearer, and just over the port bow.

The mate shouted "Hold on!" and cutting a life-buoy loose from the main rigging, hurled it out. The ketch was lying now, head in to the wind, with its sails flapping. Hamlin pulled up out of its slots the panel of bulwark which opened the port gangway and, flinging himself on his face, leaned over the side. The mate and the steward joined him, one upon his knees, the other with a boathook in his hands. From his position at the wheel Mordaunt could see nothing of what was happening, but something or someone was being lifted on board.

It was someone, a slim young man with hair as black as ebony, and a face of a pallor so thick that it could hardly ever before have met the daylight. So Mordaunt thought, until the rescued man was stretched on deck. He was alive but snatching at the air in his exhaustion. He was dressed in a grey cotton shirt, a jacket and a pair of trousers of canvas, and he wore sandshoes on his naked feet.

"Brandy," said Mordaunt, and the steward dived down the companion. He came back with a full glass and, lifting the man's shoulders against his knee, put the glass to his lips. The young man's face was long, his body where it showed at the neck and breast just bones in an envelope of skin. He took a drink of the brandy, threw back his head on the steward's knee and coughed.

"A martyr by El Greco, without a martyr's saintliness," said Mordaunt, thinking the stranger beyond hearing.

"A dago," said Hamlin the skipper.

The stranger turned his eyes on Hamlin and said :

"Damn your eyes!" in English unmistakable, and fainted away.

Mordaunt gave his orders.

"You had better get him below, rub him down with

a hot towel, give him a spare suit of pyjamas, and put him to bed in Mr. Ricardo's berth with a hot-water bottle. You don't mind ? "

Mr. Ricardo didn't mind. He was, indeed, fluttering around, trying to help and getting in everybody's way. Meanwhile a question was troubling his mind as much as he, in his efforts to help, was troubling Craston, the mate, and the steward. Why did the name of the ship, *El Rey*—" The King "—awaken some vague familiar resonance in his brain ? *El Rey . . . El Rey. . . .* No, there was no answer.

When he climbed the companion again on to the deck, the light on Start Point had been extinguished, the day had come, and the ketch had borne away upon its course.

" Mind the Skerries' buoy, sir," said Hamlin. " The tide's setting us to the east."

" I know," Mordaunt answered ; and after a moment or two, Hamlin continued :

" A queer thing. That young-fellow-my-lad must have tumbled off the stern of that ship just as she began to cross our bows. The tide brought him straight down on us. A bit of good luck, I should say."

Mordaunt grinned and shook his head.

" A bit of good timing, I should."

And with that Mr. Ricardo's memory began to work. *El Rey !* He had read about it. Certain States of South America had chartered *El Rey*—Venezuela, Colombia, Bolivia—to carry back to their respective countries some undesirable aliens. She was to call at Spanish and French ports and in England. Then she was to go on with the rest of her passengers to the Baltic and Germany. There lay the explanation of something which had puzzled them all, but of which no one had spoken. The stranger had a broad black band about his right leg above the ankle, as though a heavy iron fetter had for years bitten into his flesh.

Chapter 3

MORDAUNT WRITES A LETTER

MORDAUNT dropped his anchor in the Dart river above the ferry which crosses from Dartmouth town and the railway station at Kingswear. The morning was clear, but neither town was yet alert to it. Mordaunt felt in one of the pigeon-holes at the back of the deckhouse and drew out of it a plain yellow flag.

"Here you are!" he said and Hamlin took it from his hand. It was the flag flown by every vessel hailing straight from a foreign port, and no one, whether passenger, or crew, must leave her until the harbour authorities had given her clearance. Hamlin, the skipper, balanced the folded flag on the palm of his hand. He was thinking that Captain Mordaunt and his *Agamemnon* had sailed in and out of Dartmouth so often that no one on shore would trouble about his port of departure unless the yellow flag invited him.

"I am to hoist this?" he asked, thrusting out his under-lip.

Mordaunt nodded his head and added slowly, "Yes."

"You've a good deal to do, Captain Mordaunt, haven't you? You have to lay up the boat, travel to London, settle your affairs for a long absence. . . ."

"Still," Mordaunt interrupted, "there are rules."

They were both thinking of the stranger with the black band above his ankle who in the misty dawn had come aboard.

"He'll have to report, of course, when the Customs men come on board," said Mordaunt. "I don't see why I should be delayed."

Hamlin was still patting doubtfully the piece of bunting in his hand. It was clearly important that Mordaunt should not be held up in the Dart river by regulations at this time. Mordaunt spoke quickly.

" I'll wake him up, whilst you hoist that " ; and Mordaunt had only reached the bottom of the companion when the yellow flag flickered up the mast like a flame.

The stranger, however, wanted no awakening. He was sitting, shaved and dressed, down to his shoes, in clothes which belonged to Mordaunt.

" Your steward lent me these," he said.

" And he was quite right," Mordaunt returned with a smile.

A box full of cigarettes and an ash-tray were lying on the table and Mordaunt pushed the box over to the stranger. " Don't you smoke ? "

" Indeed, I do."

" Then try one, please ! "

There was something vulpine in the speed of the stranger's thin long fingers as they darted towards the box ; but it was not so startling as the control which stopped them at the rim of the box and set them tapping out a bar of a tune before they dropped languidly on one of the paper tubes. Yet he was starving for a cigarette ! So, at all events, Mr. Ricardo decided, as he sat unnoticeable reading, or pretending to read, an official report taken from the bookcase above his head ; and so, too, Mordaunt had decided. He said pleasantly :

" You should have helped yourself."

The man from the sea shook his head and laughed.

" That would have put me at too heavy a disadvantage."

He struck a match and lit his cigarette and, as he drew the smoke into his lungs, he uttered a little moan of delight.

" Oh . . . oh ! "

He looked at the brand on the tube.

" Turkish."

" Yes."

The stranger inhaled with his eyes closed. How many years had passed since this enjoyment had been allowed to him ? Mr. Ricardo wondered. But, indeed, it was more than an enjoyment, however sensuous. It seemed to take from him the suspicion, the fear, the expectation of an enemy in everyone, which Mr. Ricardo had observed. He sat there smoking, a man repaired. Mordaunt, with a glance of amusement at him, opened a drawer in the table.

" I have got something to say to you—by the way, my name's Mordaunt, Philip Mordaunt——"

He paused for a moment, and for more than a moment afterwards there followed a disconcerting silence. Then the stranger replied :

" And mine is Devisher—Bryan Devisher."

" Right ! "

Mordaunt took from the drawer which he had opened a letter-case and counted out fifteen pounds in notes.

" Before we talk," he said, " I should be happier if we were on still more equal terms. Will you borrow these from me ? "

Upon Devisher's white face a flush slowly spread.

" Philip Mordaunt, you said ? "

" Yes—Captain," and seeing that Devisher's eyes were wandering about the cabin, Mordaunt lifted a blotting pad with some paper upon it, placed them in front of him, and added a pencil from the table drawer. He gave the name of a club.

Devisher wrote down the address, tucked the paper away in a pocket, and did the same with the money.

" Thank you ! " he said ; and as there had been no patronage in the offer, so there was no servility in the acceptance.

"Now!" said Mordaunt. He was sitting on the couch against the saloon wall with its lockers and its high ledge, whilst Devisher was on a chair at the head of the table at his right hand. "Now, the position is this. No one must leave this ship until the Customs officers come on board. They won't be here probably for another hour. It's hardly eight yet. But when they do come, you ought to make a full statement to them."

"I see, yes," Devisher observed, staring down at the mahogany table. He could not keep the bitterness out of his voice, which already had a natural rasp, but he could, according to Mr. Ricardo, hide thus the savage fury of his eyes.

"That I fell overboard, for instance."

"Yes."

"Without a passport."

"Yes."

"From the ship, *El Rey*."

"Yes."

It was as evident to Devisher as to Ricardo on the opposite side of the saloon, that "the ship *El Rey*" meant no more to Mordaunt than information of a merely formal kind.

"With the black mark of a fetter so wide and deep around my ankle, that I am likely to wear it to the day of my death."

Mr. Ricardo sat up. No, no, he said to himself. Every word up till now had been inspired by the right spirit and used in the right place. But this reference to the chain by the man who had worn it—no, no! A lack of susceptibility to the higher tastes, an indelicacy. Fie, fie, Mr. Devisher!

Apparently, however, Captain Mordaunt was unconscious of any want of tact in his guest. He laughed as frankly as Devisher had spoken.

" That's your affair. I don't see how the Customs could make any charge, whether you declared it or not."

The words were lightly said but not lightly taken. Devisher had so far kept to the same unemotional key, but now he clapped his hands to his face and he shivered like a man stricken with a mortal chill. Mordaunt drew back in discomfort.

" I must tell you," cried Devisher violently, plucking his hands away from his face; and Mordaunt's discomfort increased. A scene—he had a horror of it, he had been at every shift he knew to avoid it.

" My name is Devisher, Bryan Devisher, yes. But it's not the name on my passport in the purser's cabin on *El Rey*."

" Then you give your real name here," Mordaunt interrupted, but the interruption went almost unheard and certainly not considered.

" I took part in a revolution over there in Venezuela," the young man rushed on, the words almost tumbling in a froth like a breaker from his mouth. " And it was high time, I can tell you. A revolution was wanted, but it failed. Vicente Gomez, the dictator won, as he always did. I lay quiet up in Caracas, but I was betrayed—and I think I know, too, who betrayed me. I spent six years dragging an iron cannon-ball in the Castillo del Libertador, an island prison in the bay with its cells below the water-line. Six mortal years until Vicente Gomez died. Then we were released. I forget how many tons of iron fetters and handcuffs were thrown into the sea. But after a time, when this ship *El Rey* was chartered, I was deported."

To both his auditors the story was true. The white mask of Devisher's face, which had felt neither sun nor wind for years, bore out his words, apart from the black ring about his ankle. And the horrors which they suggested were stark before their eyes.

"But we have a Minister there, a Consul," cried Mr. Ricardo.

"You could have appealed to them," added Mordaunt.

Devisher shrugged his shoulders.

"Not a chance! I hadn't made myself known to any of them whilst I could. Besides . . ." and his eyes fell sullenly and, after a moment or two, a displeasing sly smile twisted his face.

But Mordaunt had had enough. The sly smile had put a full stop at the end of all this palaver. Confessions were for the priest in the curtained darkness of his confessional box, not for the tiny saloon of a ketch in the river Dart on an August morning. He rose to his feet.

"No, no!" he exclaimed, and he rang a hand-bell vigorously.

The steward appeared from the pantry forward before Devisher could add another word.

"I want a hot bath, Perry, and then we'll all want breakfast."

Breakfast, that was what they wanted. They would be different men with some good hot bacon and eggs and coffee inside of them. He heard the water begin to run from the taps in the bathroom beyond his tiny cabin on his right. He stood for a moment, seized by a fresh idea. He sat down, took a block of notepaper, envelopes, and a fountain pen out of the drawer.

"Yes, whilst I am waiting, I'll write a letter"; and, pulling the blotting pad towards him, he began to write, slowly, selecting his words, a very still figure, so that no one interrupted him; Devisher perhaps because his outburst had been silenced, Ricardo certainly because he was trying to reconcile this Captain Mordaunt with the Mordaunt against whom he had brushed at so many six o'clock sherry parties. Then he had been a flibberti-gibbet of a man, querulous, caustic, defeated, the sort of man who sees others of his age leaving him behind, making their names, and complains, " If only I could find my vocation, they'd soon be surprised." But now he had authority, he was solidly sure, and it was not because he was captain of his boat and knew how to sail it. Even at Lezardrieux, Mr. Ricardo had discovered a serenity and consequently a good-humour in him which were new.

" Well, I shall get to the bottom of that," he thought cheerfully. For Mr. Ricardo counted himself a very acute observer of character.

Mordaunt had finished his letter by the time when the steward told him his bath was ready. He folded it, put it into an envelope and addressed the envelope. Then he got to his feet.

" You'll please begin breakfast as soon as it's brought in. I'm not going to hurry " ; and he suddenly turned to Devisher.

" You may have many troubles and few friends in front of you, for all I know. I should like to help you because you came to me out of the sea."

" Meerschaum," Devisher interposed, " but not half as valuable."

Mordaunt was not to be diverted.

" But I shan't be in England. So I can't. But this man can, if anyone can," and he handed the letter he had written to Devisher. " He's old, crotchety, very much eighteen-seventy, but· he's wise, and if you tell him everything, he may throw you another life-buoy."

He waited for no answer. Devisher heard the door of the cabin close whilst he was still reading the address upon the envelope. He repeated the name aloud on a note of perplexity.

" Septimus Crottle, Esq."

Mr. Ricardo, who had been rent between curiosity and

the obligation of gentlemanly reticence, gave a little jump. Devisher seemed to become aware of Mr. Ricardo.

" Do you know him ? "

" Septimus Crottle ? "

" Who else ? "

" No, I do not."

" Yet you jumped when I read the name."

" Did I ? "

Mr. Ricardo beamed. He liked people to find significance in his reactions.

" You did, but it doesn't matter."

Mr. Ricardo was nettled.

" It might matter," said he stiffly.

" Indeed ? "

Devisher smiled as he spoke, but with a polite indifference.

" Septimus Crottle is the owner of the Dagger Line of Steamships," said Mr. Ricardo.

The indifference passed from Devisher's face.

Chapter 4

" AGAMEMNON'S " BATH

MORDAUNT stripped himself of his suède jerkin, his high sea-boots, and the rest of his defences against a gale, and slipped into the bath. After the buffeting of sea and wind, the velvet caress of hot fresh water was a delight for a Roman emperor. He shaved in it, soaped his limbs, and emptied his sponge again and again over his head, wondering whether there could be anything as good as living hard and bathing soft.

But it was *Agamemnon's* bath. It is true that no lady

with a meat axe was secretly opening the bathroom door, no lads of the village listening timidly in the road were wailing "Ai, ai! That was a nasty one!" as the axe was heftily administered. But it was still, in its way, fateful. Mordaunt lay and relaxed his sinews and steeped his limbs and closed his eyes—and opened them and closed them again. From far away there was a splash of sculls, the grating of a rowing boat against a ship's side, and then a voice, thin and small, as though it spoke through a hundred folds of grey silk, but cheerful :

" So here you are, back again, Aggy boy."

Mordaunt assured himself solemnly that Aggy Boy was not a name.

" I propose to see about that," and he was apparently still proposing to see about it, when a hammering upon the door aroused him. The steward's voice spoke urgently :

" Your breakfast's getting cold, Captain Mordaunt."

And Mordaunt realised that what was happening to his breakfast had happened to his bath. He climbed out of it with a shiver, and in a quarter of an hour, and in a shore-going blue suit, he was sitting down in the saloon to a breakfast fresh from the stove.

Mr. Ricardo at the other side of the cabin was smoking a cigarette.

" Do you mind this whilst you're eating ? " he asked, waving it.

" Not a bit," answered Mordaunt. Suddenly he cried out : " Where is Devisher ? "

" He has gone, I think."

Mordaunt rose and called up the companion for Hamlin, and Hamlin came down, contentedly smiling.

" Mr. Devisher ? " Mordaunt asked abruptly.

" It's just like this, sir. The Customs didn't come on board, knowing of us well, but just passed the time of day. The two gentlemen were down in the saloon, but soon afterwards the—I can't fit my tongue to his name—the passenger from the foreign ship comes up. I was hauling down the yellow flag, and he asks what he should do now. I showed him the harbour-master's office by the slipway, and he said he would go and report if he could be put ashore. There was a boatman sculling about for a job. So I called him up to the gangway and off the gentleman went."

Mordaunt looked not too pleased.

" Just like that ? " he said. " Without a word ? "

" Oh, yes, sir. He said you were in your bath and not to be disturbed. He said he'd write to you."

Mordaunt laughed.

" All right," he said, and went on with his breakfast. " After all, he has saved us some trouble."

" And some delay," Hamlin added quickly. " We should have been kept here all day, telling the same story over and over."

It was clear both to Mordaunt and Ricardo that the skipper had edged Devisher over the yacht's side as soon as he got the chance, guessing that the last place Devisher would visit would be the harbour-master's office, or the office of any other functionary of the port. Mordaunt, however, was really troubled—and once more to Mr. Ricardo's surprise ; Mr. Ricardo could see him at a cocktail party a year ago, overshouting some other gossip to tell his story with a sardonic amusement—lest he had let loose an equivocal person, if not a bandit, on the world.

" Well, he has gone," said Mordaunt at last.

" With your letter to Mr. Septimus Crottle," Mr. Ricardo added ; and now Mordaunt laughed without any reservation.

" Old Septimus can take it," he cried. " Besides, I shall see Septimus on Sunday night, and that's before he will."

Mordaunt took a cigar from a mahogany box and split the end of it by the squeeze of his finger and thumb. He lit it and sat back smiling, as if the picture of Septimus had banished the picture of a bandit.

" Do you know Crottle ? The queerest old bird. Owns the Dagger Line, and was once a commander—a tyrant in a reefer jacket then, and a tyrant in a broad-cloth frock-coat now. Choked off any young men who came after one of his daughters, not because they were gold-diggers, but because it was the business of maidens to wait upon their fathers."

" Amiable patriarch," said Mr. Ricardo.

" Patriarch, yes ; amiable, no," Mordaunt returned, and laughed again. " You should see him on his Sunday nights. In his glory ! But he's shrewd, too. And he'd do you a good turn——" Mordaunt paused, " that is, if you acted on his advice, of course. You see, he's never in doubt."

Mordaunt was no longer deriding the comic aspect of Septimus Crottle. Mr. Ricardo suspected, indeed, that he was to hear the explanation of that change in Mordaunt which had so perplexed him. There was a confusion, a hesitation, in Mordaunt's manner.

" I never told you how I came across old Septimus, did I ? But, of course, I didn't. I was on this ketch in the Helford river. A great sailor of small boats had built his home there, and a few of us used to anchor about his house for his birthday. There were four or five yachts anchored in the pool above and below and opposite to Helford village. Septimus came in a schooner with more draught than any of our boats, and anchored down the river at Passage. Well, that evening—I don't know what made me do it—I had seen him in the garden that afternoon, an old boy, straight as a flagstaff, without any inhibitions ; and there he was, once the commander of a ship, now the owner of the Dagger Line. So that night I sent an excuse from a party on one of the yachts, dined alone, and afterwards sculled in my dinghy down to the schooner at Passage."

He had found Septimus seated in the shelter of his deck cabin, with a rug about his waist and a trifle suspicious that an upstanding young fellow should row away from a golden company to pass an hour with a solitary old crab-apple. Septimus Crottle did not ask his new companion why, but he gave him a large Havana cigar and, as Mordaunt drew a lighter from his pocket, he objected.

"Will you use the box of wooden matches at your elbow, please."

Mordaunt turned round. A small table had been placed noiselessly beside his chair with an ash-tray upon it and a box of Bryant and May's matches. So much reverence for a cigar seemed to Mordaunt to call for a response, and as he smoked, it certainly did.

"This really is a wonderful cigar, Mr. Crottle," said Mordaunt, pitching his praise high.

"It is the best," returned Mr. Crottle, simply and sufficiently. "It's mine."

Philip did not feel that his impulse had been fruitful. On the other hand, the old man, with his sharp nose and his lean chin, seemed quite content that the younger man should sit by his side and say nothing. The tide sang against the planks of the schooner. Up in the pool by Helford village the lights of the yachts threw out from their skylights a glow of jewels cased in black velvet. From one, a woman's voice, fresh and clear as a blackbird's in the dew of the morning, soared in a delight which knocked against the stars; and Mordaunt found himself pouring out in a low voice the story of his distress, the twistings and turnings in a world where he had lost his way.

He had resigned his commission when one of the

youngest captains, after the 1914–18 war, meaning to think over his life and plan what he should do. He might go into Parliament. He had a house and land in Dorset where there was an opportunity. Or he might go into business—big business—in the City. Or he might write —a comedy which would endure with "The Way of the World"; an epic, perhaps, which would stand on the same shelf with "The Ring and the Book" a novel which would make people cry Fielding Redivivus. Meanwhile, he did nothing. Some day he would begin, when he was quite sure of the road which led to greatness. But meanwhile he ran about from party to party, talking with other young men and women of the fine thing he was going to do. But one after another the young men passed him into a different and busier country. One was elected to the House of Commons, and made a first speech which was the talk of the town. A second wrote a play which stirred the critics and filled the theatre for a year. A third wrote a book which was bought as well as read. They would all come back, of course, as their squibs flickered out. But they didn't come back, and there was he, still wandering from party to party, jealous, dissatisfied, hollow as an empty tin. Septimus Crottle listened whilst the stars slid down the sky and the lights went out in the yachts in the pool. Then he said quietly :

"Great authors! To me they are the loud-speakers of God." He turned to Mordaunt. "Are you of their company?"

"How should I know?" Mordaunt asked after a pause.

"They have their labels."

"For instance?"

"They think less of the name they make than of the work they do."

Mordaunt laughed curtly. Admit that, and he was ruled out! But how could he not admit that?

" Well, I asked for it," he told himself, and thought that he might just as well, like Oliver, ask for more. So he said, rather arrogantly :

" Perhaps there are other labels."

Old Crottle was quite unimpressed by his young friend's curling lip.

" Of course." And after a glance at Mordaunt, Septimus looked out over the dark water, selecting the one which would be most suitable.

" They don't nurse long grievances," he said. " They are too busy creating. They curse and damn for five minutes and then they get on with their job."

For the second time that night Philip Mordaunt took it on the point of his chin. He took a whisky and soda afterwards and hoped that he had not obtruded too long between Mr. Crottle and his repose.

Mr. Crottle, however, confessed to having been flattered by Philip Mordaunt's visit.

" Besides," he said, standing at the gangway, " everybody enjoys g ving advice, as long as he's quite certain that the advice isn't what the advised had come to hear."

Mordaunt halted on the first rung of the ladder and stepped on board again.

" Yes," he said in some surprise, " the curious thing is that I'm not discouraged. On the contrary, I am relieved."

The sense of relief stayed with Mordaunt as he sculled back to his yacht, and was no less strong the next morning. Old Septimus had banged the door on a good many dreams which of late were darkening into torments. He had left Mordaunt to find another door for himself, and it was evident to Mr. Ricardo that somehow Mordaunt had succeeded.

Philip looked up at the clock on the wall behind the stove as he ended his story.

" You'll want to catch the Torbay Limited," he continued. " There it is, in Kingswear station. Hamlin will land you at the steps and put your bag in your carriage. I am sorry that I couldn't give you a better passage from France."

Chapter 5

DANIEL HORBURY

O N that afternoon, Mr. Horbury, Member of Parliament for the Kempston Division of London, walked from the House of Commons to his office at a few minutes after four. He had done two useful things certainly for himself, and perhaps for his country. He had asked a question and he had voted in a division. The division took place on the Government's need to occupy the whole time of the sitting, and was a daily affair, occurring just after questions were concluded. Thus a shrewd man, and no one had ever denied shrewdness to Mr. Horbury, could well within the compass of an hour establish proofs of his stern determination to fulfil his duties towards his constituents and the State. That the division was a formality, mattered nothing ; that he would not be present to vote upon the serious question for which the Government claimed the whole sitting, mattered less. He had had his name duly noted down on the division list, and it was the division a day which kept the opponent away and confirmed the constituents in the belief that they had chosen the best sort of man to represent them.

Mr. Horbury, having thus done his duty, ambled across St. James's Park to his office in King Street.

He was a heavily-hipped, short-legged, obese man who walked like a pigeon, crossing his toes. He was not noticeable indeed unless he raised his head, and then the big red face on its bull neck startled one. For his head, down to a line just below the eyes, was massive as an emperor's, and the strong eyes were noble. But below the eyes a curious blend of the animal and the insignificant disgraced his features. His nose, for instance, was small and round, his upper lip long, and the swollen jaw not so much massive as brutal—the jaw of a great ape welded to the brow of a Cæsar, set upon a torso of so slovenly a vulgarity that the man almost escaped the curiosity of the passers-by. But there were some to whom he was unknown, people no doubt a little more sensitive than their neighbours, who felt a chill if he approached, like that cold aura which, in the legends of the Sabbaths, enfolded the person of Satan. Mr. Horbury walked clumsily and slowly, round the water where the pigeons imitated his progress, to the Marlborough Gate, through a dark and exclusive arcade, and so to his fine panelled offices in King Street.

Mr. Horbury was uneasy. There was a certain danger to be eliminated. Not so very serious a danger. Daniel Horbury was accustomed to navigating shoals still more menacing than the shoals of Lezardrieux. But, in order to eliminate the danger of this afternoon, Horbury would have to relinquish a victim, a victim plump and ripe, the fruit of a golden tree, and Mr. Horbury had the greatest detestation of such sacrifices. He went through the outer office into his own sanctuary. It was panelled with rosewood. The deep arm-chairs were cushioned with a dark red damask. A great walnut writing-table, shaped in an arc and fashioned in the days of Queen Anne, with the carved pigeon-holes and little doors of its period, decorated the centre of an Aubusson carpet.

Mr. Horbury paused for a moment upon the threshold, consoled for his uneasy reflections by the sheen and costliness of his surroundings.

" Not many offices like this, Foster," he said to a clerk who was reading out a list of names at his elbow.

" No, sir."

Foster was an old-fashioned clerk from Gracechurch Street and knew Big Business to be more generally associated with worn linoleum, upright Victorian chairs, and ink-stained writing-tables.

" Will you see Mr. Ricardo at five-thirty ? "

" Mr. Ricardo ? "

Horbury became very still. Mr. Ricardo ! He had never heard of a Mr. Ricardo. And the unknown was always dangerous.

" It is not convenient," said Horbury. " This afternoon I don't wish to be disturbed."

Horbury shut the door. On the writing-table lay the last edition of the *Evening Standard*. He approached it with a careful carelessness, for there are times when a prudent man will play-act even to himself alone. He turned the pages as though they were of little interest, and came willy-nilly to the shipping news. There, at the very head of the column, the announcement stood :

" *El Rey* from South American ports passed Prawle Point at 6 a.m."

Mr. Horbury expected the announcement, yet he was taken aback. Providence should have intervened, as Providence had often dutifully done, in Mr. Horbury's affairs. There were, however, occasions when Providence, though willing, wanted just a trifle of help. Horbury must, in the parliamentary phrase, explore the avenues. He went to a cupboard and opened it. Two shelves were disclosed. On the first stood half-a-dozen glasses and a small wire-cutter ; on the lower half a dozen swelling bottles with a golden-yellow foil guarding the mushroom-headed corks and a famous year on a printed strip.

The pop of the cork was heard by the clerks and no longer provoked even the office humorist to imitate the sound of liquid hissing into a glass.

Horbury, in his sanctuary, drank half of his bottle. He lifted the receiver from the hook of his telephone and dialled LED 0045. In a little while he heard a door close noisily and, upon the closing of the door, an eager, wooing voice.

" Is that you, Beautiful ? "

Mr. Horbury smiled, showing all his teeth to the gums, but he used a pleasant voice.

" No, not more so than usual. It's just plain Daniel Horbury speaking."

At the other end of the line there was silence. Daniel Horbury really smiled this time as he pictured to himself a man shocked into speechlessness and grey with fear.

" You got my message ? " Horbury continued.

" Yes."

" Sorry I used your private number."

" Who gave it to you ? "

Horbury made a joke. At least it seemed a joke at the time.

" Mr. Ricardo," he returned. It was the last name which he had heard when he entered his office, and he rang off before another question could be put to him.

Mr. Horbury finished off his bottle of champagne, leaning back in his chair with his short legs crossed under his walnut table. He was tempted, indeed, to commemorate the name of Mr. Ricardo with a second bottle. After all, he was wont to argue, as long as you don't begin before eleven o'clock in the morning, champagne can't do you much harm. It gives a sparkle to your plans and delays their over-hasty execution.

But to-day execution was needed. He pushed his

chair back, unlocked a drawer and lifted out of it a small chart set flat with drawing-pins upon a thin ebony board. Five black pins were stuck in the chart, and now Horbury added a sixth, just seven miles west of Start Point where, at six o'clock on that morning, *El Rey* had lumbered past the Prawle Signal Station on her journey to Thames' mouth. Horbury replaced the map in the drawer. He then called up his flat in Park Lane. He asked for his wife, and when she spoke to him there was suddenly another man at Horbury's desk, one with a laugh in his eyes as well as on his lips, and even a throb of music in his voice.

" Olivia—that's you ? Yes, and the sound of you drives everything else out of my head—listen now, it's urgent—oh, by the way, I heard you called beautiful less than half an hour ago—oh, I needn't have rung you up to tell you that ?—you haven't got it at all—I heard you addressed as Beautiful over a private line," and he chuckled comfortably. There came back to him a tiny cry.

" You've been reading my letters ! "

" Would I ? " cried Horbury indignantly. " The number was given to me by a Mr. Ricardo."

" Who ? "

" A Mr. Ricardo. But don't go away. This is serious. We must go down to Lordship Lane to-night. At least, I must, and I do hope you will. We are free to-night, aren't we ? "

In a room overlooking Hyde Park a woman half the age of the obese Romeo in King Street listened and smiled.

" Yes, I'll come," and again Romeo was talking.

" We might sleep there, don't you think ? It'll be the full moon. You know how the big oaks with their black shadows make crazy patterns on the meadow ; and all the birds aren't dumb at the end of August when you're near."

It was commonplace raillery, but whoever had seen Olivia Horbury, with a tender smile trembling upon her lips, might well have addressed her as " Beautiful."

" What's the plan ? " she asked.

" Will you drive the small car and pick me up here at seven-thirty ? We might dine at the Milan Grill, and get to the house at half-past nine. And somewhere about half-past ten I'll lock the front door, and we shall be alone in that lovely silence—Beautiful."

He could hear the deep breath she drew and wanted no other answer. He rang off and settled himself to compose a speech for the September rally in his constituency. Then he bathed, shaved, and dressed for the evening in a dinner jacket. He was hardly ready before Foster announced to him that Mrs. Horbury was waiting for him. He sent the commissionaire out to the car with the chart, bidding him ask Mrs. Horbury to take care that the pins were not displaced ; and he took from a secret drawer in the Queen Anne bureau a large sealed envelope which just fitted into the inside pocket of his jacket.

He slipped on his overcoat and stood once more upon the threshold, looking here and there about the room. He was merely admiring its sheen and costliness. It did not occur to him that he would never see it again.

Chapter 6

A WAKEFUL NIGHT

M R. RICARDO arrived in London at half-past three. He had slept in the train and was looking forward to giving his friend, Monsieur Hanaud, over a charming little dinner for two, quite a comical account of his night's adventure on the mail ship *Agamemnon*, plying between Brittany and the Dart.

But, alas! though he rehearsed the scene diligently, letting the real terrifying danger leak through the amusing episodes, making much of the mate's miscalculation of the dawn, it was good work wasted. Only Hanaud's suit-case arrived in Grosvenor Square in time for dinner.

With the bag, however, there was a note of eastern abasement, written hastily in pencil at Victoria Station. Hanaud had a telephone call and a visit to make, and he must attend a conference after that with Superintendent Maltby, who would keep him to dinner.

Mr. Ricardo was torn between testiness and gratitude. On the one hand he had, in order to fulfil the duties of a host, endured through a long, dark night the impact of those black, snow-crested waves. On the other hand, even as he spread his napkin over his knees, his eyes closed and his head nodded. Mr. Ricardo, in fact, was exhausted, and as soon as the formula of his dinner was complete, he rang for his butler.

" Thompson, I shall go to bed. You will see when Monsieur Hanaud comes in that he has everything he wants. You will ask him what he would like for his breakfast. For me, after my usual breakfast upstairs at eight, I shall come down at nine-thirty. Will you please tell him ? "

" Certainly, sir." And Mr. Ricardo, revived by a glass of old port, majestically ascended the stairs. Not everyone in Grosvenor Square had passed the last night battling in a cockleshell against a gale. There had been times when Monsieur Hanaud had treated him lightly. Those times had gone. Let him give heed now ! Let him give heed and listen !

And how right Mr. Ricardo was ! If Hanaud had received one hint of the fine story of *Agamemnon* and his bath, he would have fled from Superintendent Maltby and the dubious dishes of Soho to the fastidious menu at Grosvenor Square.

Yet Mr. Ricardo, for all his fatigue, slept not so well. At some hour, about which he did not trouble himself to be precise, he was aroused by one of those penetrating conversations in whispers which people use when they are trying not to wake their neighbours.

"Really, really," Mr. Ricardo murmured drowsily. "If they would only talk quietly, I should still be asleep. But those gasps and hisses remind me of the early days of the Underground, or of First Nights when villains were villains. I can hear every word."

Addressing thus the emptiness of the room, he did gather that Monsieur Hanaud had arrived and wished to be called early the next morning.

"There is a telephone, of course, in my bedroom ? "

A pause followed, a stately pause, meant to tell Hanaud exactly where he got off. It was followed by Thompson's most glacial voice.

"I think, sir, you must have forgotten that Mr. Ricardo is sensitive to telephones."

"Ah ! He would be ! "

"There are three telephone instruments in the house, sir. One in the staff's quarters on its own line. There is a second one in the hall. From that, again, there is an extension to a third instrument in the library. I think if you are intending to confer with Scotland Yard during the hours of darkness, the hall telephone would be the less disturbing."

Certainly, Mr. Ricardo reflected with pleasure, Thompson has the most dignified modes of expression, and he fell asleep. But at some later moment, he lay again in the half-way house between consciousness and dreams and seemed to hear a muffled foot glide by his door and down the stairs. But Thompson had been wrong.

Although the library was beneath Mr. Ricardo's bed-room, the floor was of Cubitt's making, so that no sound reached to the room above. On the other hand, the hall was less furnished, it was hollow, and noises rose from it. Thus Mr. Ricardo heard a whirr, and another, and another.

" The district," he thought.

Then came four twirls of the dial.

" The number," he continued, and, adopting Thompson's phrase, he explained the matter with a smile : " Hanaud is conferring with Scotland Yard during the hours of darkness."

That Thompson, being wrong in the matter of resonance might also be wrong in the destination of Hanaud's message, he was far too sleepy to argue. He heard no words, he drifted away into another world where Agamemnon rose out of a black sea with a huge telephone machine in his hand, and cried " It's the dawning." Mr. Ricardo was aware of nothing thereafter until the curtain-rings rattled and the blinds were drawn up and his cup of tea was steaming by his bedside.

He dressed deliberately. The mere fact that his friend had arrived that morning neither hurried nor halted him. He descended to his library at nine-thirty, and was surprised. For bending over a copy of *The Times* sat Monsieur Hanaud, attired for an English day in the country. He wore a rough suit of bright yellow, football stockings, and mountaineering boots. To Mr. Ricardo his appearance was delightful as well as amusing. Even the familiar blue paper-case of black cigarettes was pleasant to his eyes, and he sniffed the acrid fumes as a Malayan returning to his native country after a long absence might sniff his first doerian.

" You have waited for me to share your work. That is kind."

But Hanaud, after greetings of a warmer character

than Mr. Ricardo was used to or, indeed, desired, exclaimed dolefully :

" But there is no work to share. There never was very much. Just a little affair to be privately arranged which would do justice to a certain Parisian and at the same time give me a chance to meet my friend. But . . ." and before he could even shrug his shoulders the telephone bell rang.

" I tell you afterwards," said Hanaud as Ricardo lifted the receiver to his ear.

Ricardo confirmed it with a nod. " The message is for you."

Hanaud took the receiver from Ricardo.

" 'Allo, 'Allo ! Ah, it is the admirable Maltby. Yes, I listen with both my ears. So ! "

And Ricardo saw the look upon his friend's face change from attention to stupefaction. Hanaud held the earpiece close against his ear. Finally he spoke :

" In half an hour ? Yes, I will come. I thank you " ; and very slowly he replaced the receiver upon its stand. To Ricardo, watching his friend's face, the room had lost its comfort. It had become very still, very cold.

" You knew him ? " Hanaud asked.

" Whom ? "

" Daniel Horbury."

Ricardo started. " I know of him," he replied. Who in London didn't ? He added cautiously : " I will give you, my friend, some information. It is said that the police are on his heels."

" Oh ! no, no ! The information is wrong," cried Hanaud. " He has no heels. He is a shark."

Mr. Ricardo looked sourly at his friend from the Sûreté. He must always have the last word.

" Well, what has Daniel Horbury done now ? " Mr. Ricardo asked sulkily.

" Ah, that is it," said Hanaud, nodding his head.

"What is what?"

"He has cutted his throat."

Mr. Ricardo pushed back his chair.

"Dead?"

"Last night," Hanaud added gloomily. "I shall go to the house. Yes. But is it worth while? To have Hanaud looking about the room? Yes, the good superintendent thinks well of it. 'He may see something, that piece of quicksilver, which we do not, to explain this suicide.' But for me, it's a tragedy." He threw up his hands in despair.

"How so?"

"There were two rogues who cheated a Parisian years ago. One Horbury, the second a younger man just released from prison and deported from South America. Without them both, we have not the evidence. With them both, we don't want the prosecution. We want the money repaid. Now Horbury has slitted his throat, and the man from South America . . ."

"Bryan Devisher," said Ricardo carelessly.

"Yes," replied Hanaud, "that's the . . ."

He stopped, staring at Ricardo with his mouth open. Never had Ricardo enjoyed such a triumph. His blood sang proudly in his veins. But outwardly he was as negligent as before.

"What of Bryan Devisher?" he asked.

"He was drownded dead yesterday morning . . ."

"Off the Start Lighthouse from the ship *El Rey*," Mr. Ricardo interrupted.

Hanaud nodded gloomily.

"I had made arrangements for a little talk with Devisher after he had landed. Then we go to Horbury together and he pays the bill. But now Horbury has slitted his throat and Devisher is drownded."

"But Devisher is not drowned dead."

Hanaud looked at him with awe. Then he seized the

telephone and dialled with ferocity, speaking the while to his companion.

"You will come with me to the house of Daniel Horbury? Yes," and into the mouthpiece: "It is Hanaud. Could I speak to Mister the Superintendent Maltby?"—and so again to Ricardo: "You will use your car, yes? And you shall tell me about this Devisher as we go. Is that you, Maltby? I am staying here in the Grosvenor Square with a dear friend who, I can tell you, has been very helpful to me on many delicate occasions," and Hanaud did not even project a wink down the mouthpiece. "Yes, I should very much like his assistance. Yes, I stay with him in the Grosvenor Square when I come to London. The most charming of hosts."

"Really, really," Mr. Ricardo tittered, blushing in his embarrassment.

"His name?" Hanaud continued. "Mr. Julius Ricardo."

It seemed that something exploded at the other end of the telephone. Was it laughter? Was it surprise? Was it joy?

"We come in his car, a Rolls-Royce. Very fast, very fine. Give me the address again." Hanaud wrote it down on a pad of paper and rang off.

"What a coincidence," cried Mr. Ricardo, beaming. "Devisher, me, you, Horbury!"

"Bah!" exclaimed Hanaud, jeering like a schoolboy.

"It might happen once in a hundred times," said Mr. Ricardo.

"But it does happen every day once in a hundred times," Hanaud replied, and he hurried off to dress himself in less outrageous clothes, whilst Mr. Ricardo called up his Rolls-Royce, No. 2, to the door.

Chapter 7

THE LITTLE AFFAIR THREATENS TO BECOME THE BIG AFFAIR

MR. RICARDO was a trifle uncomfortable as he drove with Hanaud to the Embankment. Police authorities did not, as a rule, endure easily the presence of laymen at their investigations, however simple. But he had heard the voice of Superintendent Maltby as he spoke over the wire. It was hearty. He had jumped at the name. " Mr. Ricardo ! You are staying with Mr. Ricardo in Grosvenor Square ? Bring him along, of course, my dear Hanaud. The very thing ! "

Hearty—yes. Enthusiastic even. But perhaps a little unsettling. He reflected, however :

" It may be that he has heard of me giving Hanaud now and then a tiny help where social knowledge was needed, or some delicate impression was to be felt. One never knows. But I was conscious of quite a shock. Really, I might have been a criminal " ; and Mr. Ricardo uttered a little laugh, an uneasy little laugh, as though the great doors of Wormwood Scrubs were opening before him.

" And now," said Hanaud, tapping him upon the knee, " you tell me, do you not, of Bryan Devisher ? "

" To be sure."

The car was crossing Battersea Bridge. The sunlight was glittering upon the water. Seagulls wheeled and swooped in the inimitable beauty of their flight. Above them and about them was summer, its scents, its warmth ; and against that bright background Mr. Ricardo told the story of how the waif from the sea came aboard the ketch *Agamemnon.*

" In my mind, for it would not have been polite to have said it aloud, I called him meerschaum," said Mr. Ricardo, who had done nothing of the kind. " See ? A piece of meerschaum."

Hanaud, however, was indifferent at the moment to Ricardo's witticisms. He sat upright, his broad, shaven face very serious. " No, it would not have been polite to have said anything so stinging aloud," he replied, his mind far away from his words, and he turned to his companion.

" This man Devisher. Did he really fall overboard ? "

Mr. Ricardo replied slowly : " It was thought by the men on *Agamemnon* that he took a chance."

" With the odds against him ? " said Hanaud.

" Yes."

Hanaud dug his hands into his pockets. He was obviously puzzled.

" It is not pleasant, of course, to be landed as an undesirable at Gravesend. But, after all, he would be alive."

Monsieur Hanaud took his hands from his pockets and threw them up. " It is something to be alive."

" There might be other charges against him ? " Ricardo suggested, " waiting for him at Gravesend. He told us that the name upon his passport was false."

Monsieur Hanaud waved the suggestion aside. Some other question was troubling him.

" And he went ashore at Dartmouth alone, with fifteen pounds in his pocket ? "

" Yes."

" Did he go to the harbour-master's office ? "

" He landed at the slip close to the harbour-master's office, but I think that if he had gone to the office, some official would have come off to ask whether we corroborated his story."

Hanaud nodded his head in agreement. Then he asked :

48

" Do you think the Captain Mordaunt was really asleep in his bath ? "

The question had occurred to Mr. Ricardo, but he had made up his mind.

" I do. It is true that Mordaunt was in a hurry to lay up his yacht for the winter. But he really meant that Devisher must make his position clear to the authorities."

Hanaud, however, was not so confident.

" It will be. Yes. No doubt. But I should like to converse a little with the Captain Mordaunt, none the less."

Mr. Ricardo shook his head. That would not be so easy. On Sunday, it was true, Captain Mordaunt would be present at one of the famous evenings of Septimus Crottle. But Julius Ricardo did not belong to that circle, and did not propose to do a gate-crash with Hanaud at his elbow. He said :

" There, my friend, I cannot help you."

" It is a pity," Hanaud returned, staring out of the window. And suddenly he turned back upon Ricardo.

" This Torbay train ? He arrives in London at half-past three ? "

" Yes," said Ricardo.

" And you travel on him ? "

" Yes."

" And you take the luncheon in the dining-car ? Yes ? "

" No. I slept in my compartment."

" Was Devisher upon that train ? "

" I don't know. It was a long train with many carriages. I never saw Devisher."

" So that, for all you know, my friend Ricardo, Bryan Devisher may have arrived in London at half-past three yesterday afternoon. It is agreed ? "

" Yes."

Hanaud twisted his body and shook his big shoulders and made the grunts and moans of discomfort.

"You see how it is," he cried to Mr. Ricardo, who didn't see at all how it was. "There is my little affair. I wind it up and I take a vacancy. Good! If it be. But it isn't. My friend, I do not want my little affair to become your big affair. No."

"And you're afraid of that?" replied Ricardo in surprise.

Hanaud laid his hand impressively on Ricardo's arm.

"So afraid that it gives me the gaiters," he said solemnly.

Mr. Ricardo translated correctly, but, looking into his friend's troubled face, knew that this was not the moment for correcting the translation.

"You had better tell me what your little affair is."

"I will," Hanaud replied as he pulled his blue-paper packet of cigarettes from his pocket, "whilst we smoke the Maryland." He offered the packet to Mr. Ricardo, who recoiled from it as if it were a dish of poison, and then, having lit one, continued : "It was seven or eight years ago. Daniel Horbury was in a smaller way of business, but he had his fingers in a hundred pies, and you know that a day comes when there must be real money on the table. Mr. Horbury knew the date of that day. Ten thousand pounds on the table—and he had not one sliver."

"Stiver," Ricardo corrected.

"As I said, one sliver," Hanaud agreed equably. "Mrs. Hubbard, she was naked. You understand?"

"Positively," said Mr. Ricardo.

"Good! But he has associates, not clerks exactly, and not partners. Strap-hangers, you call them."

"And sometimes hangers-on," said Mr. Ricardo.

"Amongst them, Bryan Devisher. A valuable one for the Daniel Horburys. He had good manners, good looks, youth, and he was not odd. Public School and the entrance into houses of which the good Horbury only knew the portico. You follow me ? "

" I am alongside of you," Ricardo observed with his eyes on the window. Battersea Park had been left behind. The car had skirted the Park, crossed a main road, dived southward into a street where little houses with little · gardens were succeeding terraces. They might reach the end of their journey before Hanaud had reached the beginning of his. " You would be wise to continue."

" I go." Hanaud bounced up and down on the seat, marshalling his facts. Then he raised an imperative finger.

" First an historical set of pearls disappears. Second, Mr. Devisher sells them to a jeweller, Gravot, in the Place Vendôme, for ten thousand pounds. Daniel Horbury has his ten thousand pounds on the table. Act one ! See ? "

Mr. Ricardo nodded his head.

" But the loss of the pearls is discovered," Hanaud resumed, " and Gravot of the Place Vendôme must give them back. For that is the law. Gravot gives them back, but he is out for Devisher's blood."

" I see that," Ricardo agreed.

" But there is no Devisher. He has gone. One of Horbury's little pies was a revolution in Venezuela. It was needed. The revolution fails. Devisher finds himself in the Castillo del Libertador, and is there for life, or for as long as Vicente Gomez lives. So at once there is difficulty. There is not, without Devisher himself, proof that the ten thousand pounds Horbury put upon the table were the ten thousand pounds paid by Gravot of the Place Vendôme."

" So—there's the jeweller . . ."

" Down the drain, as you say in your picturesque way.

Exactly, my friend. Oh, how quick you are! That Mr. Ricardo—who shall get by him? He wait—with his glasses not straight upon his nose. Then he pounce —the jaguar! The criminal? Poor fellow! It is over."

Mr. Ricardo wriggled and blushed and laughed—a small, modest laugh.

" Poor fellow, yes," he said, playing a little tune upon his knees with his fingers. " It is over."

" But my Gravot," resumed Hanaud after his flatteries had been enjoyed, " with him the years have passed. He wants now, not the blood, but his good money. So we try, as I told you, for a friendly settlement."

Mr. Ricardo frowned over the problem very astutely.

" Yes. No doubt nowadays Daniel Horbury could command ten thousand pounds."

" Yet he slitted his throat," replied Hanaud quickly. " Explain that to me. After all, it is not an ordinary behaviour."

" It is not," Mr. Ricardo agreed.

It was not reasonable, he thought, even if Hanaud had come. . . .

" By the way," he asked, " did Horbury know that you had come to London? "

" No."

Hanaud was emphatic. Superintendent Maltby knew and perhaps one or two officials of his service. And a lawyer. But no one else.

" As I told you, we did not wish the prosecution. I called on the solicitor Preedy, who was employed in the original case, when I left Victoria Station."

Again Mr. Ricardo was silent. The little houses with the little gardens were giving place to big houses with big gardens. There were big trees, too, chestnuts and oaks and beeches, holding up their thick lacework of leaves and branches, so that even upon the roads there was the cool refreshment of a green world. But there was clearly no comfort for Monsieur Hanaud in the pleasure of the morning.

" Tell me," he said, " Devisher—Bryan Devisher—did he talk to you on the yacht ?."

" A little, yes."

" For an example ? "

" Wait a moment."

Mr. Ricardo was being bustled, an experience which he disliked extremely. There was something said. It was at the back of his mind, almost tangible, really tangible if he wasn't bustled. And suddenly he had it.

" He said that after the revolution failed, he might have got away ; but he was betrayed."

" By Horbury ? "

Hanaud flashed the question at him.

" He did not say, but he looked as if he knew. Yes, I remember, he was whiter than ever, his eyes staring and his lips working with a curious little smile." And Mr. Ricardo shivered suddenly, as he had not shivered in the saloon of the yacht when the words were spoken.

Hanaud leaned back in the car. After a little while he said slowly : " He took a chance. Perhaps he took that chance, not because I or Maltby might be waiting at Gravesend for *El Rey* to anchor, but because Horbury might be—or shall we say Horbury's friends ? Do you see ? "

Mr. Ricardo saw very clearly not merely Devisher's staring eyes and twisted smile, but saw them lost in a great crowd on the arrival platform of a railway station. Three-thirty, the Torbay Limited ! Devisher had the advantage of the big rusty steamer by an afternoon— and a night. He had the advantage of Horbury by an afternoon—and a night—of Horbury, who had sold him into six years of hell in the Castillo del Libertador.

" But I do not want my little affair eight years old to widen himself out into the big case of Horbury," cried Hanaud, spreading out his arms in an extreme vexation. " No ! Saperlipopette, I do not want it ! "

He took a black cigarette from his blue-paper packet and lit it, and as he snapped the lighter he shook off from his big shoulders the suspicions which had troubled him.

" However, we fright ourselves for nothing at all. Men like Horbury ! They commit such follies. They are often in the odd street."

" Queer street," Mr. Ricardo corrected.

" So I said," observed Hanaud. " But you will be disappointed," and he shook his head sadly at his friend. " That Mr. Ricardo ! He likes his bit of crime," and with a laugh he nudged Mr. Ricardo in the ribs.

There were few things which Ricardo detested more heartily than these familiar nudges with the elbow. As a rule he left a sufficient space between himself and Hanaud for them to miss him. But they were travelling in his second Rolls-Royce, a smaller limousine, with no arm-rest to protect him, and the elbow jolted him unexpectedly.

" I am not the only one who will be disappointed," he said tartly.

" Who else ? "

" Gravot of the Place Vendôme," said Ricardo.

Hanaud smiled.

" Perhaps not, my friend. This Daniel Horbury had a wife. We shall see. She might wish to make the amends."

A wife ! It was the first time that Mr. Ricardo had ever heard of Horbury's wife. His horses, to be sure ! But a wife ! Mr. Ricardo was conscious of a sinking at his heart. Had he known that a wife would be present, questioned, harassed, maybe in tears, he would perhaps have sent Monsieur Hanaud on his quest alone. But he had himself to come, he reflected ; the police wanted him at their side. He recalled the hearty invitation of Superintendent Maltby over the telephone, but now he recalled it with relief. Certainly Mr. Ricardo could hardly have refused.

" England expects . . ." he said to himself—was there a cliché with which he was unfamiliar ?—and he sought an anodyne for his uneasiness in a curious speculation. Horbury had married either in his youth, when the passions were hot and the world just waiting to be turned over on its back like a turtle ; or in his maturity, when the years had given him a plump and purselike semblance. In the one case he would have married a girl of his own station, but worse educated ; in the other a white-fingered daughter of the counties, disdainful and greedy.

In neither case should I care a tuppenny damn, Mr. Ricardo thought, and giggled at the common but expressive phrase.

The car was passing upon its right hand the playing fields of a great school. The school buildings, a fine central hall linked by a covered way with two big blocks of classrooms, all in deep red brick and white stone, faced a second main high road. And this road, too, the motor-car crossed. As it entered a narrower, gently-sloping avenue, Monsieur Hanaud read a name upon a tin plate :

" Lordship Lane. It is here."

On their left hand, large villas lay hidden amongst trees, behind fences and high laurels. On the right a meadow, set here and there with a great oak or a chestnut, sloped up to a low hedge and the flank of a two-storied small white house. Behind it rose a screen of holly, so thick, so high, that it made a curtain quite isolating the house from its neighbour.

" White Barn," said Hanaud.

A policeman saluted. The car turned in at the gate and stopped in the gravelled court in front of the door. Already two cars were parked there.

Chapter 8

WHITE BARN: THE LOCKED DOOR

WHITE BARN was a pleasant oblong unpretentious house without gables or ornaments. It had neither basement nor front steps, and on the upper side, between the tall hedge and the house, a garage had been built without spoiling its symmetry. It was of two storeys only, a small manor house of some two hundred years of age. The door was in the centre of the house with a large window on either side, and it was ajar. Hanaud pushed it open.

" It is permitted . . . ? " he asked.

A man of middle age, with a pair of sharp grey eyes set in an inconspicuous face, stepped forward.

" It is desired."

" That you, the Superintendent, should be here . . ."

" Is a compliment to France."

These politenesses having been exchanged, Hanaud introduced Mr. Ricardo, and the Superintendent's inconspicuous features became at once so vivid that, according to Ricardo's fancy, they claimed the attention of the world.

" Mr. Ricardo ! It is a pleasure. We shall not ask you anything for the moment, but later you will, I am sure, help us."

Superintendent Maltby's eyes were widening alarmingly as they looked over Mr. Ricardo.

" This is Detective-Inspector Herbert," he said, pointing to a second officer in plain clothes, " and Sergeant Hughes." This was a slight, smiling man in uniform who moved round between Mr. Ricardo and the door.

" To be sure," said Mr. Ricardo, but he was not comfortable. It seemed that he had tumbled from the high pulpit of Investigation into the dock. Before he could remember any crime which he had committed, the offensive elbow caught him again sharply in the ribs.

" Really, really," he exclaimed in a fluster. He had almost cried aloud, " Not guilty, m'lud."

Hanaud, however, quite unconsciously rescued him from his embarrassment.

" It is charming this house, yes ? " he said, and Mr. Ricardo cordially agreed.

He had, indeed, been surprised when he first saw it between the trunks of the trees, by its plain, unbedizened beauty ; and the hall matched it. It was in the shape of a capital T. Where Mr. Ricardo stood, with his back to the front door, he looked straight down the long leg of the T, past the staircase, to the door of the service quarters. The broad cross-piece in which they all stood stretched from side to side of the house. On each side of the front door a big window looked upon the courtyard, and on each side, facing the window on the inner wall, was a mahogany door ; that upon Mr. Ricardo's right, or London side, leading to the room which commanded the garden and the meadow to the edge of the Turnpike Road ; that upon his left, into some chamber filled with a subdued green light by the holly hedge. The floor of the hall was a dark polished oak, whose severity was relieved by two or three Eastern rugs. A Sheraton sideboard spread its elegance under the right-hand window, a small writing-table received light from the left, and between each mahogany door and the edge of the long passage, a Chippendale chair, upholstered in a dark red silk, kept a comely balance.

" So ! The Horburys lived here ? " said Hanaud. " I should have thought Park Lane, perhaps, or Piccadilly."

Ricardo smiled. He, too, had found something inconsistent between White Barn and the hot, equivocal, noisy career of Mr. Daniel Horbury, financier.

" He did live in Park Lane," Superintendent Maltby agreed. " As for this little house, it may be that Mrs. Horbury—but we shall hear."

A door behind the staircase opened as he spoke. It was obviously a second door from that room upon the left-hand side which shortened the journey to the kitchen. A middle-aged woman, broad and stout, with a cotton frock and a large apron in front of it, waddled into the passage carrying a breakfast tray and vanished into the kitchen.

" Mrs. Wallace," explained Maltby. " She is the charwoman. She comes every day at eight, airs the rooms and makes the beds when they have gone to town. She was with Mrs. Horbury when we came."

" You have seen Madame Horbury ? " Hanaud asked. Maltby shook his head.

" I thought it would be more comfortable for the poor lady if, first of all, we got the body out of the way and the photographs and the finger prints taken. We will hear now what Mrs. Wallace has to tell us."

The charwoman came along the passage. Her eyes were red as if she had been crying and her face was mottled ; but now that the shock of her discovery was dulled, she was beginning to see herself as the one without whom the story could not be told at all. The Superintendent asked her to seat herself in one of the chairs, and she did with a sniff which might have been gratitude for his consideration or grief for the loss of " the master."

" They didn' live here 'xacly," she said, " but they use to be here when they was firs' married, and Mr. Horbury kep on the house, sort of sentimental. And every now and then, especial in the summer, they'd dine early in London and she'd drive him down in the car.

Mr. Horbury, he didn' drive at all but she's a beautiful driver. I expec' what with parties and speeches and goins-on, they came down to be quiet-like together."

" They were fond of one another ? " the Superintendent asked.

" Oh, special," replied Mrs. Wallace. " Beauty and the Beast, I use to call 'em, though it seems sort o' sacrilegious now. You could hear them laughin' in the mornin' gay as gay, and as I says you don't go laughin' proper with people before breakfast unless you've got hearts attune," she added surprisingly.

The Superintendent, whilst applauding Mrs. Wallace's philosophy of love, led her to describe the habits of the household.

" Did you know when Mr. and Mrs. Horbury were coming down for the night ? " he asked. " Did they telephone, for instance ?"

" No, sir. Mr. Horbury, he said that was making arrangements. What he wanted was or-gan-i-sation." She brought out the big word in cautious syllables. " Oh, he was a one for organisation, was Mr. Horbury. He said without organisation he wouldn't have a bottle o' Pommery '06 in the 'ouse or a penny-piece in the bank. How I did laugh, sir, 'im puttin' a bottle of champagne before money in the bank, and so did he when I pointed it out to 'im."

" Yes, that must have seemed very funny to Mr. Horbury," said the Superintendent dryly. " Now come to last night."

" I did what I always did," she replied. " There are electric fires in the bedrooms and everywhere except the garden-room. I put the logs there and the paper all ready to light. In the kitchen I prepared a primus stove with some fresh eggs and bacon sliced ready in a glass jar, and rolls and butter and corfy, if they should want a little supper, as it were. Plates and cups and saucers and glasses and knives and forks, of course. There were some bottles of the Pommery in the cupboard. They never drank nothing but the champagne and never more than one bottle, though I think he drank most o' that. Just brushed her lips with it, as you might say. Often and often I've found her glass half-full and the bottle empty in the morning."

" Did they bring friends with them ? " asked Maltby, who now let her ramble on as she willed that he might get lights from as many angles as possible on this tragedy.

" No, no, never," she replied. " They just come here to be easy. They just come to be quiet-like together. So I put everything ready and shut up the house and went away at five o'clock as I always did," she resumed, " and I came back at eight o'clock punctual this morning and let myself in with my latchkey."

" Have you got it ? " the Superintendent asked, and she produced a small Yale key on a ring.

Maltby balanced it for a moment in the palm of his hand.

" How many are there of these ? "

" Three, sir," she answered. " Mr. and Mrs. Horbury each have one."

Maltby nodded his head and gave the key back to her.

" Now, when you got in ? "

Mrs. Wallace drew a great breath. She was clearly going to put over a big performance, thought Mr. Ricardo. Not one horrific detail was to be omitted. She had gone at once to the kitchen. The primus stove was unlit, the eggs were still in their paper bag, the bacon in its glass jar, the butter in a curious glass dish with a lid, standing in a glass saucer. " Irish, Mr. Horbury says. Whatifer, he calls it and what's it fer, I calls it. Leadeny stuff. It wouldn't do for the village, I can tell you. When we wants glass, we wants glass, if you understand me."

" Yes, I do understand," replied the Superintendent cordially. His voice sounded as if he couldn't have endured a piece of Watifer in his house for a minute.

" So everything was untouched," Mrs. Wallace continued. " I hangs up my coat and bonnet on the peg behind the door, and I lights the stove and puts on a kettle of water to make myself a nice cup o' tea, and I says, ' Maria, here's a neasy day for you.' But I hadn't hardly spoken the words when I noticed that the drinkin' glasses weren't there. Two there should have been, and two there weren't. Moreover the cupboard door was open. Generally it's locked, with the key in the lock. There were two glasses missing but no bottle missing. That weren't like Mr. Horbury. Allus took the bottle into the garden-room, he did. ' So they're here arter all,' I says, ' and lucky I was to put the kettle on to boil for their mornin' tea.' I hadn't a suspicion in my mind. There ! Not one."

" No, indeed. Why should you ? " the Superintendent asked sympathetically.

Mrs. Wallace had run back along the passage to open the windows and air the garden-room. She pointed dramatically to the door in the inner wall opposite to the hall window on the right of Mr. Ricardo.

" It was ajar," she said, " and the lights still burning."

She had flung the door open with a gesture worthy of Mrs. Siddons, she had advanced a step, and she had seen " the poor gentleman " still sitting in his chair, but his body stretched across the little table in front of it, the blotting-book pushed forward over the edge, his arm outstretched. His throat was gaping, and just underneath the outstretched hand, lying in a great pool of blood, was the knife.

" A horrible thing with a long blade and a handle pale blue, just like Cambridge under Hammersmith Bridge. I shrieked," she cried, and her arms whirled in the air. "Never had I seen such a sight. Everything went black. I tottered. I was goin' to faint, I was, when I remembered that poor woman upstairs. 'My dooty,' I says to myself and after clawing to the door a bit to steady mysel, I stumbled upstairs to their bedroom door. And it was locked."

"Locked?" Hanaud cried suddenly in a sharp voice, and bowed his apologies to the Superintendent.

"Locked," replied Mrs. Wallace, glaring at Hanaud, "which it never had been before. Never! I used to take their mornin' tea into them regular as if they were the King and Queen. And now the door was locked."

Hanaud nodded, but he was puzzled. Here was something which needed explanation. Meanwhile he could not reconcile that locked door and the wife behind it, with Maria's story of the couple coming down alone to be 'quiet-like' together in their suburban solitude and 'gay as gay' the next morning.

"What did you do when you found the door locked, Mrs. Wallace?" the Superintendent asked, keeping her to her story.

"I beat on it," she replied. "I cried 'Open, please! There's horrors, Mrs. Horbury. Oh! the poor gentleman.' And I heard Mrs. Horbury say, in a low voice and quite from the floor, as it was: 'Wait! I'll let you in.' She seemed to bump against the door and unlocked it. But as she unlocked it, she said again 'Wait! Wait!' and I heard her stumbling into her bed. Then at last she said, 'Come in!'"

"And then?" Again it was Maltby who urged her.

"When I went in—it was terrible. There was the twin bed which Mr. Horbury used, turned down for him, and his fugiamas, as he called them—Japan, you know—spread out as I had spread them, and Mrs. Horbury in her bed with the blankets up to her chin, white as a sheet and shivering—oh, as if she was an iceberg in the Artic 'Ocean. ' Oh, you poor, poor darlin',' I said, just as if we were both of the same stature. I told her the truth and she said, still all frozen and her teeth chattering, ' Get me my dressing-gown. We must ring up the police.' We came down the stairs together. I pointed to the garden-room and said in a whisper, ' It's in there.' But she shook her head and rang up the police station.''

" Do you remember the message ? "

Inspector Herbert of the local constabulary answered for Mrs. Wallace. "We took it down." He turned towards Sergeant Hughes, who turned back the leaves of a notebook and read aloud : " This is Mrs. Horbury speaking from White Barn. Will you please send the proper people up here ? My husband has died—by violence."

Sergeant Hughes then took over the history of events from Maria Wallace, the charwoman.

" The message was quite clear and quite without hysteria, but the voice was urgent and distressed. We sent at once what men we had—photographer, finger-print man—and we rang up the police surgeon, Dr. Claxton. The french windows into the garden were locked and it looked as if Mr. Horbury had committed suicide. Since Mr. Horbury was a Member of Parliament and well known in business circles "—Sergeant Hughes dwelled for a little longer than need be upon that useful phrase—" we rang up Scotland Yard and tried to get in touch with Superintendent Maltby, who had not yet . . .''

" That's enough about that," the Superintendent interrupted with some hauteur.

" Certainly, sir," said the Sergeant and crossed out the offending lines. The Superintendent coughed.

" Of course," he explained, " if one sits up all night . . .''

" With a sick friend," the Sergeant interpolated, his eyes again stolidly upon the wall, and the Superintendent, who possessed a sense of humour, made a good mark against the name of Sergeant Hughes.

" By the time Superintendent Maltby arrived the drudgery had been completed," Sergeant Hughes read. " The police surgeon, Dr. Claxton, had met the late Mr. Horbury's doctor, Cornish, at White Barn. They made a cursory examination to be certain that life was extinct, and after the police had taken the necessary measurements, Dr. Claxton conveyed the corpse in the station ambulance to the mortuary, having arranged with Dr. Cornish to join him later with a view to a full post-mortem investigation. Whilst the body was being removed, the finger-prints and photographs taken, Inspector Herbert asked Dr. Cornish to look after Mrs. Horbury and prepare her for an interview with Superintendent Maltby, who would doubtless wish to ask her some questions."

" Up till now, then," said Maltby, " no one has received any account of what happened last night ? "

" No, sir."

" Beyond that Mrs. Horbury locked her door," said Mr. Ricardo, and, though the fact was known before, the separation of this fact from the rigmarole of Mrs. Wallace gave to it a new significance. There was a pause, even a stiffening of attitudes, a silence.

Mr. Ricardo, however, had up to this moment experienced no flashing revelation which he wished to pass on to his colleagues. From the first aspect of White Barn he had suffered a confusion. He could hardly reconcile Horbury with this house, and still less with his retention of it as a refuge where he and a wife could be " quiet-like together." But when he had at last accepted these details, he found them weakened, if not contradicted, in that Mrs. Horbury had gone up to her bedroom alone and locked the door.   Had they quarrelled, Ricardo wondered ? Hardly enough to account for Horbury's suicide, in any case.   Horbury and his wife— the homely background to the flambuoyant career— Pommery '06 at Bentano's in the Strand and domestic felicity in Lordship Lane. For a student of life, a fascinating case ; but, since his wife had locked the bedroom door, an enigma.

The silence was broken by Hanaud in a most deferential voice.

" May I ask a question ? "

" Of course," Maltby answered.   " We shall welcome your assistance, although I fancy we shall find the Horbury affair not too difficult."

" I thank you," Hanaud answered.

How charmingly correct they both were, Mr. Ricardo reflected, as Hanaud now turned to the charwoman.

" Was it by· means of this telephone that Madame Horbury summoned the police this morning ? "

A telephone machine was standing almost at Hanaud's left hand on the writing-table beneath the window.

" Yes, sir."

Hanaud looked at the handle of the receiver and with a little bow to Sergeant Hughes :

" I see there are traces of the powder for the finger-prints."

" We found some old marks of Mrs. Wallace's fingers which she let us take and a new, quite clear, set, which we take to have been made by Mrs. Horbury," answered Hughes.

" Then "—and Hanaud turned back to the charwoman —" is this the only telephone in the house ? "

" No, no, Mounseer. It is a French gentleman, isn't it ? This is the one which I use for ordering things— coal and food, and suchlike. But there is an extension in the garden-room which Mr. and Mrs. Horbury use when they want to use it. But that's only onct in a blue moon."

" But if they are rung up, the bell rings here ? "

" To be sure," said Maltby with a touch of impatience. What on earth had the telephone here to do with the case of a man who had cut his throat in the garden-room ? The charwoman, however, was all for giving information. When would life have another thrill for her like this ?

" Yes, Mounseer, the bell rings here and in the garden-room and you can answer from either."

" You are bound to hear it, then, wherever you are ? "

Mrs. Wallace laughed.

" You'd have to be as deaf as a post not to hear it," she said. " Bad as a firebell, I says. I can shut the kitchen door never so, but let that bell go off, and there's no being quiet-like until you've answered it."

" Quiet-like," said Mr. Ricardo solemnly, with a nod to the charwoman. " That is the key word."

" To what ? " asked the Superintendent. Mr. Ricardo had not an idea.

But Hanaud hurried to his rescue.

" Yes, my friends," he declared with a serious face, which somehow frightened everyone else in the hall, " I think we shall find that there is much which is too quiet-like in the whole of this affair."

" The locked door ? " Maltby suggested.

" That is one thing," Hanaud replied, " but only one thing."

Again there was a pause. Then Maltby, shaking from his shoulders some horror which he did not wish to believe, moved.

" Let us see this garden-room."

He walked to the door upon the right hand, opposite to the window under which stood the Sheraton sideboard. It was a thick mahogany door with a glass handle. He took out his handkerchief and wrapped it round the glass. But Sergeant Hughes interrupted him.

" The only prints upon that handle were the same as those clear prints upon the telephone on the writing-table."

" Mrs. Horbury's then ? " said Maltby.

" Yes."

" And one set only ? " suddenly Hanaud interposed.

" Yes."

" As she went upstairs—to lock her door ? Yes, no doubt," cried Hanaud. " But when they arrived in the evening, eh, my friend ? To spend an evening quiet-like together. Which of them opened this door ? "

" No doubt Olivia Horbury," said the Sergeant, politely condescending.

" Oh, no doubt," cried Hanaud, and there was no politeness at all in his voice. " And she was kind enough to save us trouble by placing her fingers on the handle in exactly the same position as she did when she drew the door to, to go upstairs to her room and lock herself in. That is curious, no ? "

Sergeant Hughes looked uncomfortable. Superintendent Maltby was troubled.

" Yes, I don't understand that," he remarked unhappily. " It might, of course, happen by chance, once . . ."

And Monsieur Hanaud cut in : " Yes, my friend, once —when the moon is blue."

Superintendent Maltby, with a gesture of annoyance, threw open the door of the garden-room.

Chapter 9

THE UNSPOKEN WORD

THEY entered an oblong room with panelled walls enamelled white. One or two girandoles and one or two water-colours decorated the panels. The carpet was thick and of a warm wine-dark red, and the curtains and pelmets of heavy silk matched it in colour. A white marble fireplace had a panel of blue Wedgwood figures below the mantelshelf. Mr. Ricardo was the last to enter, and, standing by the door, he shut his eyes tight and asked of himself :

" What message has this room for me ? "

Apparently it had none. Isolate himself as he might, no message shot tingling across his mind. And, besides, Mrs. Wallace, the charwoman, was talking volubly.

" The room was lit and the curtains drawn as though it was still night, and there was the poor gentleman sprawled across the table, and gore—you wanted to be a butcher born, you did, not to feel sickish. Then I screamed and ran out of the room."

It was not wonderful to Mr. Ricardo that she should feel sickish. He conceived that if his mind had been less alert, he might have felt a trifle sickish himself. Upon his right hand were two french windows opening on to a green and pleasant garden with the great meadow beyond a low hedge. Although birds sang no more, rooks wheeled and cawed about one of the oaks and, as the branches swayed, the sun threw an ever-changing pattern of draperies upon the grass. An idyllic place where lovers could be quiet-like together—especially at night with the curtains drawn and an aromatic log fire burning on the hearth. Now the small table was pushed forward, and blood had splashed even on the enamelled wall and coagulated in what seemed an enormous pool upon the carpet. A blotting-book bound in a buhl cover, ornamented with mother-of-pearl, had tumbled off the table and stood on its edges, like a child's tent, on the rim of the dried pool. Beside it were the splinters of a broken wineglass. Mr. Ricardo could almost see the heavy figure of the man slumped over the table and the right arm flung forward just over the spot where a cardboard cover had been placed to mark the position where the knife had fallen.

The table stood close to the fireplace with a chair, against the wall behind it, in which Horbury had been sitting. It was small and there should have been, one would have thought, letters, papers of some sort, scattered upon the floor. For a fountain pen with its nib exposed had peeped out beneath his arm.

"There were no papers," Inspector Herbert explained. "It struck me as curious."

The Superintendent walked to the fireplace and, going down on his knees, poked amongst the ashes. Then he sat back upon his heels. "Yes, it's curious," he said slowly. "If he burnt papers, he did it thoroughly. There's nothing here but an old butt of a cigar. He must have tossed that into the fire, and then put an end to everything."

Hanaud, for his part, was more concerned with the appointments of the room. The table at which Horbury had sat was on the further side of the fireplace from the door, and still further along the wall, in the corner, a cushioned chair with arms was placed. It looked diagonally across the room towards the door, and the cushion at the back of it was crumpled. A long table stood against the wall running between that corner and the windows. Opposite to the fireplace was a sofa with a back, and upon that, too, there were cushions which had been disarranged. At the end of it a round mahogany table was placed, and on it was a glass half full of champagne.

" It seems that at one moment Madame Horbury sat here with her glass of champagne at her elbow and, as that good woman tells us," Hanaud said with a glance towards the charwoman, " she took no more of it than she usually did. And there upon the floor are the splinters of Horbury's glass. But why should Horbury, of all men, have put ·the bottle back in the cupboard ? "

Superintendent Maltby nodded his head.

" We don't want to make difficulties ourselves, do we ? "

To him this was a plain case of suicide by a man of a very stormy history, who might well have found himself with no option between death or a long term of penal servitude. " These are small matters."

" Yet there is another. May I again interíere ? "

Hanaud was all smiles and deference and entirely at Mister the Superintendent's disposal. Mister the Superintendent, indeed, was beginning to wonder whether he had been wise to invite this burly Frenchman. But he tried not to show it.

" Of course," he said. " My dear Hanaud, we know of your painstaking methods. A hair on a coat-sleeve, a key lost or found . . ."

" Lost or found ! " cried Hanaud. " Was ever anything more properly, more profoundly said ? My dear Monsieur ! "

He walked lightly across the room to the table against the end wall. On it stood a telephone instrument of the modern kind, ear and mouthpiece in one, resting on a cradle, and a dial at the foot of the instrument. But it was not the telephone which had attracted him. Almost, but not quite, behind the machine, something had gleamed.

"Yes, another little matter, and that, too, out of place," and Monsieur Hanaud was not the man to keep a note of triumph out of his voice. He held up a bunch of keys, picking it up daintily by the ring.

"You will observe that there is a Yale latch-key on the ring. Is not this the bunch of keys which the good Horbury carried on a chain in the pocket of his trousers? Yes? It seems so. Perhaps Mister Herbert will tell us."

"Them's his keys," said Mrs. Wallace. "I've seen them over and over."

Sergeant Hughes, at a nod from Maltby, took the keys and went out of the room. When he returned, he addressed himself to Maltby.

"It is the key of the front door, sir."

Maltby crossed to the side table and, taking a piece of chalk from his pocket, held it above the spot where Hanaud's eye had discovered the bunch.

"That the place?" he asked.

"Yes."

Maltby marked the place and both men stood for a moment in a perplexity. After all, why should Horbury have taken the bunch off the chain on which he usually carried it?

"If the lock of the door had been stiff, for instance," said Hanaud. "Yes, it would have been easier to turn it so."

"But the lock wasn't stiff," replied Hughes. "And why should he put the bunch on the table?"

All three men stared again at the chalk mark on the table. Another little thing. But an unusual thing. And therefore needing explanation.

"It's certainly odd," Maltby exclaimed. He turned rather savagely upon the charwoman. "You never saw them off the chain?"

"Never," she declared. "Cross my thumbs!"

" But it might happen ? "

Mrs. Wallace sniggered.

" And it might rain pigs and chocolate creams," she answered, " but it don't."

" Of course "—Maltby disregarded the charwoman's nettled rejoinder—" Horbury might have wanted to telephone. Standing up straight after dialling, the edge of the table may have pressed the bunch into his thigh. He may have taken the keys from the spring hook of the chain and tossed them where they fell. A little fanciful ? " he asked of Sergeant Hughes, who looked more than a little troubled by this sudden high flight of his superior officer.

" No, sir, not fanciful at all," he replied, " but "—and he blurted out the uncontroversial fact—" that telephone wasn't used last night."

Mrs. Wallace sniggered again. But it was Hanaud who spoke, a little startled perhaps and certainly perplexed.

" I should like to be very sure of that," he said quietly.

" You may be," said the Sergeant. " That—well, that handle thing was tested for prints. There wasn't a mark of any kind upon it."

" No, and there wouldn't be," cried Mrs. Wallace, folding her arms across her body. " Not if it wasn't used last night. Yesterday morning I dusted it, I did, and when I dusts, I dusts."

" Did you take the receiver from the cradle ? "

" That I did," she answered. " I holds the spring down, see ? With my left hand. Then I takes off the handle thing. Then I slips one of the two telephone books on to them,supports to keep them down. Then I dusts the thing thoroughly—earpiece and mouthpiece and all—and slips it back again."

She contemplated Monsieur Hanaud with an aggressive face, but he answered her with a bow which was quite disarming. " Madame, I do not doubt you for a moment. The whole room is an example for housewives."

Mrs. Wallace relaxed from her indignation ; and the next moment she smiled. For Sergeant Hughes added his tribute of praise.

" That's true," he said. " I never saw furniture so clean. There are marks on Mr. Horbury's chair and table made by him, as we know, and a few on the mantel-shelf and the arm of the settee, where Mrs. Horbury sat with her glass of champagne. They correspond with the prints on the telephone in the hall. But, apart from those, nothing at all."

" Except, perhaps," Hanaud suggested, " some on the arms of that chair in the corner where the cushion is disarranged ? "

Hughes was for the moment taken aback.

" No, sir," he answered after a pause. " That's queer, that is. I was here whilst the finger-print men were at work. There were no prints on that chair at all. It may be that the cushion was thrown on to the chair, perhaps by Horbury himself from his chair behind the table."

It seemed, however, that Hanaud had lost interest in the matter.

" Very likely," he said with a shrug of his shoulders and a nod of his head. " Little things. As the Super-intendent tells us wisely, we must not make too much of them."

A bell rang in the passage and the knocker rattled upon the outside door.

" It will be the doctor," said Herbert, and Maltby nodded to the charwoman.

" Will you let him in, please, and then we need not keep you from your duties."

The charwoman brought into the parlour a minute afterwards a big-boned, loose-limbed man, with a genial, bluff manner, and a suit of dark clothes even looser than his limbs.

" Dr. Claxton," said the charwoman.

" And very many thanks for your help, Mrs. Wallace," Maltby said gratefully. " When I ring, will you ask Mrs. Horbury if she is ready to receive us ? "

Before Mrs. Wallace was out of the room, Claxton held out to Maltby a narrow longish cardboard box.

" The Inspector at the station wanted you to see this."

Maltby took off the lid and all could see the gleam of a long-bladed knife. Hanaud took a step towards it and Maltby made him an apology.

" I forget my manners. Dr. Claxton, I present you to Monsieur Hanaud of the Paris Sûreté."

" It is an honour," returned Dr. Claxton with a keen glance at the Frenchman.

" And Mr. Ricardo," added Maltby with a wave of the hand a little too careless.

But Dr. Claxton turned with a smile and an extended hand.

" Of Grosvenor Square ? " he asked, and lifted Mr. Ricardo into a heaven of delight. He wondered whether, if by any chance he should ever fall ill, it would seem unusual if he were to send to Lordship Lane for a doctor. He had no time to solve this important problem at the moment. For Maltby was kneeling down by that clotted mush of blood on the floor.

" Who would have thought the old man had so much blood in him ? " Mr. Ricardo observed, quoting from Macbeth.

" But he wasn't old," said Maltby.

" Mr. Ricardo was quoting from a standard case before the days of finger-prints," said Claxton.

Mr. Ricardo heaved a sigh of pleasure. He had been feeling rather chilly in that room. Even Hanaud had been too engrossed in some troublesome thoughts of his own to keep his friend constantly within the consultation. Now he had an ally.

" By the way," said Maltby over his shoulder. " The prints on the knife handle ? "

" Horbury's," said the doctor.

Maltby removed the cover from the blood upon the floor. The shape of the long knife was as clearly moulded in red as if it had been made in a sculptor's clay. Maltby took his handkerchief from his pocket and carefully lifted the knife from the box. It fitted exactly in the space. To Mr. Ricardo it looked the most murderous of weapons ; one side of the blade was thin and sharp as a razor, the other more than usually broad and heavy, as though it had been loaded ; and what gave to it a curiously sinister aspect was the pale blue colour of the handle. It was a weapon of death imitating a child's toy. Even so unimaginative a woman as Mrs. Wallace had noticed especially that gay bright colour—" Cambridge passing under Hammersmith Bridge."

" One of the occasions, I suppose," Mr. Ricardo ruminated, " when Oxford had been embarrassed by their long list of wins and didn't try."

He did not pursue this engaging topic for Hanaud turned a pursed and frowning face upon the doctor.

" There seems to be no hinge where the blade joins the handle of the knife."

" There is none."

Hanaud nodded his head. He glanced sharply at Ricardo and so back again to the doctor.

" I see. South American, do you think ? "

The Superintendent once more began to show signs of impatience at Hanaud's excursions beyond the strict boundaries of this garden-room ; and Dr. Claxton drew back from the dangerous game of conjecture.

" No knowledge. No theories," he announced curtly, and Maltby nodded.

" That's sound. Speculation may be the soul of conversation, but it's a will o' the wisp to a Superintendent of Police."

Hanaud was not at all abashed. He was darting glances on the floor, on the settee, on the mantelshelf, as if he had not heard one word of the rebuke.

" If it is your hat you look for, my friend, you left it in the hall," Maltby continued sweetly, and Inspector Herbert did audibly snigger. Hanaud smiled apologetically.

" My hat ? Yes, there he is. He will not run away. But, Inspector, the sheath, he does."

" Sheath ! " Herbert exclaimed.

" To be sure. The knife, since he does not shut himself, will carry himself in a sheath. It was on the body perhaps ? "

" No," said the doctor and " No," the Inspector agreed. Maltby cried :

" There is a drawer in the table at which Horbury sat. We may have overlooked it."

He went behind the table and pulled out the drawer with a little more violence than it needed.

" No," he said and he acknowledged Hanaud's question with a stiff bow. " But it must be somewhere " ; and at once everyone in the room began to search for it.

" It might be of soft leather," said Herbert.

" Or of stiff leather," said Mr. Ricardo helpfully. He was down on his knees with the Sergeant. They peered under the chairs and tables, they turned up the edges of the carpet, they swung back the window curtains. Maltby picked up the blotting-book, shook it out and replaced it. Hanaud pushed his hand down at the side and the back of the settee. The few things which Herbert had taken from the dead man's pockets—a small diary, a gold pencil, a few half-crowns, a black letter-case with some pound notes in the partitions, the steel chain with the tab at the end for the trouser-button —were all arranged upon the mantelshelf. But of any protection for that deadly weapon with the blue handle, there was nowhere any sign.

" It is just another of the little things which do perplex me," said Hanaud, and then the doctor took him up.

" But there is no doubt that this was the knife he used," he argued. " No shadow of doubt ! He had drawn it from left to right across his throat. He had severed the carotid artery. The blood must have burst from it in great gouts, as though it had been pumped. He would have died very quickly."

" When ? " Hanaud asked sharply ; and Mr. Ricardo with a jerk drew himself erect.

He knew that here was the question to which Hanaud had been working up from the first moment when he had entered the room. " When ? " Just that ! All the rest, the small particulars discovered which made suicide a verdict difficult to accept, were the knitting of a pattern to which the answer to his question was the key. He had no wish, as Ricardo knew, to see his small affair of the pearls merging in the ever so much bigger crime of murder. But the plain reason for his life had driven him irresistibly. Murder must be revealed anywhere, upon whomsoever the blame fell. When did Horbury die then ? At what hour ? Answer !

The doctor answered :

" It is not always possible to be exact. But within limits one is justified, and in this case Mr. Cornish, a famous surgeon, agreed absolutely with me. We examined the body of Daniel Horbury in the mortuary at ten o'clock this morning and we agreed that death had taken place between ten and twelve hours before."

" Not after midnight then ? "

" Certainly not after midnight," Doctor Claxton

stated firmly, " and not before ten. We cannot be more precise."

Hanaud's eyes dropped from the doctor's face, and he stood so with his eyes on the ground. Then he slipped into an armchair below the fireplace and stared moodily into the ashes. He was not acting. His disappointment was as apparent as his honesty. There was no one in that room who interrupted him, no one indeed who stirred.

" My friend, I beg your pardon," he said to Maltby very gently. " Yet perhaps, in the end,· you will say, ' That Hanaud ! He was the nuisance, but he helped.' "

" I should not say he was the nuisance," Maltby returned with a smile.

" Although one might think it," Hanaud answered. " But I will not keep you on the tip-toes. No ! I was very anxious yesterday to settle my little dispute with this Horbury. So, on arriving in London by the Continental train, I rang up his office. I did not give my name, but I said my business was urgent. Horbury was not in his office, but the telephone number of White Barn was given to me. I dined with you, my friend Maltby, and I went home to Grosvenor Square. But I could not sleep. I said to myself, ' That is a slippery one, that Horbury ! How do I know that he has not caught the night train to Rome ? ' There are reasons besides why he might. So at half-past two in the morning . . ."

" Twenty-five minutes to three," Mr. Ricardo interrupted.

" You heard me ? "

" I heard you go down the stairs and call up a number on the telephone, but what number I did not hear."

" Good ! I have the corroboration," cried Hanaud. " This was the number—White Barn."

" You called up this house ? " exclaimed Maltby.

" I did."

" At twenty-five minutes to three in the morning ? "

" Yes."

" And you got an answer ? "

" I tell you what happened. I got cluck-cluck, cluck-cluck, like a clock. Then that ceased. So someone had lifted the receiver from the cradle. · I said ' It is Mr. Horbury ? Excuse please the hour. It is most urgent.' There was no answer, and I began to wonder whether the receiver had not been lifted just to stop the bell ringing through the house. Then, after a moment or two, I heard a little rattle as the handle was replaced on the spring— and the line went dead."

Again Hanaud received the tribute of silence. Then the detective-inspector suggested :

" Mrs. Horbury perhaps ? "

Hanaud shook his head.

" You heard the woman Wallace. There are only two instruments in the house. One in the ·hall, the other here. On the telephone in the hall, there were old prints of hers and one set—mind, only one set—of Mrs. Horbury's, made this morning when she rang the police."

Nobody wished to accept the consequence of his argument. Not even Hanaud himself. He looked round the bright and inviting room with its enamelled walls, its deep cushioned seats, the delicate tracery of the plaster on the ceiling and the long windows opening on to trim lawn and wide meadow, where the sunlight and the oaks played a swiftly-moving game in black and gold.

" So then ? " Maltby challenged, himself the first to grasp the nettle.

" So then," Hanaud repeated, " at half-past two this morning, in this room—perhaps the lamps were lit and the curtains drawn and the fire bright upon the hearth ; perhaps the room was dark and the windows open to the shadows and the silver, as now to the shadows and the gold—someone stood by that table and with a covered hand lifted the earpiece, mouthpiece, what you will, and held it,—not to listen to a message, but to stop the call jangling through the house."

" Some one ? " Herbert repeated. " Mrs. Horbury then ? "

Hanaud replied thoughtfully :

" Yet I do not think it was Madame Horbury. Imagine it ! Horbury has been dead for three to four hours. Someone in this room hears the telephone, lifts the receiver, does not answer, and replaces it." He pointed across the room to the table. " Was it then, do you think, that someone tossed the keys on the table ? "

Maltby bent down.

" You have in your mind, Monsieur Hanaud," he stated rather than asked, " a picture, and perhaps the name of that someone."

" Picture, no ! Name, perhaps yes. There was one who—and again I say, perhaps—had great reason to hate Daniel Horbury."

A look of bewilderment passed over Maltby's face.

" Devisher ? " he said.

" Bryan Devisher," said Hanaud.

" But—but—we both know. At Gravesend, he was not on board. He was lost at sea during the night."

" And that also is true. But he could have been in this house last night. Let Mr. Ricardo tell us."

He swung round upon Ricardo with the outstretched forefinger of melodrama ; and everyone turned about and stared, incredulous, ready at a word to contradict.

" Really, really," Mr. Ricardo stammered. He swallowed hurriedly. He was not averse to his proper share of the limelight. But he preferred that it should glow brighter and brighter upon him gradually, that he should, as it were, slide into it. But to stand one moment obscure, and the next moment lit up like the ghost of

Sir Marmaduke—well, really, really ! It was the penalty one paid for the friendship of Hanaud. However, it was an hour to be registered. He looked at his watch. He gave himself twelve minutes, and as the clock struck twelve he finished.

" Thank you," said the superintendent warmly. " That is very important, and, if I may say so who have listened to many stories, very closely told."

Mr. Ricardo was delighted and would have been more delighted still if Hanaud had not with a bow and a smirk taken the commendation to himself. " Really I might be his ventriloquist's dummy," he reflected acidly.

Superintendent Maltby moved to the fireplace and rang the bell.

" There is no evidence that Devisher was here," he said.

" None," Hanaud agreed.

" We shall hear now what Mrs. Horbury has to tell us," said Maltby and the charwoman opened the door.

" Will you ask Mrs. Horbury if she will receive us ? " he asked and, when she had gone upon her errand, he resumed :

" It will be best, I think, that no mention of Bryan Devisher should be made, no hint given of that story of the sea which Mr. Ricardo has told to us."

These words were not a hint. They were a definite order, and Maltby looked to each of his companions in turn for a promise of obedience.

" Good ! " he said and Mrs. Wallace came back with a message that Mrs. Horbury would receive them at once. Mr. Ricardo hung back, but Maltby took him by the arm with a smile.

" You have been very good. You never spoke out of turn. Will you be my secretary for half an hour ? Let us go ! " ; and they filed out of the room.

The one word murder, of which all had for so long been thinking, had never once been spoken.

Chapter 10

OLIVIA

SHE was standing in the room with the windows looking upon the holly hedge. But there was space enough between the hedge and the windows for the sunlight to fall golden upon the gravel path between and to fill the room with a serene and quiet light.

"I don't want to distress you more than must be," said Maltby gently ; and Olivia Horbury gravely acknowledged his courtesy.

"You have your duty, Superintendent."

She was tall and dressed in a coat and skirt of dark blue and a white shirt with a collar. Her hair, which was black but had the blue sheen of a raven's wing, was parted in the middle and drawn softly back, masking the tops of her ears. Beneath its heavy mass her face was very pale and her eyes, enormous under the long, upturned lashes, were black as night, too, and as night unfathomable. Prepared as Mr. Ricardo had been for someone of a closer kinship with the house than with her gross bandit of a husband, he was none the less surprised. The broad forehead, the wide spacing of her eyes, the delicacy of nose and nostril, the short upper lip and the curve of cheek and jaw gave her beauty ; but the supple grace of her movements, the slenderness of her figure, the long white hands, made her exquisite besides. . . . She was neither of the Lambeth Walk nor of bankrupt gentility. He was inclined, with a rare spurt of fancy, to think that she was born at Sèvres, and there had got lost amongst images with the colours of pale flowers as lovely as herself. There Horbury, on an off day between Longchamps and Auteuil, bought her, noticing that she was alive and so worth more of his money than the others. Her voice, however, upset Ricardo's fairy tale. For it was not silvery and light, as it should have been, but full and low.

" Will you sit down, Superintendent—and your friends, of course."

Was there a hint of a question in her use of the word friends ? Mr. Ricardo hoped not. The very last thing for which he wished was to be turned out of the room. The Superintendent took it up indirectly.

" I don't want any misunderstanding, Mrs. Horbury," he said. " You have a perfect right to refuse to tell me anything, with or without a solicitor present. The only person you will definitely be called upon to answer is——"

" The coroner," she interposed. " But I have nothing to hide from you, Superintendent."

She sat upon the opposite side of the table, the bright green hedge beyond the window behind her. The men began to take their seats opposite, like so many directors at a board meeting. But Superintendent Maltby was not satisfied. He had his country's belief in fair play, except, perhaps, so far as Bryan Devisher was concerned.

" This," he said, laying his hand for a moment on Hanaud's arm, " is Monsieur Hanaud of the Sûreté in Paris. You might object to his presence. I am in your hands."

Olivia Horbury's eyes moved slowly towards the burly Frenchman. There was no hostility in them, no change in the stillness of her face.

" I think, of all men, Monsieur Hanaud should be here," she said. " He is far more in this "—she paused, as though she hated to use high-sounding words— " tragedy, than perhaps he knows."

Hanaud was disconcerted. He looked inquiringly at

Mrs. Horbury ; he bobbed his head at her ; he sat down rather heavily. " Dee-flated," said Mr. Ricardo, but he only said it to himself.

" I should be obliged, madam, if you would tell us what happened here last night," said Maltby, and the detective-sergeant at once produced a notebook and an indelible pencil.

" Beginning with—— ? " she asked.

" Your reason for spending the night at White Barn. I understand that it was not unusual for you and your husband to come here unexpectedly. But was there yesterday any special reason ? "

" Yes," she answered at once. " Dan rang me up yesterday afternoon from King Street."

" King Street, St. James," said Maltby.

" Yes."

" From his offices ? "

" Yes. Witherton's Rooms, where, in the thirties of last century, the select dined and gambled, and yesterday Daniel only drank a glass of Pommery '06 and gambled."

A slow and wistful smile changed surprisingly Olivia Horbury's face. It lost its hard calm and with the calm something of its pallor. A rose-leaf pink softened it and a tender humour shone in her eyes. She might have been watching, with more amusement than disapproval, the antics of a not very well-behaved boy.

" And he was in some trouble ? " Maltby asked.

Mr. Ricardo saw the tears suddenly flood her eyes and glisten on her lashes. He heard her voice check and, for a second, tremble.

" Perhaps. Would I drive him down to White Barn ? So many dangers had there conjured themselves into nothing. Of course, I would ! There were no special arrangements to be made. Daniel changed into his dinner jacket at the office. I picked him up there and drove him to the Milan Grill, where we dined. It was, perhaps, half-past seven. He told me nothing at dinner, but drank—see, I am frank with you, Superintendent! —more than he usually did. We left the hotel at a few minutes before nine. I noticed the clock in the small hall. It was the time when the theatres were filling. But beyond Battersea Bridge there was very little traffic, and I reached White Barn well before half-past nine."

" You noticed no one in Lordship Lane whom you knew ? "

Mrs. Horbury looked at Maltby in surprise.

" No. There was no one to notice," she answered at once. " Not a soul. The gate was open. It is left open. I drove the car into the space in front of the door and left it so that it could be backed into the garage. Dan got out and opened the door of the house with his latchkey."

" That was on his ring of keys ? " Maltby asked carelessly.

" Yes," said Olivia, dwelling for a second on the monosyllable. " No doubt."

" And he carried the ring in his pocket on a chain ? "

The even flow of Mrs. Horbury's narrative was checked. She did not take her eyes from Maltby's face, but suddenly they were wary.

" As so many people do," Maltby added in an indifferent voice.

" Yes, I suppose he did," she answered. " Any way, he opened the house door and came back to the garage."

It was noticeable to Mr. Ricardo, who prided himself considerably upon the nicety of his observation, that she who had been so slick—he used in his thoughts that unpleasant word—in her statement of quite unimportant details, such as the exact time at which they dined and the traffic on the roads, was now not so sure, was wondering ; not what the answer was, but what it was politic that it should be.

" And I suppose Mr. Horbury backed the car into the garage and locked it up again ? "

" I suppose so."

" He could do that ? "

" Oh, yes. He never drove a car because his mind ran off to business in the midst of Piccadilly, but he could drive," Mrs. Horbury answered. " Whilst he was putting the car away, I went into the garden-room and lit the fire. It was dark, but the moon was like gold in a clear dark sky, and I thought what a pity it was to close out the last of the summer nights. But Dan liked to be what he called snug—fire burning, blinds down, curtains drawn, and a glass of the only wine in the world at his elbow." Again that half smile of amusement and affection gave to her face tenderness.

" You did share a bottle of champagne yesterday evening, didn't you ? " said Maltby. " And by share, I don't mean divide."

Olivia Horbury bowed her head.

" Yes, but not at once. Dan came in just as I had finished lighting the fire."

" You had left the door open ? "

" Yes, and I closed it after he had entered. He flung himself in his chair at the back of the table. He pulled his fountain pen out of his pocket and opened the blotting-book."

" Before you go on, may I interrupt ? " Maltby asked.

" Of course."

" What had Mr. Horbury done with his coat and hat ? "

Olivia looked up at the ceiling as if trying to remember. Then her eyes were suddenly turned to Mr. Ricardo. Whether she saw him or not, he could never be sure.

" I don't think he had a hat at all," she explained. " But he certainly came away from the Milan Grill with a brown overcoat over his dress-jacket. I expect that he hung it up in the hall."

" He wasn't wearing it, then, in the garden-room ? "

" No, I should certainly have noticed it if he had been."

He had taken off his overcoat before he had entered the room.

" Well, you are both in the garden-room," Maltby resumed.

" My husband was in trouble. He said that, to put the lid on, Monsieur Hanaud was on his way from Paris with a criminal charge against him which, even if he got the verdict, would ruin his career."

Hanaud sat back in his chair with a look of absolute incredulity upon his face.

" But, madame, this is a lunacy. It was a small affair for him, for me, too, Hanaud. A small conversation, an injustice put right . . ."

Mrs. Horbury replied coldly : " My husband did not take it so lightly, Monsieur Hanaud," and Hanaud threw up his hands.

It was Maltby's moment to take charge again.

" From whom did Horbury hear of Monsieur Hanaud's visit ? " he asked.

" I don't know," she said. " He was in great distress and I didn't press him with questions. He jumped up after that and said that a glass of wine might help us."

" Yes ? " said Maltby, leaning forward a little. He glanced quickly at Detective-Sergeant Hughes, who was holding his notebook below the table upon his knees. " Yes ? "

" Daniel fetched two glasses of champagne from the kitchen and drank his own with one gulp."

" Just the two of you standing in the garden-room ? "

" Yes. I remember Dan saying with a sort of hysterical laugh : ' That isn't the proper way to treat a wine like that. Upon my word, I deserve all that Hanaud can do to me ! ' "

" He said that ? " exclaimed Hanaud without any apologies to the Superintendent.

" I remember it clearly," Mrs Horbury declared ; and once more Hanaud sat back in his chair, but this time with such a look of admiration upon his face that Mr. Ricardo was quite at a loss to understand it.

" It could not be disputed," he said, bowing to her ; and now she was for a moment disconcerted. " So Horbury does a thing which he had never in his life done before. He put a bottle of Pommery '06 half-full back in the cupboard."

Mr Ricardo was indignant. Hanaud had no manners. He was French, of course. You had to take that into account. But if ever a man had called a charming woman a liar to her face, that man was Hanaud of the Paris Sûreté. He just didn't believe that Horbury had put back the half-empty bottle into the cupboard. Unusual ? Perhaps. People did unusual things—he himself, for instance, who, only two nights ago, had crossed the Channel in a cockle-boat. However, Olivia Horbury had resumed her story, and it was more pleasant to listen to her low and melodious voice than to reflect how curiously wrong Hanaud could be when he was removed from the perhaps rather sordid purlieus of Paris.

Mrs Horbury was saying :

" Daniel was less discouraged. He had got out of scrapes just as awkward before. He supposed it was just returning to this house which so comforted him— but he wondered at times whether the big fight was worth all it cost——" and then, without a break in her voice, without any warning change in feature or expression, she uttered a little cry and covered her face with her hands. She bent her head forward and the tears ran between her fingers and splashed upon the table. There was no sound from her throat of a sob, but she pressed her hands tight, although they could not hold back her tears. Not one of those who saw her but was distressed. So calm and sedate she had been, she had even laughed wistfully once or twice as she spoke of Daniel ; and then came this flood of grief as though a gate had burst.

Maltby spoke with compunction.

" I am sorry. One cannot help these interviews being distressing. Perhaps you would like us to wait . . ."

" No, no ! " she cried with a sudden violence. " Let us finish ! " She took her hands away from her face and dried her eyes and swallowed. Then she made her apology for her outburst. " You are right. It is, of course, disturbing. But I am almost at an end. For, seeing that Daniel was in an easier mood, I went up to bed."

" And what time would that be ? " Maltby asked easily. " Did you notice ? "

" Certainly. There's a clock upon the mantelshelf of the garden-room. It was half-past ten."

" You expected him to follow you ? "

" Yes," she answered. " He gave me three-quarters of an hour, as a rule. But it had been a tiring evening, and as soon as I was in bed I fell asleep."

Monsieur Hanaud now covered his face, but it was to hide a grin, not a flood of tears. So far, to his thinking, Olivia Horbury had told her tale cleverly, but there was a snag just ahead of her which he did not see how she could weather.

" And you slept well ? "

" Too well," she answered remorsefully.

" Too well—because you had quarrelled ? "

Olivia Horbury was bewildered. She raised her eyes and stared blankly at the Superintendent. And then to the recognition of all of them bewilderment became deliberately intended. At first she had been surprised. Now surprise was being acted.

" If we ever quarrelled, the quarrel ended before we parted," she said, and waited for a trap to be sprung. Superintendent Maltby obliged.

" How is it, then, since you hadn't quarrelled, and since you expected Mr. Horbury to follow you in three-quarters of an hour, that your door was locked against him ? "

" But it wasn't ! "

The Superintendent jumped in his chair as he heard that calm, quiet statement. Hanaud looked down at the table ; for the smile upon his face was more pronounced than ever. She would have her answer ready, not a doubt of it, and quite a good answer, too.

" But, madam," Maltby answered, and now there was a note of sternness in his voice. He was not a preparatory schoolboy in flannel shorts who must take what is told him without contradiction. " Your charwoman, Mrs. Wallace, found your door locked this morning."

" But that's not all she told you," Olivia Horbury returned.

" No, there was more," Maltby admitted.

" Exactly," said Mrs. Horbury. " I left my door on the latch. Daniel, if he finds me asleep, is careful to make no noise. I slept until I was awakened by a scream. A scream of horror. I sat up with my heart beating. I saw that the lights were on, although the sunlight was streaming round the edges of the blinds. Then I noticed that Dan's bed had not been slept in, that the coverlet had been turned down, and that his pyjamas were spread out upon it, waiting for him. Something terrible had happened. I sprang out of bed, afraid, and I turned the key without thinking. I heard Mrs. Wallace sobbing and crying out bits of words which I couldn't understand, and I did "—she shrugged her

shoulders—" the fool thing which women do. I fainted.
I know. For when I came to my senses I was lying
on the floor and Mrs. Wallace was banging on the door.
I can only have lain there for a few seconds, but "—and
she shivered as she recalled the moment—" I felt as cold
as ice. I unlocked the door and told Mrs. Wallace to
wait until I got into bed again."

She sat with all their eyes upon her, intent upon
telling her story without unnecessary lamentations. If
ever a woman was speaking the whole truth, and nothing
but the truth, Mr. Ricardo was certain it was now. If
the telephone had rung at half-past two in the morning,
she had not run down the stairs to answer it. Mr.
Ricardo put his hand in his bosom ready to swear it.
Even Maltby seemed to be impressed.

" I see," he said slowly. Then, like one turning to a
lighter subject : " Will you carry your mind back to the
hour or two when you and your husband were in the
garden-room ? "

" Yes."

" Did Mr. Horbury, during that time, take his keys
off the chain in his pocket ? "

Mrs. Horbury's forehead wrinkled. She drew a deep
breath or two.

" I don't think that he did."

" Thank you," said Maltby. " There is just one last
question which I must ask you. But I am afraid it is
the most trying for you of them all." He held out his
hand to the Detective-Sergeant.

With a little gasp, Olivia whispered : " That can't be
helped."

The Detective-Sergeant put into Maltby's hand the
long, white cardboard box. It was ornamented with
gold lines. It was gay and gleaming, the sheath of
beauty's buckler and weapon, a dainty flickering toy to
exploit a pair of passionate eyes or make malice of an

admirable mouth. But the prettier it looked, the more Olivia Horbury dreaded it. Maltby set it down on the mahogany table and rather slowly, with his eyes upon Olivia, " Now ! " he whispered. Really, he might have been a conjuror, Mr. Ricardo thought. And then Maltby suddenly whisked the lid from the box, and there was no luxurious fan of painted chicken skin with a handle of jade, but the long, blood-crusted blade and the straight handle of Cambridge blue.

Olivia set her hands against the table's edge and thrust her chair back. The knife might have been a cobra and she the rabbit, so helplessly she stared at it.

" Have you ever seen that knife, madam ? "

Olivia shook her head once and a second time more violently. But Maltby must have the word spoken and duly recorded in Hughes' notebook.

" You mean, madam, that you have never seen it before," he said, polite but insistent.

" I do mean just that," she answered, and, as Maltby covered the box again with its lid, she uttered a sigh of relief and suddenly swayed in her chair. Mr. Ricardo uttered a cry. He saw her slipping down by the bed-room door. " She will fall," he cried.

But however caustic Hanaud might be in words, he was very quick on his feet when succour was needed. He was already at Olivia's side and supporting her.

" You know what I think ? " he asked.

" I do not," replied Maltby.

" I think that a bottle of the Pommery '06 would be the best thing for Mrs. Horbury."

Mrs. Horbury sprang up at once.

" No, please ! I am quite well." She turned to Maltby. " If you have done with me, I will go home."

Maltby bowed to her.

" I have to thank you very much for answering my questions. I shall have to lock up this house for the moment and leave the constable in charge." He turned to Inspector Herbert. " Mrs. Wallace must go, too, and will you take her latchkey ? "

Herbert went off upon his mission. Mrs. Horbury said :

" No doubt you will want mine, too, Superintendent ? "

" I should prefer to have it. Should you need anything here, you have only to name it to me or Inspector Herbert."

" Thank you," said Olivia.

She took a dark blue hat which had been lying on a chair, pinned it on in front of a mirror, and drew down a veil which hid her eyes. They gathered in the hall : Mrs. Horbury, the charwoman, Maltby, Hanaud, Mr. Ricardo, Herbert and Hughes. Mrs. Wallace was the first to go.

" The detective-inspector has your address," said Maltby. " You will be wanted at the inquest, of course. Notice will be sent to you."

She went away on foot and then the garage door was opened by Herbert.

" You have petrol enough, madam ? "

" More than enough," she answered as she opened the door and climbed into the car. She drove the little car out into the open and stopped again.

" Monsieur Hanaud," she called, and Monsieur Hanaud advanced from the group at the garage door. " It is not private," she added, and Hanaud stopped so that all might hear. " You spoke of some injustice to be put right."

" Yes, madame."

" You must give me a few days."

" Certainly. It is ages since I was in a vacancy. I will give myself one now until you are ready."

Olivia Horbury stared for a moment.

" I should like your address."

Hanaud smiled. It was the moment for an off-hand

93

gesture, an address hardly worth giving, so certain it was that he must lodge there. " The Grosvenor Square. The corner house."

" Oh ! " cried Olivia with a little twist of her lips. " Have they got one in Grosvenor Square now ? " and she drove out past the policeman at the gate and turned her car towards London, her face losing its humour as the chestnuts and the gardens disappeared. The flat and arid life of the town—she must get used to that now that Dan, with his rogueries and his good humour, his preposterous politics and his queer truth to her, had gone. That, sooner or later, he might go to prison for a long time she had felt sure, even before she had married. But death—violent, bloody—Dan hated the sight of blood—this sort of death above all ! And as she drove across Battersea Bridge and past the Houses of Parliament yet a third, and this time a passionate, expression began to burn in her eyes.

*   *   *   *   *

The police officers returned to the house. In the upper rooms, a bathroom, two servants' rooms, a dressing-room for Mr. Horbury, and the big double bedroom, nothing new was discovered. The windows of the garden-room, its door, the doors of the dining-room and the kitchen—everything was made safe.

" There will be a man in the house, as well as one outside, until the inquest's over," said Maltby, as he handed over the keys to Inspector Herbert.

" I have arranged for it at the Station."

They were in the hall, and Maltby was opening the front door, when Hanaud cried :

" 'Arf a mo ! There is somethin' we forget ? Yes, no ? "

He dashed across the hall, and a rather condescending smile at the antics of the foreigner which had begun to broaden over Maltby's face was suddenly frozen there.

Hanaud went straight to a cupboard in the wall. It was not locked. He pulled it open and there, for all to see, a brown overcoat of a light weight, and a white silk scarf hung upon a hook.

" Ah ! " he cried. " The Horbury's coat ! "

He turned it so that the lining showed and the inside pocket in the breast. He stood up on the tips of his toes to peer into it. Suddenly he whipped the silk scarf from the hook, shook it out, and spread it over his palm. He felt in the breast pocket of the overcoat and stood for a moment or two afterwards with his back towards his companions, and in the poise of his head and the stoop of his shoulders there was a bitter confession of defeat.

Mr. Ricardo, indeed, feared that he was going to disgrace the whole confraternity of the Sûreté by a shameless attempt to hide his discovery. But it was not unusual for Mr. Ricardo to be wrong. Hanaud was double-dyed in his vocation. He would follow relentless through the dark labyrinth of a crime ; but he never pretended when a stiff barrier had to be climbed ; and never denied failure when one simple fact, which could not fairly be explained away, brought him up all standing and closed the case. He knew the difference between a full-stop and a semi-colon. So now he came slowly to his colleagues, holding and hiding his treasure in a scarf. A semi-colon ?—at the least. A full-stop ?—maybe.

" It is over," he said, holding forward his swathed hand.

Maltby looked puzzled.

" The Case—if it is a Case ? " the Superintendent asked.

" Yes. For the Coroner at all events "—the semi-colon, so to speak—" it is over."

Hanaud turned back with deliberate care the folds of the scarf. Lying upon it, across the palm of his hand, was the thick, stiff sheath of a long knife. It was decorated at the wider end with a pattern in thread of Cambridge blue.

" And in Horbury's top-coat, eh ? "

" Yes."

Maltby looked with a smile of relief at Inspector Herbert.

" That settles it, then."

The knife on the ground beneath Horbury's hand and his finger-marks upon the handle ; the sheath in the pocket of the overcoat in which Horbury had driven from London : facts. All else was wild surmise.

" For the Coroner, yes," Hanaud repeated as he handed scarf and sheath to the detective-sergeant.

But for the Red Judge ? The full stop ? He was not so sure.

Chapter 11

THE BLIND MAN'S DOG

ON the gravelled enclosure where Mr. Ricardo's second Rolls Royce stood side by side with the swift but inconspicuous police car, Hanaud spread a large white hand over his paunch.

" I rumble," he said. " It is the luncheon gong."

Mr. Ricardo bowed eagerly to Superintendent Maltby.

" I shall be honoured if you will join us," he exclaimed, but the Superintendent shook his head. " I must go back to the Yard. There are other matters awaiting me." He noticed the gloom gather on Hanaud's face and hurriedly went on : " You may be assured that we shall not neglect the interesting points you have raised. Inspector Herbert will submit a full report, of which you shall have a copy at the corner house in Grosvenor Square." Not by the twitch of a muscle did he express his pleasure in that unusual address. " And I think you should come with me to Mr. Horbury's offices in King Street. At half-past three ? Will you and Mr. Ricardo call for me just before the half-hour ? Meanwhile, I'll send out a call for Bryan Devisher, on the chance that he will have something to tell us. And I hope to find all ready for us at the Yard, some particulars of Mrs. Horbury's history."

Hanaud's face had been growing happier and happier, now that the file was not to be closed and put away upon its shelf.

" I thank you," he said gratefully.

Maltby was carrying a key with a linen tab tied to it. He called the constable on duty at the gate.

" This is the charwoman's key. You will be responsible for it, and Inspector Herbert will see that you are relieved. You will allow no one to enter the house without his or my leave."

The constable saluted and took the key.

" No one, sir ? Not even Mrs. Horbury ? "

Hanaud gasped audibly.

" That woman ! Above all, no," he whispered, and Maltby took up the words at once.

" Above all, not Mrs. Horbury."

The constable saluted again and retired to the gate. Maltby glanced curiously at the Frenchman.

" I thought that you were rather on her side," he said.

And, for a moment, Hanaud hung in a suspense. Should he speak ? Shouldn't he ? But he was effervescent. He simply had to.

" That woman ! " he cried, and admiration was loud

in his voice. " She is a oner ! She is the goods ! I tell you. She is out of the top of her drawers."

" Really, really," cried Mr. Ricardo, quite shocked.

" An idiom, my friend. I use him," said Hanaud affably.

" Use him properly then," Ricardo remonstrated. " She is out of the top drawer."

" So I said, my friend," Hanaud returned. He continued enthusiastically : " And how she lied ! Mind you, she will give back the money of Monsieur Gravot, even if she starves. In the name of the Place Vendôme, I honour her for it. But how she lied to us ! And with what aplumbing ! The woman screamed, and she jumped out of bed half-awake and turned the key of her door and fainted. Did she ? Oh, no, no ! " and his face lost all its humour, and his voice all its excitement. " Oh, no, no," he repeated in a whisper, and the lids of his eyes half closed, as though he were watching somewhere a long way off a scene of horror which nothing could prevent.

" I was looking very sharply, my Maltby, when you placed the long cardboard fan case down on the table in front of her. I think that already she knew what was in it. It was not surprise she betrayed. There was no staring up into your face to read what startling discovery you had made. No, she gazed at the case, she gathered herself, her feet pressed upon the ground, her hands gripping each other, to meet with nothing more than a shock of horror, a recoil of disgust, her second view of that brutal weapon. She pushed her chair back—yes, with the proper violence, and no doubt there was nature enough in the violence, but there was no surprise."

Undoubtedly both Maltby and Herbert listened with discomfort. It was not merely that Hanaud's words strengthened an unwelcome suspicion of their own.

But through his heavy features there shone a light, even in his whispers there sounded an authority which could not but arrest their judgment.

" You think she knew already what the thing in the cardboard box was ? What it had done ? " cried Ricardo.

" I do," Hanaud returned slowly. " I think that she was present when a great crime was committed——"

" By Horbury," cried Maltby.

" By Devisher," Mr. Ricardo amended.

" I don't know," said Hanaud.

" And, if she knew, why should she keep silent ? " Maltby asked.

" Again, I don't know," Hanaud repeated.

But he was not abandoning his inspiration. If anything, it grew stronger. For he looked about him, and in that noonday sunlight, with the blackbirds and the thrushes calling from the garden, he suddenly shivered.

" I wish I knew," he cried, a man in distress. What happened here when even this house was silent, and nothing moved but the shadows on path and meadow and lawn, as the moon drenched the world in silver ? " Let me tell you what I—see. Her, Olivia Horbury, when the crime was done and the house empty, climbing the stairs to her room. It was not yet midnight—and all the long night to live through. She must go to bed, leave the light on to help the man who needs no more helping. She turns from one side to the other until— surely it is close on dawn ?—suddenly the telephone rings through the house, shrill enough even to wake that sprawling figure in the room below. Did she look at her watch and note that the night was not half spent ? And suddenly the telephone stops. Too abruptly, too quickly ! Someone is in the house besides herself and the dead man. A friend ? No. The murderer returned, not trusting her word, to make sure. To make sure by a second crime. Imagine her panic, if you can! She sprang out of bed, she locked the door between her and death, and so fell fainting to the floor, to be awakened hours afterwards by the screams, the banging upon the panels."

He stopped and a silence followed upon his words. Maltby was the first to shake off the obsession, but he was troubled, none the less. Although he strove to speak lightly, his voice betrayed him.

"Facts, Monsieur Hanaud! Facts we must cling to. Not imagination, however subtle."

Hanaud answered with a smile.

"Yes, facts, my dear Maltby, and a little imagination to interpret them. Imagination on a leash—he is the blind man's dog."

He mounted into Mr. Ricardo's car and produced his blue packet of abominable cigarettes.

"Just before half-past three, then!"

"Just before half-past three," cried Maltby from the window of the police car, "and, my dear colleague, I shall hope for some more idioms from you in the course of the afternoon."

Chapter 12

BIG BUSINESS AND SWITCHBACK BUSINESS

AT a small table for two in Signor Bentano's restaurant in the Strand, Monsieur Hanaud tucked the end of his napkin between his collar and his neck and drank a glass of Porto as an appetiser. It was a restaurant famous for its cuisine, which was hampered in the evening by an orchestra in a gallery and a crowd on its way to the theatres. But in the morning the clients were for the most part of the more jovial and sporting business men.

"So it was here that the Horbury lunched," said Hanaud, looking about him. "Good! So we get the atmosphere, and that is enough. We eat and we keep our eyes open, and we talk of the ballet and whether the *filet mignon* is as tender here as at Larue's."

And in that way the meal was eaten pleasantly enough, with a bottle of Clos de Tart to keep it company. At the end of it, Hanaud produced his inevitable blue packet of black cigarettes. But Mr. Ricardo was firm and stern.

"You shall not," he said. "There are limits. On the borderland of the Clos de Tart there are Hoyo de Monterrey cigars, but not your revolting cigarettes."

Monsieur Hanaud was, having been well fed, docile. He lit his cigar.

"Am I allowed a peppermint?" he asked.

Mr. Ricardo smiled indulgently.

"You are. A simple glass of Signor Bentano's brandy will do for me."

Hanaud smiled affably as he sipped his peppermint.

"What did your Mr. Gladstone say in 1884?"

"That will never be known," Ricardo declared firmly. He was not prepared to argue. By three o'clock Signor Bentano's clients had gone back to their amusements or their business. At a quarter past, Mr. Ricardo paid his bill, and the pair travelled in the Rolls-Royce to Scotland Yard. Maltby and Herbert were waiting, and Maltby handed an envelope to Hanaud.

"You will find in that a copy of all we know about Olivia Horbury. It is much what you would expect, I think."

Hanaud put the envelope away in his pocket, and the half-hour had not struck when they were on their way to what had once been Witherton's Rooms in St. James'.

They were received in a small office of unnoticeable appointments by a long grey man, as thin as a question mark and almost as bent. He was handsomely dressed in a dark grey suit with a cutaway morning coat, a stiff white collar and a grey silk tie. He had a thin grey Chinaman's moustache, of which he would lure the ends into his mouth and by biting them assure himself that there was something he need not question. He had so few qualities akin to the boisterous roguery of Mr. Horbury's career that all the four men counted him as a watchdog, put in by a firm which was owed money. The grey man, however, rose to his feet and made a small bow.

" Superintendent Maltby, I believe. I have been instructed to put the office at your disposal."

" Mr. Foster, then ? "

" Yes."

" You have been Mr. Horbury's manager for five years ? "

There was still some surprise in Maltby's voice and it brought a sardonic smile to Foster's mouth.

" His managing clerk," he answered, lifting a hand in correction. " Mr. Horbury's business was, in the main, personal and conducted by himself. I fancy that I owe my length of service and my very good salary to the fact that I was honest and that, however uncongenial some of his activities may have been, I did not pry into what didn't concern me."

" I see," said Maltby dryly. " It's no use coming to you for secrets."

" No. For I don't know any," said Foster. He crossed the room to a door and, with something of mockery in the gesture, flung it open. " This, gentlemen, was Mr. Horbury's private office."

They went into it one by one and stared. Maltby pursed up his lips and whistled. Rosewood panels decorated the walls, the furniture was upholstered in red damask, leather arm-chairs stood on each side of the Adam fireplace, and in the centre, on a thick Aubusson carpet, stood a beautiful big walnut writing-table, with a semi-circular top of pigeon-holes and drawers.

"Queen Anne," Mr. Ricardo thought, looking at it with envy.

"Yes, all sheen and costliness," said Mr. Foster, in answer to the Superintendent's whistle. Maltby, however, was less concerned with the glitter of the office than with his need to reach more familiar terms with this difficult managing clerk. He had not noticed the irony in Foster's voice, and was led consequently to make the most unfortunate mistake. He looked about him with admiration.

"Ah!" he exclaimed. "Big Business, eh?" and saw disdain completely occupy Foster's face.

"Forty years in the City have led me to associate Big Business with furniture which invites you to go away as soon as your business is concluded."

The Superintendent's approach had been faulty. But he had still one other pebble if he could fit it somehow into his sling. At the present moment, however, Foster was not mixing his metaphors. He was driving straight on.

"Mr. Horbury himself, who had the most redeeming sense of humour, knew quite well that Big Business had nothing to do with the style of this room. For I ventured, falling, if I may say so, into your mistake, Superintendent, to expostulate with Mr. Horbury upon it, and he answered, 'My good Foster, the sort of clients you are used to will no doubt shudder, but the sort of clients I expect will imagine this is the replica of a nobleman's study.'"

Mr. Ricardo felt internally a sort of warmth. It is, after all, always pleasant to see a policeman put in his place.

" Big Business," continued Mr. Foster, warming to his theme. He crossed the room, unlocked a cupboard and flung open the door. On one shelf stood glasses, capacious goblets of thin glass. On the other bottle upon bottle of Pommery '06. " Look ! " cried Mr. Foster, and he added with the most assertive waggings of his head, " Cocks don't porp in Big Business."

Mr. Ricardo here felt constrained to intervene.

" Mr. Foster means, of course, that corks don't——" but he was allowed to get no further.

" No, no, my friend," cried Hanaud. " I like him as he is. Cocks don't porp in Big Business. There is a profundity there." He turned with a bow to Foster. " I thank you, sir. I use him."

But Mr. Foster was staring curiously at Hanaud. He said to the Superintendent :

" You did not, I think, present me to these gentlemen."

" I am sorry," Maltby answered with a little discomfort. " This is Monsieur Hanaud of the Sûreté of Paris."

He paused, his eyes watching the clerk keenly, but on Foster's face there was nothing but bewilderment, no realisation that here was Horbury's enemy ; not even any recognition of the name.

" Monsieur Hanaud ? " he repeated with an inquisitive glance at the Frenchman. " But as I told you, Superintendent, Mr. Horbury worked alone." His eyes came quickly back to the Frenchman's face. " Might I ask you, sir, whether we owe to your sudden arrival the—the crisis of last night ? If my question is incorrect, I beg you to forget it."

" Your question is incorrect to the last degree," Hanaud returned with a smile. " But I am glad that you asked. For everywhere I see eyes of suspicion and hear ditto voices. I came from France yesterday, the complete incog of the wheel. No one knows me. I came to see the Horbury, it is true, but on a small matter of business."

Foster's gaze passed doubtfully on.

"And this," said Maltby, "is Mr. Ricardo."

"Oh!" cried Foster. "That is interesting. You rang up Mr. Horbury yesterday afternoon."

"I did!" exclaimed the astounded Ricardo.

"Yes," said Maltby keenly. "I want the details of that call, Mr. Ricardo."

Ricardo stared blankly at the Superintendent.

"You knew about it?"

"Certainly I did. At my first contact with this office I was told that an unknown Mr. Ricardo had rung up yesterday and obtained from some incautious clerk Mr. Horbury's address in the suburbs. Come, come, sir! You have been very quiet about it all, but we have been waiting for you."

Superintendent Maltby, Mr. Foster the clerk, and Inspector Herbert were all closing in on Mr. Ricardo with determination. He seemed to hear the handcuffs jingling, he almost looked round for the ewer of his prison-cell that he might wet his throat.

"Take out your notebook, Inspector, and set down the business Mr. Ricardo had with Horbury yesterday afternoon."

"I had no business with Horbury," Ricardo persisted.

"And why he wanted the address in Lordship Lane," he exclaimed.

"What time was it when Mr. Ricardo rang up?" Maltby asked.

"Immediately after five," Foster returned; and a great light shone in upon Ricardo's troubled mind.

"Yes, of course, and he rang up from Victoria Station," he declared, gazing at Monsieur Hanaud with indignant eyes. "The Continental train was no doubt punctual."

Hanaud was seldom abashed.

" Evidently I rang up from the Victoria Station. I did not wish my visit to excite the fear, so I did not give my name."

" That's no excuse for giving mine. And why should people be afraid of you ? " Mr. Ricardo straightened his knees and scoffed at Hanaud's self-importance.

The Frenchman shook his head in melancholy reproof.

" So ! You trample on the poor Hanaud, the alien, the humble one. Yet how you are unjust ! It is a mixture, a jumble up. If I say it is someone who stays with the fine Mr. Ricardo of Grosvenor Square it becomes, before you can twinkle a bedpost, Mr. Ricardo himself. You all see that, I am sure."

What Mr. Ricardo saw was that the prison walls were fading into air : what Superintendent Maltby saw was that a hopeful clue to the suicide of Horbury, upon which he had set some store, was dead as a doornail.

" Yes, it is a puzzle," said Foster frowning thoughtfully at Maltby. " You see we are not Big Business, but Switchback Business. Sometimes we are up, up, up . . ."

" With cocks porping," Hanaud interposed.

" And the Banks smiling. Sometimes we are down, down, down, with the creditors filling King Street and Mr. Horbury invisible—and perhaps Superintendent Maltby not so far away."

" And what was it this time ? " Maltby asked quickly, but Foster was equally quick to avoid an answer. He shrugged his shoulders.

" It was, as I told you, a personal business. We shall know when the accountants make their report," he said frostily. " But do not expect Big Business. Even those fine gentlemen," and he pointed to a photograph of a horse hanging upon a nail, " never won a race except at Ostend."

" Ah," cried Maltby, seizing his opportunity at last,

" I'd sooner see a Rugby football match at Twickenham any day."

Foster gasped. Under the solemn aspect of Superintendent Maltby, he had found a brother.

" Would you ? " he cried.

" Rather ! Wouldn't you ? "

Both faces went back to the Ostend champion, but their thoughts had nothing to do with the sport of kings. Mr. Foster was turning over in his mind pictures of finely fought football matches. Maltby was saying prudently to himself, " You've hooked him. Play him carefully ! " With invariable care, he had left a direction early that morning for a check-up of Horbury's staff, and of the few discoveries this was apparently the most valuable. It established him on a brotherly footing with the old clerk.

" Do you remember the last England and Scotland match ? " Foster asked eagerly.

" My word, yes," Maltby exclaimed ecstatically. He had never seen a Rugby game since his boyhood. " That was a match ! "

" Just a run away from the beginning."

" To the end," Maltby was about to add, and fortunately saved his prestige by smiling at the ceiling.

" Until the last two quick goals saved us," cried Foster. He laughed aloud. He almost stood upright. Every Saturday he hurried from the office, drank a glass of beer, swallowed a sandwich, and passed an afternoon of enchantment, watching heroes. He turned to Maltby and grasped him by the arm.

" I'll show you what is puzzling me."

He led the Superintendent to a panel of the wall where a large—map, was it ?—or cartoon ?—was wound up on a spring roller. Foster pulled upon a string, unrolled it and made the string fast to a nail ; and, as if a military command had been given, everyone in that room took a step backwards and stared. Maltby was the first to find his tongue.

" It's difficult to surprise me, but if not Big Business, then Hot Stuff ! "

Mr. Ricardo, though he sought for a pointed and devastating phrase, could not achieve it. No doubt he was stunned.

" Really, really, what vulgarity ! " he stammered.

Inspector Herbert said nothing and made a note. Perhaps Monsieur Hanaud was the only one of the four to appreciate it properly. A laugh of enjoyment, if so thin a sound could be so described, tinkled suddenly.

" He was a—what you call him ?—a gamin, a monkey, an urchin, that Horbury ! How I would have liked it if he had lived."

Foster swung round, surprised, and in spite of himself pleased. He was not as a rule in favour of foreigners. Finicking people who would be frightened by a good square meal off a saddle of South Down lamb, and hadn't learnt how to be beaten at games. Yet this one had got nearer to the truth than any of his visitors.

" That's right, monsieur. A touch of the gutter boy in him, to be sure. Always winked at himself, whatever roguery he was up to."

The Wembley Stadium had noticeably diminished the correctitude of the clerk, who chuckled and rubbed his hands. " Half of that was just fun to him," he cried, pointing to the wall on which the big cartoon blazed. It represented a crowded House of Commons, Horbury standing in the Prime Minister's usual place at the Treasury Bench, with his hand on a red box and an incredulous face turned towards an opponent who had dared to inter upt him, and the Speaker on his feet with a shocked expression and these words enclosed, as it were, in a bubble issuing from his lips : " Order ! Order ! If it's in Horbury's Newsbag, it is so."

" Pretty crude, the colours," said Maltby with a grin.

" No doubt, but it would nobble the public," Foster returned.

" Horbury's Newsbag," said Maltby. " A newspaper ?"

" A weekly," returned Foster.

" But I've never heard of it."

" You were going to," Foster replied. " Switchback business. A big lottery on the Derby in Switzerland put us up. Horbury's Newsbag was going to put us higher. In a fortnight that poster was going to glow on every hoarding big enough to hold it which Horbury could lay his hands upon. A week afterwards the first number was to be published. He had got his staff for it. There were to be competitions with tremendous prizes. All the political stuff he was going to write himself. I warned him that he was overdoing it. But he wouldn't hear a word. He just looked at that cartoon—I told you he had a sense of humour—and cried with a grin as broad as his face, ' I tell you, Foster, Horbury's Newsbag is going to be Horbury's Nosebag, and pretty full too ! ' Now mark me, Superintendent "—and Foster sat down in one of those too easy chairs and shook his finger at the Superintendent—" and you too, the detective of France. Horbury said that to me less than a week ago. Well then, explain to me last night ! "

Maltby nodded his head thoughtfully and Hanaud sat himself down at Foster's side.

" There was real money in the bank ? " he asked.

Foster answered him a little more stiffly than he would have answered Maltby.

" Lots of it. The accountants, Trenlove and Timmins, a firm of the highest integrity, will no doubt supply you with a statement."

" You were up, up, up," said Hanaud, " with the cocks porping."

Foster agreed with a smile. " That little joke amused

you, eh ? " and he added with a shrug of the shoulders, " but there have been times when the car rushed headlong down the curve, and there, perhaps, was the Superintendent at the bottom of the curve, waiting for the smash, and the razor perhaps not so far from the throat But last night—no ! "

Ricardo was oddly affected by the scene, so that he felt always on the edge of a revelation, but a revelation which never broke. Maltby, greatly annoyed that a simple verdict of suicide was becoming less and less acceptable, and at the same time honestly troubled as to what dark mystery the evidence was leading to, stood alone, staring now at the preposterous cartoon, now at the portraits of Horbury's second-class racehorses. And in the two armchairs, side by side, Hanaud and the clerk talked in low voices quickly together. Anyone who has stumbled into an accidental witticism and finds it credited to him as intentional, will regard with favour the man who has made this pleasant error. Altogether, what with this engaging Frenchman and the comrade of Wembley, Foster was now inclined to give all the help which he had meant to deny.

" Apart from his lottery and the nosebag," Hanaud asked, " was there, do you think, any private affair which troubled him ? "

Mr. Foster shook his head.

" Any enemy getting nearer and nearer to him ? "

Foster looked sharply at Hanaud and pondered and pondered in vain.

" Did you ever hear him mention Bryan Devisher ? "

Foster sprang at the name. Here at all events was something definite, even if it was definitely to be denied.

" I never heard the name before you spoke it."

The hopefulness died out of Hanaud's voice and Mr. Ricardo recognised that the moment had come for him to encourage his friend.

" But Mr. Horbury, no doubt, was a man of many secrets," he said.

" Secrets is it ? " cried Foster. " To be sure, there were secrets ! His, mind you."

" Yes, his, of course. But sometimes perhaps these secrets had outward signs with them ? "

Superintendent Maltby had swung round upon this question and stood, holding his attitude, afraid lest a movement catching the eye or ear should distract Foster's attention.

" Outward signs ? " Foster repeated.

" Such as an unlikely visitor and a long conference ? "

Mr. Foster reflected, heaved a sigh and shook his head.

" Some unusual thing he did and hid ? "

Mr. Foster sat up straight.

" Oh ! " he said. " I wonder," and then he sat so long erect with his eyes bright and his head on one side like a bird that patience herself could hardly have borne it. " I wonder," he whispered to himself, and every head was bent towards him. But he only relaxed in his chair. He was still seeing something that no other of them could see.

" And hid, you said ? "

He turned towards Hanaud.

" And hid," Hanaud confirmed.

" Did and hid ? "

" Did and hid," repeated Hanaud.

" Yesterday," said Mr. Foster suddenly, and of the four, three started and smiled, and were warned by a movement of Hanaud's wrist.

" Yesterday," Hanaud whispered.

Foster rose from his chair and crossed the room to the walnut writing-table. There was a row of pigeon-holes with drawers underneath them and in the middle a small locked door with walnut wood pillars on each side.

Underneath the table there was a long drawer across and two smaller drawers, one on each side. Foster pulled at the brass handle of the smaller and lower drawer on the left-hand side and found it locked. He looked up at Maltby.

" You have Horbury's keys ? "

Inspector Herbert advanced, he took an envelope from his pocket and the bunch of keys from the envelope.

" Thank you ! "

Mr. Foster tried one or two before he lit upon the right one. It might have been play-acting, but, to Ricardo's thought, the man was feverishly eager now to reveal the secret of that drawer.

" Now we shall see," and he pulled it open. He peered into it, he thrust his hand into the furthest end of it, and drew it out again with a cry of disappointment. The drawer was empty. He sat back in Horbury's chair and looked from face to face, bidding them notice how the fates played with men.

" But it was there. I saw him put it away when he had done with it and lock the drawer before he went to his bath. Ah ! "

He sprang up, passed through his own room along a corridor. At the end of the corridor a dressing-room led into a bathroom. A charwoman had evidently cleaned the room after Horbury had dressed, for the clothes he had worn in his office lay neatly folded on a couch.

" Oh ! " cried Mr. Foster and he darted forward. " To be sure ! To be sure ! I had forgotten." He turned round, flourishing triumphantly a copy of an evening newspaper above his head.

" Was that what you were looking for ? " Maltby asked glumly.

" Oh no," he admitted, dropping at once to disappointment. Mr. Foster was rather like a rock which expands in the sun and contracts sharply in a frost. " No, and

I don't see it anywhere at all. However, we have got the evening paper," and once more he flourished the paper. He had found it carefully folded like the clothes and half hidden beneath them. " And that may help ! "

" How ? " asked Mr. Ricardo.

But Mr. Foster was lost in thought and to Ricardo's idea, most provokingly.

" I have a notion," Foster exclaimed, and he turned to the corridor.

" What we want is a fact," Maltby returned.

Over his shoulder Foster called out, " A notion is the cocoon of a fact."

He hurried down the passage back to Horbury's office, seated himself importantly in Horbury's chair and, after a definite poise of his left hand to make clear to all the momentous thing which he was doing, he struck a gong upon the table with the flat of his palm and sat back, his arms folded.

" Napoleon," Hanaud whispered. " Something will come of it."

A boy came of it. He sat in the general clerks' room, behind Foster's and appeared by a parallel doorway.

" John," said Mr. Foster with dignity.

" John yourself," said the boy. " Mr. John Urwick Esquire to you, please ! "

So quickly had the discipline of Daniel Horbury's firm disintegrated.

" Mr. John Urwick, will you ask the commissionaire to step here for a moment ? "

" I don't mind, seeing it's you," John Urwick answered as he swaggered by. But he swaggered by Mr. Ricardo too, and he, incensed by so much impertinence crowning so many failures and delays, was carried to the very extreme of violence. " Really ! Really ? " he cried and, swinging his leg, he landed Mr. John Urwick Esquire a real one in the right place with the right foot. John with a yelp flew across the room, dropping the Mr. on one side and the Esquire on the other. He dashed out of the door and with a speed which marked a new era in his life, brought in the commissionaire and slunk away behind him to his office. Mr. Ricardo, however, rather pleased with his resource, was completely occupied by the commissionaire, who stood at attention before Mr. Foster.

" Brown, you saw Mr. Horbury go away from the office yesterday ? "

" I did, sir."

" Did he take anything with him ? "

" Yes, sir."

" Do you know what it was ? "

" I couldn't help knowing, sir. I was a petty officer in the Navy."

" Oh ! " and Mr. Foster was not the only one of that company who was startled by the answer. " What was it that he took away ? "

" A chart, sir," and Foster's hand thumped down upon the table. " Of course ! " and for the first time the Superintendent and his companions began to learn something of that missing article which had so intrigued the secretary.

It was a small chart pinned at the four corners on to a flat ebony board by ordinary flat brass drawing-pins. It was easy enough to carry and it might have been carried under the arm, but for a difficulty. Pins had been pricked into the chart as if to mark out a course—only a few of them, but long ones, black ones with glass heads in the shape and colour of white ensigns.

Mr. Foster's memory responded to this extra flick. His hand darted to a small flat box of white cardboard. Within a decorative wreath on the outside was the name Hamley, and an address. Mr. Foster lifted out the box from the pigeon-hole in which it lay and opened it.

" Like that ? " he asked, holding up just such a pin as Brown had described.

" Exactly that," Brown answered.

Maltby closed the box and took it up from under Foster's nose. Not a very considerate action, in Mr. Ricardo's judgment, but to be expected. Fortunately, however, Foster's fingers were still holding the pin which he had taken out of the box for Brown's inspection. Hanaud stepped noiselessly forward.

" One for me, please ! " and he snatched at it.

But he only scratched a red line across the back of his hand, for which the managing clerk made no apology.

" Later on, no doubt," he said, waving the pin backwards and forwards and using familiar words to answer familiar questions, but with his mind lost in other matters.

" Horbury was sitting where I am," they heard him say; " and I came in behind him from my office with some letters for him to sign. Yes. He hadn't heard me come in. He was bending over something in front of him, which I now know to be a chart, hunched over it. But where does the evening paper come in ?—wait a bit—I know. Horbury grabbed at it. It was lying on the top of the desk above the pigeon-holes. He turned over the pages, hardly read a line at the top of a page, and drove in a new pin rather viciously. Did he turn the pages of the paper back again—— ? "

" No," Monsieur Hanaud broke in.

Maltby turned round, half jealous, half friendly.

" How do you know ? "

" Look ! "

Hanaud pointed to the top line of the page.

" Shipping news," and underneath it, " *El Rey* passed Prawle Point at 6 a.m."

Maltby recognised the name and all that it meant in the shape of further investigation. He heaved a sigh, reluctant to abandon the simple verdict of suicide. But he was honest down to the soles of his boots. He smiled grimly at Hanaud.

"Yes, that was the ship which carried Bryan Devisher. And seven miles farther on, Devisher took a header into a rough sea. Yes—but damn!"

The oath came from the heart of a busy, overworked public servant who couldn't have shirked the least item of his job even had he wished to.

Mr. Foster had no ears at this moment for either Hanaud or Maltby. He was sunk deep in his recollections.

"I was standing"—he looked round—"just where Brown is standing. There was, yes—I think I can say that—a little gasp of fear when he looked at the evening paper, and he jabbed rather viciously the last pin into the chart. By the way—" and he turned round with a smile. "All right, Brown, that will do," but when Brown had gone, the smile was still upon his face. "Did you notice those pins? Black pins with the White Ensign flying. Very characteristic of Horbury. All for King and Country. The old rogue—you couldn't but like him. He must have gone out of his way to the toy shop in Regent Street to get those pins. However, there he was jabbing his pin in, and he was suddenly aware of me behind him. He just flung himself over the chart and said: 'You can leave those letters on the little table by the fireplace. I'll sign them before I go,' and he pulled out the lower drawer on his left hand, as if he were going to replace the chart as soon as I left the room. But, you see, he took it away."

Mr. Foster swung round in his chair.

"Yes," said Maltby.

"Yes," said Hanaud.

"Yes," said Mr. Ricardo

"Yes," said Inspector Herbert.

They stood in a semicircle about Foster's chair, brooding upon him. Mr. Ricardo could imagine nothing more intimidating than the group they formed, and, indeed, felt some secret pleasure that he was one of the intimidators. Foster was undoubtedly affected. He rubbed the palms of his hands together, leaning forward in his chair.

" There, that's all," he cried, throwing himself back and meeting Ricardo's gaze rather than the gaze of any of the others.

" Ah, ha ! he looks at you. You are the magnetic one," said Hanaud in a low voice.

Ricardo wished that the charge were true. " I accuse him less," he answered regretfully.

" It is curious, though, that Horbury should have taken that chart away with him to White Barn," Foster resumed carelessly. He was seeking an opportunity of breaking up that arc of intimidating bodies and faces and slipping out of it. But Hanaud was too quick for him.

" It is still more curious that not a fragment of the chart, not a splinter of the ebony board, nor even one of the drawing-pins was to be found at White Barn."

" Yes, that is more curious still," Foster admitted. " Someone must have taken it away."

" Then you admit a someone," said Maltby sternly.

" No, I do not," cried Foster agitatedly, and then surrendering : " Kamerad ! "

He took the bunch of keys from the lower left-hand drawer where it dangled and, fitting one to the lock of the small chamber in the middle of the pigeon-holes, he said :

" There's a letter. It won't help you. I didn't mean to mention it because it could clearly have nothing whatever to do with your case. It is written to really big business, you know. I was more than a little astonished that Horbury should be writing at all to this person. However, he was, and a long letter, too."

" Do you know what it was about ? " Maltby asked.

"Not an idea," replied Foster. "But it had enclosures, I remember noticing that."

"And the address?" said Hanaud.

"Oh, yes. The address, of course. Horbury made no secret from me that there was such a letter, you must understand. If anything happened to him—you know the way men talk—I was to see that it went."

"He said that?" exclaimed Mr. Ricardo. "If anything happened to him——"

"I think the material words were I was to see that it went," replied Foster. "For he said them with a wink . . ."

"A wink?" repeated Hanaud.

Foster nodded. "A bit phoney, eh? But you'll be able to break the seal and see for yourselves."

"It was sealed, was it?"

"Yes, black wax. Horbury pointed that out to me and winked again. Suggestive, eh? Hot stuff, I think, my late employer."

"That's all very well," said Maltby. "But that little cupboard you've opened is as empty as Mother Hubbard's. There's nothing in it."

Foster grinned. "It's not as easy as all that, you know. There's a little wooden latch in the roof of it." He felt with the tip of his middle finger and shot back a wooden peg. Then he stretched his hand in to the back of the cupboard where a hole had been cut in the side wall. "Here she comes!" He was now able to slide forward the pillar on the left side of the cupboard. It was seen to be a narrow drawer set vertically, so that the opening was at the top. He took it out, turned it upside down and shook it. It was as empty as the cupboard. He tapped the sides and shook it a second time. He peered into it.

"It was there!" he cried. "He put it away for safety."

Superintendent Maltby took the drawer and examined it.

" Anyone who knew the trick might have stolen it," he argued.

" No. He would need to open this little door first, and for that he would want the key."

" Can you tell when he took it away ? "

Foster nodded his head.

" Yesterday," he answered. " Horbury was very busy with his first number of the *Newsbag*. So it was only two days ago that he had an hour or two to spare. He made up his packet and sealed the envelope and put it away ready in the secret drawer the day before yesterday."

" Yesterday, then," Maltby agreed. " And ready for use, if the person whom it affected was not amenable, eh ? "

Mr. Foster set back the secret drawer in its place, shot the wooden latch into its place, locked the cupboard drawer, and, with a great formality, handed back the keys to the Inspector. He was once more the managing clerk, official and discreet.

" I could not for a moment, Superintendent, subscribe to any such suggestion," he said, and Monsieur Hanaud rose with a smile from his chair.

" No, no, my friend, that is clear, and the Superintendent never meant that you should," he said gaily. " But one thing, you can tell us, the great boum to whom the package was addressed."

" The Big Noise," Mr. Ricardo said usefully to a rather perplexed managing clerk.

" Yes. You certainly have a right to the name," the managing clerk replied. " It was the name of Septimus Crottle, the Head of the great Dagger Line, and it was addressed to him at his private residence, 41A, Portman Square."

Chapter 13

FEARS, DOUBTS, CURIOSITY

DINNER was finished. The windows were open and the road across Grosvenor Square was quiet as a country lane. Yet even so, it was hardly more quiet than the dining-room where the three men sat about Mr. Ricardo's round table. Four pale blue candles, set in tall, painted candlesticks of Battersea enamel burned, and no other light. The three men had pushed their coffee cups aside ; they were smoking ; but they were not talking, until Mr. Ricardo, embarrassed by the silence, must needs break it with a not very happy fancy.

" My four candles burn in the dusk like little flaming spears, the brighter as the darkness grows. I have two flaming spears one on each side of me, and the blacker the problem, the more brilliantly they will pierce it."

Hanaud shook his head. It was difficult for Ricardo to gauge the hooded look of his face, but he replied with a gravity in his voice which Ricardo had heard only once or twice before.

" For myself, I could find a better image in one of your candles than a spear pointing to the truth."

" Yes ? "

" A heart turned upside down."

Julius Ricardo was as much startled by the quiet voice as by the strange figure which he used.

" By what ? " he began, but he felt Maltby's hand close upon his arm. Hanaud, however, answered the unfinished question.

" By fear."

And for a moment the darkness seemed to deepen and the illumination of the candles to grow dim.

" I have been feeling like a man who is sent to find a number in one of the narrow corridors of your new hotels. You cannot find it, and at the end the corridor turns, and again the corridor turns, and again you cannot find the room. But for me, I meet fear."

Once more there was silence, but Ricardo no longer wished to interrupt it, and Maltby's hand was withdrawn from his sleeve. Then Hanaud resumed :

" Permit that I tell you how it grew. First we have a suicide, a thing simple, and with the Horburys almost natural. The razor close to the throat, as the good Foster said. But not now. The business is up, up, up. Horbury's *Newsbag* becomes Horbury's nosebag. The great poster will be on all the streets. Laughter and money and cocks porping—yes, yes, yes. But suicide. No ! "

" There was the chart," said Maltby.

" The chart Horbury leans over to hide from the Foster eyes, I do not forget him. One cannot doubt what he represented with his black glass pins with the white ensign, and the last pin jammed in angrily opposite to the Prawle Station. It marked the journey of that old steamship *El Rey*, the ports she had put into to deliver back her unsatisfactory visitors, the Lloyds Stations she had signalled. A trouble, yes. A danger, perhaps ; but to be met to-morrow. That night, no danger at all. *El Rey* was still upon its way. It was rounding Beachy Head."

" That's quite right," Maltby agreed. " There was a clerk from Horbury's office at Gravesend to meet *El Rey* in the morning. Horbury couldn't have expected Devisher."

" Yet he took with him to White Barn the chart ? " said Hanaud, pursuing his own thoughts. " Why ? "

" Oh, that's easy," answered Maltby. He leaned back and drew at his cigar with a greater ease than he had shown before. " He had tried to hide it already from Foster. He wanted to get rid of it."

" And he certainly did," cried Mr. Ricardo, clenching the matter finally with a rather irritating laugh.

" How ? " asked Hanaud swiftly.

" There was a log fire," Mr. Ricardo replied no less swiftly.

" Saperlipopette ! " cried Hanaud, beating with his fist on the table. " That will not do. That tough white paper of which the charts are made. That little flat ebony board. All burnt up in a small log fire so that not an ash of blackened paper, not a splinter of the board, not even a brass drawing-pin is left to tell us here it was burnt. I am for the miracle, yes ; but miracles must be reasonable."

It did occur to Ricardo that the question whether a miracle could be a miracle if it was reasonable might be a diverting subject for a debating society. But Hanaud was too much in earnest. He had never known Hanaud utter that explosive outrage of a word—Saperlipopette—unless he was in his most serious mood. So without flippancy he suggested :

" That chart may have been overlooked in White Barn."

Hanaud shrugged his shoulders.

" My dear friend ! The English police ! They may be accused of the want of imagination, perhaps, but they do not overlook things, no, not anything. And a little chart nailed on an ebony board with glass pins pricked in ? No, no, let us be serious."

" All the more serious," added Maltby imperturbably, " because a second search was made in White Barn after we had left Horbury's office this evening and nothing was found."

"Very well." Mr. Ricardo would accept the disappearance of the chart by another agency than the log fire. The explanation was to be found with the explanation of Horbury's death in Hanaud's hinted theory of the morning.

"Very well. The man Devisher comes to White Barn. It is the address of Horbury which he remembers. He comes late, he quarrels, having good reason for a quarrel. He murders—that was your fear—and, taking the chart with him, he goes——"

"Where ? "

The abrupt question shot at him across the table brought Mr. Ricardo to a stop. After all, that was to be considered, and at once a mountain of difficulties confronted him. Devisher had arrived probably at half-past three in London, in a borrowed suit of clothes, what was left of fifteen pounds after his fare and his luncheon had been paid, and no luggage. He had found his way to Lordship Lane, if the theory of a revengeful murder were accepted, unnoticed, and had unnoticed got away in the middle of the night to some place where he could lie in safety.

"Ever since you gave us his name and description, the search has gone on," said Maltby gloomily. "Hotels, lodging-houses, shelters—a man without passport or luggage."

"Add that he has not been in England or in touch with anyone in England for seven years, shall we say ?— and then that he disappears as easily as if he had a place in every thieves' kitchen in London—that is hard to believe."

"But it might happen," cried Mr. Ricardo, "and perhaps it might be the more likely to happen if he were unaware that anyone was looking for him."

Monsieur Hanaud threw up his hands.

"We lose ourselves in the dialectic. We make up

the fairy tale. We sober policemen! I tell you my trouble."

He pushed everything away from in front of him— plates, cups and saucers, table-mats—making an empty space as though he were about to deal a pack of cards.

"In the first place, there is no reason for suicide. The excellent Foster makes that clear. In the second, Horbury has a poor little wretch whom he has injured, due to arrive in England this morning. Horbury has made his arrangements that the man shall be met. That he was afraid of him there is no sign. But the man was already in England. It may be that he made his way to White Barn last night. It may be that he murdered Horbury—just settling his account. I do not say no. But I do not say yes. I say that if he was at White Barn, taking a desperate chance, he blundered in upon some much bigger affair, and must be safely hidden away now."

Superintendent Maltby pushed out his underlip and glowered at the mahogany table.

"I haven't got that," he protested. "Devisher was not alone, or, at all events, ceased to be alone? Of course, his disappearance, a man without money or luggage or friends—yes, I suppose you might infer that there were others, or one other, who was concerned in seeing that he got safely away."

"And the wife," Hanaud added quickly. "Olivia Horbury. Let us not forget her. Whatever we told her, whatever we showed her, she was not startled. Full of horror, as anyone would be who was forced to live over again some dreadful hours, but surprised—no. She knew. She was present. Yet she would not speak."

"Perhaps she had been cowed . . ." Ricardo began, but he suffered his very frequent experience of never being allowed to finish a sentence.

"Ah! Ah! Ah!" exclaimed Hanaud. "I see you.

But she was not cowed to-day with the police at the gate and in the house. Then what was the compulsion which shut her lips ? Something grim—something brutal. The sure knowledge that if she spoke, she would follow on the husband's road. Oh, there was someone else at White Barn last night, and that someone returned."

" Devisher ? " Mr. Ricardo suggester " To recover the chart on the ebony board."

Hanaud nodded his head once or twice, dissatisfied but unable to disregard the argument.

" It may be. He would not want the chart discovered. It points too clearly towards him."

" But you yourself think that someone else came for something else ? " said Maltby.

There was amusement in his voice and, at the same time, respect. It was amusing that Hanaud should so shut his eyes to the obvious explanations of Horbury's death, suicide or murder by Bryan Devisher ; that he should chase in his mind some phantasm of his own creation. And yet, he had the power to leave one uneasy. That image of a narrow corridor, and another, and another, and at the end—fear. Maltby certainly did not like it.

" You think Mrs. Horbury is in danger ? " he said.

" That, I think, could be," replied Hanaud.

" From Devisher ? " Maltby persisted, and Hanaud suddenly thrust forth his hands, palms outwards.

" No, no, no ! My Maltby. I am not here to make the confusion, to tickle you with the red-hot poker. Joey in the woodpile. No ! I abandon you for your delight and go upon my vacancy."

And the three men lost at once their tension. Cigars were renewed, a business-like decanter of Armagnac went forth upon its rounds. Maltby, Ricardo, both were at pains to discover the ideal place where Hanaud might pass his vacancy. " Margate," said Maltby. Ricardo plumped for Brighton. But the unaccountable Hanaud had already his own plan.

"Cathedrals," he said. "I like to sit on the pavement under a stripy awning at a marble table and look at them. They are solid. If I cross the road to one and say, 'I arrest you,' it does not mind. It just says, 'Here is that foolish little Hanaud,' and very far away, in the depths of her, I hear a chuckle. Yes, I shall go to see a cathedral to-morrow. I am told she is very beautiful."

It was astonishing, even to Ricardo, to discover so much romance under the practical urgency of Hanaud's character, but he was startled to hear the Frenchman add:

"She has what is rare, perhaps, the flying buttocks."

Maltby jumped in his chair. Mr. Ricardo looked coldly at his friend.

"A French cathedral, no doubt," he commented acidly.

"No, no!" Monsieur Hanaud was as serious as a man could be. "I shall not give you the laugh by pronouncing the barbaric word of the city which she makes beautiful. No, I shall lead a porter at the railway station to a board. I shall point with my stick, I shall press money into his thorny hand . . ."

"Horny," said Mr. Ricardo.

"And I shall say," continued Hanaud, without paying the slightest attention to Ricardo's interruption, "'Please to buy me the go and return ticket to that unpronounceable place. For I am now upon my vacancy.'"

Superintendent Maltby stubbed out the butt of his cigar into an ashtray.

"I should like to see the porter's reaction to your request," he said, and then the smile left his face.

"So you give up?" he cried with a challenge in his voice; and, indeed, that was to Ricardo the most astounding factor in the whole case. Hanaud gave up. He would go on a vacancy and moon under a stripy awning on Gothic architecture.

"Yes, my dear Maltby. You shall have your way. You shall make that amusing Horbury a fellow of the sea. It shall all be as you wish. And yet I hope that when I come back and have my little meeting with the adorable Madame Horbury and carry off my cheque for the patient Gravot of the Place Vendôme, you, as you say good-bye, will tell me something I much wish to know."

"Oh?" Superintendent Maltby put his interrogation suspiciously. "And what is that something?"

Hanaud shrugged his shoulders. He flapped a hand and flung the subject away. Yet he was curious.

"Yes, I would like to know what switchback business had to write to big business. What Horbury's *Newsbag* had to say to the great Dagger Line of Steamships. And what Daniel Horbury enclosed to Septimus Crottle in so carefully sealed an envelope."

"But that letter has disappeared," cried Ricardo..

"Precisely, my friend," Hanaud returned. "That is why I am curious."

Chapter 14

A MEETING IS ARRANGED

W HEN the unobtrusive Thompson slid into Mr. Ricardo's bedroom the next morning with his morning tea, carried over land through how many countries, lest one tang of the sea should tincture its fragrance, he carried in upon the tray a note from

Hanaud. Mr. Ricardo was grateful. No man was less
hail-fellow-well-met in the morning, than he. Rosy-
cheeked people who hardly knocked before they bustled
in, nephews and nieces and such-like modern importu-
nities, were not allowed. The act of getting up was a
slow and quiet ritual, to be conducted without words.
Not until he was afoot and dressed would he consider
with what rocks and stones and trees he was to be rolled
round in earth's diurnal course.

It was, therefore, with a desire to do what he could
for his friend that he opened his note. Mr. Ricardo
read that Hanaud had put off his visit to the unpronounceable city owing to the persistence of a surprising
idea. He himself must see this Septimus Crottle. He
had no authority by which he could claim an interview.
He was of no account in this Horbury affair. It was
even possible that Septimus had never heard the name
of Hanaud, for nothing was more curious than the small-
ness of the orbits within which fame was circumscribed.
As Mr. Ricardo had himself observed, no one could
answer what Mr. Gladstone had said in 1884. Well,
then, it would be desirable that Hanaud should have an
introduction to Septimus Crottle, and who could give it
but that excellent Mister the Captain Mordaunt, who,
one might think—No ? Yes ?—had a passion for intro-
ducing strangers to Septimus Crottle. Monsieur Hanaud
threw himself at the feet of his dear friend. *I understand*, the note concluded, *that Septimus Crottle is difficult,
but as you know I am at my best with difficult people.
You have seen me at work. I am inspired, I soar,"* and
he signed in his usual style as a peer of the realm.

Mr. Ricardo derided the signature and scoffed in his
mild way at the vanity of the writer. But he, too, was
reluctant to leave this odd matter of Horbury's letter
to Septimus Crottle undiscovered. He wanted to know
the answer to a host of other questions besides. Who

had come to the house and lifted the telephone receiver in the early morning? Why had Olivia Horbury locked her door? And when? And why, with Horbury's *Newsbag* ready to become Horbury's Nosebag, had Horbury drawn that unusual blue-handled knife across his carotid artery—if he had?

Mr. Ricardo accordingly rose, dressed with his usual circumspection, and found Captain Mordaunt preparing to eat his luncheon at his club and more than a little worried. He drew Ricardo into the bar as if he had been his dearest friend.

"A cocktail before we lunch?"

The invitation was, in the modern phrase, telescoped.

"I'd rather have a Manzanilla," said Mr. Ricardo, and the barman gazed at him with the awe due to a customer who knew of a drink unknown to the barman.

"We're just out of it, sir," he said. He thought of embroidering his statement with the news that there had been a great run lately on that there drink, but the theme was dangerous.

"A glass of your driest sherry, then," said Mr. Ricardo, and with Uncle Pepe the barman walked on solid ground.

At luncheon, Mordaunt began whilst Mr. Ricardo was still twittering. Maltby had called on him this morning, Maltby with an infernal fellow with a notebook. Where was Bryan Devisher? Why wasn't his arrival notified to the authorities? Etcetera, etcetera.

"I am bound to say that Maltby was pleasant," Mordaunt continued. "He seemed to know already all that I was telling him."

Mr. Ricardo smiled wisely.

"He was checking up the statement I had already made."

Mordaunt stared at his companion and leaned forward eagerly.

"Perhaps you can help, Mr. Ricardo. I must leave

England on Monday. Ticket taken, cabin booked. All that could stop me would be the police."

"You're not involved in any way," said Mr. Ricardo confidently. "You did all that a reasonable man in a hurry could be expected to do. I am here. We told the same story, no doubt. I am sure that Maltby won't want you to stay."

Captain Mordaunt was greatly relieved. His voice lightened, his face lost its gloom and, as he looked at the trim and decorous Mr. Ricardo, a smile came and went upon his lips.

"So there is an affair of a kind ? " he suggested.

Mr. Ricardo seemed to weigh his inclination to tell against his reticence as an unofficial sleuth.

"Yes. I can say so much—there is," he said darkly.

"And you are in it, of course."

In a whisper, attended by a knowing smile, Mr. Ricardo replied :

"Up to the neck."

"Crime, then ? "

Crime, the wonderful word. It drew the two men together in a net. That crime fascinated Mr. Ricardo was known to all his acquaintances. But were they not fascinated, too ? Let a man say in any company that he has been present at the Old Bailey when an obscure crime is being probed and established, a silence will follow upon his words, however carelessly he may speak them. He may be merely the dullard, the last-wicket-rabbit brought in to make up the party, but at once he becomes the cynosure. He will be plied with questions. He will not relapse into obscurity until all that he can contribute on the characters, the passions, and the events which have woven the dark pattern, has been brought to light. And even then each one of the party will, with a small pang of regret, reflect : " If only I had been in his place, I should have noticed so much more."

So now Captain Mordaunt, though his hopes were cast overseas, leaned forward with shining eyes.

"Yes. You are known to be a student of crime, Mr. Ricardo."

At such moments Mr. Ricardo was apt to become a trifle fatuous. He laughed affectedly.

"Not really? A dilettante, perhaps. But a student? Well, perhaps others might say so."

"Maltby said that you had got the little Frenchman with you."

"Little! My dear Mordaunt! He's as big as a bull and quite as obstreperous."

"I'd like to meet him," said Mordaunt; and there was a great deal more than mere curiosity in the warmth of his voice.

"My dear fellow," said Ricardo, "nothing could be easier."

He had his cue, and over the luncheon table he told Mordaunt all that he knew of the Horbury puzzle.

"Devisher has disappeared. Yes, an ominous fact. Yet Hanaud seems to set as much—no, I am inexact—more importance upon the sealed letter with the enclosures addressed by Horbury to Septimus Crottle. Has he received it? If so, why does he keep it to himself? Does he know nothing about it? Hanaud would very much like to make Crottle's acquaintance."

"Septimus Crottle is a queer old bird," said Mordaunt doubtfully.

"A crotchety patriarch, I think you called him," Mr. Ricardo added. "Hanaud is aware that he must tread gently."

"Yes, but the old man doesn't," replied Mordaunt. "He's a trampler." He thought for a moment. "I tell you what. We'll have some coffee and a cigar upstairs whilst I see what I can do."

They went upstairs to the smoking-room. Coffee and

liqueurs of brandy were put beside them on small stools.

"Cigars," ordered Mordaunt, and at once Mr. Ricardo broke in.

"Claro, please! At this hour not a Colorado."

"Good God, man," Mordaunt exclaimed, "I'm not offering you a beetle"; and, having established Mr. Ricardo in comfort, he went off to the telephone office. He returned in a quarter of an hour.

"It is all right. I didn't mention the letter or, indeed, anything about Horbury's death. I should think he'll go straight up in the air when he hears that Horbury has written to him at all. But that's your pigeon. All I said was that Hanaud and you want to have a word with him."

"And he's willing?"

"Yes. A nice bit of crime, you know! I am going to him on Sunday evening and I'll take you and the Frenchman with me. But I warn you. You have got to fit in. Sunday night is his company night. There's a ritual. The family, one or two friends. We have a glass of port, then someone reads a book, then the girls —there isn't one of them under thirty—are sent off to bed, and then you'll get your conversation. You're not to dress, and you have your dinner before you go. I'll come to your house at ten minutes to eight."

Mr. Ricardo drew back. The order of the day was not to him a phrase for committees.

"Then we must dine at seven!" he exclaimed incredulously.

"Yes, the old man moves with the times," said Mordaunt. "When he was captain of the steam-packet *Tunis* he dined at six."

Chapter 15

SEPTIMUS READS A BOOK

SEPTIMUS CROTTLE lived in a big Victorian house in a big Victorian way. There was now no outward sign upon him that he had not lived upon the land all his life. The weather had faded from his cheeks, and neither an eye of steel nor an aura of tremendous authority are qualities limited to sea captains. It might, indeed, have been Mr. Dombey who received his three new guests at eight o'clock of the evening in his dining-room in Portman Square. He wore a long frock-coat of broadcloth, and above the folds of a black satin neckcloth, decorated with a single pearl of great size, two sharp points of white and glossy collar clipped his face.

"You will drink a glass of port, gentlemen," Septimus said. "Mary, set some chairs and glasses."

There was no manservant in the house ; patriarchs, after all, are waited upon by maidens. Mary cleared three places at the long table, one upon Crottle's right for Monsieur Hanaud and two upon his left for Mordaunt and Mr. Ricardo. The ladies, of course, had already retired to the drawing-room.

"I welcome you to my house, Monsieur Hanaud," said Septimus, holding up his glass of wine.

"It was gracious of you to invite me, Mr. Crottle," Hanaud returned, holding up his.

Both men bowed and drank, and Hanaud, as he put his glass down, exclaimed in an ecstasy :

"And this is a wonderful glass of Porto which you are giving me."

"It's the best," said Septimus, quite simply. "It's mine. George, fill Monsieur Hanaud's glass."

A fair-haired youth upon Ricardo's right obeyed with a broad grin upon his face and a twinkle in his eye.

"The guv'nor decanted it himself from his own private bin, Monsieur Hanaud," he said genially. "There aren't many to whom he shows that consideration."

Hanaud tasted his wine and looked up at the ceiling. He tasted it again and held it for a long time in his mouth, and swallowed it at last slowly, with his eyes closed. Mr. Ricardo was disgusted with his friend's behaviour. To Hanaud, Porto was Porto, and the blacker it was and the stickier it was, the more Hanaud enjoyed it. "Look at the hypocrite," Mr. Ricardo said to himself. "He's obsequious."

But obviously Septimus was pleased.

"I shall offer you a cigar," he continued, "but I am afraid that must wait until after our reading. Meanwhile I should like to present to you my nephew, George Crottle. The gentleman sitting on the other side of Captain Mordaunt you may perhaps know."

Hanaud looked at a thin, tall, narrow man with a grey moustache.

"Yes, yes," he said with an air of surprise as he held out his hand. "I certainly have had the honour to meet him."

"Mr. Alan Preedy is one of the Line's solicitors."

"But in a very small way," Preedy put in modestly. "I don't aspire to famous cases."

"No doubt they will come," Hanaud protested.

"But not, I hope, in connection with the Dagger Line," said George Crottle in mock dismay.

"I think that is unlikely," said Septimus, with a touch of irritation in his voice. "I have another nephew "— and the irritation was still audible—" who apparently is not giving us the pleasure of his company to-night."

" I beg your pardon, sir," Preedy interrupted rather eagerly, as if he recognised that a smooth relationship between the elder and the younger branches of the Crottle firm was one of his duties. " I fancy Mr. James arrived a moment ago."

Septimus turned his head and listened.

" I can't hear a sound," said George. " Old James has carted us, this night of all nights, when our Uncle Septimus is reading."

Septimus looked at his nephew with approval, but Alan Preedy still appeared for the absent one.

" It was a taxi stopping at the door which I heard, and the passing of change makes the driver, as a rule, undress himself by several layers of clothes. Ah, there he is ! "

Alan Preedy had hardly finished before the housebell rang, but he had finished. Mr. Ricardo looked with admiration at the lawyer, upon whose face there rose a blush.

" Yes," said George gaily to Ricardo, " if I wanted to listen at a keyhole, I should brief Preedy as my sub-stitute. It's quite a gift."

Monsieur Hanaud seemed to be concentrating his attention upon his Porto, and said nothing.

James Crottle, a tall, dark and grim young man entered the room. He made his apologies to his uncle, clapped Preedy heartily upon the shoulder, and said with a laugh :

" The law's delays are nothing to a taxicab's."

He nodded to Mordaunt, was introduced to Hanaud and Ricardo, and took his seat at the table on the side of the Frenchman. The difference between him and George was remarkable. George, the fair-haired youth, seemed by comparison with him of almost feminine good looks. There was a supple grace in his slim figure and a friendliness in his smile and eyes which James was with-out. James leaned a little forward and said to Hanaud :

"My uncle did not tell us that we were to have the honour to-night of meeting anyone so distinguished as you."

There was just a hint of a question in his words which Septimus took up :

"Monsieur Hanaud has, I gather, some matter of importance which he wishes to talk over with me afterwards."

Coffee was brought in on a great silver tray, and Ricardo, under such security as the clatter of the cups granted him, said to his neighbour, Alan Preedy :

"This is to me the greatest blessing of the evening so far. For keep my head from nodding during a reading, that I cannot do."

"Septimus isn't so bad," Preedy returned. "It's his turn to read to-night, thank the Lord ! You'll see, he'll probably keep you awake."

At that moment the parlourmaid entered the room and anounced to Septimus that the ladies were assembled in the drawing-room and that the clock had struck the hour three minutes ago.

"Then I suppose that we had better go, Mary," he said with a smile.

"Yes, sir, and the room all prepared as if it was for a Church Service," she answered.

For perhaps a minute Mr. Septimus did not budge, a little colour rose into his face, the smile remained upon his mouth, and a sparkle of fire revived the youth of his eyes. He looked and smiled straight ahead of him, savouring in advance the small ritual of the assembly, the resonance of his voice, the stillness of his audience as he held it in a magic web. There was romance in these Sunday nights for Septimus Crottle. At this hour, once in every fourth week, he recaptured some shadow of the thrill and glory of his first command. When he opened the book, he stepped again upon his bridge. He was no longer the owner of the Dagger Line, concerned with questions of policy, he was the young Lord and Master of his ship, of its passengers, its crew and its cargo. He stood at the pilot's side in Southampton Water with his eyes fixed upon tropical harbours, where after weeks of vigilance he would hear the thunderous rattle of the anchor chains in the bows. He rose from his chair, his old wrinkled face eager and radiant.

" Let us go ! " he cried on a rising note.

Mordaunt noticed the change and smiled. " He has dropped his pilot. He has set his course between the Spithead Forts for the Nab. Has he the clusters of palm trees in his vision, a scent of strange perfumes in his nostrils, the sing-song of coolies in his ears ? And he's only stepping from a dining-room to a drawing-room in Portman Square."

But this was Mordaunt's thought and his alone. It was prompted by the same instinctive sympathy which had once made him row down Helford River to Passage to hear some home-truths from this redoubtable old man.

Mr. Ricardo was not given to such fancies. He was simply troubled by the knowledge that for an hour, in a room where every curtain, every piece of furniture was certain to offend the eye, he must listen to this old fellow droning out the pages of a book. Monsieur Hanaud, for his part, was puzzled, and he was showing that he was puzzled—showing it so much indeed that as he walked towards the door of the room, he felt a hand upon his sleeve. He turned and saw George Crottle at his elbow.

" Something, I can see, is perplexing you, Monsieur Hanaud. Can I help ? "

Hanaud was at once all contrition and apology. He stammered, he spread out his hands.

" It was an impoliteness. . . . I beg you to forgive.

. . . The habit grows of itself. . . . One asks oneself the questions, and suddenly one is guilty of an inconvenience."

" Not a bit," George replied. " I could see you looking from James to me and from me to James."

Hanaud was more confused than ever.

" I had no right to make the comparison," he said. " No. And I should not have been surprised. So often one sees it—in brothers——"

" Who don't seem to belong to the same litter, eh ? " George returned with a laugh. " James ! " and the dark young man turned back from the door.

" What is it ? " he asked, not too pleasantly.

" All is discovered ! We are lost ! " George resumed, and he turned again to Hanaud. " You are right, Monsieur Hanaud, we are not brothers at all, and, what's more, our names aren't even Crottle."

James uttered a small cry of impatience and followed the rest of the party out of the room. George, however, detained the Frenchman. He burst into a laugh as he watched James's abrupt departure.

" You may as well have the facts, Monsieur, especially as they throw an amusing light on Uncle Sep's quarter-deck style."

Uncle Sep's sister Maria had married William Martindale, and had had one son, George. But William Martindale was already a widower with a stepson by his first marriage, James Urquhart. Thus both James and George were in no blood relationship to each other. William Martindale was himself a partner in a shipping firm of small prosperity, and upon his death, Septimus bought up the Line, added the few good cargo ships which it owned to the Dagger fleet, and took both boys into the management. James was by three years the elder, but George was the actual nephew, and it was generally understood that on Crottle's death or retirement, George Martindale would become Chairman of the Line. James, however, was to be left substantially in it, a director and a partner.

"Then one morning," continued George, "we both woke up to read in *The Times* that we had changed our names to Crottle. It isn't what you'd call a pretty name and, as you could see, James is still peeved about it—all the more because the old man, neither before nor since, has ever said a word about it to either of us. He just did it—the bit of brimstone in our treacle, but there's such a lot of treacle that I, at all events, didn't notice the bitter taste at all."

Monsieur Hanaud thanked him for the explanation, and added :

"It is, after all, natural that Mr. Crottle should like to leave his name associated with the great Dagger Line. One day, no doubt, he will be Lord Crottle."

"Not he," cried George with a laugh. "He's Mr. Crottle of the Dagger Line—and proud of it."

But they were in the doorway of the drawing-room now, where conversation was exchanged in low voices, as if they were all in the porch of a church. Monsieur Hanaud was presented by George to the three daughters of Septimus. It was Mordaunt's story that the Patriarch had turned a most deliberate back upon suitors for their hands. Certainly all three of them were in their thirties. Anne, the youngest, a large handsome woman with a high colour and pronounced features ; Audrey, smaller, prettier, but beginning to look a little like a horse ; and Agatha, the eternal spinster, angular, acrimonious, awkward. Her hair, gathered in a tight bun, was already grey, and her face, with its high thin nose and a bitter mouth, had lost, so worn it was and tired, any pretension to charm which it might have had. She gave Monsieur Hanaud a hand so thin that it caused him a little shock, as though he had shaken hands with a skeleton; and whereas the other two sisters had shown some little excitement, not at meeting him, but at the recurrence of this weekly ceremonial, she greeted him with a dull eye and a languid voice.

" I hope you won't be too bored."

" I ? " exclaimed Hanaud. " But I am never bored, even when there is reason to be. So how could I be bored here ? "

Mr. Ricardo caught the words and once more whispered " hypocrite." The room was just what he expected. Not one artistic nerve in him but twanged distressfully. The curtains were of crimson rep with pelmets disfigured by yellow rectangles; the chairs of black painted wood, with thin gold lines, were upholstered tightly in black and green silk with buttons sunk in little pits; and wherever an antimacassar could be hung, it was hung. One particular piece shook Mr. Ricardo to his centre : a cabinet without a curve, made in black painted wood. There was an oblong bevelled mirror in the raised central back, and below the level surface two cupboards with bouquets of roses painted on the doors. His eye, indeed, rested with pleasure upon an oval mahogany table, a Regency cabinet in white and gold in a corner of the room, and an arm-chair by Chippendale in which Septimus was to sit. An electric lamp with a green shade burned upon the table, and the book from which Septimus Crottle was to read lay closed within the circle of light.

" All ready ? " asked George of the company, and each one took the seat arranged. The chairs were grouped in an irregular curve. Thus Hanaud was sitting almost behind old Mr. Crottle's shoulder; two daughters, Anne and Audrey, came next; the lawyer, Preedy, sat at the head of the table, and Agatha was at his right. Mr. Ricardo sat at Agatha's right and beyond her Mordaunt. George occupied the end of the table fronting Alan Preedy, and between George and his uncle was an empty place for James. Thus, in a free space, sat Mr. Septimus Crottle of the Dagger Line.

It was remarkable how clearly that order was established in Ricardo's mind; for his was not a tidy mind. Yet he had hardly to shut his eyes, before he could see each one of those ten people sitting upright and stiff, side by side. It is, perhaps, still more remarkable that Ricardo grasped exactly why the positions were so accurately registered in his memory.

" All ready ? " asked George at the table; and at once, by gesture or word, assent was made. Mr. Ricardo expected that now the book would be opened and the reading begin. But George cried over his shoulder " Go ! " and James switched off the lights of the room. There was only one left burning, that of the lamp with the green shade upon the table. James slipped into the empty chair. The room sank to darkness, the ugliness of its equipment vanished. Above the coats of the men and the dresses of the women an arc of faces gleamed, all set towards the one lamp, faces lifeless and pallid as masks; and Mr. Ricardo understood that, however dull the book and however inadequate the reader, not once would his head nod or his eyes close until the reading was finished.

He was conscious of an excitement which ran through his veins and throbbed in his ears. For a moment or two he could not trace it to its source. · There was the old man with his wrinkled features in the full bright light and, in spite of his frock-coat and upstanding stock, of some obvious brotherhood with the sea. There was, above the green shade of the lamp, the circle of white dead faces. But to neither of these causes was due the expectancy racing through him. He came to the explanation at last and, though he knew it for an illusion and the merest of accidents, it did not lose its hold. The book which lay upon the table directly beneath the lamp was bound in cloth of exactly the same pale blue colour as the painted handle of the knife which had caused Horbury's death. It shone in the gloom of that room ; it alone shone : it claimed the eyes ; it seemed to Ricardo to make a promise—or perhaps a threat. More likely a threat, since it was with a definite relief that he saw the old man's thickly-veined hands open the book somewhere towards the end where a ribbon marked the place.

Septimus began to read. For a little while Ricardo did not notice the theme of the book. Words followed words in the rhythm of prose—so much he observed, but he was too surprised by the voice of the reader to take to himself their meaning. The voice was clear and musical and muted to the compass of the room, but it was troubled, so troubled that the reader seemed to find in this far-off story of Marie Antoinette—for here and there her name came and went amongst the words—some quite personal and startling application. Mr. Ricardo began to listen now to what was read, and it was read so faithfully that the stodgy room in Portman Square vanished altogether, and he moved in the squalor of the Conciergerie, amongst ruffianly gaolers and elegant dandies and great ladies awaiting, with a jest to hide their fears, the creak and rumble of the tumbrils at the door. Against that background the wail of a boy rose and fell like a tide.

Marie Antoinette had paid for the folly of her tongue and her inadequate life. Septimus read of the Dauphin —a boy, sickly, spoilt, but punished by such drawn-out cruelty as, even in these days, few boys have endured. He needed playmates of his own age, he was allowed none. He wanted fresh air, open fields, sunlight and good food. He was given instead the foul, overbreathed vapours of the Conciergerie, a small cell with a high small window on a hall, and once a day a word or two of abuse from his gaoler as his food and his jug of water were brought in to him. The Dauphin of France was too dangerous a magnet for all that was left in France or abroad of the old regime. But he couldn't be tried He couldn't be sent to the guillotine. Even the rabble shrank from that abominable horror. What the most abject slander could do to asperse his character was done. But it was not enough. He must disappear. So he was left, locked up in his cell, a child without books, without clean linen, without a doctor, without a mother, to get through each day and night and the next and the next as best he could. Finally the gaoler ceased to show his face or utter a word. Once a day a panel was opened, food and water were pushed through, and the panel was closed again. That was all. And after an eternity—of what torrents of tears, of what gusts of passion, of what lonely despair !—neither the plate of food, nor the jug of water were touched. For twenty-four hours, 'for forty-eight hours they were left, and then for the first time in weeks the door of the dark cell was unlocked.

Old Septimus read so far, controlling his voice, but stopping now and again to control it, and bending his head a little lower over the page. Then suddenly he stopped, closed the book, and raised a face so ravaged with horror, so old beyond all age, that it imposed silence upon all that company. It was a silence as heavy as a pall, and it was broken at last by one deep sigh.

Every head had been lowered or shaded by a hand or fixed upon the reader, and all had been a little dazed. That one deep sigh must have seemed to have been breathed by a corporate voice, to have issued from the blended emotions of them all But it was a shock to all. It jarred upon all except Septimus Crottle at the table. He was still in the Conciergerie, standing at the door of the cell as the key at last grated in the lock. But to the rest it was grievous. There had been no pity in it, no horror, no refusal. Construed into words it meant "At last!" Something long sought for had been discovered.

Septimus finished before his hour was up, but at the end of a chapter, so that it was natural that he should halt there. He closed the book slowly after marking the page with the ribbon, and said in a voice which surprised the audience, so unmoved and ordinary it was once more:

"I think we can stop this book here and choose another one for our next Sunday."

He rose, and the bright sheen of the blue cover moved out of the circle of light, to Ricardo's relief. Septimus walked to a table which stood under a window at the end of the room. It had a drawer with a couple of gilt handles. Septimus pulled one of them, but the drawer remained closed. For a moment he was puzzled, and a frightened voice cried:

"Father, it's locked."

The cry sprang from the mouth of Agatha. She jumped up and, pushing the chairs apart, hurried to the mantelshelf. But she was too late. For even while she was fumbling in a china box set on a ledge by the mirror, Septimus pulled the handle again. But this time it was a tug, a jerk, and with a crack the drawer burst open.

"It was locked. Why?"

"The key caught in one's dress."

Agatha showed the key to Septimus. It was rather long.

"You see how it juts out. I took it from the lock."

But Septimus had still one foot in the Conciergerie. He nodded his head.

"The drawer's no use to me now," he said, and Hanaud was already at his side. Cumbrous though he was, no one moved so swiftly, so unsuspiciously as Hanaud when he chose.

" Can I help, Monsieur Crottle ? " he asked, and he laid his hand upon the top of the open drawer.

" No, the lock's broken," interposed Agatha. " It's a gimcrack affair, any way " ; and as in the room the lights were turned up she shut the drawer so violently that Hanaud had barely time to snatch his hand away.

" Did I catch your fingers ? " Agatha asked, staring at him angrily, and obviously hopeful that she had.

" No, no, mademoiselle." Hanaud' returned with a smile. " You would have to be quicker than that."

He turned towards Crottle, who walked to the one solid piece of furniture in the room—a Chippendale bureau which stood against a wall opposite to the cabinet. It had a bookcase with shelves and glass doors on the top and below it a front which could be let down to make a writing-table. Septimus Crottle let the front down, pushed the book in, locked up the front again, and pocketed the key. He said in a curious, hard, resentful voice, which astonished no one who had heard him reading, and would have astonished anyone who had not :

" I never want to see that book again."

He was once more Septimus Crottle, the owner of the great Dagger Line. He stepped out to Mordaunt.

" You're off to-morrow, Mordaunt, and I'm sorry to say not on one of my ships. But my ships sail on Fridays, so it couldn't be helped. I'm going to tell you that your letter put you up a peg or two in my esteem." A sudden smile made his face very pleasant and friendly. " This is your last night in England, so you will have letters to write. I am to talk with these gentlemen "— he waved a hand towards Ricardo and Hanaud—" so I'll say good night and good luck."

He shook hands with Mordaunt, but for a few seconds did not move. Then he said " Yes," and took a step or two towards the door ; and again he said " Yes," adding, as once more he moved on, " If there's anything we can do for you, write to me," and this time he reached the door. But there he turned, having made up his mind. He came straight back into the middle of the room, challenging them all to blame him if they dared.

"Meanwhile, Mordaunt, you might perhaps do something for me."

His voice was now firm but gentle, and Ricardo wondered afterwards whether something of the pity which he had felt and imposed upon his audience for that young victim of a nation's revolt was still working within him.

"My youngest daughter—Rosalind. She was lovely to look at. She said she was stifled in this house. I didn't understand that. She married against my will. Leete, the name was. She may be still where you are going. I think the marriage has turned out ill. God knows, I take no pride in that! So, if you meet her, will you tell her that her place is here—and empty."

So it was not pity which had moved him, not even compunction, Mr. Ricardo thought, but just the patriarch's feeling that, owing to the wrong-headed folly of one of the family, there was an uncomfortable gap which should be closed.

"Of course I will, sir," said Mordaunt, and at once voices broke out in a babble. The only words Ricardo distinguished were spoken by George Crottle enthusiastically :

"It would be fine to have Rosie back again."

Septimus turned with an apology to his two new guests, and he included in his smile Mr. Alan Preedy.

"But these are family matters. You have something to say to me, Monsieur Hanaud. Will you and your friend come along with me to the smoking-room ? George, and James too, perhaps, since in so much they take my place. To everyone else, good night."

He led the four men to a room along the corridor behind the drawing-room.

Chapter 16

HANAUD SMOKES A CIGAR—OR DOES HE?

IT always gave Mr. Ricardo a pinch, as it were, of malicious pleasure to see Hanaud's discomfort when he drank a whisky and soda ; and a still stronger and more satisfactory pinch to watch his inability to cope with a big cigar. Hanaud would so much sooner have smoked one of his own black abominations. Thus Mr. Ricardo's spirit, which had been undoubtedly depressed by the reading in the drawing-room, rose with a bound when Septimus, standing by a tray which held bottles of soda-water and a black, pot-bellied bottle of whisky, invited his guests to drink.

" A whisky and soda, Monsieur Hanaud ? "

" What would be an English evening without it ? " Hanaud returned with a flourish. He took a tumbler from the tray and held it out to Septimus. But, even so, there was a twisting of his nostrils as the smell of the liquor reached them, and a gentle writhing of his features, as he realised that he must actually drink it, which was reminiscent of the Christian martyrs. Worse, however, was to come. As Hanaud stood with the tumbler in one hand and the other fumbling in his pocket for a cigarette, Septimus produced a large box of cigars from a cabinet.

" But that is a big box, Monsieur Crottle ! "

" They are big, big cigars," Ricardo replied gleefully.

" They look wonderful," said Monsieur Hanaud.

He stared doubtfully into the box, advancing and withdrawing a hand ; rather, Ricardo thought, like a young lady in the days of his youth on the steps of a bathing machine dipping her toes into the water on some bleak summer morning.

"They're the best," Septimus explained. "They are mine."

Hanaud quivered as he took a cigar of a length associated with one English aristocrat and two English statesmen.

"You'll spoil me," he said, holding up a warning finger to Septimus; and, indeed, Mr. Ricardo fancied that that might really happen before Hanaud had reached the end of his cigar. However, diplomacy meant doing a good many repugnant things with an air of extreme pleasure, for the sake of establishing a position, didn't it?

"Have a light," said Septimus, and he struck a big wooden match. "You wouldn't, I am sure, insult that cigar with a briquet."

"I would not, indeed," cried Hanaud, hastily withdrawing his hand from his pocket. He carried his cigar and his tumbler to a chair which really was easy and settled himself into it with deliberation. He was marking time. Certainly there was a little noise outside the room for which, indeed, Hanaud was to blame. He had been the last of the five to enter the smoking-room and he had not latched the door. The front door closed once, gently, as Alan Preedy, quiet, as gentlemen of the law should be, departed. Then followed a rustle of skirts and a couple of high-pitched voices on the stairs. The ladies were going to bed—or two of them, at all events.

"Now, Monsieur Hanaud, in what way can I help you?" said Septimus, upright in a straight-backed chair.

"I shall tell you frankly," Hanaud replied, and he felt in his pockets. He looked at Ricardo. "You can oblige me. I left, or I think I left, a little diary in a topcoat in the hall."

" I'll get it for you," Ricardo answered readily. He had, in truth, not needed the quick glance which Hanaud had thrown at him. He was really wanted now !

" It's the grey coat," said Hanaud.

" I remember," said Ricardo.

He didn't remember at all, but he went out of the room. In front of him stretched the long corridor to the inner of the two hall doors, empty—but not quite silent. A strange sound made itself faintly heard as he listened. What it was that Hanaud wanted of him, he could not imagine. All the more reason, therefore, to miss nothing, however infinitesimal. The strange sound was rather like the bleating of a sheep. And it came from the drawing-room just in front of the smoking-room, through the open door. And the room was still lit, although the girls, as Septimus had called them, had gone up to bed.

But Ricardo had only heard two voices. Was the third bleating in the drawing-room, and which of the three would it be ? He advanced stealthily, noiselessly. He, Julius Ricardo, of Grosvenor Square, was primitive man-trapper, Redskin with the scalping-knife—Mr. Ricardo loved the picture—or perhaps not primitive man at all, but the man of to-day, acute, erudite, the sleuth—Mr. Ricardo liked the picture still more. He held his breath ; he moved on tiptoe—and stopped. From the spot where he stood he stared through the doorway into a long oblong mirror against the drawing-room wall. He saw reflected in it the gimcrack table with the gilt handles, and the drawer once more open and, in front of it, seated in the chair which she had used during the reading, Agatha. But not the Agatha of the reading. This was a woman stricken. She sat with her hands to her face, shuddering. At times the shuddering mounted to a sob of horror and so stopped altogether. But it began again, and again so ended. Ricardo noticed that there lay upon her lap a card which had been torn across in two pieces; and even from where he stood he could see that there was writing on the card.

As he watched, he was aware of a change in her. Instead of the horror there was now uneasiness. She moved her shoulders, the hands fluttered upon her face; and he was warned. People who do not know that they are watched, sometimes by some instinct suspect it. He himself was the cause of her uneasiness. He stooped low. He had time to see her snatch her hands from her face, stare with a violent shiver at the torn pieces of the card, and then drop them into a wastepaper basket by the side of the cabinet. The carpet was thick and he made no noise. He stood straight up now, pulling down his coat. He said in a voice no louder than was natural:

"The grey topcoat? All right."

He walked forward past the door of the drawing-room, humming a little tune to himself. He was extremely careful not to direct one glance into the lighted room; and as he reached the contraption by the hall door, with its hat- and coat-rack and its tin trough for umbrellas, he so rattled it that only the most obsessed people in the world could have been unaware that he was pretending with every artifice that he was not pretending. However, it was one of the most obsessed people whom he had to deceive; and whilst he was fumbling in the empty pockets of a coat, he heard a click as a light was switched off, and a moment later the hiss and rustle of a dress upon the stairs.

"There's nothing," Mr. Ricardo was saying aloud. Really, he was playing his part admirably. "I can't understand it." He heard a door shut upstairs. Then he stopped at once his untheatrical piece of theatre. But he waited, listening for that door perhaps to open again; it did not. Now he hurried back along the corridor. He slipped into the dark drawing-room. Enough light crept in from the hall to define the plan of the room. But he must not stumble over furniture and he must be quick. He slid between the chairs to the wastepaper basket. A great fear was troubling him that the basket might be full with the litter of the day. But his fingers assured him that, except for two small pieces of pasteboard, the basket was empty. He snatched those pieces up. Above his head he heard a woman's heels tapping. He slipped out and returned to the smoking-room.

"I can't find it," he said. "I am very sorry."

"Oh!" said Hanaud, disappointed. "Well, I've no doubt that I can remember all that's necessary," he added encouragingly, and Ricardo, with confidence, shut the door.

Hanaud was leaning forward to speak, when Septimus said :

"You have let your cigar go out, Monsieur Hanaud."

"And if you think that's a good beginning, my friend, you are wrong," Ricardo commented silently.

Even Hanaud realised his fault.

"I have, indeed. It is not to be pardoned. But with a wooden match, I light him again. So."

"Now blow once."

Monsieur Hanaud blew.

"Now you can smoke it."

Hanaud drew in a breath. "It is delicious," he said.

"Of course," replied Septimus.

"But I waste the time. There was a man of whom, Monsieur Crottle, you will only have heard. Daniel Horbury."

From neither James nor George was there a start nor any movement.

"He committed suicide," said Septimus.

"So it is said."

"An inquest will be held on Tuesday."

"And that same verdict will probably be given."

"But you don't believe it, Monsieur Hanaud?"

There was no shrugging of the shoulders now in Monsieur Hanaud, no flourishing of arms.

"I don't believe it, Monsieur Crottle."

"And whether it was suicide or murder—I take murder to be the only alternative——?"

Crottle paused, but his eyes met only a face of wood, and he resumed: "How am I concerned?"

"He wrote a letter to you, sir."

The sentence was thrown quickly at Septimus—a grenade to produce an explosion. All it produced was a smile of amusement on Crottle's old pippin of a face.

"They all do."

Hanaud was clearly puzzled.

"They?" he repeated.

"Horbury and men like him," Septimus repeated.

"What is it, then, they want?"

"A passage on the Dagger Line, Monsieur Hanaud, to the land of their dreams—a land where there are no extradition treaties."

"But there were enclosures in the letter."

"There would be. Passages must be paid for."

"And he didn't send the letter at once. He kept it by him."

"That, also, they all do—for Mr. Micawber's immortal reason."

"Something turning up," Mr. Ricardo interpreted.

Hanaud was disappointed. He refused to accept the obvious and practical conclusions of Septimus Crottle.

"But Monsieur Crottle, you will pardon me. Horbury was not in distress. In fact"—if it came to idiomatic phrases, Hanaud could hold his own—"in fact, he exclaimed triumphantly, "he was upsidaisy."

"Financially?"

" Yes. We have the evidence, eh, my friend," and he turned to Ricardo. " Horbury's nosebag."

" But was he upsidaisy with the police, Monsieur Hanaud ? " Septimus answered with his eyes twinkling.

Hanaud, however, was ready for him there.

" The Superintendent Maltby had no intention to arrest him."

Septimus Crottle smiled.

" It might be that the Superintendent Maltby didn't explain, even to you, Monsieur Hanaud, all that he had in his mind. I am afraid that, after all, you have found a mare's nest."

" And I, no doubt, am the foal," Hanaud returned quickly.

Mr. Ricardo was in the mood to applaud the witticism, even though it was founded on a mispronunciation. He did not like to see his friend so put down. Even Septimus began to laugh, but corrected himself immediately. Instead of a congratulation, he implied a censure. He said :

" You have again let your cigar go out."

" It is the excitement," returned Hanaud. He rose, and young George Crottle was in front of him with a match-box in his hand. For a moment Hanaud stared at him as if he had forgotten his presence. Then he looked from him to James. Then he said : " Oh, yes, Mr. George Crottle ! Mr. James Crottle ! You agree, of course, with your uncle ? "

The question, though out of keeping no doubt with the times, was quite appropriate to this particular uncle and nephews, so masterful the one, so debonair or amenable the others.

" Yes, I should say old Horbury wrote the letter," replied the debonair George, " and put it away on the chance that he might some time want it in a hurry. There it was."

" But there it isn't," replied Hanaud.

" It has disappeared ? " asked James. He looked quickly at his uncle.

" Without trace. We have searched the office, Horbury's desk, his blotting-pad, and his house."

" White Barn ? " said James Crottle.

" Yes," answered Hanaud, and Septimus appeared surprised.

" You know the house ? " he asked of his nephew.

" The name was in the evening papers," George explained.

" There is no reason that I can see "—and Hanaud, who had started smoothly, now halted and pronounced slowly each word, as if he had just begun to see—" why Horbury should have taken the letter to White Barn. But he may have done."

" However, it wasn't there, and, mind you, we looked everywhere, Maltby and I."

" In the blotting-book ? " James asked.

" The one on the floor ? " said Hanaud, and George Crottle chuckled loudly.

" I've heard that Horbury did a good deal of his business over a bottle, or bottles, of Pommery, but I never thought that he couldn't stand up to it and had to keep his blotting-book on the floor."

A little long-winded, Mr. Ricardo thought. Rather silly, too. George Crottle, with all his good fellowship, might become a rattle, when a gaffe had been made, to cover up the man who had made it. But the rally of dialogue was swift enough to cover more than a gaffe. Moreover, Hanaud chose that moment to close a subject which had become interesting to Ricardo. He flung himself away from George Crottle and the big offending box of Bryant and May.

" In a moment I ask for the match, Monsieur George, the splutter, the flame. Yes, I shall ask for them," and with a laugh he challenged George to contradict him. "But at the moment"—he turned, still smiling, to Septimus—"it is to you, Mr. Crottle, that I would like to tell all, if you will have the patience to listen to me."

"Of course," replied Septimus.

"I have little concern in this affair," and Hanaud explained the case of Devisher and Gravot of the Place Vendôme. "That is all settled. I shall carry back from the widow Horbury in notes of the Bank of England the money owed to him. But I went with Maltby"—and he described with a quiet force what he had seen and what he had inferred; the sudden determination of the Horburys to spend the night at the house in Lordship Lane, the manner of Olivia Horbury itself—"to read what people say is one thing, to hear them saying it is very much another"—the locked door, the telephone receiver lifted and replaced in the dark of the morning, the absence of all the natural fingerprints on the furniture, the want of any reason why suicide should have been committed, the disappearance of Devisher. "Yes, and something more, the disappearance of a little chart, fixed on an ebony board."

"Chart?" exclaimed Septimus, sitting forward.

"Chart?" George Crottle echoed.

"Chart?" James Crottle repeated.

They were men of the sea, the three of them. Charts were part of their business. There were rolls of charts in the cupboards of the offices of the Dagger Line. It was inevitable that the Crottles should sit up and wonder what in the world Daniel Horbury was doing with a chart.

"Yes. It was marked, too, with pins, little black glass pins, with a white ensign on the top, such as you may buy at a toyshop. They seemed to mark the passage of a steamship—*El Rey*, which brought Devisher home."

" And the chart has disappeared ? " Septimus asked.

" Yes," replied Hanaud, " with the letter."

" Burnt, no doubt," George returned.

" Cartridge paper," said Septimus with a shake of the head.

" And the ebony board, too ? Yes, it is possible. There was a small fire at White Barn. But why should Horbury be so anxious to burn so carefully that not a splinter of the wood nor an edge of the cartridge paper should be left for us to find ? And after so much trouble to stretch his chart flat and prick it day by day ? It doesn't sound reasonable."

Septimus Crottle nodded his head.

" No, it doesn't. But this man, Devisher ? He was rescued by Mordaunt's yacht. He left Kingswear by the Torbay Express "—once more Septimus went over the old ground. " Devisher is the man to look for."

" No doubt," said Hanaud. " Yes, no doubt, and Maltby is looking for him."

Septimus Crottle was watching Hanaud's face closely.

" But he has disappeared ? "

Hanaud nodded his head.

" Yes. Like Horbury's letter to you, the marked chart and the ebony board."

" With them, perhaps," suggested George Crottle, and Hanaud swung swiftly round to him.

" Then Devisher was at White Barn on Thursday night," returned Hanaud, and George Crottle's face flamed red. He began to make in a kind of hurry some faltering suggestions which seemed superlatively foolish to Mr. Ricardo.

" Then he will have taken the letter."

" From the blotting-book on the floor ? " Hanaud interposed with a grin.

" And the chart," James Crottle added without re-

marking upon the interposition, " and gone off according
to his plan."

Hanaud broke in again, shaking his head as if thus
he shook all the plans away into the air.

" How can he have made plans, Mr. James? He
arrived in London by the Torbay Express. He had
no luggage, no friends, a borrowed suit of clothes, and
ten or eleven pounds, and he had been at least six years
away, buried in a foreign prison. Yet, within a few
hours, he has made such fine plans that he can commit a
murder in Lordship Lane and make a vanishing that all
the police in London cannot explain."

Septimus Crottle was as interested now as if some
baffling crime had been committed on a ship under his
command.

" But he has disappeared, Monsieur Hanaud. That's
the fact, the impossible fact which is always happening."

" I do not lose sight of him. It is one of the facts
which make me think he did not murder on Thursday
night. I think that somehow he fitted in with other
plans—maybe Horbury's, if, indeed, Horbury did the
slitting, maybe some unknown murderer's."

He turned with confidence to Ricardo.

" My very good friend and consultationist "—Ricardo
shivered a little at the coinage of that new and, alas!
adoptable word—" Ricardo was for some hours on
Mordaunt's boat with Devisher. Tell us what you
thought of Bryan Devisher, Mr. Julius."

Among the innumerable irritations which vexed the
even flow of Mr. Ricardo's spirit, perhaps none hurt so
much as liberties taken with his name. To be " Mr.
Julius " was to be a younger son addressed by a superior
being—like a butler, say. He was being bidden to speak
up and tell his little story. On the other hand, his good
name as a man of observation was at stake, and that

was more important than irritation. Mr. Ricardo spoke up.

"He did not seem to be revengeful. He was hard, yes. But six years in the island dungeon had killed, I think, the spirit in him. To lie soft and easy was the idea, and ·he saw a way of realising it, so long as he could get away from the steamer *El Rey* without reporters and the police checking up on him. No, I agree with Hanaud, I doubt if he was the man to commit a murder."

"So the murderer escapes," said George Crottle with a smile of sympathy. "I am afraid we all prefer a laugh at the police to the capture of a criminal."

Hanaud took up the statement very good-humouredly. He laughed with George Crottle.

"Yes, to be sure, that is so. But why do we all prefer a laugh at the police? Because, in our heart and soul, we know that the criminal will not escape, after all."

"He will do it again, you mean?"

"I mean more. The little offences, if they escape, at once there is some bad example and some harm is done. That is all. But the big crimes like murder, they may not escape. Once or twice, in the blue of the moon, there may be a nobility and it never fails to be recognised. Oh, never! But, as a rule, Monsieur George, accept the creed of an old tracker, the two remarkable characteristics of the big crime are its meanness and its cruelty."

Septimus Crottle was undoubtedly interested. He nodded his head, sitting upright in his high-backed chair.

James Crottle said with a trifle of cynicism: "It would need a bold man to hold out against you and Mr. Ricardo."

"I hope that one day, Monsieur Hanaud," Septimus added, "you will come on some other than a Sunday evening and tell me in detail a few of your cases."

" I hope," cried Hanaud, " that I may give you some day the whole story of the night at White Barn in the Lordship Lane."

As this was spoken, it took on a more important meaning, certainly in Hanaud's ears, no less certainly in Mr. Ricardo's. Hanaud glanced slyly at George Crottle and James.

" It may be, after all, that I make a mistake. Once I made one. In this case, however, I am sure."

" Although the coroner's jury will say suicide ? " James Crottle asked.

" Yes."

" But in that case it is over."

" No. You see, Mr. James, Maltby is not satisfied."

" Oh ? "

The exclamation came from Septimus. What this flibbertigibbet of a Frenchman, who hadn't the stomach to let him smoke a Romeo and Juliet Corona cigar, thought, was one thing—of the mere weight of a cigarette, say. What the Superintendent Maltby, of the tenacious, deliberate mind, thought, was quite another—of the weight of a Romeo and Juliet Corona cigar, in fact.

" Therefore, if the letter from the late Horbury were to reach you," Hanaud continued, as he rose from his chair, " it might, perhaps, help to send it on to Maltby."

" I will do so," said Septimus, accompanying his two guests to the front door.

Hanaud drove home uncomfortably by Ricardo's side in the Rolls-Royce No. 1, which had that evening arrived by way of Cherbourg. He had many postures, but no words, and experience had made Mr. Ricardo too wary to provoke them.

Chapter 17

THE TORN CARD

ONCE the two friends were seated in the study of the corner house, Hanaud had to speak.

" A peppermint *frappé* ? " he asked, and added, rather proud of what he thought to be a humorous phrase, " Can do ? "

" I should think nothing is more unlikely," Ricardo returned as he rang the bell. " Thompson, could you manage a peppermint *frappé* at this hour ? "

Thompson came as near to a smile as his code of manners permitted.

" Monsieur asked for one once some years ago and caught us at a disadvantage. A few moments, monsieur."

So Hanaud sipped his peppermint *frappé* and smoked his black cigarettes, whilst Ricardo reflected on the oddities of friendship.

Suddenly Hanaud smiled :

" You shall tell me what you saw when you were kind enough to search for the diary I had not left in my topcoat."

Ricardo made a grimace.

" It was not pleasant."

" The Miss Agatha, then ? "

" Yes."

Ricardo described her shuddering in horror with the broken drawer open at her side and the torn pieces of a card upon her lap.

" She swept them into the wastepaper basket," he continued, " and after I was in the hall she turned out the lights and went up to bed."

" Dropped them—just like that—in the wastepaper basket ? " Hanaud mused, " and turned out the lights."

" But that didn't baffle me," cried Mr. Ricardo triumphantly. " I knew Miss Agatha might perhaps hear the snap of the switch if I turned the lights on, so I didn't touch it. I knew she might wonder if a chair or a table were overturned, so I slipped like an eel between them " ; and Mr. Ricardo, to make this piece of sleuthing as admirable and vivid to Hanaud as it was to himself, twisted and slid towards the table ; and undoubtedly Hanaud did admire—little cries of admiration broke from him. He had hands raised ready to applaud. Mr. Ricardo loved that moment, and to complete the movement with a most dramatic finish, he plunged his hand into his trouser pocket and flung the two pieces of pasteboard below Hanaud's eyes upon the table. . . .

Well, where were the words of praise ? Or, if not of praise, of thanks, for a most difficult example of the detective's art ? Mr. Ricardo opened his eyes. He had closed them as he had flung the pasteboard fragments—and he saw Hanaud staring at those fragments in consternation.

" You picked them out of the tub ? " he said quietly.

" Of course. Wasn't I right ? "

" No, my friend."

" But there was a word written on the card."

" I read it when Septimus jerked open the drawer."

" I am sorry if I did wrong," said Mr. Ricardo tartly.

Hanaud was swift to reassure his friend. It was not that Mr. Ricardo had done wrong. No, no ! On the contrary ! He had done too much right. Miss Agatha's agitations, they were suggestive, and described with a particularity only to be found in a master—and with an economy, too—it is so rare to use few words when many would do. It did not really matter so much that he had removed the two pieces of card.

" In any case the servants would have emptied them into the dustbin in the morning," said Ricardo, once more smiling.

" No, no."

The contradiction came like a slap in the face.

" Why no, no ? "

" Because," said Hanaud sweetly, " at this moment, perhaps, or perhaps in an hour or in two hours, Miss Agatha will wake uneasy. And in a little while she will understand why she is uneasy. That torn card—it should be burnt. She will creep down in the dark, with a torch, perhaps—and the pieces—they have gone ! Oh, in the long run it does not matter. Very likely she will think, ' Oh, it is that inquisitive one from France, he was at the elbow of Septimus,' and she will be more discreet. But . . ."

" But what ? " Mr. Ricardo demanded impatiently.

Hanaud finished his peppermint and stubbed out his cigarette. " I should not be quick to destroy those two pieces of card," he replied slowly. " It is for you, of course, to say. . . . For me, I wait upon the exquisite Madame Horbury to-morrow morning, and in the afternoon I return to Paris. But, my friend, if I were you, I should lock them up. One never knows."

He stood up and, with a complete change of tone, added :

" We go to bed, no, yes ? We will not lose the sleep ? We meet at the luncheon, when I say to you farewell. What I owe to you ! " and Hanaud betook himself upstairs.

Mr. Ricardo took the ashtray on which Hanaud's cigarette still smouldered and emptied it into the fireplace. As he replaced it on the table, he saw the torn pieces of the card ; and it flashed across his thoughts that he had never read the word written across them.

He fitted them together. It was a word, of course,

but it was more—a name. And as Mr. Ricardo read the name he was seized with a discomfort, the same sort of discomfort as had seized upon Hanaud in the motor-car. Fear, in other words. The fear a man might have as he looked down into a pit. For the name written upon the card was—Horbury—with an initial in front of it—D—yes, of course, D. Mr. Ricardo was half inclined to let those two pieces of card follow the cigarette ash into the fire. But in his mind's eye he saw Hanaud's face again, serious and alarmed. He locked the pieces safely in a drawer of his private desk.

Chapter 18

THE HOLLY HEDGE

THE flat on the first floor of Audley Court had neither the elegance of White Barn nor the opulent glitter of Horbury's office. It was not furnished to a period. A Sheraton writing-table stood side by side with a marqueterie cabinet. Comfort was the note of it, and quiet colours, restful to tired eyes. Hanaud's first thought, indeed, as he moved into the sitting-room and across to the window and looked over the tree tops of the avenue to the wide grassland of the park, was that here was a refuge for a far-thinking statesman rather than for a double-dealer in the equities.

"Mrs. Horbury will be here immediately," said the butler with a bow.

Hanaud beheld his broad shoulders and his lean strength with contentment and, as the man turned away, he said firmly :

" 'Arf a mo' ! "

The butler, used to all conditions of men, turned about stolidly and waited.

"You've been a sailor," said the perspicacious visitor.

The butler complimented Hanaud with as much of a smile as he allowed himself on duty.

"Admirals at sea and generals on land wouldn't agree about that, sir. But name of Hanworth to both."

Hanaud was puzzled and then especially pleased.

"I have him. A marine."

"Yes, sir."

"We have them, too. Les Fusiliers-Marins—yes? They are much thought of and they think much of themselves. Good! Then you stay here?"

"I don't know, sir, whether Mrs. Horbury will require me."

"But if she does——?"

"Her service is a pleasure, sir," Hanworth replied.

A little sententious, no doubt—the super-marine on duty—but, however you looked at it, good marks for Olivia Horbury.

"Ha!" said Hanaud to himself as Hanworth left the room; and "Ha!" he said to himself again, drumming on the window-pane contentedly; and a quiet voice with a tremor of amusement broke in upon his contentment.

"The name was Gravot, I think, Monsieur Hanaud?"

He swung round. Olivia Horbury was seated at a table under the second of the two windows.

"Ah, madame, you make the heart beat," he said.

"You flatter me, Monsieur Hanaud."

"Yes, that way, too. But at the moment it is the noiselessness."

"Monsieur Hanaud, do you wish me to believe that you belong to the day when women's gowns whispered and their bangles rattled and all the birds in the garden piped ' she is here, she is here ' ? "

"I try, madame, to be of my day and the Code

164

Napoleon——" He broke off, noticing that she sat with an open cheque book in front of her.

"No, please, that is not possible now. I had hoped to return to Paris with one like that. But now there must be lawyers and hindrances." He pointed to the cheque book. "Instead, perhaps, a little signed letter on the crested paper that as soon as the probations are over a cheque will be posted."

"But, Monsieur Hanaud, that's what I was doing." She put a slender forefinger on the twopenny stamp. "Perhaps you don't know that that was Daniel's crest."

She smiled as she spoke and Hanaud laughed, and Olivia laughed again.

"What a woman!" Hanaud exclaimed to his soul. "She can make the joke about the good Horbury's honesty, but none the less yesterday she was in tears for him." Indeed, as he watched her writing the cheque, her laughter dwindled to a whimper and the tears once more filled her eyes.

She scribbled a note, put it into an envelope with the cheque, sealed it, and rang the bell.

"I have drawn the cheque on my private account. The branch of the bank I deal with is on the ground floor of the next block of flats. I have already arranged with the manager. Hanworth will bring you back a draft upon the Paris branch."

She sent Hanworth off with the sealed envelope.

"He will not be five minutes."

Hanaud felt a trifle uncomfortable. After all, it was a large sum of money.

"It may be months before the estate is finally wound up," he said.

"A year, monsieur. And since there is no reason that Monsieur Gravot of the Place Vendôme, who has waited so long for his money, should wait for another year, you shall take it back to him."

She got up with a swift movement and invited him to a chair.

"I don't want you, Monsieur Hanaud, to misunderstand me. Daniel and I were the very best of friends. Lots of people, no doubt, will give you quite another picture of him, and theirs may be true from their points of view ; I'll go further, and say it is. For me it was all different."

There was a suggestion in her tone that he could have her story if he wished ; and at that moment there was nothing Hanaud wished more. A younger daughter of an impoverished family, she had been carefully educated so that she might earn her living as a teacher in a high school.

"I was almost learned in those days," and she spoke of them as so remote that they were difficult and astonishing to remember. "But it wasn't any good, for I couldn't teach. I could chatter, but I couldn't instruct. I could get enjoyment myself out of Virgil, say—oh, yes, you needn't look so surprised, Monsieur Hanaud, it's not, as you might say, a politeness—but I couldn't impart it. So I thought that I would go on the stage."

"Ah !" said Hanaud.

"Yes," said Olivia, taking up his exclamation relentlessly. "You think Daniel might have noticed me in the back row of the chorus, but could hardly have had the *entrée* into a high school."

That is exactly what Hanaud had thought, but, having once been chided for his manners, he did not propose to fail again.

"No, no, Madame Horbury," he cried. "It was that I saw you myself upon the boards—the lady of Scotland coming down the stairs with the candlestick."

"Yes, and both acting equally well—no, I am wrong," she answered, and again her lips curved in good humour and her eyes for a second danced, "for the candle had

166

a flame and I hadn't. I was no better on the stage than I was in the high school. But I didn't believe it, of course. I wanted my opportunity. I was playing small parts, maids, you know, with the tea-tray—I suppose that I didn't look so impossible——"

Here Monsieur Hanaud broke in with a flourish:

" Every great lady must have prayed for such a maid ! "

" Hadn't we better say every great husband ? " she replied dryly. " Anyway, you are quite right. Daniel was dabbling in theatrical management, and I sat next to him at a supper party. He was full of—fun, perhaps, isn't the right word—jocularity's better, and very sympathetic. My opportunity would come. Not a passionate part, no, a static part—arranging everything for the passionate ones, without leaving a trace of one's mascara on one's cheeks. As you see, he knew that I couldn't act. Yet "—and there came a tenderness into her voice, whilst neither her eyes nor her lips lost their humour— " yet he put up a play for me."

" Because he hoped that the quiet looks and the quiet part might draw the town ? "

Olivia shook her head gently.

" No, because he wanted me to marry him, and he knew that if I did, without failing in a big part, I should always feel aggrieved that I had never had my chance."

" The play did fail ? "

Olivia Horbury shivered, and half of her shivering, even so long afterwards, was serious.

" I was scarified. I wanted to put all the dramatic critics into a bag with a couple of cats and throw it it into the Bosphorus. Daniel filled the house with paper for a month, but that wanted more canvassing than ever he did to get into Parliament. We got married immediately afterwards."

That had been six years ago. Olivia had been twenty-two years old at the time of the marriage, and for the next two years they had lived at White Barn in Lordship Lane.

" I fell in love with the house as soon as I saw it."

" The holly hedge ?   It was already there, of course ? "

Olivia's face grew soft.   Her eyes beamed.

" I am glad you remembered it," she said warmly. " It was there, but it was ragged.   It was like a man who wants his hair cutting.   And there were holes coming in it.   I looked after it myself.   Days and days in the autumn I stood on a ladder and clipped it.   We had a gardener to look after the flowers.   But the holly hedge was my job.   I let nobody else touch it.   I saw it grow glossy and the holes fill up until it was a great high evergreen wall."   She laughed happily.   " Even now I drive down and spend delightful days looking after it."

" Even now ? "

Hanaud pressed the question with a smile.

" Even now.   Still no one must touch it except me." She checked her eager speech rather suddenly and turned towards the window.   Once she threw a swift glance towards him and saw that he was watching her.

" But though we took this flat afterwards, when we had money," she resumed quickly, " it was because Dan had to see people.   We wanted to keep White Barn for ourselves.   So perhaps, Monsieur Hanaud, you can understand my willingness to settle the account of your jeweller in the Place Vendôme.   Whenever we were on number seventeen with the *carrées* and the *transversales* and seventeen won, a good wedge of the winnings was handed over to me.   Of course, it was borrowed again, fairly often at the beginning, but of late Dan was on seventeen quite often."

Hanworth returned to the flat with the draft upon the Paris branch of the Bank.   Olivia looked it through and handed it to Hanaud.

" It is correct ? " she asked.

"It is oke," he returned, as though indeed it were something more, and taking from his pocket-book a receipt by Gravot et Cie of the Place Vendôme, he laid it upon her writing-table. Then he bowed over her hand.

"So," said she, "it is all ended."

"Yes."

He turned and walked towards the door. But he walked ever more slowly, and when his hand was on the knob of the door he stopped altogether.

"For my friend, Gravot, yes," he repeated.

"There will be other claimants? Maybe," she asked and answered behind him.

"I was not thinking of claimants," he replied, and he turned round towards her rather swiftly and dramatically. It was a disservice to Hanaud that, although he could keep drama out of his thoughts, he never could out of his actions; and generally it was transpontine drama. He saw a young woman without any of the tender humour which had moved her a few minutes ago, wary and suspicious.

"Of whom, then?" She was as curt as she was wary.

"I cannot say for sure."

"In other words, you don't know."

"I don't know," Hanaud agreed.

No three words were more repugnant for Hanaud to utter amongst little people in connection with a small case; and none easier when he was coping with big problems and intelligent minds. And at all events Olivia Horbury was—relieved?—yes, relieved by his ignorance. Her face grew less tight, her eyes less wary; she drew a breath. Hanaud had expected dismissal. He was invited to continue.

"I do not for one moment think that Horbury used that blue-handled knife himself," he said, and saw her lips twitch and a gleam of horror in her eyes as he thus described the weapon. "And my good friend, the

Superintendent Maltby, begins to think with me. But, see! I am in a special debt to you. Moreover, though now you stand all queenly and prickles, I will say it."

Suddenly the smile for which Hanaud had ceased to hope glimmered again upon her lips. She sat down in a chair.

" You shall," she said.

" At White Barn, I was moved. There was something I did not understand, something in all this grim tragedy, pleasant and disturbing, of which I now have a tiny hold." He was discovering a Titania permanently in love with Bottom, though of that couple he had never heard. If Racine had imagined such a pair, Hanaud would surely have quoted him, for he was well up in Racine. But, unfortunately, Racine only dealt in the heroes of Troy and the ghosts of Sophocles, and with these Horbury and White Barn had no connection.

" So I will say, I beg you to be careful." He nodded his head.

" And why, Monsieur Hanaud ? "

The question was gently, but firmly put. Olivia was guarding her secrets. Hanaud hesitated over his answer. But he felt, and felt strongly, that he could speak more exactly to Olivia than he would have dared with weaker vessels. He said :

" Because there may be danger for you again."

Olivia did not move, and there was more deliberation than surprise in her face.

" Again ? " she asked.

" Yes. There was danger when, in the middle of the night, a telephone receiver was lifted from its cradle in an empty house and you locked your door."

Olivia's face grew white as a plaster mask. Even her lips were bloodless. But in her eyes there was fear. And yet, for Hanaud, not enough fear. She was keeping her secrets, and Hanaud felt the danger grow and seep into this room like a miasma and fold about her till darkness grew between them. Olivia got up from her chair. If the danger was not to end, talk of it should.

" I thank you," she said and her voice was warm.

Hanaud accepted her decision. But he had a practical word.

" You keep the marine ? "

There was urgency in his voice. A *fusilier-marin* of twenty years' service with the honourable discharge ! To be fostered, yes.

Olivia's voice broke into an open, joyous laugh.

" Of course ! If he will stay and wait upon a lone woman in Lordship Lane."

" You go back there ? "

" As soon as the formalities allow."

She waited now for him to give the sign that their interview was ended and, as he bowed to her, she rang the bell. As she heard the front door close she said slowly, " I have lost a friend."

But Hanaud was a persistent animal and was not so sure.

Chapter 19

THE IMPORTANCE OF BEING O. AND NOT D.

L UNCHEON was over at the corner house. Hanaud ate the last of his brandied cherries and, with a sigh of content, brought forth his cigarettes.

" To-night I shall be in Paris. My vacancy is past. The cathedrals which I so much wished to see——"

" From a café opposite with a striped awning," Mr.

Ricardo interposed with more of regret than sarcasm in his voice. Hanaud from time to time opened a door upon a different and intriguing world, and now the door was to close. But more than the closing door he regretted its tiler. Strict but impish, relentless yet kind, Hanaud seasoned Mr. Ricardo's ineffective days and raised him at times into high consideration. The corner house would be very empty after the four o'clock express had steamed out to Folkestone. Mr. Ricardo foresaw himself suffering a nostalgia for the smell of the black cigarettes from the blue paper packets and—he actually coined a portmanteau word—the argotistical flourishes of Hanaud's speech. He felt that, but for Thompson, he would have tried a peppermint *frappé* last thing at night. He summed him up, at all events, in the lingo Hanaud might have used, " He's a one."

" A cognac with your coffee in the study ? " Mr. Ricardo suggested.

" Superb ! " answered Hanaud ; and in a few minutes, seated in a comfortable chair with a Maryland between his lips, his coffee smoking at his elbow and an ancient goblet of fine glass, worthy of its little pool of condensed sunlight, in his hand, he was gazing across the square. His luggage was packed. Thompson would book it to Paris and find a seat for him on the train. He should have been at ease, but his shoulders twitched and his eyes were gloomy, and even when he set the golden pond gently swirling just beneath his nose, it released no sunlight on his face.

" I do not like things unfinished," he exclaimed. " Pictures which trail away to a corner like the train of a lady's dress, books which another author completes, crimes which are not solved—especially crimes which are not solved because other crimes come after them."

" Imitation crimes," said Mr. Ricardo, and it is deplorable that he, so fastidious and indeed finicking, should at this moment have committed the vulgar crime of using a noun when an adjective would be correct.

"Not only those," Hanaud answered, concerned with facts and indifferent to grammar. "They are not so difficult. But the crimes which follow because someone has a glimpse into the crime which is not explained."

"And you have that glimpse?" Ricardo was startled into asking.

"I have," Hanaud answered simply as he exhaled a little cloud of smoke. "Yes, I have him, but not enough of him to paint the rest of the picture or write the last chapters of the book." He shrugged his shoulders. "But, after all, he is Maltby's pigeon."

"Then the jeweller of the Place Vendôme must still whistle for his cheque?"

Mr. Ricardo was sorry. When Hanaud failed, he felt that he lost a few plumes himself.

"No, no."

Hanaud pulled his pocket-book from the breast of his coat and slipped back the band of indiarubber which held it shut.

"See! An envelope. Inside the envelope a banker's draft on Paris and a little note for Gravot of Madame Horbury's regrets."

He showed them to Ricardo and replaced the draft in the envelope, whilst his friend's eyes lingered over Olivia's apology."

"O. Horbury," Mr. Ricardo said as he came to the signature.

"Yes," Hanaud observed with a good deal of significance. "We have seen that name written before—you and I."

There was a note in Hanaud's voice which puzzled Ricardo. As if they two had been especially privileged.

"We? You and I? No!"

For answer Hanaud pointed to the drawer in which

were locked away two torn halves of a pasteboard card.

"But 'D. Horbury' was the name written," cried Ricardo. "D for Daniel." He was straining his eyes, as if he could force the name to take shape upon the air. "Yes, D for Dan——"

He got up and, taking his keys from his pocket, opened the drawer. He brought the two pieces of card to the small table by the side of his chair and fitted them together.

"D. Horbury," he insisted. "Of course, my dear man! D. . . ." and his voice weakened.

The name was written in some sort of flurry. The initial was attached to the name, as if the writer had written it without lifting the pen from the card; so great was the need to write it out and have done with it for good. Suppose that you started to write O, beginning at the top and following down on the right-hand side and up on the left, and then made a twirl at the top so that the pen might run away to the first letter of the surname, H., you might indeed mistake it for a D, as he himself had done. The more he looked at the writing, the surer he felt. O for Olivia, not D for Daniel—yes, but why?

Mr. Ricardo was not very alert to whispers from the dark pools of fear where knowledge ends, but here was something which troubled him, for which he must find, if he could, some quite simple and comfortable explanation. He had seen Agatha Crottle's face at the exact moment when the lock was broken and the drawer, with a sound of splintering wood, burst open. There had been such a look of terror in her eyes, such a sickly convulsion of her features as he hoped never to see again. He had slammed a shutter across that vision in his mind and by no word had reopened it. But it was in front of him now.

"You saw her that night when she was alone," said Hanaud with a challenge in his voice.

"I saw her in a mirror. But her hands covered her face. Tears were falling between her fingers and running down the backs of her hands. She was in a storm of misery. Why?"

Hanaud could explain it. He had sent him on a pretence just to see and bring back that story.

"You expected that I should see what I did," Ricardo cried.

Hanaud shook his head gravely.

"I was not sure."

"It was—it was frightening."

And now, as gravely, Hanaud nodded.

"Yes, that is the word," he said. "You have heard of people who hate enough to summon death to help them. They use a sort of witchcraft."

Hanaud's voice dropped as he spoke, and to Ricardo the room, even on that day of late summer, had suddenly grown cold.

"They write the name of their enemy on a card, and they lock it away in a drawer where no one will see it. They make of that drawer a coffin. And it has been known—whether by chance or some dreadful power of evil—that the victim has fallen sick, has faded until, in an agony of remorse, the would-be murderer has unlocked the drawer and torn up the card."

"As she did—Agatha?" cried Ricardo in a great relief.

"I wonder," Hanaud replied sombrely. "One of the name of Horbury has died violently. But not the woman. She had never unlocked the drawer. She did not mean it to be unlocked. Are you sure those passionate tears were not tears of bitter anger? Isn't it even possible that she thought that she had killed the man when she had meant to kill the wife? In that extremity she might have believed it."

Mr. Ricardo, of course, chose the obvious explanation of the words.

"But you can't mean," he gasped, "that Miss Agatha had set her heart on that fat rogue Horbury!"

"I don't," Hanaud answered with a grin upon his face in which there was neither humour nor amusement.

"Upon someone else, then?"

"Obviously," replied Hanaud.

"Who—oh, I see—who had set his heart on Olivia Horbury?"

"So it would seem."

So here was Mr. Ricardo faced with the triangle of the dramatists. Two women and a man or two men and a woman. It was a triangle of the first sort in this case. A man pursued by Agatha who had set his longings on Olivia.

"Who is it?" cried Ricardo.

"I wish I knew," Hanaud returned, and the lines of disappointment deepened on Ricardo's face. After all, what's the use of a walking *Who's Who* if it doesn't answer your questions?—he asked of himself indignantly. But the Frenchman continued:

"The unknown man. Perhaps my friend, the murderer. There is now something we did not have before, a reason for murder."

They had Devisher, to be sure, or they would have, if they could lay their hands upon him. But neither Ricardo, nor Hanaud, nor indeed Maltby, had any real belief in the guilt of Devisher. Ricardo was thrown back upon his disinclination to accept the picture of Agatha Crottle presented to him.

"She is middle-aged. I can't believe she ever had a lover," he cried. "She is of the kind which finds its consolation in religion."

And there Hanaud wholly agreed with him.

"Yes, yes, she goes to church, no doubt of it, and

prays with all her soul. But to such, what is the witch-craft of the locked drawer but a more desperate prayer? She is helping. Oh, I have seen them, the religious ones, the unconsidered ones, the world's faded, pitiable wallflowers, when passion comes to them for the first time in middle-age they can be dangerous."

And so quietly, yet with such significance, did Hanaud let that word fall from his lips that once more Ricardo gazed into a black pit with horror in his eyes.

But Thompson, the unfailing, brought the grim con-ference to an end. The Rolls Royce (No. 1) was at the door. He himself was now starting in the second car. A quarter of an hour and they should follow.

"I shall come with you," said Ricardo, and he stood by the train's side after Hanaud had taken his seat.

"You will come back, I hope," he said.

Hanaud shrugged his shoulders.

"It may be," and he suddenly leaned out of the win-dow. "I will tell you a little thing. Maltby will press at the inquest for an open verdict. This affair is not ended, my friend."

"And there will be danger before it is ended," Ricardo declared.

But this danger struck first of all where neither of them expected it.

Chapter 20

MORDAUNT READS A SIGNAL

IT was Mr. Ricardo's way when some high narrative of fact or fancy was acclaimed, to discover some detail or episode, which no one else had remarked, and to applaud it to the exclusion of all other details, and indeed, of the whole pattern. The detail or episode may have been quite insignificant. That did not matter. His concentration upon it made strangers wonder for a moment whether he were not a very deep fellow. And, indeed, Mr. Ricardo enjoyed that pleasant sense of equality with his betters which comes from travelling first on a second-class ticket. Thus it was he who noticed what a vastly important part in the explication of the Horbury Affair was played by the one who had the smallest concern in it. " Mordaunt," Mr. Ricardo would say, standing on his hearthrug before the fire and nodding his head sagely like a mandarin in ivory, " Please don't forget Mordaunt." He should have added " *verb. sap.*", and perhaps we might add it for him.

For on the morning when probate of Horbury's will was granted to his widow—that is a few weeks after Horbury's death—Philip Mordaunt was walking along the street of Nubar Pasha, in Cairo. It was half-past eleven. The wide platform of Shepheard's Hotel was as yet sparsely occupied and he passed it with a distinct pleasure. He had the time but no longer the wish to explore it. He passed the Esbekiyeh Gardens and crossed the head of the road leading to the great Bazaar. Later, when the platform outside Shepheard's was filled and the alleys of the Mouski empty, he would walk that way, but for the moment he had a happier task. He continued along the straight broad avenue of Abdul Azziz. Upon his left hand the great sand cliffs of the Nile Valley were closing in. Just behind this street the houses were thinning out on the rising ground. Spaces of brown earth, broken walls, an Arab cemetery replaced them ; and then it came into view—the village of Elaoui.

It hung like a cage under the high edge of the cliff, tiny, yet, in that clear air, distinct—three sides of a square rather like Lezardrieux, except in one particular, and an awkward particular. At Lezardrieux the road from the square down to the river ran backwards and forwards across the slope in reasonable gradients, sometimes invisible under a cliff, sometimes in full view on a plateau. From Elaoui one road, straight as the blade of a sword, dropped like a precipice from the outcrop of rock on which centuries ago the village was built. It dropped for a mile in length till it joined the desolation of broken walls without which no eastern city is complete ; and throughout that mile not a building nor a tree cast a shadow across it. Moreover, it was lighted at night at the top, where it passed between old brick walls into the village square, and half-way down, and, most usefully for a keen-eyed watchman in the square, at the bottom where at last it swerved amongst the ruins and was lost. Mordaunt could see it, plain as a panel painted white in a wall of pale red. Not a car, however swift, could ascend that road without advertising its approach. And it was the only road, as the village about the square was one house with a hundred tunnels and passages ; for the inhabitants of the village were one close-knit, remote family. A formidable village under the eaves of the high Mokattam Hills—an island with a single causeway, always watched, and time to spare !

Mordaunt took his first look at the Elaoui village, as he walked along the street of Abdul Azziz, with as much indifference as he could counterfeit, and suddenly came to a halt. Straight ahead of him, the owner of a little bar had set out a few iron tables and iron chairs on the pavement ; and at one of these, facing him, sat a man he knew. A man whom he had last seen on his yacht in Dartmouth Harbour, wearing a suit of his clothes and with fifteen pounds of his money in his pocket. Devisher ! Yes, Devisher, but now a Devisher whose face had begun to fill out, who wore white flannel trousers and white buckskin shoes and a grey coat and waistcoat suitable to the season and the place. It perplexed Mordaunt for a moment that, although they were face to face and the distance with each step that he took narrowing between them, Devisher did not see him. Mordaunt laughed, and the laugh brought no look of recognition to Devisher's face.

"Well," Mordaunt reflected, laughing again at the image of the dead-and-gone Mordaunt which rose in his mind, "that would have annoyed me a few months ago. I couldn't have believed that anyone who had once seen the Mordaunt who was shortly to electrify the world, wouldn't have known him again."

There was a vanity, too, even in that reflection, as Mordaunt began to recognise. But he was too beset by curiosity to continue his analysis. Devisher did not see him because all the senses that he had were gathered and blended into one. He was listening as the blind listen, to hear something far away beyond the hearing of the men with vision. His eyes, a little down-turned, were empty.

Mordaunt was already abreast of the table, but instead of passing on he dropped his hand sharply on Devisher's shoulder and slid into the iron chair opposite. Devisher's reaction to that clap of the hand was astonishing. With a yelp which was sharp with terror, Devisher sprang to his feet. He looked around wildly and brought his eyes down at last to Mordaunt's face.

"You?" he gasped, and then cried sharply: "What are you doing here?"

Philip Mordaunt answered meekly:

"Cairo—early October—mayn't I? Or do you already own the town?"

Devisher laughed a little uneasily, but he was bringing his nerves under control and made a shift to excuse his cry of fear.

"You might have realised, Captain Mordaunt, that for the residents of the Castillo del Libertador, the laying on of hands was a rite seldom associated with pleasure."

"I am sorry," Mordaunt answered. "What are you drinking?"

"Beer. Not so bad."

Mordaunt rapped upon the table and two long glasses topped with snow were set before them.

"Here's luck!" said Devisher as he drank.

"The skin off your nose!" replied Mordaunt.

"I, too, take in the Sunday newspapers," said Devisher, and Mordaunt produced a cigar case. "Will you?" he asked, holding out the case.

"No, thank you."

Mordaunt pinched the end of one of the cigars and put it between his lips and felt in his pocket for a box of matches. But the box was hardly out before he heard a tiny click and a spirit-fed lighter was burning under his nose.

"Why waste a match? Try this!" cried Devisher with a curious urgency.

Mordaunt had it on the tip of his tongue to answer that he preferred a wooden match, but a startling conjecture suddenly struck him dumb. It wasn't probable; it was hardly tenable at all. But if it were true? It explained the expectancy and concentration of Devisher, the eager offer of his cigar lighter, his presence at this hour, at this bar, in this broad street under the hanging village of Elaoui. Did it explain, too, Devisher's presence in Cairo? Mordaunt must discover the answer to that question. It was not busybody's work. It was his appointed work. But he must approach it cunningly and he was a novice in the art.

Luckily for Mordaunt, Devisher was not at his ease. He had a question or two which clamoured for answers.

"You know," he began as he lit a cigarette and put his lighter back into his pocket, "when I saw you in the cabin of your yacht—whether it was something you said or just an impression that I got—I thought you had evolved out of your experiences a sort of complete new pattern to which you were going to fit your life."

"I had?" asked Philip, apparently as much at sea now as he had been on his yacht.

"Yes," Devisher added, with just a hint of disdain for the man who made a plan but couldn't act on it. "And then, a month or so later, I find you strolling along a street of Cairo, the complete tourist, a walking poster for Mr. Cook."

Mordaunt's face flushed. The contemptuous good-humour stung him and he leaned forward sharply to show Mr. Bryan Devisher how wrong he was. But he showed nothing. A warning bell was beginning to ring rather urgently in his brain. Devisher's scorn was meant to sting, and to sting him into admissions, if admissions there were. Mordaunt lowered his head. He drank his beer silently, shamefacedly. The rush of blood into his face might as truly have expressed his shame as his anger.

"You are quite right," he confessed. "I had made a plan. I was going to do wonders. But you know what I did do?"—and he uttered a harsh little laugh—"I fell asleep in my bath. That's me, I am afraid."

He leaned back in his chair, with now and then a jerk of amusement, and now and then a pull at his beer, and now and then a puff at his cigar.

"The complete tourist. Not so bad for you, Mr. Devisher, but too hard a stroke to be pleasant to me. After I had had the nerve too, one night on the Helford river, to give old Septimus Crottle a full history——" Mordaunt broke off suddenly. He had been tilting his chair on to its back legs. He brought the forelegs down

with a bang upon the stones. " Of course," he cried.
" I gave you a letter to old Septimus, didn't I ? "

Devisher was not prepared for that question being
flung at him. He was distracted, too, by the crash of
the chair legs upon the stones. He could listen and
talk, but he couldn't listen as he wished to listen if the
talk was to be punctuated by these exclamation marks.

" Yes, you did."

" And you used it, I hope."

Devisher jumped at the suggestion. It explained at
once his presence in Cairo, his means of livelihood. He
would have been compelled to offer some explanation to
the man who had seen him last in such distressful circum-
stances. Here was a providential explanation provided by
this simpleton. Devisher smiled and spread out his hands.

" Well, you see. I am here."

" Permanently ? "

" To be sure."

" The Dagger Line ? "

" Thanks to you."

And Philip Mordaunt began to doubt. Septimus ?
Was there anything in the world so dear to that old
man's heart as the Dagger Line ? Its prestige, the
beauty of its ships, their efficiency and speed ? Mordaunt
had written a fair letter to Septimus, concealing nothing
which he knew, not even the deep black ring round
Devisher's ankle. To try such an applicant out in an
office under his eye—yes, that the old tyrant might do.
But to send him at once abroad to a place so important
in the shipping world as the Canal—that didn't sound
like Septimus at all.

" You're stationed at Port Said, I suppose ? "

" No, here. The Line has an office in Cairo."

Well, that might be so. Mordaunt leaned back in his
chair, and Devisher said with a smile.

" It looks as if the old man has taken a risk. But

that isn't the case really. I have merely routine work. As you saw, probably, I didn't want responsibility. Checking up on passages, passing the time of day with Cook's and the travel agents. And I'm not alone in the office. It just suits me, and if it doesn't run to cocktails at Shepheard's, it does to a decent glass of beer in the street of Abdul Azziz."

He had hardly finished when a match was struck upon the other side of the street. Devisher did not turn his head, but he heard—Mordaunt was sure of it. There was a quick flicker in his eye—Mordaunt classed it with the scratch of the match upon the emery paper—and a relaxation of his face. A signal had been given and taken. Mordaunt, for his part, could look across the road. He saw a tall youth in an Arab gown standing outside a cheap provision shop with a cigarette in his mouth which he had just lighted, and a big box of Bryant & May's matches in his hand. The young Arab drew at his cigarette to make sure that it was alight and then, putting the match-box into his pocket, strolled away.

High up above their heads the village of Elaoui clung under the rim of the hill. Mordaunt was tempted to draw Devisher's attention to it and watch confusion trouble his face. But he bethought him of a better way which would not betray himself.

Devisher was looking at his watch.

" Twelve o'clock ! " he said, and he finished his glass of beer. " That will give me just the hour I want before lunch." He looked around for the waiter and summoned him. " I had a glass before you came," and as he paid for it, Mordaunt said blandly :

" I'm very glad that we met, and I'm very glad, too, that things have smoothed themselves out for you. I'll write to old Septimus to-day and tell him that I've met you and thank him."

Now he saw more than confusion rise in Devisher's face. He saw fear. He heard a quick gasp.

"I've already done that," exclaimed Devisher.

"But not for me," Mordaunt returned with a laugh. "I wish you could. I hate letter-writing. But this one I must write myself."

He watched Devisher hurry away. Septimus and the Dagger Line could not blend with Elaoui and a young Arab striking a match in the street of Abdul Azziz. The sooner he wrote to Crottle to thank him for giving Devisher a chance, the better. That was all that he need do ; and, indeed, he wrote the letter and posted it that evening.

But it was already too late.

Chapter 21

THE HOUSE WITH THE TAMARISKS

MORDAUNT sat for a few minutes longer at his iron table. The functions of Devisher in Cairo and the unlikely action of Septimus Crottle were put aside. He rose a little reluctantly and turned back to the great Bazaar. Midday had emptied its narrow streets. He stopped once at a small booth and bought a packet of cigarettes from an old white-bearded Arab in a blue cloak. At a corner he turned to the north-east and walked into a quarter where the indifference and quiet of decay followed with an astonishing abruptness upon the noisy bargainings of the Bazaar. He came to a silent open space.

Mordaunt had seldom seen anything more desolate. Once, no doubt, it had been built upon. For it had certainly never been laid out as a garden or a place of

ornament and rest. Here, for instance, a wall began
for no reason, continued for a few yards, crumbled, and
for no reason ceased. Here a mound of bricks with a
floor of bricks spread like an open fan about it showed
where a house had slipped to the ground. Everywhere
the earth was uneven and in colour of a dull yellow,
and was withdrawing, it seemed, from sight under a
yellow pall made of its own dust. Were there a flint
upon that ground, it had no facet from which the sun
could strike a spark. The whole place was melancholy
and more silent than the desert, as all places will be
where dwellings are relapsing slowly into the shapeless
earth from which they sprang.

As Mordaunt leaned forward he saw on his left hand
two trees of tamarisk which stood within a wall at the
path's side. He had begun to hope that he had missed
his way. But his courage sank now. The house with
the tamarisks !

He went forward to it. It was a large house with a
gate and, within the gate, three brick steps led up to
the door. Again the hope that he had been misled
encouraged him ; so little sign was there that anyone
for many years had made a home of it. But he had
instructions nowadays. He opened the gate, mounted
the three steps, and smartly knocked upon the door with
the crook of his stick.

To his surprise, it was opened so quickly that he
seemed to have been awaited. A young woman, indeed
she was little more than a girl, stood in the doorway
with a look of eagerness upon her white face. Never had
anyone in Mordaunt's experience appeared so out of place
as this girl in this dusty area of ruin. She was slender,
dressed in a coat and skirt of dark grey, shabby, no
doubt, but as trim and tidy as when it came first from
its George Street tailor in London, and with nothing of
Egypt in her dark blue eyes. Mordaunt had not a doubt

that here his walk ended. But there was obviously no such conviction in the woman in the doorway. There had been a welcome for someone, but it had faded into bewilderment at the sight of him; and even that bewilderment had not been able to master her disappointment. She was very white. The youth of her face was spoilt by her fatigue and under the broad forehead her eyes brooded upon him incuriously.

"You have come to the wrong house, I think," she said.

To Mordaunt, this gracious English voice was lovely as music, however commonplace the words.

"I am sure not," he answered. "In a way, no doubt, I am sorry, but in a way perhaps I am glad." If Mordaunt had been at pains to replace her distress with a return of her bewilderment, he could hardly have done better. "You are Mrs. Leete."

Now, indeed, she was surprised. The white brows drew together under the swathe of fair hair which crowned her head.

"Yes."

In the admission there was a question.

"When I left London, your father, Mr. Septimus Crottle, asked me to bring you a message."

For a moment her face softened. A smile almost flickered across her lips, as though she saw Septimus suddenly in his frock coat with the points of his high white collar cupping his cheeks. All that she said, however, was again "Yes?" but now in a voice less hostile.

"Mr. Crottle wished you to know that your place was always kept for you in Portman Square."

Once more the smile almost curved her lips and the ghost of a smile glimmered in the dark pools of her eyes.

"Next to Agatha's, was it? Do Sunday nights still go on?"

"Rather," Mordaunt exclaimed, commending them.

"Yes, riotous, weren't they?" she answered dryly, and added thoughtfully: "I ran out—that was the phrase—but I may come back—to 1870—if I wish." She remained silent, and then threw up her head. "Wouldn't it have been better for all of them—Anne, Audrey and Agatha—if they had run out, too!"—and recovering from her outburst, "I should, of course, very much like to hear all you have to tell me. But to-day——" and again distress took her by the throat so that her voice broke "If you will give me your address, I'll write to you."

Mordaunt pulled out of his pocket a small diary with loose leaves. He was saved one awkward moment; it was all the more welcome since there were many others ahead. He wrote his name and title on one leaf and handed it to her.

"Yobosci," she began as she read. "That's captain, I think. Captain Philip Mordaunt——" and as her eyes ran along the written words, she stopped abruptly and began again. "The Coastguard Directorate. I see."

There was no resentment in her voice and no suggestion that Mordaunt had set a trap for her. "I see," merely meant, "It was expected." Mordaunt, however, took the words to himself.

"No doubt I should have put my duty first," he stammered.

"We are all recommended to do that," she answered gravely.

"What I said was true," he exclaimed.

Rosalind Leete looked puzzled.

"No doubt," she replied.

"I mean—your father's message. He did send it."

She looked—and again with a trifle of amusement—at his face, so troubled lest he should be thought guilty of a despicable subterfuge.

"I never thought for a moment that you had made the message up."

"Thank you," said Mordaunt fervently, and so began to stammer again. "As for the other matter"—no other matter had been mentioned but neither pretended that it didn't exist—"as for this other matter—it's—well—it's different."

"It would be," said Rosalind Leete. Clearly she had to help him out. "As you pointed out, it's a matter of your duty and it should have come first."

Mordaunt caught at the word.

"Yes."

Rosàlind stepped aside in the hall and he crossed the threshold. She shut the front door and threw open the door of the room which looked out upon the empty space. Mordaunt walked into a room, meagrely equipped but clean as soap and a scrubbing brush could make it. One or two cotton mats were spread upon the bare floor. The furniture was of painted deal and upholstered in brown plush, a sofa, an arm-chair and half a dozen straight-backed chairs—a suite in fact from a Cairene Bon Marché. But more pitiable than any sign of poverty was the absence of any of those trifles which, through their private associations, will make a home out of the barest lodgings. Septimus had declared that the marriage had failed. Mordaunt had thought, "There spoke the architect of his family, angry because a brick had fallen from its place." But clearly the marriage had failed. There was not a photograph in the style of ten or fifteen years ago, not some little toy or book which linked the grievous to-day with a pleasant schoolroom, not some small picture or statue on which one hangs a dream. Mordaunt's face was compassionate as he stood in that inhospitable room. He had a queer vision of the girl setting those small memorials out when she and her husband came first to live there and removing them one by one as the shadows darkened upon their lives ; until the room became the cold waiting-room of a railway station.

" Now," she said.

" I want to see Professor Leete."

That the title was no longer Leete's by right, Mordaunt knew, but still to attach it to his name might give her a momentary comfort. It seemed, however, that she would have no pretences.

" Then you didn't know ? " she cried.

But the cry was so wild, the look so amazed, that more must have happened than the loss of Leete's professorship. Rosalind clapped her hand suddenly to her mouth to stop the hysteria in which her voice was rising. But she succeeded. She drew away her hand and let it fall by her side.

" What else should I know ? " he asked.

" What you shall know," she answered.

The words were not clipped. There was nothing whatever dramatic in her gesture. She walked to a door at the side of the room and opened it.

" He is here," she said.

Mordaunt followed her into a bedroom as mean in its equipment as the parlour. But it had a dignity which the other room had not. For in the bed a dead man lay swathed already for the grave. He had the likeness of a man of middle age, with black hair growing thin and a face so discoloured and emaciated that it was shocking to see. Moreover, there was no peace in it.

Mordaunt bent his head towards Rosalind.

" I was abrupt. I am sorry. This—you were quite right—I didn't know," and he looked at her full in the face. " Can I help you ? "

" I don't think so," she answered quietly.

" It happened——? "

" This morning at five o'clock."

" You had a doctor ? "

" An Egyptian. Dr. Achmed Agami. He has been attending my husband. He is very kind. You know that here there must be no delays. He is arranging everything."

There were possibilities of delay, a simple form of embalming, but no doubt the doctor had explained that. If there were no friends to escort Leete to his grave, and Mordaunt thought that he had shaken off all of them except this girl, delay was little to be desired.

" The actual cause was, I suppose, malaria ? "

Rosalind Leete looked at him with surprise.

" Yes. How could you tell that ? "

For one might have thought that he had starved to death, even with those wrappings about his throat and neck.

" It ends that way so often," said Mordaunt gently.

And it begins so easily, so pleasantly. Perhaps as a reward for a day's overwork, perhaps idly as an experiment, perhaps, as with the fellaheen, to gratify a lust. There were a thousand entrances into that fatal Enchanted Cavern.

" It began in Luxor ? " he asked.

" In the Valley of the Kings," she answered. " He was sent out with an American Mission. Why it began, I don't know," and for the second time her voice broke. " I hope that it wasn't my fault."

Mordaunt wondered how much of truth there was in that self-reproach. It might have been that she had " run out " to escape from the sea-discipline of the house in Portman Square rather than from any love of her professor. Somehow disappointment had come.

" You went to him straight from your father's house ? "

Even as he spoke, he realised the question's impertinence, but she answered at once.

" We had arranged everything on tiptoes. We were

married in St. Bride's, at the back of Fleet Street, on a Friday morning and left by the boat-train for Brindisi."

Had he looked for so much more from her than she, with all the promise of her youth, had to give him ? For she must have been glorious three years ago before poverty and shame had reclothed her in distress. It was certainly distress rather than grief, distress and a gnawing sense of guilt, which numbed her now.

Mordaunt could read the history of their marriage easily enough, once the lure of the drug had caught him. The man's loss of interest in his most fascinating work, his long absences, the growing slovenliness of his dress and his looks, the whispers which became open talk, the loss of discipline amongst the men employed, the dismissal, the flight to a native quarter in Cairo, the growing urgency for the drug, the diminishing means to gratify it, more boracic to less heroin—until in the end it came to an Arab in a back room of the Mouski using an hypodermic needle which was never disinfected. Hence malaria and this polluted skeleton of an outcast who had once ruled men and held his head high.

Mordaunt turned towards Rosalind Leete.

" You are alone here ? " he asked.

" There is a woman. She is buying food now. She has been very helpful."

" But she doesn't sleep here ? "

Rosalind Leete looked about the room.

" We have nothing worth anybody's while to steal."

Nevertheless this grim morning had been foreseen. It was properly humbling to Philip Mordaunt to realise that all the high services which he had begun to watch himself rendering to the hapless daughter of Septimus Crottle had already been discounted. Rosalind had sufficient money to pay all that was due, she had taken a room in an English boarding-house in the Sharia Abdin.

She had been working in the Museum for Henry Scobell, one of the greatest of English Egyptologists, owing to a certain skill which she had acquired in photography and typewriting.

"So you have been the breadwinner in Cairo?" he said.

"He was too ill," she answered, and the noise of wheels broke in upon her voice.

She looked out of the window as a van stopped before the house and a sharp movement warned him that here, after all, were friendly offices which a deputy might take over.

Mordaunt was the only mourner besides herself at the burial in the English cemetery that afternoon.

"I am grateful," she said as they walked away, "and in a day or two I should like to talk to you. I shouldn't wonder if I could help you," she added with a ghost of a smile.

"Did you ever hear of the village of Elaoui?" he asked.

She repeated the name. "No."

"Nor of a match struck at a certain hour in a certain place?"

"No."

"Yet I think we might help one another, nonetheless," he said as he left her at her door.

Chapter 22

MORDAUNT MAKES A BRILLIANT SUGGESTION

O N a Sunday morning Mordaunt waited anxiously in the gardens of Gezireh for the coming of Rosalind Leete. He would hardly have admitted anxiety. For he could find no excuse for it in the help which so far she had given him. A few small tradesmen, like the little Arab with the white beard and the blue coat from whom once Mordaunt had bought cigarettes, had been gathered in for selling slippers of hashish, and a few more important dealers in carpets for selling the more deadly heroin. But the profits were so great that there were always others to take the risks.

There was the troublesome business that, although just when at one time the traffic in drugs seemed to be mastered, it had broadened out with a violence and a fatality too big, it seemed, for the private trafficker and most difficult to explain. It was thought—no, it was believed—and surely it was more than believed, it was known—that a great and bloody-minded nation which called crime culture and theft civilisation and enslavement hegemony, had, as a wise policy, set out to corrupt and destroy the Egyptians by the illicit smuggling of drugs into that country. It was no longer a case of this or that man, or this or that company, running hashish or heroin or cocaine into Egypt for profit at the risk of penal servitude for its officials on the spot. It was a national policy aiming at a national destruction. It was the curse of the fellaheen that he would starve rather than control his lusts, leave his family to starve and himself, within a few months, die, an idiot and a pauper. However carefully he had tilled his land and paid his dues, however many the hours he had given to the tiny canals and ditches which had watered his fields and secured some sort of a livelihood for his family and himself, they would have no memories to restrain him. There were no cords which would bind him to the mast of his daily work, once the siren music condensed within those dark blue paper bags was allowed to swell. All would go, industry, food, life. Colossal! One of the great signal posts from which the world's traffic was controlled would lie open for a great and worthy nation to use it entirely for its own advantage. . A people would have perished—well, great nations march to their destiny over roads ballasted by corpses. That was dutiful!

So the slippers of hashish and the envelopes of thick blue paper, filled with the sparkling white crystals of heroin, were sunk in waterproof bags off Mersa Matruh, or were carried across Sinai on the back of camels, and were ferried across the Canal. But a centre was needed where all this vital fodder could be collected in safety and distributed with as little danger as was possible. For a national policy, and so magnificent a policy as the destruction of another nation by the most corrupt and vicious incitements, organisation was needed—good, careful organisation, such as this high-class, A.1, sedulous nation had always at its command. It was a short-sighted nation, physically, and something of that short sight had crept into its plans as well as into the eyes which passed them as perfect.

The centre had been found, the clearing-house, in the village of Elaoui. Approached by a single road which could be watched night and day and whence ample warning could be given, that honeycomb of houses was the best hiding-place near Cairo. It had moreover a most saintly mosque, dating from the twelfth century, of which one of the Elaoui family was the priest. That this sacred building did, in fact, hide those dangerous cargoes, no one of the authorities concerned could doubt. But the mosque could not be searched. Another point of junction must be discovered, where the village under the rim of the hill touched the great city by the river.

And it was discovered after a great deal of patience.

The family of the Elaoui held itself strictly aloof. If a member of it went down into the city, he made his home there. He was not an outcast, but he had lost his place in the home circle. He remained on terms of friendship with his kinsmen and, when occasion served, he did business with such as descended to do business with him. There were a good many of that upland family who had married and made their homes in Cairo and, carrying on tradition, they cultivated a secret clanship. With the gradual storage of the forbidden drugs in that unassailable village, the opportunity for mutual service arrived. As soon as enough had been gathered in those rambling dwellings and that saintly mosque to soak the town, a youth strolled down from the village to the street of Abdul Azziz and at twelve o'clock noon precisely struck a wooden match in front of a certain provision shop. There was no crime in that. But it was the sign for the Elaoui men in the city to make their secret bargains with the actual dealers, a carpet seller with a big shop in a main street, or a lesser one, like the seller of cigarettes in the blue cloak on the edge of the great Bazaar ; and in a day or so the traffic was in full swing. At times a dealer was caught and disappeared for years into the grim convict prison. But he never talked. At times a youth was seen to strike his match at the appointed time in the appointed street. But if a man couldn't light a cigarette in a public place at midday, what was the world coming to ? The secret of the distribution had been kept, and with that problem the new and unknown officer in the Coast-Guard Directorate was set to deal.

Mordaunt thought over his problem as he waited for Rosalind on a bench in that long avenue which leads at last to the Anglo-American Hospital. So far fortune had served him. He had seen the match actually struck. He had noticed expectation in the bearing of a man whom he knew before the match was struck and relaxation afterwards ; and the man himself was suspect. Mordaunt wondered whether he had been wise to inform Bryan Devisher that he would write to thank Septimus for his kindness. There had been a quite unmistakable flash of fear across Devisher's face. Yet who but Septimus could have appointed him to a seat in the offices of the Dagger Line ?

Mordaunt shrugged his shoulders. The question was not worth a minute of debate. For Mordaunt had written on the evening of his encounter with Devisher thanking Septimus for so readily helping his acquaintance and hoping, without any great conviction, that good would come of it. The letter should have reached London now. It would probably be delivered on Monday morning at the office of the Company. He had addressed his letter to the Chief Office rather than to Portman Square, since it was upon a business matter. Well, in ten days, if not before, he would have an answer ; and, as he pushed the trouble away from him, a small hand fell lightly on his shoulder and he looked up to find some other trouble waiting to take its place.

" I am late," said Rosalind.

" There is always an excuse for it," Philip replied as he rose from the bench, " and to-day I'm afraid a reason."

Rosalind nodded and sat down beside him.

" Yes. I had to decide. It was difficult. James thought, that since I had got this job with Mr. Scobell, I might as well get on with it."

" James ? " Mordaunt asked, rather at a loss. " Is he the successor to Septimus ? "

" Not that I know. I suppose George and James are equal. But James saw no reason why I should go back. I couldn't help. George, however, is a real Crottle. We ought to be together, the lot of us, in one room ! "

Her lips twisted a little crookedly even at this moment as she thought of the code of the Crottles. But Mordaunt knew her well enough to be assured that her trouble was real. She sat with her hands folded in her lap, very quiet, looking straight ahead of her.

" What has happened ? " he asked.

" My father."

He hesitated. But her face was troubled and perplexed, rather than grief-stricken.

" He is ill ? "

" Not unless he has lost his memory," and she swung round to Mordaunt, " and can you imagine Septimus doing that ? "

" No," Mordaunt answered, and now the nature of the disaster was clear. " Septimus has vanished ? "

" Yes. He is lost altogether. Of course we always say that such things can't happen nowadays. But they always are happening."

Mordaunt sat and stared at Rosalind. He was never very quick to recognise and separate the sets of complications which one event might cause. And several questions were struggling to take form in his thoughts. One came first, and he asked it of her rather breathlessly.

" When did Septimus disappear ? "

Rosalind gave him the date and Mordaunt traced it back to a day which began forty-eight hours after a match had been struck in the street of Abdul Azziz— and after Mordaunt had warned Devisher that he meant to write a letter of thanks to Septimus. Meanwhile Rosalind explained.

" I got this telegram this morning from George. The Line has two offices, the main big one in Leadenhall Street and a smaller one in Whitehall, which father, of late years, used. You know how he lived ? "

" By watches."

" He had no fixed rule as to the hour when he went to his office, but he left it at six every day, from Monday to Friday."

This was his daily walk, whether fine or wet, whether winter or summer. On this Friday—it was a Friday and the footpaths, for that reason perhaps, a little

less crowded than at six o'clock they usually were
—he would have walked up Whitehall until he was
opposite the mouth of Downing Street. There he
would have crossed the road, passed through Downing
Street, traversed St. James's Park to the Mall, and walked
up the slope of the Green Park to Piccadilly. At times,
if the weather was very fine, he would prolong his consti-
tutional to Hyde Park Corner and the Marble Arch,
but as a rule it came to an end in Piccadilly opposite to
the Turf Club. Here he hailed a taxi and was driven
home to Portman Square.

Now on this Friday night a fog was settling like a
brown blanket on the town and the month being October,
the nights were closing in. Septimus was recognised
by a policeman under the lamp-post at the entrance
to Downing Street—and was never seen again. The
nephews waited for some days on the chance that some-
body would have met and recognised Septimus, but now
George had thought it wise to telegraph the news to
Rosalind and summon her home.

" And you are going ? " Mordaunt asked, and when
she agreed he nodded his head once or twice like someone
reckoning that here was a disaster to be added to the
rest.

" I am not going for any but rather mean reasons,"
Rosalind continued. " They have always expected me
—my family, my father, too—to come crawling home,
asking for shelter and the run of the cupboard. I want
to go back and show them that one needn't necessarily
fail. I want to wave a flag—yes, it's beastly and boastful,
I know—for five minutes. Then I shall come back
again."

" And find me packed off on an easier job, I expect."

Suddenly Rosalind struck the seat with the palm of
her hand.

" No, no ! " she cried with a curious violence. She

sprang to her feet. " We have had failures, both of us. But we are not to continue having failures. We are going to do well—both of us." And she turned away abruptly to hide perhaps the colour which rushed into her face. She was aware, quite unwittingly, of a community in their lives. She had paraded it too flambuoyantly, she had brandished it. She turned back again to Philip with quite another impulse.

" You will still be digging into your problem," she cried. " I want to see the end of it. If you are ready to blow the Last Post outside the walls of Elaoui, wait, please, until I can hear the notes, however far away I am."

She had the eagerness of a child, she was so certain that the great cause must prevail, that Mordaunt laughed with her on a wave of confidence.

" I'll try. As you come steaming into Cairo in three weeks, you shall hear them faint as fairy chimes from the edge of the hill."

They were moving away to take their luncheon for once in the grill-room of Shepheard's when the great idea came into Mordaunt's head. It was such a scintillating and illustrious idea, such an idea amongst ideas, that Mordaunt wondered how he came by it. He stopped dead on the bridge between the island and the city.

" My word ! " he cried.

If ideas were to come to him of such beauty, why, he might solve the problem of Elaoui before Rosalind came back.

" But I wouldn't like that to happen, Rosalind," he exclaimed.

" No, Philip, it wouldn't be pleasant," Rosalind returned, and it was noticeable perhaps, although neither of them noticed it, that this was the first time that in talking together they were using their Christian names.

" No. I want you to be in on it," he said.

" Nothing could be more lucid," replied Rosalind.

" Of course," said he, and he suddenly began to walk forward at a great rate.

" Philip, I can't keep up," she replied ; and he stopped again, full of remorse.

" It was the idea."

" Yes, ideas do run away with one," she answered.

" And this one, oh, I want it to be ever so clear."

" It's certainly a little involved at the moment."

" Then I've put it wrong," said Philip.

" You haven't put it at all," replied Rosalind.

Philip Mordaunt stopped and stared at her.

" No, I suppose I haven't," he conceded. " But we'll go along slowly——"

" We are not moving at all now," Rosalind interposed.

Mordaunt looked at the bridge as if he expected it to be a staircase on the Underground Railway.

" No, we're not," he remarked with surprise.

He walked on again with Rosalind at his side, but now more discreetly.

" Your boat leaves Port Said ? "

" To-morrow evening."

" You'll get off at Marseilles ? "

" Yes."

" And take the Blue Train ? "

" Yes."

" Right. I'll tell you what, Rosalind ! I'll get it all clear in my mind and whilst we are lunching I'll reel it off."

" That would be a change," said Rosalind and, with a little gurgle of amusement, she walked by the side of her frowning companion up the long street to the hotel. They had a wash, they drank a cocktail, they sat down to luncheon in the grill-room, and Mordaunt was ready with his idea.

" I took to Portman Square the last time I saw your father, an acquaintance of mine, Julius Ricardo."

" He was on your yacht with Bryan Devisher."

" Exactly. And with Ricardo, a friend of his, a French detective of mark, Hanaud."

" Yes."

" Hanaud was a big, heavy man with thick black hair and a blue jowl. He looked rather like a French comedian. He appeared to be as clumsy as a rhino, but he moved as lightly as an antelope, and he had quiet eyes which saw everything and a voice which was of no account and suddenly had all the authority in the world. I watched him whilst Septimus was reading—a book about Marie Antoinette's boy, the young Dauphin of France, and it seemed to me afterwards that if I had wanted an account of that queer evening, with nothing left out, I might have got it from him."

Rosalind Leete was listening now and with much the same concentration as Hanaud had shown. She no longer interrupted.

" Hanaud was very interested in the death of Daniel Horbury. He had a question or two to ask of Septimus which I didn't hear, and he was, I think, inclined to believe that somehow Bryan Devisher was concerned in it."

" Oh ! " She recoiled ever so slightly. " Bryan Devisher," she repeated.

" That's the man to keep in mind," said Mordaunt cheerfully. As long as you kept him in mind, it seemed that all the inferences would come trotting up one after another by themselves. " From the moment he deserted *Agamemnon* in Dartmouth Harbour to the moment when I found him by chance in the Sharia Abdul Azziz, he disappeared altogether, although the police the next day were searching for him."

" He disappeared with a letter from you to my father ? "

" Yes."

" A letter of recommendation ? "

" No. Of introduction, yes. I gave what I knew of his history."

" The black rim round the ankle ? "

" Yes."

" The Horbury swindle over the necklace ? "

" I didn't know of it when I wrote the letter."

Rosalind nodded at him with a frowning brow.

" There's a lesson for you not to write letters to other people's fathers recommending engaging scoundrels."

" You weren't other people. You aren't other people. Devisher wasn't engaging. And the letter wasn't delivered," he countered, and then came dolefully to the honest conclusion : " Yet I am beginning to be afraid that that letter did all the harm."

" How ? "

" I suppose because I am only just beginning to think things out," he said so contritely that Rosalind's hand slipped across the table and gave his arm upon the table a friendly and comforting shake. " You see, he couldn't have delivered the letter because he couldn't have done it until some time on the day when the police net was out for him—the Friday."

" Still, when you found him here, he was engaged in the office of the Dagger Line," she argued, and Mordaunt took her up at once.

" All the more reason to suggest that he hadn't delivered it. The Dagger Line was almost the Holy Grail to Septimus. To put an unknown man out of a prison straight away into the Dagger Line here—in Cairo—no, Septimus would never have done it. If I hadn't been sure of it at once, I ought to have been absolutely sure the moment I saw the terror in Devisher's face when I told him that I should write to Septimus and thank him."

"But you did write that day."

"Yes, I wrote," said Mordaunt emphasising the word. For it condemned him. He pointed towards her handbag at her elbow. "You received a telegram. I gave him a week, a clear week, to telegraph or telephone."

A silence followed whilst Rosalind followed out the possibilities which that difference of time suggested. This was how the story ran then : Devisher had friends who were expecting him in England, rogues of quality, the Horburys in fact. They had hidden him, obtained for him somehow this cover in the Steamship Office and sent him to take his profits and risks in the drug racket in Cairo. But if Mordaunt's letter of thanks ever reached old Septimus Crottle, the whole scheme would be blown sky-high. Therefore Septimus must be kidnapped, removed, got out of the way somehow, until Mordaunt's letter could be surely intercepted and destroyed.

Rosalind shrank from facing that tragical dilemma, but she did face it. Septimus Crottle came of a tough yeoman stock. He could face—he had faced—disasters and conspiracies. She knew of no secret flaws in that old and stubborn man which would defeat him. And such a hue and cry would be raised that all England would be searching for him and not searching in vain.

This was the legend which commended itself to those two novices over the luncheon table.

"I will write carefully a letter to Hanaud explaining everything, the striking of the match, what it means, Devisher's recognition of it, my foolish letter to Crottle—everything."

"Yes," said Rosalind.

"I'll give you the letter this evening in an open envelope. You will read it and then gum it down so that no one else can read it. I'll send Hanaud a telegram saying that you will leave the Blue Train at the Gare du Nord on the morning when you arrive, and that you will call on him at the Sûreté that morning and go on by the afternoon train to England."

" But "—Rosalind asked doubtfully—" you say he's important. Will he see me ? "

" I introduced him to Septimus. Of course he will," Mordaunt replied. " Besides, he's interested in the letter Horbury wrote to Crottle which was never delivered. Oh, he'll see you," and as if to make sure that a meal so dismal should not end in frowns and gloom, he added : " If you have any luck you'll meet Mr. Ricardo."

Chapter 23

HANAUD RETURNS AND ANOTHER

FAITHFUL to her instructions from a more experienced traveller, Rosalind continued in the Blue Train from the Gare de Lyon to the Gare du Nord. At the Gare du Nord she descended and followed a porter, who carried her two travelling cases up the steps to the small hotel in the station building. A letter was handed to her by the manageress in which Hanaud begged her to make no fixed arrangements, assured her that his debt to his English friends would not be diminished by the utmost help which he could give to her, and that by the time she had made herself comfortable and taken her little breakfast, a messenger would come for her. By his signature, he was still a member of the Peerage.

Rosalind enjoyed an admirable hot bath, a change into a well-tended black suit, a white silk shirt with a frill of lace, a pair of beige silk stockings and shoes as admirable as her bath, and took an equally admirable little breakfast in the restaurant. When she had finished her cigarette a messenger bowed before her. Monsieur Hanaud was at her disposal. She followed him to a car in the courtyard and was whisked away through the traffic by a driver, who used his gong rather as a musical instrument playing a coloratura solo than as a motorist's signal, across the bridge to the *Cité*. In an office looking out upon the quay and the river Monsieur Hanaud received her.

" You will see in England that dear Mr. Ricardo," he said as he held open an agate cigarette-box. " Will you, please, at some time suitable, indicate to him that I do not offer to my friends those deplorable black cigarettes in a blue paper cover which hurt him so much when he smells me smoking them. A match ? So ! You have a letter for me I think ? Thank you ! Will you sit here whilst I read it ? "

He put her into a comfortable chair whilst he read the letter, and it was not in order to make her feel more at her ease that he read it with, now and then, an exclamation of pleasure. When he had finished it, he laid it down and thumped it with little blows of his fist.

" So-o-o ! " he exclaimed slowly and he became aware of his guest. He had gleaned something out of that letter more than they knew who had sent it.

" Madame, the letter is helpful. I sympathise with you over the absence of your father, Mr. Crottle, but I do not think it will be for long. Meanwhile, I say that you and the good Mordaunt torture yourselves without the reason if you think the kidnap was to anticipate Mordaunt's letter of thanks."

" Then you are acquitting Bryan Devisher of having any share in all this trouble of the Horburys and the Crottles ? "

" Oh, I am ? Am I ? I plead at all events that we

do not exaggerate the share. Listen, as they say in the films," he continued, hitching his chair forward and then casting his glance in a wide sweep about the room. He lowered his voice, he nodded his head with the sagacity of an alderman. "I will tell you the truth. The negro in the firewood is a bird of another colour."

"Oh, I thank you!" she cried warmly. "That does make everything so clear."

Hanaud had the grace to blush. He had intended to save himself from a young lady's questions by making the young lady feel foolish. All that he had succeeded in doing was to make himself look ever so much more foolish than she could have felt. However, he was not a man of grudges. To get your own back was not really a necessity. He laughed with friendliness.

"I tell you, madame, something more. You are the first to link with the affair of Crottle the affair of Horbury. Yes, they are one. What happened on that moonlit night at White Barn? Who was there? And why? Hours afterwards, when all was over and the moonlight growing grey, who lifted the telephone mouthpiece from its cradle to silence it? And who silenced—oh, something ever so much more important than the telephone. . . ?" He was following his own fancies and forebodings as they had crowded in upon him that August morning in the white house beneath the beech trees and the oaks.

"Who or what silenced Olivia Horbury? Why did she lock her door? For how long did she lie in a swoon against it? Only when we know all that happened at White Barn between the great holly hedge and the toll-gate road on that night of late August—only then shall we put an end to the chain of crimes which began there. Daniel Horbury is murdered. That is no great harm, you may say. But Septimus Crottle disappears—and next—ah, what comes next?"

He broke off with a shiver of the shoulders, so violent, so unexpected, that Rosalind was shocked by it.

"Unless we are quick," Hanaud continued. He folded Mordaunt's letter to him without noticing what he was doing, slowly and carefully, so that each crease crossed the paper exactly as it had done; all his urgency rang in the whisper of his voice.

"Yes, unless we are very quick."

Hanaud looked up. He saw Rosalind Leete with a pair of startled eyes staring at him from a face as white as paper. Was it she? Or that other woman of whom he dreaded to hear? He moved to bring himself back from that corner of London. Outside the window those cries were rising from the quay, that flashing silver flood was the river Seine under the midday sun. Besides, this one's hair was of the colour of a summer sunset. That one's hair in London of the midnight.

"I frightened you," he said remorsefully.

"You did."

"I am sorry."

"You will come to London perhaps?"

There was an insistence in Rosalind's question which made him smile.

"Yes, I must pay for frightening you," he cried and was met with frowns and disfavour.

"I am serious," she said.

Hanaud opened a drawer and produced a passport, a special request from the Sûreté that all help needed shall be granted to him, a special authorisation from the Home Office and finally a ticket.

"As soon as Captain Mordaunt telegraphed to me of your coming, I wrote to my friend the Superintendent Maltby and at once everything was made easy. But I must say frankly that there is nothing which I can do which Maltby cannot do. We had many talks together.

I think in the end we saw with one eye. But frankly, too, I do not like unfinished things."

Hanaud was preening himself upon the nobility of his character, whilst he disclaimed all superiority to his English colleague. He had a false modesty which earned him jeers and sarcasms and disparagements and a true modesty which kept warm for him the loyalty of his department. It was the false modesty which was talking now, mimicking a humility which he did not possess and depreciating the social value of his calling.

"Now you, Madame Leete, by what route do you travel ? "

" I proposed, if I was free, to travel by the afternoon train."

" Arriving at ten-thirty or so ? "

" Yes."

Hanaud sat for a minute without speaking. Then he proposed to her a change.

" If you do not arrive to-night," he said, " I do not think that anything we fear can happen. You are expected to bring important information ? "

" About Bryan Devisher, yes."

" But no one knows yet what your information is. It may be of more importance than anyone thinks. Therefore it will be waited for."

" Yes."

" But if you arrive to-night, you do not know who will meet you or how many there will be in the house to hear your story ; and before that awkward hour of midnight it may be known that you have not so much to tell after all."

Rosalind sat back in her chair. She was breathing rather quickly. She was still frightened. Nay, she was more frightened than ever. She felt so near, as this man talked to her, to some grim lake of horrors writhing just beyond her feet.

" What do you want me to do ? " she asked.

" Keep for us this night safe."

Monsieur Hanaud did not much like the sea. He preferred the shortest Channel crossing. But, if he had affairs to wind up, he could sleep without malaise on the steamer from Havre to Southampton. It was convenient. There was time to dine on arrival at Havre and time to dine well. There were private cabins on the ship, one of which he would procure for Madame, as well as change her ticket. " La Gare d'Orléans, Madame." A clerk should accommodate her ticket at Mr. Cook's. And to-morrow morning Mr. Ricardo should meet them on the quay in his Rolls Royce No. 1, and drive with them to London.

Hanaud rang the bell and consigned her to his clerk. But while that man waited outside the door, the truth forced its way to speech.

" We are neither such clever ones, nor such fools as people think. A crime may be committed. Such crafty plans may be invented to hide it up that we could never unravel them. But very often a little accidental thing happens, a change of weather, the departure of a train changed by an hour, some unexpected visitor at a late hour of the night. Ah, if we are quick to seize upon that small scrap of grit which blows in from the window and spoils the smooth fine machine, to know it for what it is, then Madame "—no, he couldn't keep it down, the other side of him must have its turn—" then, Madame Leete, one becomes Hanaud."

At all events this should be said. By travelling on the Havre packet to Southampton Rosalind did more than save a night. She saved a life.

* * * *

There were warm salutations by Hanaud and a deprecatory reception of them by Mr. Ricardo on the quay side. The rest is silence. It was, besides, early in the morning and the rugs folded in Rolls Royce No. 1 were appealing. Rosalind had drunk tea and Hanaud what passed for coffee on the ship. Mr. Ricardo had done as much at the South-Western Hotel. Hanaud's papers had wafted the two travellers through the Customs House. The car flowed round Bargate and along the street Above Bar to Winchester.

"We breakfast here, the English breakfast. Yes, I am the cosmopolitan. I like him. I eat him. The eggs, the bacon, the sole, the mutton chops and the Oxford marmalade. The night was untroubled?—yes "—this with a glance of enquiry towards Mr. Ricardo. " So for half an hour ! Then we go on to London. We send Mrs. Leete home in a cab from Waterloo Station. We collect Maltby : over the luncheon at the Corner House we hold the council of war. Then perhaps we stretch out the hand—and make an arrest," he was going to add. " But," he stopped and heaved a prodigious sigh—" we are in England. Prisoners will not keep in the cell here. They must be aired in public before the magistrates at once, yes, and the police must be ready with their case, pronto, pronto."

Mr. Ricardo, who was prepared like any true-blue to enter the lists for *habeas corpus*, regarded his friend's lament as a tribute rather than as a challenge, and the car drove on through the woods of Hartley Wintney whilst the shadows were folded away. It was broad daylight when they dropped down the hill to Cobham and swept up the left-hand turn on to the open Fairmile. Gorse and heather and the straight white road running through, and not a soul to be seen. At least, so it seemed.

There was no one visible ahead. Monsieur Hanaud, who was sitting opposite to Mr. Ricardo with his back to the bonnet, asked suddenly : " You permit ? "

Without waiting for an answer, he turned and rapped

upon the glass panel and within a few yards the car stopped. Hanaud turned towards Rosalind.

"Mrs. Leete, I beg you to answer me a question."

"If I can."

"Of whom was Miss Agatha enamoured?"

Rosalind listened. She was amazed, then she was intrigued, then she was wildly amused. She broke into a laugh.

"Agatha! Oh, poor Agatha!"

There was no malice, no scorn in the laughter. It was sufficiently affectionate to persuade her audience that she would have wished a lover on Agatha if she could.

"Of no one, then?"

Rosalind took the question seriously. Her thoughts ran back to olden days. She shook her head.

"It's six years since I ran out. There was no one then. No one was ever expected by the rest of us. . . . Perhaps we made it obvious—you know how cruel women can be without meaning it—and she——"

Hanaud, who was listening in an excitement which no other in the car understood, broke in:

"So that was it, perhaps. She was told too often that she was the spinster, that there was no man for her, and she invented one. Oh, it is no new thing."

Rosalind, however, would not accept the calumny.

"She was religious. No! If there were a love story, even if it were only a dream of a love story, it would have a real live person for its hero. And I think," Rosalind added, looking out of the window, "such an apparition would have so astonished her—at the beginning, at all events—that she must have had very good reasons for believing in his sincerity."

"Oh!"

This fantastic story of the coffin and the locked drawer began to slide out of a grim fairyland into the land of fact.

" Then Miss Agatha is rich ? "

" One might call her so. She was the first child. My mother left her what she had, shares in the Dagger Line, when they were worth very little and they are now worth a good deal."

" Rich in her own right ? "

" Yes."

" To be signed away over her own hand ? "

" If she so chose."

And the coffin slid out stark before Hanaud's eyes. The outrageous improbability became solid. Someone in desperate need of money had advanced, had pretended, had prolonged the pretences in the hope of eventual escape, had inspired a passion, had betrayed in what bower his hopes really had their home. Hanaud raised his hands and let them fall rather helplessly. If only he knew what had happened between the holly wall and the turnpike road on that night of ending August !

" If there has been anything, it began after I had gone away," said Rosalind.

Hanaud smiled gratefully.

" You have told me, not for the first time, more than you think to have told me. I should have asked you this question before."

" Why ? " she asked bluntly.

" Because, if I had waited for another five minutes, I should not have had the chance ever to ask it of you at all."

To the surprise of everyone, he tapped again upon the glass, and, sliding it to one side, gave an order to the chauffeur.

" Back the car slowly with the least fussiness possible, until I tap. Then stop ! "

The chauffeur looked behind him. No car was approaching. No one stirred at all in all that wide expanse of heath and road and sky except one old man resting upon a bench at the edge of the common above the road, with his hands to his face and his elbows propped upon his knees.

The car slid gently past him below, but he took no notice of it. It seemed at first that he was in an abstraction, staring at the ground with his temples between his fingers. Hanaud tapped gently on the glass and the car stopped without a sound. It was seen then that the tips of the old man's fingers were working.

Hanaud leaned forward and noiselessly opened the door of the car at the side of the bank.

" Madame Leete," he said, " there is your father. I saw him as our car passed."

Chapter 24

AN UNLIKELY MEETING ON THE FAIRMILE

THE man on the bench certainly did not recognise the voice and it is doubtful if he heard the words. He was occupied. On the ground between his feet lay a small pile of strips of sticking-plaster ; and now and again his fingers added to it from his brows and the sockets of his eyes. " Father," Rosalind repeated ; but the old man was not ready, and the small group stood about him and waited. It was curious to Mr. Ricardo, rather horrible to Rosalind, and quite comprehensible to Hanaud that this sticking-plaster covered no wound ; the skin below it was patched and discoloured, but there was no mark of a knife or a blow ; and one of these patches, crossing the lips diagonally from a nostril to the chin, showed to what purpose the plaster had been put. His eyes had been hooded and his mouth had been gagged.

He lifted his head and became aware of the group about him. He looked at Ricardo and at Hanaud and at Rosalind, and then sat back and drew in some great breaths of air. Then he looked again at Rosalind, and suddenly barked out with a resentful note in his voice :

" Rosalind, eh ? "

Then he laughed as she shrank a foot or so away from him. " There, my girl, I'm not barking at you for leaving the ship, but for seeing me in this humiliating condition when you come back."

He held out a hand to her, and with the help of his other hand and the back of the seat he managed to struggle to his feet. He looked at Hanaud and then at Ricardo, balancing himself with difficulty. There was very little in him of the Septimus Crottle whom they could remember. He was shrunken now and a good decade had been added to his years. But the very spirit of the man had gone. They could see it by the way he clung to his daughter's arm for protection—he, the patriarch !

" Mordaunt sent you—Mordaunt, who thought—what was his word ?—that I had no inhibitions, that I was free of the terrors, of the weaknesses, of the degradations under which other men fall—I ! " and his voice rose in a scream suddenly, as a car rose up above the hill at Cobham and raced forward towards the group. He sank down upon the bench behind them. But the car went past without slackening. There were people in it, men and women laughing and talking. Septimus watched it between the bodies of his friends, at first only with his eyes, then with a trembling finger until it disappeared in the dust, and then until the dust itself had cleared away.

" All my life I have had that fear," he went on, communing with himself rather than talking to his companions, " of being shut away in a silent place——"

" Like the Dauphin of France," Hanaud exclaimed suddenly

" A small dark place, where no one came, where no one spoke, whence you couldn't escape," he continued, " until—until you died all by yourself. All my life I had been afraid of it. That's why I liked the bridge of my ship. The wide air and the stars in front of me! I tried to laugh the fear out of me—to bully it out of me—and then it happened."

" How ? " asked Hanaud, and Septimus Crottle drew back. He tried to throw a great deal of surprise and scorn into his looks.

" What ! Don't you know ? You and your friend Maltby ? The police ? " and then, in a panic of shame and fear : " Strange that I should remember names, but of what happened to me that night—nothing."

To Mr. Ricardo it occurred that there was a question still more important to be answered. How did the old boy come to find himself alone on the Fairmile in the early morning with his face visored and latticed with sticking plaster ? And, arising out of the answer to that question, whatever it might be, was it wise for them all to be standing in plain view on the high footpath above the road ?

He suggested that Mr. Crottle might find the cushions of his car more comfortable than the hard rails of the park seat by the roadside. But Crottle was suspicious on the instant. He looked at the great car, at the white empty road, at Mr. Ricardo.

" How do I know ? " he asked, and his head twisted from side to side.

" You can trust me, sir, in any case," declared Hanaud. And Mr. Ricardo reflected how seldom Hanaud seemed to be important when he most cried himself up to be ; and how remarkably dominant and inspiring he could grow when he was not thinking of himself at all. Yesterday, in Paris, he had been an expert speaking out of his knowledge and of the wisdom which knowledge had brought. To-day it was Hernani, and not a very good Hernani either.

Mr. Ricardo's suggestion was obviously reasonable, and the whole party moved to the car. But, even in those few moments, it became still more noticeable how his experience had crippled Septimus, how swift and complete his disintegration had been. He walked irresolutely with his shoulders bowed and eyes which, despite his will, searched at every rustle for an enemy. Even in the car he must sit with his hand upon the lock of the door and the long stretch of road visible ahead of of him and the driver's mirror well within his vision.

" We will go forward slowly ? " Hanaud asked.

And suddenly, with a flash of cunning, Septimus replied with another question :

" Where to ? "

Hanaud nodded with some satisfaction. He had his own answer to that question and wanted no conflict with Septimus over it.

" Let us see ! "

He made a sign to Mr. Ricardo and, as the car moved on towards London, Septimus Crottle was questioned as to what he remembered of his disappearance.

" I left the office—it's almost at the corner of Parliament Street—at six, as I usually did. There was a thick fog, turning brown, and night coming on. It seemed to me the moment to shorten speed, eh ? I've crept across the Bay in my young days in that sort of weather. There was a street light opposite to Downing Street. I remember crossing there. There was a policeman standing just under the light."

" There was," Hanaud agreed.

" I crossed, walked through Downing Street, descended the steps at the end, and passed the Memorial to the Guards opposite to the Parade——"

At that point Septimus Crottle came to an abrupt stop.

"Well?" Hanaud asked, and, shaking his head, Crottle answered in a sullen voice:

"I remember not one thing more. The Guards Memorial, yes. I crossed the road, wondering whether I was going to be run down by a car. I crossed quickly and I almost ran into the stone of the Memorial. But I didn't. No, I didn't. But I don't remember one thing more until——" and the old man began to shake. A few little cries, they were less cries than the sobs of a child lost in some jungle of horrors, broke from him and grew in loudness. His hand fidgeted with the handle of the door. He looked about him as a man looks, caught by his enemies. He whimpered.

"We shall leave it there," Monsieur Hanaud cried cheerfully, "until we collect the admirable Maltby," and a shadow of a smile brightened Septimus Crottle's face.

"If my case is in his hands," he cried.

"But it is, Mr. Crottle," said Hanaud. "We have talked together, he in the Scotch Yard and I in Paris, over the vanishment of monsieur and of something else which I, the obstinate, congregate with it."

Septimus looked up curiously and bowed.

"But there is now a little thing, is there not?" and he made his two fingers run along the arm of the seat and spring into the air. Hanaud was nervous, Mr. Ricardo decided. Now, why? There was a problem, or—to adopt the humorous slang which Mr. Ricardo thought it modern to approve—or was there? But he was nervous. Yes. Once more the fingers ran daintily along the arm at his side and sprang into the air.

"Yes, there is a small——"

"Don't do that, please," cried Septimus, watching the two nimble fingers. "It confuses me. What do you mean by it? Do it again and I'll jump into the road."

The old man, suspicious of this unusual if harmless

manœuvre, was watching Hanaud alertly, one hand upon the lock of the door.

" It's all right, father," said Rosalind, and she turned apologetically to Hanaud. " I expect that any new movement disturbs him."

" Yes. Certainly any movement so typically French," added Mr. Ricardo sternly but with a warm inward satisfaction.

" Yes, it was French," Rosalind confirmed. She was eager to make discomfort comfortable for her good friend of the Sûreté. She had no reason to realise that if there was one point outside his profession upon which Hanaud prided himself, it was his anomalous internationalism. " It was just the Frenchiness of the gesture which worried him."

Mr. Ricardo hugged himself with pleasure, and who shall grudge it to him ? Hanaud's ears would burn. So English wasn't he ? " *Mon pied !* " Mr. Ricardo exclaimed silently—and aloud :

" It'll be all right when we get hold of Maltby."

" Ah, yes, Maltby," Mr. Crottle repeated happily.

Mr. Ricardo nodded towards Hanaud.

" We will drive straight to the Yard. Maltby will not dance his fingers along the arm of the seat. At the Yard——" and a blank determined negative came explosively from the most unexpected quarter :

" No ! "

It was Septimus who uttered the word. He was looking from one to the other with just that bright flash of cunning in his eyes which they had all noticed before when he was sitting on the garden seat.

" Maltby, yes—with Monsieur Hanaud, to whose kindness I am deep in debt," Crottle continued, " but privately. It is the full morning now. If we drive into Scotland Yard we may be seen. There will be many on the Embankment."

" At home, then ! " cried Rosalind, but still Septimus shook his head.

" I have servants. I have three daughters—beside you, Rosalind. Within an hour the evening correspondents would be knocking at the door. It is not known that I have come back. I shall go to a nursing home, where no inquiries would be answered."

With an " Ouf ! " Monsieur Hanaud showed them as radiant a face as a man of his sallow complexion could.

" The nursing home, it is good. But better still is the house of my good friend Mr. Ricardo."

There was a pause. Mr. Ricardo was not quite sure that he welcomed this interruption of his routine. Also, if the invitation had to be offered, he would, on the whole, have preferred to offer it himself. But Hanaud rushed on. There was an entrance through the Mews at the back of the house. Also, since it would quickly be seen that he, Hanaud of the Sûreté, was visiting once more his old friend, it would be natural for the good Maltby to call. As for visitors, Thompson, the invaluable, would reject them, and no doubt Maltby would lend a fine young fellow who could fit himself into one of Mr. Ricardo's liveries. There were many spare rooms in the corner house. No one would be so pleased as Mr. Ricardo to help in this affair.

Mr. Ricardo could do nothing but agree. He certainly did object to the lack of ceremony in the requisition of his house and perhaps still more to the trifle of malice in Hanaud's smile. If Maltby was necessary before the necessity for silence could be explained, so, too, was Mr. Ricardo's fine house in Grosvenor Square.

" Ah, ah, you make fun of your poor Hanaud. Well, well ! " Hanaud exclaimed gaily. " After all, we are twins."

" Personally, I should prefer to say ' quits,' " Mr. Ricardo replied acidly.

Thus, in any case, it was decided. Septimus was smuggled unnoticed through the Mews at the back of Ricardo's house and the car was driven on to Waterloo Station with Rosalind and Hanaud.

" I take you out of your way," Rosalind protested, but Hanaud shook his head and got in beside her.

" We must be sure that the appearance of papa has not altered the story to be told," he argued. " You are to say that Mordaunt saw Bryan Devisher in the street of Abdul Azziz and drank a bottle of beer with him ? "

" Yes."

" That Devisher said that he had presented Mordaunt's letter of introduction to Septimus and that Septimus had appointed him to a position in the Cairo office of the Dagger Line."

" Yes."

" That Mordaunt had written to Septimus to thank him for his kindness."

" Yes."

Hanaud nodded his head.

" And that Devisher was really concerned with a nation's policy to rot the Egyptian people with drugs."

Hanaud swung round to the girl. He frowned, he pursed his lips.

" You would say that ? " he asked. " Because a match is struck in a street ? "

Rosalind was astonished. He had listened to her in Paris without seeming to doubt a word of the story she told.

" Would it be fair to say the match was struck because heroin had come to Elaoui ? " He was drumming on his knees, troubled by a doubt whether he was fair to a possible enemy. Rosalind found it a little difficult to identify Hanaud with this extremely scrupulous officer.

" You think that I should forget that circumstance ? " she cried.

" Ah, circumstance—yes, the convenient word. But suppose the true word is coincidence. Then you tell your story and this poor man—ouf ! "

Rosalind glanced at him again. She said firmly :

" I will not mention the matchbox, nor Elaoui, nor Philip's idea at all."

Monsieur Hanaud's relief was curiously great. It was all very well to wish to be fair, but to wish for it so much, as first his anxiety and now his relief established, Rosalind did not believe. She was not, however, given time to debate the question in her thoughts. Hanaud chattered to her about her sisters until they reached the station. They had to discover a train from Southampton which would fit in with her arrival in a taxi at Portman Square. They were fortunate there, for a train was due in ten minutes.

" Shall I say you crossed with me, Monsieur Hanaud ? " she asked as he stood by the door of the taxi.

He shook his head.

" No, madame. You can, I am sure, find a friend whom you wished to seize the opportunity to visit. Or, better still, you went to the Paris office of your father's Line to find out whether they had news of him. So you missed the boat train."

He stood back and drew a long breath of relief as Rosalind's cab drove off. He sent Mr. Ricardo's Rolls-Royce back to Grosvenor Square and took another cab to Scotland Yard. He took a hurried luncheon with Maltby at a little restaurant in Soho, and at half-past two he looked at his watch.

" Septimus Crottle has something to tell us," he said.

" Let us go," said Maltby ; and, finding a taxi at the door—in those days such miracles happened—they drove to the corner house in Grosvenor Square.

AT ARKWRIGHT'S FARM

Chapter 25

AT ARKWRIGHT'S FARM

INDEED Septimus had something to tell. He sat in
an arm-chair in a big room overlooking the Square and
overlooked by none. He was bathed, shaven, dressed
in clean linen borrowed from Ricardo, with a dark-blue
dressing-gown over all. But the marks of terror were
still engraved upon his face and his eyes were the eyes,
so unmistakably explicit, of one who has passed through
the shadows of death. They tell no story, they deny
that they have a story to tell, but they inspire the prayer,
" God forbid that I should suffer as this man has ! "
And he was years older, shrunken in his spirit and his
courage as much as in his frame. He was like, too, some
sharp and watchful animal of the forests and the heath.
The simplest little unexpected sound set him quivering
and, still worse, cringing, as if there were no end to the
new horrors which stood darkly about him. That this
man had ever commanded a great ship through gales
and reefs, across the wide oceans of the world, and
brought his cargoes and his passengers safe to far ports,
seemed to the most unimaginative of his visitors beyond
credulity itself to believe.

Happily Mr. Ricardo had an inspiration from a kindly
heart. He came into the room with Maltby and Hanaud
at his heels, carrying a box of Havana cigars. It was
all very well for Septimus to tell the world that his
cigars were the best, but they were no better than
Ricardo's. And, as he held out the box, Ricardo
said :

" I thought that you might like to lunch alone, Mr.

Crottle, after these stormy times, but these I hope you will enjoy in company."

The old man's face lit up with the cigar. Mr. Ricardo could have done nothing more wise. The smoke curling upwards, the fragrance which comes from nowhere but Havana, with all its associations of ease and pleasurable moments, brought comfort and a smile to Septimus Crottle.

" I thank you," he said warmly to Ricardo, and Hanaud must add his comment.

" He has the tact, my friend Ricardo. Not from the books of the deportment writers. No, no, he has it here," and he laid his hand admiringly upon his heart.

Septimus, however, was finding his recollections crystallise more easily into speech, now that he had a cigar between his lips.

" When I became conscious, my eyes were covered," he said with a shiver of disgust. " I was aware we were in a car—a man—I think—I can't be sure, but I doubt if my instincts would lead me astray—a man of the sea and a woman." He was silent for a little while, and went on choosing rather meticulously his words. " Afterwards—I can't say more than that now at all events—there was I with the nightmare of a lifetime discovered and made true—oh, yes, discovered ! When the nightmare began, I can't remember, for I've always remembered the nightmare,"—he shut his eyes and shivered, looking back over years of watchfulness and years of imagined horror.

" To be confronted with it, eh ? " he looked at Hanaud and from Hanaud to Ricardo, perhaps with some vague idea that they, who had been present when his voice had broken over the dreadful history of the young Dauphin, would picture to themselves with what ghastly detail that history had been staged again.

" They had a lanthorn, which they set upon a white

deal table. They emptied my pockets. They took everything from me except two things. This," he took out of his waistcoat pocket a small thin diary with a small thin pencil in a sheath. " They were very jocose about it. It would pass the time for me to read in the daylight by the chinks of the shutters the engagements I wasn't going to keep. Oh, very jocose they were, and unwise. And the second thing was this. They were funny about this, too."

The second thing was an old battered silver watch with an old strap and buckle, which he took from his watch-pocket. It was as big as a turnip, thick and round, and indeed, to modern eyes, looked comical enough. But Septimus Crottle handled it as fondly as if it had been a jewel fashioned by Cellini.

" I bought that when I was an apprentice in a clipper. Very funny they were about that, too. What a fortunate thing it was for me that, when I wanted to know the time, I shouldn't have to ask a policeman ! Very funny, and still more unwise." He looked at the clock. " Listen," he said.

The hands made the hour to be three and the silence was broken by three faint little silvery chimes from Crottle's watch.

" A repeater ! " exclaimed Ricardo.

" A repeater. They didn't know. It was just a piece of luggage. They left it with me and slammed the door and locked it. I was in the dark with the watch in my hand and, as I stood there, I heard above the roof of the house the drone of an aeroplane, the throb and pulse of its engines, the rush overhead and the swift decline to silence. Even at that moment it was pleasant, companionable, a promise. I asked my watch the time. It was midnight."

The next morning, by a ray of light, a golden ray on which the sun danced like Blondin on his tight-rope into the black room, Septimus had ticked off in his diary the day, October the eighth, on which he had been taken, and this new day which had come. That night, too, the friendly aeroplane roared at midnight a friendly " Here I am," and was gone. Septimus Crottle could test his watch by its passage. There was a water-tap and a basin and a bucket and a straw mattress in his shuttered room besides the deal table. At times—and with difficulty he blurted out a word here and there— he must stand silent with his face to the wall, whilst the room was cleaned and his food brought in. But no one spoke and, like all prisoners, he began to live for little things, and, above all, for the moments when he could tick off the day in his diary and when the aeroplane announced from afar its approach, thundered overhead and died away.

" In a little while I was able to expect it," he said, " sitting in the dark. Then I would hear it and press the spring of the repeater. It was punctual like the postman, sometimes on the tick of twelve, sometimes a few seconds later. I think that waiting for the noise of it kept me alive all through that first week. And then one night it didn't come at all."

To each one of his auditors, so completely were they held by the sombre fire of his eyes and the simplicity of his tale, the sudden drop of his voice to a whisper brought the same shock of catastrophe which the absence of the aeroplane had brought to him.

" Even later on . . . ? " Hanaud began in a hush.

" That night it never passed overhead at all."

" You are sure ? "

" I lay awake until the morning was a grey mist in the room."

" And what morning was this ? " cried Maltby with a curious violence.

Old Septimus opened his diary.

"The fourteenth of October. Look! I put a ring about the line which marked the day. For it looked as if I had lost my only friend."

Maltby almost snatched the diary from his hand.

"Yes, the fourteenth. But you heard it the next night?"

Septimus came to life again. There was a smile upon his face, a kind of lilt in his voice.

"Yes, I heard it the next night. And every night for the six nights which followed. I heard it even yesterday."

But Maltby had not waited to hear the end of that sentence. He was out of the room. They heard his feet running down the stairs to the hall; and a moment afterwards his voice upon the telephone.

But they distinguished none of the words; and now that Septimus had come to the end of his narrative, the fatigue of his adventure was upon him and his head nodding on his shoulders. A bedroom, however, had been prepared for him and Mr. Ricardo's housekeeper, a matron and such as one could count upon in that household, was at the door.

"A nice sleep, a nice dinner in bed . . ."

"And another nice cigar after the dinner," said Crottle with a grin at Ricardo.

"And the gentleman will be himself again," observed Mrs. Ffennell, the housekeeper, "if he isn't that already."

But there was still some knowledge for which Hanaud could not endure to wait until the next morning.

"Before you go, sir," he exclaimed, throwing himself in front of Septimus and his hands flapping signals of distress to Ricardo.

"Let us finish with it. You are wondering how you came to find me on a bench half-way along the Fairmile?"

"But exactly," cried Hanaud.

"Well, I can't tell you. All I know is that these

people, the man and the woman, talked late. I heard their voices through the floorboards. Then I heard the motor-car being brought from somewhere. I used my watch. It was three in the morning. They came up the stairs almost immediately afterwards with the lanthorn. But I was not able to see much, as you know," and now there was more anger than horror at the indignities which he had suffered. "I was no match for them, even if I had possessed my usual strength. I got up and dressed, whilst they hurried me."

He stopped for a moment whilst he straightened out his recollections.

"Yes. They were frightened. It gave me a sudden shock of pleasure," and Crottle's face cracked with a grin more blissful than any which Hanaud could remember. "Their hands shook. They spoke too quickly to be understood, as if the hangman were at their heels."

Again the old man's voice dropped to a whisper.

"When I could see nothing, nor speak, they were busy with the room. There were nails torn out of the shutters and the shutters folded back. The mattress was pulled out of the room. It all took a few minutes. I think the room was dismantled Then I was taken down to the car. They spoke in whispers. We drove off quietly and slowly. Then we drove faster and for hours. But whether we went backwards and forwards, or straight, is more than I can tell. They turned me out about seven o'clock—a little later perhaps."

He stood for a moment. Mr. Ricardo was looking at his diary. Summer time would end in a couple of days now. The dawn would just be showing when Septimus Crottle was pushed out of the car at the edge of the common.

"Yes, we passed about eight," Mr. Ricardo declared, but Hanaud did not answer.

"That's all I have to tell you," said the old man.

Mr. Ricardo sprang to his feet and went with him to the door. There Mrs. Ffennell, the housekeeper, and Thompson awaited him and led him to his room.

"That was interesting," said Mr. Ricardo as he came back into the room. He saw Hanaud still seated in his chair, his face troubled and perplexed.

"Yes," he continued, "a terrible story. Did you follow Crottle's reactions? Now that old fear was at the top of his mind, now the mishandling, the affront to his dignity."

Mr. Ricardo was excited. He was living great deep moments. He took a glance at the window. Outside, in the Square, men and women were going about their ordinary business, unaware of all that was happening up here just above their heads. An old man telling a story of cruelty, and Hanaud and Maltby and himself launched out to catch the criminals.

"A strange, grim story, my friend," he cried with pride. He almost added, "Find its equal in France, if you can!"

But, before he could utter so outrageous a boast, Hanaud quietly interposed.

"Do you know what I find most curious? They were frightened. The man and the woman. In the middle of the night they must take the old fellow away, dump him somewhere along an empty road and fly off. They were frightened. Why? No one challenged them. Why?"

He was still pondering this question when the door was flung open. Maltby came back into the room and his face was alight.

"Mr. Crottle?" he asked.

"He has gone to bed."

"Good. There will be a plain-clothes officer in the house to-night. He will run no danger."

Hanaud looked up at him.

" You have news ? "

Maltby nodded his head. Mr. Ricardo could have shaken him. He had no vivacity, no emotions ? But at last Maltby spoke.

" The Western Air Company flies a nightly service from Heston. It stops at Taunton, Exeter and Plymouth. It leaves Heston at eleven. On the night of the fourteenth of October the engine failed a quarter of an hour after it had taken off. It was able to return to Heston. There was no service to Plymouth that night."

Chapter 26

TWO OF THE LITTLE ACCIDENTS

THERE were not many travelling by the Airway on that night, and the three men at the back of the car could talk and watch without interruption. Two nights had passed since the moon was full, but the black curtain was rolled back from the sky now, and more and more clearly the tranquil countryside reached out below, great trees and their shadows on fields of silver-grey, long rounded ridges of turf and rock which sprang high and broke off, rivers like glistening highways. And now and then they sank low enough to imagine that by holding their breath they could hear the lowing of cows.

" We could hear of no other service which missed a beat, as you might say, on the night of Thursday, October the fourteenth," Maltby declared in answer to a question from Hanaud.

" Ten minutes now," said Mr. Ricardo looking at his

watch, and Hanaud fetched out of his pocket the clumsy silver chronometer of Septimus Crottle. He laid it face upwards on the table between them, and all three bent their heads over the white face.

"Twelve minutes, by the old man's repeater," said Hanaud.

Mr. Ricardo was regarding his friend with awe. He looked round suspiciously. There were three naval officers on their way to Plymouth, a journalist bound for Exeter, and a couple of holiday folk for Cornwall. But they were all to the front of the car. He turned back to Hanaud.

"I should never have thought of that," he said, reproaching himself, "if I lived till I was a hundred. You actually borrowed the watch from Mr. Crottle?"

Hanaud shook his head.

"I took it when he wasn't looking."

Whether borrowed or taken, the watch was an advantage. It gave them an absolute precision for their arrangements.

"If you, Monsieur Hanaud, will watch on this side of the plane, Mr. Ricardo and I will look after the other."

Maltby moved across the aisle and drew back the curtain. Ricardo placed himself in the seat in front and both stared down through the moonlit air. The aeroplane was travelling along a big whale-backed ridge like one of the Berkshire Downs. Here and there the smooth turf was broken by a black outcrop of rock; here and there in a scoop of the sides there grew a little spinney of larches. Below and along the three men watched with a concentration which spread through the car and provoked the curiosity of the other travellers, so that their conversation ceased and they, too, began to look downwards, but for what they did not know.

On the table in front of Hanaud the monstrous watch of Septimus ticked, it seemed to Ricardo, louder and louder with each second. He saw now, beside the dark surface of the down below him, flat meadows to his right, with cut ditches in which water gleamed, and a long way forward and to his right a sprinkling of lights which betokened a town. Bitter thoughts came into his mind: " We are on the wrong air-line. There will be another company running a different service. Perhaps, if Maltby hadn't booked us as ordinary passengers ! In front there, in the pilot's cabin, a man would see more clearly." Why was it so important to hide their movements ? Secrecy—hush, hush—there could be too much of it.

Mr. Ricardo was beginning to boil with exasperation, when suddenly Hanaud's finger closed upon a spring and the clear, yet tiny chimes, chimes of the little people, tinkled with a strange incongruity through that most modern of carrier wagons.

" We shall miss it," Ricardo cried, and even as he cried he saw it, just ahead, just before the down broke off abruptly in the plain. It stood in the open upon a slope of ground, with a break like a quarry in the side of the down behind it, a farm-house without a light in any window, and not another house visible in its neighbourhood. Ricardo turned excitedly towards the Superintendent. " Do you see ? Do you see ? " he asked in a whisper, and the rudder of the aeroplane gave a wriggle. The machine was turning, so that it would move straight over the house towards the grouped lights of the city. In a second Hanaud would see it upon his side. Mr. Ricardo rushed across the cabin. Hanaud was sitting with his face at the window and his hands curved about it to shut out the light above and behind him.

" Look ! Look ! "; and the aeroplane swung clear of the down and swept across the fields and dykes of Sedgemoor to the airport on the edge of the city.

" Did you see ? " asked Ricardo.

Hanaud picked up the watch and tucked it away in his pocket, a little embarrassed by his friend's excitement. But Maltby cleared the air with a most unveracious story.

" The house was probably not that house, but one of an earlier date. But certainly Monmouth was taken there. His men had broken before Colonel Kirke's pikes on this flat land. Monmouth, I think, was found under a truss of straw in one of the outbuildings."

Maltby noticed the other passengers turning away with a smile from these historical enthusiasts, and the aeroplane took the ground.

As they dismounted a big man in a blue suit advanced towards them.

" Superintendent Maltby ? My name's Lance. Inspector Lance."

The two men shook hands.

" There are rooms for your party engaged at the hotel," said Lance, " and I would rather talk there."

A car was waiting, and a few minutes afterwards Inspector Lance, in a comfortable sitting-room warmed by a bright fire, with a hot grog at his elbow, was administering, not without a certain pleasure, the coldest of cold douches to his colleague from the Metropolis.

" I am afraid that you have wasted your time, Superintendent. If I had only known before," and he sighed as he looked into the coals.

" You couldn't, because we didn't," Maltby answered.

" Yesterday, for instance," said Lance slowly.

Maltby smiled.

" If we had known yesterday, I should have been able to give you a much more complete account of how much we needed your help than I could over the telephone this afternoon."

Inspector Lance admitted by implication to have had his plumage a trifle ruffled.

" The call sounded a little abrupt."

Nobody could be humbler than Maltby when something was to be gained by humility.

" It must have," he agreed remorsefully. But there had been no time for the courtesies. He had only just that moment learnt what air service failed on the night of October 14th. " But perhaps now you will, over another glass of this excellent whisky, allow me to tell you a little more particularly of our need."

He rang the bell, and on the appearance of the Boots —for it was then half an hour after midnight—said " Repeat ! "

The Boots looked at Hanaud, and, whether he was naturally sympathetic or just wished to spare himself an unnecessary journey up and down the stairs, pointed out :

" The foreign gentleman has drunk nothing."

" I want nothing," Hanaud snapped. As if he couldn't pass for an idiomatic Englishman anywhere !

Maltby was suddenly afraid that here again the proper courtesies had been neglected.

" This is Monsieur Hanaud of the Sûreté in Paris," he said, addressing the whole room. He tried to gather a few bouquets from his recollections, but once again the notice was too short, " of whose activities you will not need me to remind you."

It was not very good, no, and Hanaud was justly annoyed.

" You will not join us, monsieur ? " asked Lance, and Ricardo seized the moment gleefully.

" Hanaud is partial to a peppermint *frappé*, which he is unlikely to get at this hour of the night in the west of England. So perhaps a glass of Porto or a cup of coffee ? "

" Ah ! Coffee ! " cried Hanaud, and the Boots went away upon his errand.

Meanwhile Maltby filled in those details of the history of Septimus Crottle which he had not had the time to give over the telephone. When he had finished, Inspector Lance threw his hands up in the air.

"The luck of the thing! Of all the unchancy businesses," and he swung round, now thoroughly mollified, to his companions.

"Arkwright's. That's the name of the place. A farm once, and not so bad. But the owner, old Mrs. Destries over to Bridgewater, sold off most of the land, and the house stood there unlet for a long time."

In the end a man, Frank Barnish, with his wife, had hired it. It had a few acres of grazing land, which they let, and made do with a vegetable plot, a small orchard, a couple of pigs and some chickens. He had been a sailor, it seemed, but they made no friends; he, a hulking big fellow, cantankerous and sullen, and she a good match for him. They gave no trouble but nobody liked them. They never fitted in. They were just solitary people in a solitary place. They had some money of late weeks, and had bought somewhere in London an old motor-car.

"A battered old blue thing to look at," said Lance. "But once I saw her coming into the town, and she could go."

He looked straight at Maltby and added:

"So it's just your bad luck, Superintendent."

Maltby was tired by now of vague assertions that his luck was out. He answered shortly:

"What is?"

"That you didn't come yesterday."

"They have gone?"

Inspector Lance nodded. He got up and offered a cigarette to Maltby, began to offer one to Monsieur Hanaud, but, seeing what he was smoking, fell back aghast, and was offered and accepted a cigar for himself by Ricardo.

" Yes. Upon receipt of your message—sounds like old days, doesn't it, Superintendent ?—in accordance with instructions, I proceeded, etcetera, etcetera . . ."

" The people who put through the message to you from the Yard don't seem to have used very much tact, I am afraid," Maltby replied dryly.

" Oh, that's all right. Urgency and good manners have different patterns," said Lance. He conveyed to everyone in the room a pleasant sense of enjoyment. Here were two important officials from London and Paris and a *tertium quid* all of a flutter, who had flown down to teach the West Country yokels their business, whereas if they had only talked with reasonable clarity over the telephone. . .

" You see, we sent out a police-officer upon the receipt of your message to keep an eye upon Arkwright's, and he reported that there was no one about."

" When was that, Inspector ? "

" About seven o'clock."

" And where did he report from ? "

" Arkwright's."

The Barnishes had a telephone in a living-room which they never used, except perhaps for telephoning. The police-officer had found the door on the latch and not an answer to a cry.

" I told him to hold on and I would send him another man to keep him company. Empty houses at night are creepy things. We shall find the two men there in the morning. There's obviously nothing more that we can do until then."

Inspector Lance picked up his hat and threw the stump of his cigar into the fireplace.

" No, indeed," said Hanaud, at his sweetest, " and should ever fortune send you on the air to Paris, may I do no less for you ! "

Inspector Lance looked a trifle doubtfully at Hanaud,

as though he were not quite sure how to interpret that sentence. He bowed, however, and remarked :

" I hope that you'll all be comfortable."

He was just opening the door when he came to a halt. He clicked his tongue several times against his palate in annoyance, shut the door, and marched back into the centre of the room.

" It is by our mistake, perhaps, that the Barnishes have escaped you. I hope not. We had our local duty to do, and no word from you earlier, I think, than four."

Hanaud leaned forward. What little pellet of discomfort was the Inspector now going to discharge upon them ? One fairly potent in aroma, Hanaud gathered from the slow-savouring smile of penitence which waited upon his speech.

" We knew nothing until then," Maltby declared. " We telephoned as soon as we knew."

" Yes, but what a pity ! You see, a farmer who grazes his sheep on the down at the back of Arkwright's sent in the morning before a shepherd to complain of a dog which had killed some of his ewes. The man thought that the dog was an Irish wolf-hound. Well, you gentlemen of the Yard will know that an Irish wolf-hound's like a German. He can't be cured. So, naturally, we got to work and, naturally, Arkwright's was the first objective."

" Oh ! "

Hanaud jumped from his chair.

" Arkwright's was the nearest house. Also, Barnish was a morose, unfriendly man. It might, perhaps, give him a sullen sort of pleasure to injure a neighbour, especially with some cruelty added. Moreover, if he had a dog, he hadn't something else which went with it—a dog licence."

" And when did you send your officer ? " Hanaud asked.

" Let me see. The shepherd reached us about twelve. We sent Cox out—yes—as soon as he had had his dinner. He went off upon his bicycle at two o'clock or thereabouts."

" Yesterday ? " said Maltby.

" Well—conveniently but incorrectly," Inspector Lance replied, and he looked at the clock on the mantelshelf. " It's getting on towards two o'clock in the morning ; yes, we'll call it yesterday. Cox bicycled out to Arkwright's at two o'clock on the afternoon of Tuesday."

" Tuesday," said Mr. Ricardo with approval. He did not mean to be a cipher in these agreements and explanations, even though, whenever he did put in his word, everybody else turned and stared at him as though he had only at that moment materialised in the room. " Tuesday afternoon at two."

" Barnish was at home," Lance continued. " It's a curious old house, shingle and bricks and little windows. There's an archway through to the yard at the back, and the front door, as you might say, is on the right-hand side under the arch."

" Then Cox got off his bicycle," Mr. Ricardo suggested, to help a rather lame story on to its climax, and met a thoughtful glance of the Inspector.

" Ah, now, did he ? " the Inspector asked. " Did he get off his bicycle ? Or did he just stop at the door like, with one foot on the ground and the other on the pedal ? We'll have to consider of that. It didn't occur to any of us that you gentlemen would think the point important."

There was only one action for Mr. Ricardo to take, and he took it. Hadn't the Duke of Wellington once gone on his knees to a ridiculous Spanish General who had felt himself insulted ? " The matter being important, down I plumped," wrote the Duke and, fortified with that example, Mr. Ricardo grovelled.

"I won't interrupt again. I apologise, Inspector, on my knees," he said meekly.

Inspector Lance was mollified.

"He did get off, I think, for as he was propping his bicycle against the wall, the house door being a bit open, he heard a chair flung back and a dish clattering on the floor, as if the Barnishes had been fairly startled, and in a second Barnish was blocking the doorway, with a face like thunder. He began with a quarrelsome, 'What do you want?' and then saw Cox's uniform. Cox said he turned quite sickish in colour, but looked better when he was asked whether he had an Irish wolf-hound or any sort of dog."

Barnish said that he had none, and stood in the doorway as if that ended the matter. But Cox was pertinacious and said that he would go in and have a look round. For a moment it seemed that Barnish would hinder him, as, of course, he had a right to do, but he stood aside at last.

"'All right,' he said. 'But you people in your uniforms, you upset women, you know.'"

And certainly when Cox pushed his way into the kitchen he saw a very frightened woman. But there was no dog, though he looked into the cellar to find him. Cox did not go upstairs. First, because the stairs weren't visible from the kitchen. They were behind a door at the end of a corridor. Second, if the animal were locked up anywhere, it would be in the outbuildings. Cox searched the outbuildings beyond the arch, with Barnish and his wife treading upon his heels, and it had none of the pleasure of a treasure-hunt. He was very glad to make sure that there was no dog upon the premises, get upon his bicycle again—this last the Inspector underlined with a formal little bow to Mr. Ricardo—and report at headquarters.

"Cox wasn't comfortable about his visit to Arkwright's," Lance continued. "There was something about the two Barnishes which he didn't understand—something which gave him gooseflesh, he said, and Cox isn't the man to get queer fancies. Then, at four o'clock to-day, you telephoned."

Inspector Lance walked to the door.

"You would like to see Arkwright's, no doubt," he said.

Hanaud directed an imploring glance towards Maltby, and Maltby understood and replied accordingly:

"Very much, if it could be early."

"We'll make it eight o'clock if you like, and you could catch a fast train up to London at nine-fifteen."

Thus it was arranged. Hanaud stood looking into the fire after Lance had gone with a curious smile breaking the composure of his face and then vanishing and recurring again. He was remembering the speech he had made to Mrs. Leete in Paris, and how pat this example had come upon it. A plot was worked out, watertight, undiscoverable, with its sequences and rehearsals; a foggy night, a kidnapping, a lonely farm where, sooner or later, release could be arranged, unless, happiest consequence of all, madness solved all the troubles and made truth an acrostic which none could ever read. But for two small accidents! An aeroplane crossing the sky each night above the prison house at midnight, and a sheep-killing dog which brought a policeman from the town.

"No doubt," said Hanaud, "Barnish and his wife thought the game was up, the dog licence an excuse for the snoop, and, one, two, they get rid of their prisoner and disappear. The little accidents one cannot foresee, they burst open perfect crimes."

But the morning was advancing, and no one, not even Mr. Ricardo, was willing to listen further.

"Yes," said Maltby curtly. "Rouse and two people who walk a mile or so home from a country dance. And a newsboy sent back one morning for a fresh batch of papers who passes a door three times, and sees it shut, and finds it open, and next time it's shut again. Oh, yes! Suppose we go to bed!"

To bed they went. And a few minutes after eight that morning they were trampling, with a little more noise than perhaps was necessary, about the squalid house and precincts of Arkwright's Farm. Why they were noisy, no one of them was quite sure, no one would have admitted it if he had been sure. Horror and fear and suffering had left behind them in that house an air which was heavy and charged with dim threats. For no reason, each one looked quickly over his shoulder when he had passed a door, or, if he turned a sharp corner, made shift to return upon his steps in silence to see whether he was followed. And in one room the three of them halted with one accord. It was a bare room with no furniture in it but a deal table in a squat tower with a broken window over the back yard and a little hatch upon the corridor.

All eagerly agreed with Lance that it was the service hatch which had turned their suspicions into certainties. But it was nothing of the kind. As they stood in the wretched room, they knew that they had reached the end of their search. There was an oppression which weighed upon their brains, a cruelty which clutched at their hearts until they hurt. Maltby stepped forward, but very quietly, like a churchwarden in a church, and, pulling forward one of the shutters from the clip which held it to the outside wall, showed them where the screws had fixed it to the window frame.

" Yes," he said, as though he were confirming something they were all agreed about, " it was here."

" Yes, the room is hateful," said a voice which Ricardo hardly recognised as Hanaud's, so quiet and yet so respectful was the sound of it. But no more was said. Inspector Lance was looking at his watch.

" If you gentlemen want to catch the nine-fifteen——"
and Hanaud started again into animation.

" I think we do," said Maltby, and to Hanaud : " You
agree ? "

But Hanaud's face was so smoothed out with relief
that no words were needed from him. He uttered them
none the less, and they remained for a long while stark
in Mr. Ricardo's thoughts.

" What I see and smell and touch through all this
house, and, above all, in this empty room, is cruelty.
We ought to be quick."

Chapter 27

SHATTERING QUESTIONS

" THE first thing to do always," said Maltby, " is to
put people in their proper places."

" The difficulty is to know what are their proper
places," Hanaud complained.

" Well, I know mine," said Septimus. " I am Chairman of the Dagger Line of Steamships, and my first
business is to know what sort of hash my young directors
have made of my business during my weeks of absence."

He pressed the butt of his cigar down in an ashtray
and looked towards Maltby. " And perhaps you, Superintendent, could find time to come with me and learn
whether any demand for ransom has been made ? "

" Ransom ? Ah ! That is an idea. Yes," Hanaud
cried with a bright look, as though the suggestion of a
ransom was one of those original strokes of genius which
suddenly illuminate a mystery. " You will go to your
main office in Leadandall Street ? "

" Leadenhall Street," Mr. Crottle corrected.

" Yes, so I said," Hanaud replied. " Then if I come with you, perhaps, Mr. Crottle, you will tell a clerk to find a cabin for me on a nice big ship to Cherbourg ? "

Mr. Crottle turned with a little disappointment in his face. " You are returning ? "

Hanaud shrugged his shoulders.

" You sail on Fridays. I remember that you said so."

" Yes, but to-day—this morning——" Maltby exclaimed in perplexity, " you spoke very seriously."

" I am a serious person," said Hanaud.

" You spoke some other words," Maltby hesitated to repeat them in Mr. Crottle's presence. " And after them, ' We ought to be quick.' "

" So, you see, I shall only have a few hours to roll with my friend Ricardo."

For a moment there was the silence of stupefaction. But Mr. Ricardo was an expert interpreter :

" He means to loaf," he explained ; but it was not the alluring picture of Hanaud and Ricardo rolling in each others arms across Grosvenor Square which had brought Maltby so sharply up. He and Hanaud were staring at one another. Quite slowly Hanaud nodded thrice, and the doubt cleared away from Maltby's face.

" Very well."

Now, all these vague sentences and vaguer glances which had been spoken and exchanged since Hanaud had asked Septimus for a passage to Cherbourg were intelligible enough to Mr. Ricardo. The affair would finish before to-night. The whole affair. Horbury as well as Crottle. That was clear. But the conversation up to that moment was a different matter altogether.

It took place after luncheon in Ricardo's dining-room. The three—Maltby, Hanaud and Ricardo—had got back to the house to find Septimus up and dressed and impatiently walking an imaginary bridge in Mr. Ricardo's library; and whilst Julius was ordering luncheon and the appropriate wine to go with it, and causing as much delay as was possible, the other two had some kind of a conference with Septimus Crottle. From that conference resulted undoubtedly Crottle's proposal to present himself at once at his head office with Maltby, and Hanaud's decision to seek at the same place a passage to Cherbourg. The conversation, however, seemed natural and spontaneous enough, but there was no debate, and to Mr. Ricardo, who liked now and then to enliven his language with a slang word, it all sounded phoney. It gave him the impression that he was being deliberately excluded from the climax. He didn't like that at all.

"After all, where would they have been without me?" he asked of himself indignantly. He had noticed things every now and then. He had been the first to distinguish Arkwright's Farm, hadn't he? And here they were leaving him at home. In fact, here was Septimus holding out his hand to him.

"I thank you very much for your hospitality," he said. "From the office I shall go home to Portman Square, where I shall look forward to the pleasure of seeing you."

It was almost worse to hear Maltby observing with a kindly nod: "You will, perhaps, let me disturb you again when we have put our heads together with the young directors?"

Mr. Ricardo, indeed, was almost in tears. An outsider, he! The mere caretaker of the corner house! And at that, as Crottle and Maltby were going out of the door, the voice of Hanaud fell upon his ears like balm upon an open wound.

"Let them go first in a taxi. We follow in the Rolls Royce. It will be easy."

"But it's in the garage," cried Ricardo in despair.

Hanaud shook his head with a beaming smile.

" I took the liberty. I spoke to Thompson. It was not my place. You forgive ? "

" But I am grateful," Ricardo explained ; and the taxi was still in sight across the square when the Rolls Royce slid noiselessly to the door. It was not Mr. Ricardo's habit to look with any complacency upon intruders who took upon themselves to ride his small thunders and direct his storms, but he rejoiced that they were easily able to keep the taxicab within their vision.

" It is the fault of Monsieur Crottle," Hanaud explained, rather nobly to Mr. Ricardo's thinking. " He cannot forgive me for that I prefer the peppermint and the cigarette."

Mr. Ricardo must answer nobility with nobility.

" No, no, my friend, blame me and Maltby. It is not formal and correct that I should be here."

And so, disputing gracefully, they drove up to the door of the Dagger Line in Leadenhall Street on the number plate of the taxi ; and Mr. Ricardo stepped nimbly from the car to the annoyance of Superintendent Maltby. But he said nothing. For Septimus walked straight from the street into the big front office.

By the door a commissionaire sat at a small desk and at the sight of Septimus he uttered a cry. Then he rose to his feet and stood with his hand at the salute. And that was more than enough. Behind a long counter which ran from wall to wall there were many desks. From each of those desks there rose a man with some warm exclamation of welcome in his mouth. They crowded to the long counter. One or two of the chief clerks held out their hands, and as Septimus, for once in a way openly moved, grasped them and said with a smile of mock surprise, " Well, upon my word, I seem to be popular with my officers," there broke forth laughter and rapping on the long mahogany board, and a lift of voices which were obviously going to end in a rousing chorus of " For he's a jolly good fellow."

But the welcome never rose to that height. For, just when all Leadenhall Street was about to ring with a celebration which really belonged more to Lloyds across the way, a bell rang and an angry voice shouted through the room on a loud-speaker :

" I can't hear myself speak."

Septimus stepped back and all the joyous clamour died suddenly. Mr. Ricardo noticed a change in Crottle's face which baffled his understanding. It moved in a second from good humour to an anger so violent as to pass belief. That so much fire could blaze in old eyes, or that an old face, carved by time, could twist into a shape so malignant, was the strangest of metamorphoses. It was the flash of a moment, like some swift scene in a moving picture, so swift that it was almost invisible, but so vivid that it left a memory more real and complete than a mountain of detail could have done.

Crottle lowered his head then, so that none could see his face, and stood as still as a statue in a silence which had grown constrained and somehow rather alarming. Then, in a quiet voice, he said :

" That complaint came from my room, I think."

The head clerk flushed and stammered.

" Yes, sir. They moved in there."

" They ? "

" Mr. George and Mr. James."

" I see."

It was more than a trifle shocking to Mr. Ricardo to see how deeply the old man was moved by this encroachment of his nephews. They had been tactless, culpably tactless, too ready to assume that Septimus's chair was empty and too quick to share it. The business of the Dagger Line had to go on, that was evident, but they could have controlled it for a few weeks without changing their offices. They wanted all the trappings at once It was not very clever. At the same time, the old man's rage was quite extravagant.

"I'm glad I didn't serve under him," was one of Ricardo's thoughts, and, "Upon my word, Rosalind was quite right to run out," another. For still Septimus dared not show them his face and, though his body was quiet, his voice shook.

"Well," he said at last, "it's a good rule to take the first of the tide. Only the tide don't always run true," and in an effort to smile with good humour he contrived the ugliest grimace which Ricardo had ever seen.

A clerk lifted a flap in the counter.

"I'll tell the young gentlemen that you have returned, sir," he said, and at once Septimus stopped him.

"You won't, indeed," Septimus replied; and now there was some pleasure in his voice, a rather acid pleasure. He laughed. "We'll surprise them. You, too, Mr. Ricardo. I'm glad that we didn't leave you behind after all."

Septimus was chuckling with enjoyment. School-boyish, perhaps, and a grim sort of schoolboyishness at that, Ricardo reflected. Septimus was preparing his surprise with all the dramatic effects and an audience into the bargain. He would relish his little triumph, but Ricardo would have bet a large slice of his fortune that not a glimpse would Crottle give to either of his heirs of the misery and torture which he had endured at Arkwright's farm.

"Come," said Septimus, and he led the way into a passage at the side of the main office.

"The first door's my room," he said, stopping before it. "The next door is theirs. You'll be able, in their room, Monsieur Hanaud, to select your cabin to Cherbourg."

He looked about him to make sure that his audience

was complete, and then gently opened the door and stepped inside. The two nephews were seated opposite to each other at a big leather-padded table, George with his back to the door and James with his face to it. But his face was bent upon his papers and George did not turn.

" I didn't ring," said James without looking up. " Mr. George objected very properly to the noise."

" No doubt my welcome home was a little obstreperous," said Septimus, and at the sound of his voice James dropped his papers and sprang to his feet. He was as white as a sheet.

" George," he cried sharply. For George had not risen, had not even turned his head, so engrossed was he upon his work.

" I am sorry," he said, looking up towards James. But the attitude and the pallor of his stepbrother's face startled him. He came out of a dream, a dream of ships and cargoes. " What is it ? " he began, and he turned round with a perplexity so marked upon his face that he seemed hardly yet aware of any new big crisis in the affairs of the Dagger Line. But now he saw Septimus standing two feet from him. He reeled back against the desk. His voice rang out in a cry of delight, his face beamed, and if he didn't hold out his hands it was because they clutched the edge of the table behind him to hold him up.

" You, sir ! At last ! Thank Heaven ! We've wanted you ! "

" And my room, too," said Crottle drily—a reply which, to Mr. Ricardo, lowered the whole dignity of this welcome home.

" Well, we had to find our way, sir, through so many complications which you naturally had kept under your own control," George explained apologetically. " You have been away a long time."

" A fortnight," answered Septimus.

" A fortnight, yes," said George. " A long time, sir, for the Dagger Line with a jury-rigged rudder," and he laughed and made a little bow. " We were afraid," he explained again, " that something had happened to you. You were staying . . . ? "

And Septimus took him up in the same cordial tone.

" At Arkwright's Farm. A few miles from Sedgemoor."

" Sedgemoor ? " George repeated with hardly a stammer, and " Sedgemoor," James Crottle repeated again, idiotically. " Why, that's where. . . ."

" Yes, where Monmouth was defeated, wasn't it ? " added George.

Septimus nodded his head.

" I think we might read about it on a Sunday evening. It would make kindlier reading than the history of the Dauphin of France."

" My word, yes," said George Crottle heartily, and Septimus took a step forward.

" By the way," he asked easily, " do either of you remember that we employed a man named Barnish on one of our ships ? "—and at Ricardo's side even Hanaud jumped a little.

James Crottle was obviously troubled, but less by the name, Ricardo would have said, than by the oddity of the question.

" Barnish ? " James echoed, and again " Barnish ? " but on different inflexions.

" Frank Barnish," Septimus repeated and, as George Crottle shook his head, he turned and drew Maltby into the room. " But it doesn't matter. This is Superintendent Maltby of Scotland Yard," he explained. " The Superintendent will see if the staff can turn up his name," and with a pleasant nod he dismissed the Superintendent upon this business. Then, as though he had just noticed Hanaud and Ricardo for the first time, he called them forward.

"Monsieur Hanaud and Mr. Ricardo, you do know. Monsieur Hanaud pays us the compliment of wishing to return to Paris via Cherbourg on one of our ships. If you," and he looked towards Hanaud and Ricardo, "will go into the office which my nephews use as a rule, Jenkins will see what he can do for you."

He waved his hand to the head clerk, who was standing just within the doorway, and then unlatched a communicating door between his office and that of the nephews.

George moved forward.

"I had better see that they are comfortable . . ." he began, but Septimus interrupted him with a laugh.

"Oh, they will only have a minute or so to wait. Jenkins will go along to them. It's obvious from what you said when I first came in that we have a bit of work to do, and the sooner we confer about it, the quicker we'll get it done."

He opened the connecting-door and invited Hanaud and his friend to enter. He shut the door behind them and, seeing that Jenkins had already gone and closed the door upon the passage, he drew up a chair to the table.

"Now let's put our three heads together," he cried, relaxing into some sort of gaiety. Indeed, neither of his two nephews could ever have seen the old man in a more genial mood.

*   *   *   *

There were two tables in this second room. Into a chair by the nearest Hanaud dropped, exhausted with admiration.

"But he is superb," he cried, "absolutely superb ! And it was shattering, mind you, all of it quite shattering. But none the less, he was superb!" and, putting the tips of his fingers to his lips, Hanaud blew a fervent kiss to so glorious a comedian.

Julius Ricardo was inclined to think the applause a little too French and explosive, but he realised that some tribute from himself was due. So he said:

"Yes, he was remarkable, especially after those dreadful days he must have spent at Arkwright's Farm," and he did not notice the open-mouthed stupefaction with which Hanaud received the comment.

It was natural indeed that he should not. For Hanaud was already engaged in a kind of visual catalogue of the room's contents. A big single knee-hole table for James, another like it for George, a filing cabinet, a bookcase in which some Admiralty Guides kept company with some naval almanachs, some chairs, a shelf against the wall, on which stood a chronometer in a mahogany box and—just what Hanaud was looking for.

"Ha!" said he, and he was out of his chair and across the room with that light, swift step, which, after all these years, Ricardo could never quite reconcile with his cumbrous build. Behind the chronometer, on the shelf, was a roll of big charts. And suddenly Ricardo was aware that Hanaud had a pair of fine indiarubber gloves upon his hands. But when he had slipped them on, he had not one idea.

Hanaud lifted the charts carefully from the shelf and brought them over to the table.

"Listen for Jenkins in the passage," he said, "but I think he'll give us time."

Hanaud unrolled the charts and they sprang back into a roll.

"There are some paper weights."

He nodded to two which he had pushed aside—heavy things of bronze and malachite. Under Hanaud's direction, Ricardo placed them, one at each corner of the lower end of the charts. He unrolled the charts again from the bottom and held them flat. The one uppermost was a big chart of the English Channel. Hanaud let it slip from his fingers and it rolled itself again down to the paper weights. The next one was of the Indian Ocean, and the third of the Mediterranean Sea, and the fourth of the Great Barrier Reef on the coast of Australia. They were in no sort of order at all, and from the clean look of them and the speed with which each one rolled itself up the moment it was released, it looked as if they had not been examined for many a day.

Hanaud looked at, and let go, seven of them quickly, and then stopped with a little cry. From the side of the last sheet, so quick to hide its secrets, the corner of another paper was sticking out—and, of course, just at that moment Jenkins must knock upon the passage door.

Hanaud swore, and not his favourite polysyllabic oath.

"Will you stand in front of the table, please, my friend?"

He ran to the door and opened it. But he planted himself in the doorway and thrust his hands in his pockets.

"You can arrange for me? So! That is good. The *Formosa*. On the Friday, to be sure."

Mr. Ricardo, with some surprise, heard Hanaud making his plans, but it was altogether a surprising day for Mr. Ricardo.

"Then you will make out for me a ticket and I pick him up at the desk as I go out. Yes? I thank you. You are the kindness itself." He closed the door upon Jenkins. "And please to keep the snotty nose out of this room for the future."

"Really, really," said Ricardo, who disliked such phrases. Monsieur Hanaud, on the other hand, was radiant because he had used this one so appositely.

" It is not a pleasant word ? " he asked.

" It is not," said Mr. Ricardo with severity.

Hanaud nodded his head vigorously once or twice.

" I thought so. It was used upon me once in my early days by an English chauffeur who thought I was examining too inquisitively the interior of his good lady's motor-car. However, work, not words—how often do our good statesmen tell us so ! "

Hanaud was again at the table. He uncurled the seventh map and there, lying upon the centre of it was a much smaller chart with, here and there, pin-points marked upon it.

" Do you see ? " he asked in a low voice. " Do you see the corners where it has been stretched out and fixed by drawing-pins to a board ? "

" Yes," said Ricardo. " I do."

It was a small chart of the western seaboard of Europe ; the southern coastline of Spain, Gibraltar, Portugal, the Bay of Biscay and the English Channel.

" Look where the pins were set. Cadiz first, then round on the west at Lisbon, next up at Vigo. *El Rey* had landed her undesirables in Spain and Portugal. Then straight across the Bay to Brest, where she discharges her French load. Then across to the Start, just after she made her number. Do you remember Foster, Horbury's clerk ? On the afternoon of the night when he died, Horbury, reading in the *Evening Standard* that *El Rey* had made her number at Lloyd's station at Prawle Point at six in the morning, stuck in his little black pin with the white top there, at the Start lighthouse, just by, and chanced a final one opposite to Selsea Bill—see ?— which he reckoned *El Rey* to have reached just at that moment."

" *El Rey* ? " exclaimed Mr. Ricardo, staring at the map. He remembered very clearly that rusty old iron boat in the dim of the morning floundering amidst a welter of white foam at the end of the bowsprit of *Agamemnon*.

"And here, just beyond Start Point, you picked up the passenger with the black rim round his ankle."

"Yes—Devisher," he cried.

"Bryan Devisher," Hanaud agreed.

"At last we know," Ricardo exclaimed, "the murderer of Daniel Horbury."

Hanaud choked suddenly and swallowed and came to himself. He made a low bow.

"As your proverb says. *The costumier is always right.*"

But Hanaud had not yet finished with the chart. Whilst talking to Jenkins he had slipped off a glove in his pocket, and he began to press the ungloved fingers of that hand upon the chart.

"Now yours, please !"

"Mine ? "

Mr. Ricardo hesitated, wondering whether or no he was condoning or implicating himself in some great crime. But Hanaud seized his hand and dabbed it down upon the paper in one place and in another.

"There ! " he said, and he began to roll up the charts again with great care. "They must look just as they did.'

"They ? " said Mr. Ricardo in a hushed voice. "Yes. But what have we done ? "

Hanaud carried the roll back to the shelf and meticulously replaced it behind the chronometer.

"We ? " he asked. "Why, we have left our evidence quite beyond all challenge that we saw the Horbury's chart with the pin-pricks, slipped, as we expected to find it, in a sheaf of other charts in the office of the younger Mr. Crottles.

Mr. Ricardo stepped back.

"Oh ! " he whispered.

He was in a maze. He was also conscious, proudly conscious, that the presentiment which had so stirred him at Lezardrieux was true. He was engaged in the elucidation of a great and mysterious crime.

" Oh ! " he said again.

He looked at the door which communicated with the office of Septimus Crottle. He pointed towards it.

" You did not expect that you would be interrupted from that room ? "

" No," Hanaud answered. " I thought that Mr. Septimus would prevent it."

So this was the explanation of those secret conferences before luncheon at the corner house. It was reckoned a possibility, perhaps more than a possibility, that the small chart which had disappeared from White Barn on the night of Horbury's death might be found in a roll of charts in one particular office of the Line. It had been arranged that Hanaud should have time to search for it.

" It was one of the nephews, then," said Ricardo in a whisper.

Hanaud did not pretend to misunderstand him.

" Which ? " he asked.

" Why not both ? " asked Ricardo.

" Why not ? " Hanaud echoed.

" We must find out," Ricardo urged.

" I think we shall to-night," replied Hanaud. " Now we ought to say that the ticket is arranged."

He went to the communicating door and knocked upon it and entered. Septimus was seated at the head of the table discussing genially with his young partners the affairs of the Line. Was it possible that those two young men, or one of them, had murdered Horbury and planned the sequestration of Septimus, and that Septimus knew of it at this moment ? Ricardo could hardly believe it.

255

" It is fixed ? " cried Septimus. " We carry the great detective to Cherbourg, do we ? "

Septimus is untrue to Septimus, Mr. Ricardo reflected. There's something in it. Aloud, Septimus continued :

" That is good news to compensate for our bad news."

" Ah ! " Hanaud replied. " My sincere regrets. It is not, I hope, serious."

Septimus was obviously not overwhelmed.

" Not very serious, but troublesome, as all new arrangements are. Preedy has left us."

The statement took both Hanaud and Ricardo by surprise. Preedy ? It was almost an effort to remember him. Of such small importance had he seemed to be in the great affairs of the Line.

" Why has he gone, Mr. Crottle ? " Ricardo asked, and, with a touch of malice in his tone, Septimus answered :

" He saw the red light."

Both George and James ducked their heads a little over their papers.

" He is in trouble with his lungs. He is leaving—I think, George, that you said he had left—for Switzerland, and will be away for two years."

" That is unfortunate," said Hanaud, and Septimus agreed.

" Preedy was a very useful ally. These Barnishes, for instance. It looks as if they had got away. But Preedy would have laid his hands upon them. Well, it can't be helped ! I shall see you at my house to-night " ; and with a wave of his hand Septimus dismissed them.

Ricardo had entered the corridor by the second door. He saw Hanaud emerge from Septimus's room, close the door, and lean against it.

" Preedy ! I never gave a thought to him ! " he muttered, his mind disturbed. " Should I have ? For what reason ? "

Although he only communed with himself, his last question reached Ricardo's ears and he answered it :

" Preedy had a special gift."

Hanaud answered : " Yes, to be sure."

They walked slowly along the corridor to the main office. Ricardo had, in fact, answered Hanaud's question better than either of them knew.

At the counter in the outmost office Hanaud asked for and received his ticket by the s.s. *Formosa* to Cherbourg. And that again stirred Mr. Ricardo indescribably. Hanaud, who hated the sea, who never travelled to England except by the shortest passage between Calais and Dover, meant actually to sail on an ocean-going steamship to Cherbourg. Oh, certainly Mr. Ricardo was in the way of great events.

Chapter 28

HANAUD BORROWS ROLLS ROYCE NO. 2

SEPTIMUS arrived in a small car, with a constable on the seat by the side of the driver, at the corner house half an hour after Hanaud and Ricardo. Maltby had sent the car for him, and it was as well, Ricardo reflected. For it was no longer the Septimus whom anger had inspired to establish his old authority and sow confusion amongst his partners. He was tired ; the fire had gone from him ; he was that haggard and humbled man on the bench above the Fairmile.

" Maltby told me that he would be here," he complained in a weak, querulous voice, as he was shown by Thompson into the library.

" A cup of tea, sir," Ricardo suggested, and the old

man had hardly raised the cup to his lips before Maltby
hurried in.

" I have some news," he said as Ricardo handed a cup
to him.

" Good ? " Hanaud asked.

" It fits in."

He leaned forwards to Septimus.

" Frank Barnish was the bo'sun of your first oil-driven
ship."

" The *Acropolis*. Was he ? " exclaimed Septimus with
a sudden smile. But the smile was for that adventure
in new ships rather than for her bo'sun.

" Yes, sir. He gave trouble, drank too much, resented
orders, and, once the voyage was over, was not signed
on again. It was a grievance which he didn't forget.
He had the reputation of being a revengeful fellow and,
though a capable seaman, never held up a job for long.
It must have been a blessing for him when he was put
in to Arkwright's Farm."

" That wouldn't have been a long job, either," said
Septimus. " More than that, it wasn't meant to be a
long job."

And he sat for a moment or two shaking. He was
back in that shuttered room at Arkwright's.

" Come, sir, that's all over," Maltby declared. " We
are looking after you now."

" Yes, yes," Septimus cried eagerly, and he caught
Maltby by the arm. " I have great confidence in you
Maltby. You were to give me some instructions, I think."

He asked for them rather pitifully.

" I think you should go home, sir. There is a constable in the front of your car. There will be another
outside your house. I shall be obliged if you will refuse
to discuss your absence at all, but just take everything
easily. If you will leave it all to us, we will keep in
touch with you."

Words—and words which meant nothing at all—but they satisfied Septimus. He rose from his chair with some difficulty and went downstairs on Maltby's arm. Ricardo, at the window, watched the car drive away in the darkness. In old age, he thought, how swift the change can be from great authority to exhaustion and how permanent! It was the horror which Septimus had suffered that filled his mind now, no longer the audacity of the crime nor its authors. Maltby spoke at his shoulder in attune with his thoughts:

"It's a new family that the old gentleman will find in Portman Square. One of the daughters ran out, did she? Well they've all run out now. New clothes, a theatre or two, friends to entertain. A little cruel it sounds, perhaps. But after those years of submission and boredom and orders and what not, to be expected, what? Pretty natural. I don't think he'll round them up again. Patriarchs don't go down in the twentieth century. Or do they?"

"And Miss Agatha?" Hanaud asked suddenly from the room behind them. But Maltby merely shrugged his shoulders in surprise. He had no answer to that question; and now that Septimus had been packed off home, he was anxious and hurried. Hanaud pointed to the chairs.

"In a dry we finish everything."

Maltby was puzzled but took a seat.

"He means in a sec," Ricardo explained, and took another. Maltby nodded and turned to Hanaud.

"So you have found something?"

"That chart."

Maltby sat back in his chair.

"The chart with the black pins which Horbury brought from his office to White Barn on Thursday, August the twenty-sixth."

"And which Devisher took away?" said Maltby.

" But he didn't take it away," cried Hanaud. " We found it this afternoon slipped into a greal roll of charts in the office of the young Crottles."

" You are sure ? " Maltby exclaimed. He was more astounded, more troubled than Ricardo expected.

" So you see. The affair of Horbury and the affair of Crottle—they are one."

It was Hanaud's old point once more enforced upon unwilling ears.

" There is the vanishing of Devisher, too," Hanaud continued, ticking off the points on his fingers.

" Still . . ." Maltby doubted.

" The man without money and without friends. There is his reappearance, besides."

" I know, but . . ."

" There is the telephone which was lifted and replaced. There is the blotting-book. There is the door which was locked."

Hanaud was rushing back through the events of that night of death, Thursday, August the twenty-sixth.

Still Maltby was not convinced, though what course Hanaud was urging upon him, Ricardo could not tell.

" And there was another night. Oh, if you had been there you would not doubt—when, in a deep silence, a sigh was breathed."

Maltby stared between his knees at the carpet.

" There is not enough," he said, shaking his head.

" Not when we add to-day the finding of the chart ? "

Maltby rose ponderously to his feet, whilst Hanaud watched his every movement with hopeful, eager eyes.

" We must be quick," he said.

Maltby nodded his great head.

" This is our one night. After the old man's appearance at his office, to-night there will be action," Hanaud argued.

Maltby flung back his head and swore.

"If only we had the Barnishes!" he cried.

"The Barnishes!" cried Hanaud in almost a scream of disdain. "They are nothing."

Maltby frowned gloomily at the Frenchman. A man who had to decide between peace and war might look like that. So might a youth who had to choose between a blonde and a brunette. He heaved a great sigh. He made a great resolve—to hesitate again.

"I must go to the Yard," he said, and as disappointment deepened on Hanaud's face: "I shall make all the arrangements, however—you know." He nodded portentously. "And I shall come back. Let me see!"

Ricardo interrupted.

"But, my dear Hanaud, you are dining with Septimus. He said so in his office."

Hanaud swept the interruption away.

"Comedy, my dear friend. The false invitation which leaves me free. It was arranged."

"I shall come back with full authority," said Maltby, his breast swelling, "but . . ." and he relapsed again into doubt. "A little before eight, then. That will give us time—if we move," he said, looking at his watch.

"Then perhaps you will dine here?" said Mr. Ricardo, and Hanaud took him up at once.

"Yes, yes, we will dine! But not the big dinner, no. Some hors d'œuvre, perhaps, the joint, the sweet, the coffee. Admirable."

"Really, really." Mr. Ricardo addressed dumbly the vacant air. "Do I keep the inn, The Policemen's Rest?"

But Maltby was clattering down the stairs, and Hanaud was urging him to hurry. Hanaud came back to the library and dropped into a chair, limp and dejected.

"It is but and but and but with that man!" he exclaimed moodily. "He will never—no, never—come up and be scratched."

Whether Mr. Ricardo was still contemplating himself as the appointed innkeeper to the police, who shall say? He cried indignantly, for he had the strongest possible views upon this necessity of the times:

"I bet you he has been vaccinated over and over again."

Hanaud stared at him.

"The vaccination? You talk of this at this hour!"

He danced in a rage about the room and suddenly slipped, tame as a cat, to Ricardo's side.

"It is not yet six of the clock, no. And at the moment when I most need his friendship, I gibe. Yes, I gibe fatally!"

Smooth, soft words, and the voice so remorseful, so tender.

"What do you want now?" Ricardo asked laughing, though he did not wish to laugh.

"The Rolls Royce."

"What!"

"Not the Rolls Royce No. 1. No, no, my friend! I ask for no such enormity. But the Rolls Royce No. 2. the wee, wee one."

He smiled like a child asking for his father's second gold watch and confident that he would get it.

"I have no wee, wee car," Mr. Ricardo said firmly.

But it was clear to him that Hanaud was passionately anxious to go somewhere. After all, he wanted help.

"I doubt if I shall have a chauffeur waiting," he objected. "I have given no orders."

"A chauffeur!" cried Hanaud, and he thumped his chest. "I, Hanaud, I am the best chauffeur in Europe."

There was no answer to this statement, except the most direct of negatives; and Ricardo had no authority to make it.

"Come!" he said.

He led Hanaud to the back of the house and to the

garage in the Mews. He threw open the doors whilst Hanaud climbed into the car.

" You go to Scotland Yard ? " he asked.

" Perhaps," said Hanaud, fiddling with the instruments.

" And you will drive on the wrong side of the road ? "

" I will."

Ricardo stood at the side and saw Rolls Royce No. 2 dash out into the street, scatter a handful of people in the roadway and disappear.

" It may be that he is the best driver in Europe, but there are no signs of it," he said to himself. However, what did it matter, even if Rolls Royce No. 2 became a scrap heap ? Agitations were here. The world was bubbling. Great criminals sitting at their ease would feel the handcuffs on their wrists. If only Maltby had the courage. " But, but . . ." Mr. Ricardo could take it to his soul with pride that he had never said " But . . . but . . ." when Rolls Royce No. 2 had been commandeered. He had let it go to a man who must drive on the wrong side of the road, if he was to survive.

Ricardo shut the garage door and returned to the front of his house. He ordered the short dinner which Hanaud demanded. It was to be on the table at eight, with the Burgundy—say the Musigny, a lighter wine and more fit to precede a nocturnal expedition. Coffee to follow and perhaps a glass of Armagnac. He did not want fingers to tremble on the trigger of a pistol ! Mr. Ricardo waited. The clocks chimed—the hour of seven, the half hour which followed ; and Hanaud tumbled into the room, his dress dishevelled, his face dirty, his hands scratched and bleeding, yet with so proud a look of conquest in his face that Mr. Ricardo thought of Napoleon at Marengo, and, being English, of Wellington on the mountain of Bussaco. His eyes sparkled, his arms were spread out in an ecstasy. But Ricardo noticed, above all, the lines of dirt upon his face, the torn collar, the blood upon the knuckles, the dust upon the clothes.

" You have had a smash ! " he cried.

" No, I am not hurt," Hanaud answered, " but I thank you for the thought." It was not for him to recognise that Ricardo's thought was for Rolls Royce No. 2. " It was nothing Just once I was on the right side of the road and I meet a taxicab. But I was quick—oh, I surprise myself. The driver he threw a name at me— the name—not nice. I forgive him with a wave of the hand, and I drove on. I keep on the wrong side of the road carefully, and Rolls Royce No. 2, she has the right to be proud. Look, it is seven-thirty. We have a quarter of an hour before Maltby arrives."

" Yes," said Ricardo eagerly. He was to hear, no doubt, the story of Rolls Royce No. 2's adventures. " Over a glass of Porto, you shall . . ."

But he got no further.

" But first the wash ! " Hanaud exclaimed. " I disgust myself. I change the clothes. But not the smoking. Nor for you, my friend. It will not be but but Maltby, but Maltby, winner of the Derby Round. You shall see ! To-night we prowl ! "

Hanaud was half-way up the stairs to his bedroom before he had finished talking. Ricardo delayed following his example for just the time it took to order Rolls Royce No. 1 to be ready at the door by half-past eight. Washed and dressed in inconspicuous clothes, the two men descended into the study with five minutes to spare before the time of Maltby's arrival.

" A Porto," Ricardo cried gaily as he filled Hanaud's glass. " For me the Manzanilla ! "

There was just time, he reflected, for him to hear the story of his friend's adventures and the reason for all his excitement.

" There's something I want to tell you very much,"

said Hanaud, as he lit a cigarette and sipped his Porto.

"Yes, you would wish it!" cried Ricardo. "Such old compères as we are," and with a most unusual gesture he clinked his glass against Hanaud's. But, alas! he was to be disappointed.

"There was much misunderstanding. I was hurt. 'He makes a jest of me,' I said, whereas Maltby explained that his mistake was to imagine that I understood English which, as you know, I do."

Ricardo sank back. He was to be told, after all, nothing more than the tale of some ridiculous squabble which he and Maltby had in olden days. He could have groaned.

"But the first day, when I came on Gravot's account and dined with Maltby in Soho, all was put right."

"So you told me," Ricardo answered acidly. And he had lent the man his Rolls Royce, too!

"But I did not tell you the story of the misunderstanding." Hanaud leaned forward smiling, so urgently did he feel that he must tell it.

"Fire away," said Ricardo with resignation. " I'm here to be shot."

"The fact is," he said to himself, " I'm not audience enough for the real thing. He wants Maltby and myself to be paralysed together."

Hanaud fired away accordingly.

"There was a dead Frenchman in Golden Square with a bottle beside him . . ."

That was as far as he got in this never-to-be-told story, when the door was opened and Maltby announced.

Chapter 29

THE LETTER TO SEPTIMUS

THEY stood about the fireplace, Ricardo upon one side, Maltby on the other, and Hanaud, serene, masterful, in the middle. The Manzanilla and the Porto were forgotten. It was the scene of three men, Ricardo realised ; the inevitable great scene of the plays of Sardou ; and this one stage-managed—produced was the modern word, wasn't it ?—by Hanaud, chief dramatist of the Sûreté Française.

" I have a present for you," said Hanaud, smiling.

" There is only one present," Maltby grumbled.

" And here it is," said Hanaud.

Slowly he brought out from the inner pocket of his jacket an oilskin wrapper fastened with a button. He offered it to Maltby with a bow. For a moment Maltby stared at it. Then he raised his eyes to Hanaud's face. Then he pounced upon the present. He carried it to a small table farther back from the fire, and the group of three was formed again about it.

Maltby unbuttoned the wrapper and took from it a folder of morocco leather, which might hold perhaps a button-hook, a penknife, a nail file, a pair of tweezers, such as a woman travelling light might take in her suitcase. This he unwrapped and disclosed, folded lengthwise on the washleather lining, a letter in an envelope, so folded that the seal was not cracked.

With a little cry Maltby tossed the morocco case aside and flattened the letter upon the table under the palm of his hand. It seemed that he was afraid to reveal even to himself the name of him to whom the letter was written, so long he looked from one face to another, so firmly he held the envelope flat upon the table. At last he lifted up his hand sharply and there was the name for all three of them to read :

"Septimus Crottle, Esq.,"

and the address in Portman Square.

On a writing-table by the window a tortoiseshell paper-knife with a silver handle was gleaming. Maltby fetched it and pulled up a chair.

"Let us see where we are!" he said, tapping the letter with the tortoiseshell blade. "This is presumably the letter which Horbury took away from his office on the afternoon of Thursday, August the twenty-sixth."

"With the chart," cried Hanaud.

"Yes," Maltby agreed.

"Which we found this afternoon in the office of the younger Crottles," said Hanaud.

Again Maltby agreed. He took the paperknife and slit the top of the envelope.

"It ought to have gone to Mr. Septimus before I opened it," he said remorsefully.

"But since you have opened it," Hanaud suggested, and he had no twinges of conscience.

"We might as well read——" said Maltby doubtfully.

"What that old rogue Daniel Horbury had to say to him. Yes, yes!" cried Hanaud, and he turned to Ricardo. "You agree, my friend? To be sure. Yes."

"I think," said Ricardo, "that you are the most lawless person in the world. Still, I agree."

And Maltby, with his forefinger and his thumb, slipped out of the envelope a letter with two enclosures folded within it. He flattened his hand upon the enclosures as they dropped on to the table.

"Horbury's letter first, I think."

"Yes, yes," said Hanaud, and though he sat upright

at the table, his feet were dancing with impatience upon the carpet.

Maltby read it through without the omission of a word. It was written in Horbury's dutiful style. He was a public man and a Member of Parliament. His first thought was that his obligations demanded in no uncertain manner that he should communicate the enclosures at once to the Crown Prosecutor for such action as he deemed fit. On the other hand, he could not shut his eyes to the high prestige of the Dagger Line and its importance as a commercial asset to the country. On the whole, then, he had determined, though with some heavy doubts, that the patriotic thing to do was to send the two documents straight to Mr. Septimus Crottle, as Chairman of the Line, and leave them in his hands. He remained Mr. Crottle's obedient servant.

" Send them straight, to be sure," said Maltby with a grunt. " So he keeps them in the secret drawer of his desk. The damned old blackmailer ! "

He dropped the letter with disgust upon the table and took up the two enclosures. As he read them his face grew very grave, and he nodded his head twice or three times to Hanaud.

" Yes, these are enough," he said.

The first was a receipt for three thousand pounds made out to Kapitän von Kluckner, Military Attaché, and signed George Crottle. The second was an undertaking that s.s. *Harold*, a freight carrier of the Dagger Line, would call at a certain port in the Adriatic Sea and take on board two hundred kilogrammes of hashish and five hundred grammes of heroin from Sofia for Egypt. And this undertaking, too, was addressed to Kapitän von Kluckner and signed by George Crottle.·

Of the three, Ricardo alone was plunged in confusion. George ? George Crottle, drug-runner in the pay of a foreign Embassy ? The kidnapper, then, of old Septimus ? George, with his charm and his slim figure and his bright fair hair. It was not possible ! But Hanaud and Maltby kept exchanging glances as though they met at last on friendly ground. Maltby packed Horbury's letter and enclosures away in his pocket-book ; and Thompson at the door announced that dinner was served.

It was a meal taken in haste and seasoned with little conversation. The presence of Thompson prevented all discussion but that of world affairs, and nobody at the table was for the moment interested in them. Coffee was served in the dining-room. An extraordinary habit, Mr. Ricardo reflected, that of drinking black coffee and liqueurs after meals when obviously there was work waiting to be done. Cigars were on the way round, too. Then we shall never get off ! A small fellow for Maltby —that was sensible. Hanaud only ate his own black cigarettes. Well, he might as well smoke a small cigar himself and, like Maltby and his friend, sip this very seductive yellow Chartreuse. Even Mr. Ricardo realised that there was no need for hurry, and he was inclined to resent the strokes of a nearby clock. Maltby counted the strokes.

" Nine," said he.

Hanaud looked at his watch.

" Nine," said he.

For both men the search was ended, conclusions had been reached, action was now to be taken, peace of mind had come. They might be wrong, but the question was for others to decide, not for them.

Thompson entered.

" Sergeant Hughes is in the hall, sir."

" Sergeant Hughes ! " Ricardo repeated. For some vague reason the name was familiar.

" We wanted a young man," said Maltby. " I got him moved up to the Yard."

He remembered now the young officer in uniform who took notes at White Barn.

" Why ? " he asked.

" I liked his cheek," Maltby replied with a grin. " Shall we go ? "

Sergeant Hughes saluted as the three men descended the stairs.

" All quiet, Sergeant ? "

" Up till I left, sir. There's a journey proposed for to-night."

" So I supposed," said Maltby.

" But," and Sergeant Hughes looked puzzled, " it's a short journey with no luggage."

" Just as far as White Barn and back," Hanaud suggested, and Maltby smiled.

" Yes, that criminal stays and fights," and Ricardo had reason afterwards to reflect how wrong these great men could sometimes be.

A small black police car stood in front of the Rolls Royce.

" Hadn't I better give you and Sergeant Hughes a lift ? We shall otherwise leave you behind," said Mr. Ricardo grandly.

Hanaud sniggered—a malicious snigger. Maltby answered.

" We don't look much to be sure, by the side of your elephant, Mr. Ricardo. But we can go—I don't say faster than the wind, for the wind's quite out of date as a comparison, but faster than an empty army lorry in a crowded street " ; and he doubled himself up into the black car with Sergeant Hughes, whilst Hanaud and Ricardo climbed into the elephant. There was a man in plain clothes by the driver and no address was given. The cars started, kept their distance like ships in line ahead, and they did, to Hanaud's delight, pass an empty army lorry in the Brompton Road.

In a quieter road the cars stopped ; and as the occu-
pants alighted, a uniformed constable saluted Maltby
and spoke a few words to him. Maltby beckoned to the
rest of his party and went forward. On the right-hand
side of the road a crescent of small and attractive Regency
houses curved about a garden. The houses were lit up
for the most part and the blinds drawn. But in front
of one of them a small car stood with its lamps unlit.

Suddenly there was a cluster of the uniformed police
about a gate which led through the garden to a front-
door. The room to the right of the round white stone
arch of the portico was lit. Maltby walked up to the
door and rang the bell. The shrill sound of it rang
through the house, but there was no answer, no movement at all in that lighted room. Ricardo had in his
mind the picture of a man there suddenly stricken by
that bell as by a stroke of paralysis. There was not a
lift of the blind, not the shifting of a chair.

Maltby rang a second time with a louder insistence.
From inside the room a shadow was cast upon the blind.
A man stood with the light behind him. Then he moved
somewhere to the back of the room so that no shadow
was any longer shown. Even then a few unnecessary
seconds passed before a door into the passage was opened
and steps approached. The front door was unlatched.
There was no light in the passage except the panel which
glowed from the open doorway. The young man had
withdrawn into the darkness behind it.

" My servants are away for the evening. Will you
kindly come to-morrow ? "

" Mr. George Crottle," said Maltby.

" I, too, have an appointment. I shall be obliged . . ."

" I am Superintendent Maltby. My business won't
wait," Maltby stated.

There followed a few seconds of silence.

" You will make it, please, as short as you can,"

George Crottle replied pleasantly. " Will you come in ? "

He led the way into a sitting-room, furnished with comfort and elegance. It was brightly lit and a writing-bureau from which the chair had been thrust back filled a corner of the room. Maltby was followed by Hanaud, Ricardo and Sergeant Hughes. Crottle, as he closed the door, saw two uniformed constables in the porch.

" Rather a large escort, Superintendent, haven't you ? " he said coolly. His face was pale, but his voice was composed, and the only sign of disturbance which he showed was that only now, for the first time, did he recognise Hanaud and Ricardo.

" Oh ! " he exclaimed, nodding at them with a smile ; and some wariness was now audible in his tones. " I had the pleasure of meeting you, I think, in Portman Square. Will you sit down ? "

Maltby, in a formal voice, cut across these politenesses.

" Mr. George Crottle, I must ask you some questions. You need not answer them unless you wish to. But I must warn you that if you do, your answers will be written down and may be used in evidence."

In fact, Sergeant Hughes had already a large notebook open and a pencil in his hand.

" You may sit down if you wish," Maltby continued.

" Of course," Crottle answered, but he remained standing.

" You are George Crottle, employed by your uncle, Mr. Septimus Crottle, in the service of the Dagger Line of steamships."

" No," cried George Crottle, and it was only now, when all was relaxed, that those present realised under how much tension George Crottle had preserved his calm. He had seemed at ease before, he was at ease now.

" No, no, Superintendent, that won't do. I am a

director and a partner. The old boy was in a fairly black rage when he turned up this afternoon and found that my stepbrother and myself had annexed his office. I thought that he would pay us out in some way. But, my word, it's pretty hot to suggest that I had anything to do with his disappearance."

George must have been either completely innocent of any share in the abduction of Septimus, or completely sure that the Barnishes were safe from the police.

" For I suppose that's what the patriarch has been doing ? " he added. And now he did sit down and took at random a small cigar from a box on a table at his side, pinched the end and reached out his left hand for a box of wooden matches lying on a sofa.

" No, sir," said Maltby solidly, " we have no charge from Mr. Septimus. I must ask you what you were doing on the night of Thursday, August the twenty-sixth ? "

George Crottle sat with the match-box still in his extended hand.

" August the twenty-sixth ? That's a long time ago, Superintendent. I can't remember off-hand. But there's a day-book on the desk in the corner which might tell us."

He pointed with the matches towards the bureau where he had been sitting. Maltby turned his head towards it, and during that glance George Crottle put the cigar between his teeth. Hughes found the book upon the flat surface of the bureau and flipped back the pages to the month of August.

" There is no entry on that date."

George Crottle shrugged his shoulders.

" It was the day before the steamship *Sheriff* sailed from Southampton," said Maltby.

Crottle frowned, looked at Maltby as though the answer were to be discovered in his face, and shook his head.

" No," he said between his teeth, " No."

Maltby took a step nearer to him and, taking his letter-case from his pocket-book, showed to Crottle an empty envelope sealed with a black seal, but slit open at the top.

" You know this envelope ? "

" I have never seen it."

" But you know the handwriting ? "

Crottle leaned back in his chair.

" Yes."

" It is Daniel Horbury's ? "

" Yes."

These monosyllables were uttered with a most convincing perplexity. He closed his hand over the matchbox and with a sly smile began to draw it to his chest. But whilst his hand was still moving, Maltby struck his arm with a swift and violent blow and snatched the matchbox from his hand.

" George Crottle," he said, " I arrest you for the murder of Daniel Horbury at his house of White Barn on the night of the twenty-sixth of August."

Mr. Ricardo felt the floor turning underneath him. He was prepared for George Crottle's arrest for the abduction of Septimus, or for conspiring with the Kapitän von Kluckner, but on a charge of murder, no. If, however, Mr. Ricardo did not know where he stood George Crottle certainly did. With a backward jerk of his head, he drew the whole length of that small cigar between his teeth. He crushed it with a snap of his jaws. A tiny tinkle of glass was heard, for a fraction of a second his face was convulsed with all the agony of the world and then he fell dead into the arms of Maltby and Hughes.

In Crottle's pocket was found a flat black silk cord with a slip-knot which ran very easily and smoothly ; and in a locked drawer of the bureau a manuscript.

Chapter 30

STRAWS IN THE WIND

THE manuscript which Maltby found locked in George Crottle's bureau offered a complete account of the crimes without a sign of remorse. On the other hand, it was very vain—youth's passionate cry for authority over age alternating with youth's despair at age's authority over youth. He had completed the inevitable drudgery which precedes mastery in either the arts or industry, to find himself in the end a cipher in a counting-house. Septimus Crottle should have handed over the Dagger Line years ago to nimbler wits and wider views. But he had not : and this is what had come of his obstinacy—a perpetual maddening threat which he was going to get rid of to-night.

" I go out to-night to play my last hand. If I succeed I shall destroy this manuscript, although its logic might hold a lesson for students and its narrative another for authors."

The statement cleared up those difficulties which Hanaud and Mr. Ricardo had been unable to resolve. But it contained disclosures which affected not merely the high prestige of the Dagger Line, but the policy of the Realm. It was, therefore, after earnest consideration, suppressed. George Crottle could not, after all, be brought to trial, the two Barnishes had disappeared, and, although Mrs. Horbury was amenable to the law for her secrecy, there was no certainty that the verdict would condemn her. An inquest was held in due course, at an early hour, and, coinciding with the proximity of a general election, provoked little attention. Maltby, however, had a copy of the manuscript and bade Hanaud and his friend to a luncheon on the next Sunday at his cottage at Thames Ditton. They were bidden to come early so that the manuscript might be read and finished with before luncheon. Hanaud was able to prolong his vacancy until Monday, and thus on a Sunday of early autumn the great Rolls Royce No. 1 rolled down to that pleasant village at eleven o'clock in the morning. Maltby, in his riverside cottage, was an amiable host, a trifle too fussy perhaps. He set out a great jug of ale and glasses on a tablecloth of pink and white squares, pulled up some comfortable chairs, invited his friends to take their seats, and took from a drawer a few typewritten sheets of paper taped into a blue cover.

" Will you read it, sir ? " he asked of Ricardo, and Ricardo responded instantly.

" Certainly not, my dear Maltby. The story is yours, and I want to listen to it."

There was a noticeable relief in Maltby's voice as he accepted the task and quickly drawing up a chair to the table he began to read :

" I was dipped. Horses which never won, women who always lost and cards which never dealt you a full house without giving to your neighbour four of a kind. I didn't know where to turn. There was only Septimus, and to confide in him meant humiliation which I was not prepared to endure, even if he were prepared—a thing I very much doubted—to overlook my ill-fortune.

This is some years ago now—the actual date isn't necessary. I was crossing the Green Park one lovely day of early June when a very young voice ordered me to stop. I obeyed at once. I was in the mood to find an omen in any occurrence, however trivial. My name was called, " George ! George ! " I looked round, only to be once more disappointed. The call had come out of the air, a clear bell full of promise. But there rose up from a seat my cousin Agatha.

" I want you to come with me," she cried in the breathless way she had—at all events when she talked with me.

I guessed a church or a picture gallery, but I had hardly the time to shake my head, when she added :

" To the Caledonian Market."

Could any proposal be more crazy ? Yet just for that reason more appealing. The Caledonian Market, where junk jostled treasures, or so they say. Of course, I would go, and the blood rushed into her face when she clutched my arm as I told her so. We stopped a taxi in the Mall and drove out past Smithfield. I was careful, you'll understand, not to ask Agatha the reason for her choice. Only fools analyse inspirations, wise men act on them. There might be something in those old Arabian stories.

" Suppose I found a bottle with a genius in it ! " I said, laughing heartily.

" Oh, dear, I wish you'd always be like this to me," she answered. Boring ? Yes, but Agatha did bore.

In the market it was junk, junk all the way, and imitations under my feet like mad. No doubt there were pieces of Ming under the Doulton, but there was no stoppered bottle from the dreams of Scheherazade, and I couldn't see the Ming. I was feeling deflated when, looking up from a job lot of culinary articles, I saw a man whom I knew, Herr Kapitän von Kluckner, the foreign Military Attaché. I should not probably have paid to him any attention had he not met my eyes with a frown of displeasure and changed his quick, purposeful step into the saunter of an idle foreigner, sneering at the oddities of London. I watched him curiously from a distance and was still more surprised to see him entering a barber's shop on the east side of the market.

" Now, what in the world induces the elegant Military

Attaché to come up to the Caledonian Market to get himself shaved ? " I asked, and Agatha, for once on the spot, pointed to the name above the shop, and said :

" Do you think that Mr. Straws alters his name and writes music in his spare time ? "

A week or so later I began to meet the Herr Kapitän here and there at luncheon or at dinner. I suppose that he had his spies poking their noses and their sharp ears into all sorts of places. Anyway, at one house where I had been losing a great deal of money, he took me aside for a drink and talked. It was absurd that there should be any enmity between the two countries. In fact, they could now help each other very considerably without compromising each other's independence. Each country stood primarily for itself—that was clear. But, apart from that clear principle, there were many smaller opportunities of mutual help. " For instance . . ." he began, and broke off as others approached us. He talked for a few minutes, and then said he must be off, for he had a busy day in front of him. " I must get myself shaved, too," he said with a laugh as he smoothed his chin, and away he went. He had made an appointment with me. That's what it came to. I had long since made up my mind that the barber's shop was a letter-box in which spies could post their letters. But it was more than that. It was a house of assignation, and I felt that it was a duty to discover what the Herr Kapitän was up to.

But he wouldn't know my motive and it was like his impertinence to expect me. A curtain covered the doorway of Mr. Straws's establishment. It led into a passage at the side of the shop, and a man was waiting in the passage. He marched off to the back of the house without a word and, in a room too mean and undistinguished for a design so vast, a proposal was made to me. The destruction of a race. The death of Egypt.

Not by shells or bombs or fire but by subtler weapons. Heroin, cocaine, hashish! Children would not be born, work would not be done, starvation would follow, and a decadent people would make place for the legions of the North.

I was dazzled. England would share, of course, and England, in contributing the Dagger Line, could pull an oar. It was a nightmare turned into an idea. It was colossal. It was a prairie fire with its rolling smoke, its roar and its crackle and its glare, eating up the dead dry grass. I walked out with a good fat cheque in my pocket and my head up.

It wasn't so difficult. We had freighters as well as passenger ships. I had served in both the South American and the Eastern trade, and knew the routine of the ports. We shipped a good deal of furniture, most of it sound, of course, but, betwixt and between, pieces which held a fortune. We had help, too. A consul would want a new consular outfit—not that he, good man, was ever aware of it. But the outfit would arrive all right in a fine big trunk and would be collected on the quay by a dragoman (of sorts) who could pass his stuff through the Customs without examination. Sometimes it was a case of books, which never reached the library of the Minister who didn't expect it. We picked the cargo up in our small freighters from surprising places. Sofia gave us—when I say gave, there was no giving in that trade— a good deal at ports in the east of Europe. But, of course, notes had to be written, commitments acknowledged, receipts sent. The trading bills were all Sir Garnet, of course. But, keeping pace with those bills, there were more intimate acknowledgments to be made. My Herr Kapitän saw to that.

I don't think that I was careless. There was once a letter which I wrote in Pevensey Crescent and which I thought that I had posted. I had a new servant just about then. There was another which was not received, a little too frank about some freight from Sofia which we were to pick up at Salonika. These two letters worried me a little, and I got rid of my servant, thinking that the carelessness was his. Until one morning a message came over the telephone from Horbury. It came to Pevensey Crescent. He said that he had two interesting documents upon which he would be honoured if I would give him my advice. I was alarmed. I didn't know Horbury, but I knew that blackmail was his business, and the fact that I was comfortably paying off my debts may well have attracted his attention. But I did know Olivia. I had met her at supper parties and at dances more than once. I couldn't believe that she had married that pigeon-toed old beetle for anything but his money. She was always easy to look at and she had moments of great beauty. I had nursed an idea that one day, when I had a bit more time, we might see a good deal more of one another. So I thought that it might be prudent if I probed her a little before I answered Daniel.

So I called on her in her ormulu flat in Park Lane that afternoon. As a rule with women I have been fairly astute. I have made my approaches with discretion and, on the whole, I have not been unfortunate. But this time I was out of breath, as it were, and I rushed my fences.

She was difficult. I stammered a few love passages and she supplied with a kindly smile the words for which, in my passion, I was supposed to be at a loss. Disconcerting! I gave her my private telephone number at the office and I told her that I gave it to very few. She wrote it down carefully in a little book, saying, " Harem, I suppose, is the operative word."

I asked her casually whether Daniel had spoken to her about me, and she replied " Oh, no," as if I were not

nearly grown up enough to interest Daniel. Then she
gave me a cup of China tea and a cucumber sandwich
and sent me away. I ought to have left in a rage, but
I felt like a cat. If you say " Puss, puss, puss, lovely
pussie," it just walks away, but if you pull its tail
and turn your back on it, it rubs itself against
your legs. I began, in fact, to ring her up on my
private line.

But I had, nevertheless, to make an appointment with
Daniel. He had the receipt and the details of the cargo
at Salonika, and there was no getting round them.
Horbury was formal and grave. As a legislator, he had
his duty to do. I must see that. He ought to send
these papers straight to the Public Prosecutor. But he
had no wish to be hard, and if he sent them to Septimus,
the harm would be stopped, and I should escape a long
term of penal servitude.

" Why not say a stretch ? " I inquired, foolishly
disdainful.

" Because a stretch is only a year, and I couldn't
promise you that," he answered.

" Boys will be boys," was his next line, " but happily
you can't sin without payment, or civilisation would be
down the drain." Oh, Daniel Horbury knew his stuff,
and I left his office a slave. What I got from Herr
Kapitän Peter I had to pay to Legislator Paul, and the
more the better. But that wasn't the worst of it . . ."

Here Maltby lifted his eyes from his manuscript.

" We can realise, without reading of it, the perpetual
terror which George Crottle endured. So I come at once
to his account of the Thursday night when he obeyed
Horbury's summons and paid his first visit to White
Barn."

Hanaud sat forward on the edge of his chair ; his
perplexities were to be resolved. Mr. Ricardo saw the
gulls swooping and wheeling over Battersea Bridge on

the sunlit morning when he drove out of London to Lordship Lane. Maltby turned over a couple of type-written pages of lamentations and resumed his tale.

Chapter 31

THE GRIM WORD

I DIDN'T intend murder. I had played with the grim word sometimes during the last months, no doubt ; and I had the blue-handled knife. I bought it a long time ago in Uraguay, and, being at the age when what you want to do you want to do one plus, I got proficient in throwing it. It had lain in an old box, but I got it out. Did you ever notice how many commons there are close to London with small woods on them where you can wander most of the day and never meet a soul ? I had reason to, for I acquired a greater proficiency than I had ever had. I could pin a strip of white paper round the trunk of a tree, walk away with my knife in its sheath within my breast pocket, turn, and it seemed that as I flashed my hand the white paper split and the knife was quivering in the bark. I carried it about with me always. But that was not because I definitely meant to use it, but because the possession of it, the sense of it against my ribs, made me feel less paltry.

Of course the idea must have been in my mind. I had, in fact, prepared a hidey-hole for myself in the West Country in case it should be necessary. But I had never formulated a time or a place or a definite point of the dialogue which I should reach before—before the collar of white paper split. Certainly I did not on this Thursday evening. For I took Preedy with me. Preedy was a smart, quick, sedulous small-job attorney who had been very useful in resisting claims when I was in trouble and in settling them when I was better off. I had managed, in return, to slip him into the company's affairs. A few small cases which he handled very well did his reputation a world of good. He was devoted to me, and I certainly should not have taken him to White Barn had I definitely meant to turn the grim word into fact. Indeed, he was so angry that I had allowed myself to be blackmailed without consulting him, that I seldom mentioned Horbury to him at all.

There's only one answer to the blackmailer—no answer. A lagging, like God's sunlight, hots it up for the blackmailer as well as the blackmailed, and the blackmailer knows it.

But this particular summons, made, of course, over the telephone to Pevensey Crescent, hinted at mutual benefits and a settlement. Preedy wanted to go first and look round before I came. We had neither of us visited White Barn before, but Horbury had given me the bearings so accurately that a mistake could hardly be made. Preedy arrived in his small car a few minutes after half-past nine. A small garage stood on the left-hand side of the house, but the door was locked and the little courtyard was empty. A light, however, was burning in the hall and Preedy, leaving his car on the right of the yard, rang the bell. The lock, he noticed, was of the Yale kind. A man who was undoubtedly, to Preedy's thinking, Horbury, opened the door and silently contemplated a stranger.

" This is Mr. Horbury's house ? " asked Preedy.

" But there's no fishing," said Daniel, and he began to close the door.

" George has not arrived ? " Preedy asked again quickly.

" No," said Horbury, " but we are expecting the Dragon

along at any moment," and he closed the door a little more.

" I am on the staff of the Dagger Line," Preedy hurried to explain, " and I am George Crottle's private solicitor."

For a moment Daniel Horbury was disturbed. Then his face cleared and split with a grin.

" Upon my word," he said heartily, " in George's place I should have brought my solicitor with me, too. Meanwhile, come in and meet the wife."

Mr. Alan Preedy looked and looked again, and drew a deep breath. Olivia laughed and blushed.

" I must apologise, Mrs. Horbury," said Preedy.

" For the most honest compliment I have ever received," and then Preedy says, to the surprise of them both, he lifted up a finger.

" Crottle's here," he said quietly, and with so much certainty that, after a moment of stupor, they began to peer into the corners of the room. Preedy smiled.

" He has just crossed the Turnpike Road into the Lane."

" Has he now ? " cried Horbury, suddenly, as he thought, tumbling to the joke. He listened and nodded. " He's wearing shoes with crêpe soles."

" He's driving an Austin twelve," Preedy corrected, and suddenly a small car drove into the courtyard and stopped.

" My word ! " said Horbury. He saw vistas of high service done for him by Alan Preedy. The man might hear the most valuable conversations from impossible distances. " You and I must have a talk, Mr. Preedy, one of these days," and, as if to emphasise the wish, the front-door bell rang sharply.

It was I who rang. The season was the season of full moon, and a silver light, daylight almost without its harshness, made the world suave and nearly kind. Preedy's car stood to the right of White Barn, and there

was room for me to park mine between his car and the
door.

Horbury came to the front door. He did not offer to
shake my hand, but his voice cooed: " Your first visit
to my refuge, Mr. Crottle ? You'll hope, no doubt, that
it will be the last." He opened a cupboard by the side
of the front door and I saw his light brown overcoat
hanging on a peg. " What, no overcoat ? You boys !
Your friend Preedy's just the same. Wish I could risk
it."

" So Preedy's before me ? " I said as I hung my hat
next to Horbury's overcoat.

" Yes, he's talking to Olivia in the garden-room."

I stood, a little startled.

" Mrs. Horbury is here, too ? "

Horbury nodded his head.

" She knows nothing of our little secret and there'll
be no necessity to go into details. But I'm no chauffeur,
and the fewer people who know of our meeting here, the
better. Olivia drove me down. Romantic, eh ? Back
to the old house in the suburbs ! We shall sleep here
to-night after you have gone. Just the two of us in
the empty house. Beautiful ! " And he reached up and
snapped the light off in the hall. Horbury's little speech
was steeped in malice and the grin on his face was impish.
He stood very still in the black hall, listening to me
breathing and no doubt savouring it with enjoyment.
Playing with fire ? No, but with a long, heavy, blue-
handled knife. No doubt it was very tempting.

" Might I hear what you have to say to me ? " I said
quietly. " The nut, after all, can't be expected to enjoy
the cracks of the crackers, even if they are wisecracks."

Horbury threw open the door of the lighted garden-
room.

" Beautiful, you know Mr. George Crottle, don't you,"
said Horbury with a chuckle. " Isn't it a disgrace to

me that you thought of this wonderful name for Olivia
before I did ? "

He knelt down by the fire and warmed his hands.

" Chilly, these nights," he said as he stood up again.

I didn't answer. On the floor, by the side of a table,
a small chart was pinned on a board. But I wasn't
curious about that. I saw Olivia come forward from
her corner. She was dressed in a black gown of satin
with a short coat of white ermine which, as the room
grew warm, she had thrown open. Against the background of fur, the slender white neck and throat rose
from the black gown, too slender, it seemed, for even
that small head with its heavy coronal of hair. She was
as delicate to the eye as china, rose-white, with the
velvet of the crimson rose upon her lips, a creature of
health and fire. And I hated her. So they've made a
joke of me ! Robbed me and laughed at me. A harle-
quin on a string—that's what I am ; and quite slowly
I slid my left hand down the breast of my jacket. The
comforting hard feel ! Beautiful ? Yes, she was at that
moment, with a look of concern upon her face and a
quest on in her eyes. Very likely she knew nothing of
this blackmailing business, knew only that I made love
to her and laughed at me for my pains. I think that
I began to hate her at that moment.

" You go over there, Beautiful," said Horbury, " and
smoke a cigarette whilst I have a word or two with
these gentlemen."

Olivia moved away to a cushioned chair at the corner
of the wall. Horbury invited me to a seat on the divan
and sat himself on a chair with its back to the wall and
with the little table in front of him with a blotting-book
upon it—a lady's blotting-book from a suburban drawing-
room. Buhl and mother-of-pearl. Preedy—you have
to take note of him, if you please—he found a chair with
arms like the chair at Horbury's table, a good chair of

Chinese Chippendale with a seat of crimson brocade,
and moved it a little so that he sat with his back to the
wall on the side of the fireplace opposite to Horbury.
Thus all three, Preedy, Horbury and Olivia, were sitting
in a parallel, facing the garden windows. I alone sat
with my back to them. Not that that mattered, for
the blinds were pulled down and the curtains drawn
across them. Horbury, Preedy and I, on the other hand,
made an isosceles triangle, of which I was the apex,
Preedy and Horbury the angles at the base.

Horbury then told us the story of Bryan Devisher,
which Preedy, with his lawyer's eye for facts, condensed
into a few sentences.

" There was a lady with a very rich husband in a very
big house in the Bayswater Road. She loved the graceful
Bryan, and he pinched her pearls, lovely pearls, milk
and moonlight. This, remember, was before the Japs
had taught the oyster their barbarous efficiency. He
sold the pearls to a French jeweller. I think he tried
the usual trick of substituting a lump of coal, but it
didn't work. Where the cash went, it is, perhaps, not
necessary to state.

" And how do you know all this ? " Horbury exclaimed,
startled.

" The lady who loved so unwisely brought her secrets
to me in the Gray's Inn Road," Preedy returned.

" And you advised her . . . ? "

" To make a clean breast of it to her husband." He
smiled idiotically. " A happy metaphor, what ? "

" You mean, you advised her to confess to her husband
that she had loved and been robbed ? "

" I did," said Preedy, and I blew a long whistle of
derision.

" I hope," he said with dignity, " that I should give
the same correct advice to erring wives on all occasions.
But I am bound to admit that there were special reasons

in this case. Devisher had been spirited away; and although strong suspicions pointed to certain people, there wasn't actual evidence."

" And she took your advice? " I asked.

" She did. There was the usual uproar. The police were called in. The husband was going to have a divorce, a resonant, shattering divorce. Wasn't he just? Then it died down. The pearls came back, you see. The French jeweller had to give them up, since that's the law. Then the husband recollected that he had run out of the course once or twice himself and that he wanted to get into Parliament and reckoned that it wouldn't help to let the electors see what his wife thought of him. Finally came an evening when he had a good dinner, and a successful game of bridge, when his wife looked her best in her prettiest frock, and we ring down the curtain on a domestic scene."

" And what has all this to do with me? " I cried.

" Wait, sir, if you please," said Preedy, and then, " Ah! " as Horbury stooped and picked up the chart from the floor.

Horbury glanced again at Alan Preedy in surprise.

" Then you know of this, too? " he asked, tapping the ebony board.

" Yes."

" How? "

" Hanaud, the French detective, called on me at five-thirty this afternoon. He came straight from Victoria Station. But continue, please! My friend's impatient."

Daniel Horbury described the journey of *El Rey*. " I marked on this chart, from Lloyd's reports, the harbours at which the ship discharged its undesirables. It signalled Prawle Point at six this morning and will discharge her English batch at Gravesend to-morrow morning. One of that batch is Bryan Devisher."

He stood up and, laying the flat of his left hand upon

the blotting-book as if he needed its support, took from the mantelshelf a thin little dark blue book. When he sat down again he was aware of a change in the room, a tension, a greater depth in the silence. He looked sharply towards me and saw that my eyes were fixed with more than a little concern upon Preedy. He had been sitting up straight and fairly stiff against the wall, but was now stiffer than ever and withdrawn into some solitude of his own. His face was shuttered, his eyes blank, he gave me the impression of some lonely lighted house in the country which has suddenly gone black at the distant wail of a warning.

" You weren't listening to me ? " cried Horbury roughly.

He obviously liked to be listened to, as a Member of Parliament should be. Preedy's eyes—I can't say opened—for they were open before, but they lived again and a smile took the severity from his face and deepened the wrinkles at the corners of his mouth.

" Believe me, I was listening," said Preedy. " You are proposing a deal, I think ? "

Horbury leaned back in his chair.

" You are quick, Mr. Preedy."

" We have to be in the Gray's Inn Road," Preedy retorted. " You want a cabin."

" Yes."

" On the Dagger Line."

" Yes."

" For Bryan Devisher ? "

" As soon as can be."

" Whither ? "

" I don't mind as long as it's far away and there's a job for him at the end of it," said Horbury.

" On the Company's staff ? "

" That would be desirable," said Daniel Horbury.

" And what do you offer in return ? "

Horbury's replies had been thought out, but they were no quicker than Preedy's questions, which came rattling on the answers like the sharp bursts of a machine-gun. Horbury relaxed now, smiling contentedly.

" Ah ! There we are ! " he said.

" Are we ? "

" To be sure."

Daniel had no doubts. If there was no eagerness in Preedy's face, there was enough of it in mine.

" I propose that a couple of letters which, if I had strictly regarded my duty to my country, I should have sent to the Public Prosecutor, but which I have addressed to Mr. Septimus Crottle, should be handed over for delivery to Mr. George Crottle."

I interrupted here with a good deal too much fervour to please my solicitor Preedy.

" We have a ship, the *Sheriff*, sailing from Southampton at five o'clock to-morrow afternoon. We have a cabin or two free. One of the firm usually goes to Southampton to see the firm's ship off and it's my turn to-morrow."

No doubt I was a little too ready to agree. I was indeed ready to invite the unknown Devisher to travel in my car to Southampton, when Preedy objected :

" Even so, he'll want a new passport, won't he ? "

Daniel Horbury handed him the small blue book. Preedy turned it over and opened it.

" The photograph was taken more than six years ago," agreed Horbury.

" When you sent him gun-running to Venezuela," Preedy replied. He turned to the page with the photograph and nodded his head.

" Yes, I expect that that will get him on board, especially if he motors with you."

He gave me a nod and a smile. There was, after all,

very little which got by Alan Preedy. But he had, nevertheless, not done with his difficulties.

" But will he go ? There's no case against him. The pearls are back, the wife and husband reconciled."

" But he doesn't know that," said Horbury. " Besides, the Frenchman's here, you said."

" Yes."

" Acting for Gravot of the Place Vendôme."

Again Preedy grinned at Horbury.

" I see you know the name all right. Curious, isn't it ? "

But Horbury was not the sort of man to be offended by a little sarcasm. He didn't even blush, and Preedy continued.

" Hanaud says Gravot has cooled down, too. He doesn't want any extradition. He wants his cash back."

" But Devisher doesn't know that either. Besides, he probably hasn't got a farthing, and a pleasant cruise on a tip-top liner with a comfortable easy job at the end of it—not too bad," Horbury explained anxiously. " Further," and he looked down at the table and added with a hard note in his voice, " he's obnoxious to me."

Preedy laughed.

" Obnoxious is an excellent word. A dandy of a word. All right ! When you hand over to me the letter to Septimus Crottle. . . ."

" On the quay-side."

" I see."

Preedy tucked the passport away in his pocket.

" You'll go down by yourself ? "

" Yes."

" Then I'll go in George's car and hand over the passport to Devisher as you hand the letter to George."

Horbury beamed. " Good ! " he cried. He sprang up

from his chair and, still supporting himself with the flat of his left hand, took a cigar from the mantelshelf and bit off the end.

"The ship is the *Sheriff*," I said, and I gave the number of the quay at which she berthed.

Horbury took a pen from his waistcoat pocket, lifted a tiny corner of the blotting-book and wrote the name *Sheriff* upon it. Then he put the pen away in his pocket, lit the cigar and blew a ring of smoke into the air.

"There!" he said, a man conscious of a rather virtuous day's work. "Now it's all Sir Garnet."

I suppose that since I have already used it, I got that old phrase from him. Anyway, he folded his fat arms across his chest and concentrated on blowing exactly rounded rings of smoke into the air. I expect that he was wondering why we didn't get up from our chairs, say "Until to-morrow, by the *Sheriff*," and take our leave. I was wondering that, too, but, after all, if you bring a solicitor with you, you're a mug if you don't use him. I watched Preedy. He sat stiff and still against the wall and looked as if he didn't mean to move until the Day of Judgment. He was puzzled, too, and annoyed. Finally he seemed to flare up.

"What I don't understand, Mr. Horbury, is why all the flummery? Why all the pretence? Surely we can fix everything now and have done with it?"

"My dear fellow!" cried Horbury. "My dear fellow!" and even to me, Preedy at that moment seemed a daunting figure. He sat up so inhumanly straight, he spoke with so impersonal a tone, he gazed with so unwinking a stare across the room. One of the gods or kings from the Old Nile come back to sit in judgment.

"My dear fellow, I wouldn't of course bring those letters here, no, not I"; and the way in which he held tightly pressed against each other the covers of his blotting-book proved to me that there was a good deal more than the word ' *Sheriff* ' between the leaves.

I couldn't help wondering for a moment whether, for all his effectiveness, I had been wise to bring Preedy. If Horbury and I had been alone, those infernal letters might already have been in the fire and an order for a cabin on the *Sheriff* in Horbury's pocket. But we were two men against one, and the rules of the game which we were playing excluded neither violence nor any kind of treachery.

" They are safely locked away where they can't be found," he exclaimed with a slobbering sort of laugh, and Preedy cut in across his words very quietly now.

" I wasn't thinking of your bits of paper," he said.

He moved at last. It was curiously startling to see. His head turned round until he faced Horbury and he asked, with the annoyance most people feel when they see someone complicating a perfectly simple question :

" Why on earth don't you let him in ? "

In reply to Horbury's look of bewilderment, he stretched out an arm with his forefinger pointed towards the curtained windows across the room. Even then no one except Olivia at once understood. She had been sitting not far away, forgotten in the urgency of our deal, but alert to each step of it and to the three characters who were conducting it. She rose from her chair and turned towards us. Was there something protective in her attitude ? In her mere rising from her chair ? Something which cleared the fog from Daniel's brain ? His eyes followed the line of Preedy's arm, straight as a bar to the finger's end.

" Let who in ? "

" Devisher."

Horbury tried to scoff. " Rubbish ! " he cried, and laughed, but the laugh was more of a sob of anxiety than a laugh. " Devisher is at this moment tumbling

up and down in an old iron ship off Beachy Head ";
and then in an appeal for confirmation, " Isn't that
true ? "

Preedy's answer came at once, not to be denied ; and
the very gentleness of his voice made it more than ever
implacable.

" I have heard the footsteps of a man for the last half-
hour. I could almost draw a n ap of your garden from
the sound of them."

No other words could have so affected Horbury. They
were the drops in the laboratory phial which change in
a second the red to blue. Terror swept over him. He
saw a panther slinking, padding his garden paths, waiting for the guests to go—Devisher. It was one thing
to send an agent to Gravesend who would promise com-
pensation, claim *El Rey's* passenger as his friend, wrap
him in the favour of a Member of Parliament and bring
him along to King Street, St. James's, in broad daylight.
It was quite another thing to find him hiding in this
quiet garden for a solitary interview with him in an
empty house. Horbury uttered a little screech and his
face turned yellow. The whole casing of the man col-
lapsed, his small mouth dropped open—it looked horrid,
obscene, and his eyes could not turn from the curtains.
There was no doubt why he was afraid. He had sent
Devisher out of the country and then betrayed him to
that soft-hearted man, the Dictator of Venezuela. He
had imagined himself free of him until the Judgment
Day : and here he was in the moonlit garden of White
Barn, with six years of the Castillo del Libertador behind
him. I had never seen so much fear made visible. And
I enjoyed it ! My word, how I enjoyed it !

" You are afraid, Mr. Daniel Horbury," I said with a
chuckle of pleasure. " You don't mind facing a body
of shareholders thirsting for your blood. A mellifluous
voice and silky-smooth words, and they want to give

you what you've left them. But one man with a nasty account to settle, waiting in a lonely garden—that's quite a different affair."

And quietly, just as quietly as Preedy talked, Olivia came across the room to Horbury's side.

"Hold your tongue," she said to me.

Why couldn't she stay in her corner? It wasn't her business we were discussing. She had been told to stay there. But he was throwing out his left hand to her and she took it and held it and willed him to resistance.

"Well, if he is here—I don't see how he can be—yes, we had better get him in," he quavered, "whilst we're all together. Then, when we've settled everything, Mr. Preedy, perhaps, will take him back to town."

Nobody said a word. Nobody doubted that somehow, translated from the moonlit Channel, Devisher was waiting in the moonlit garden. Olivia put an end to the tension. She uttered a little cry of revolt.

"I can't bear it!"

Preedy's arm fell straight to his side—a decision given and not to be gainsaid. Olivia moved—did she ever walk?—across the room to the curtains.

"Let us make quite sure first," Horbury quavered.

"You must put out the lights, then."

"Oh, no," Horbury wailed, but no one took any notice of him at all.

There was but the one switch to control all the lights in the room, although, here and there, the walls were plugged for standard lamps, and that switch was at the side of the door into the hall. I stood up and, after turning round, walked to the door. It was set in the wall at a right-angle to the garden wall. I turned. Preedy still sat stiff against his wall like the effigy of a god. Horbury had been smoking a cigar when the warning of Devisher's presence had stunned him. The cigar had fallen from his mouth and bounced upon the table. He had put it into his mouth again and, just in order to do something, was drawing upon it, though only the tiniest grey spirals of vapour curled up from an edge and the end was as black as that ebony board on which the chart was fixed.

Olivia stood by the curtains.

" Wait ! The fire," she said.

" It is out," I answered, but the grate was obscured from me by the back of the divan.

" Then go ! " Olivia ordered, and I turned down the switch. But I had been wrong about the fire. As the darkness fell, one of the logs sent forth a little spurt of flame which strengthened into a flickering blaze and gleamed upon the white ceiling and sparkled in every polished panel in the room. I heard a small gasp of relief from Horbury—how he was petrified by this ordeal ! —and though I took no stock of it, I noticed that the spiral of smoke from his black cigar was a trifle heavier.

The log moved in the grate, the spurt of flame died altogether, the fire was out and the last glimpse of Daniel Horbury was gone.

" Now," Olivia whispered.

Without letting one ring rattle upon the pole, she drew the curtains apart so that one panel of the long glass door was exposed from the lintel to the ground. A thin curtain of brown linen hung over it and the moon made of it a sheet of silver and dappled the floor about its edges with pools of silver, but left the hollow of the room black with the depth of a Rembrandt.

Except for the shadows of some boughs of the oak trees in the meadow beyond the garden, the screen was blank. Yet so completely had Preedy taken the mastery of our minds that no one holding his breath in the darkness of the room doubted that he had only to wait in order to see it occupied.

One could not see or hear Olivia move, but a sharp click rang like a pistol shot through the darkness. She had unlocked the glass door. Again one could not see or hear Olivia move, but I know now that without touching chair or table she slipped back to her seat in the corner of the room. I remained by the light switch at the angle, and suddenly a figure was on the blind, to me at all events it looked gigantic and grotesque. Daniel Horbury yelped—there is no other word for the sharp, queer cry of pain which broke from him. But the figure advanced and the nearer it came, the less formidably supernatural it became. It was now no more than a huge man, clumsy but dangerous still, for it lurched this way and that, a night bird scouting for a victim. And now, as he advanced yet nearer, he was slender as a youth and his twistings mere hesitation and timidity. He wore a felt hat and, since his back was towards the moon, it was impossible to distinguish his features. As if he were tired of waiting for the cars in the court-yard to take their departure, he came forward on tiptoe across a gravel path and laid his ear against the glass pane of the door. Satisfied, apparently, that the room was empty, he tried the handle and the glass door swung open at his touch. He stepped over the threshold silently and easily into—of course—an empty room.

" Who's there ? "

This wasn't the challenge of the buccaneer. His voice was a whisper, his question an appeal.

" Devisher ! " cried Horbury.

No one answered him. But Bryan Devisher had not spent six years in the dungeons of the Castillo del Libertador for nothing. He knew his mistake as soon as he had made it. There were others in the room besides Horbury. He sprang to one side out of that picture frame of moonlight.

" This is a trap, what ? "

And, by the most wondrous luck, Horbury's cigar glowed red. He had puffed and drawn the black thing into life, unaware of what he was doing. Devisher flung the curtains across the glass door. There was no caution about the rings on the pole this time. They rattled like all the clogs on the French market stones. His voice changed to anger.

" A trap ! " he repeated.

Oh, it was Devisher—and my great moment. Never did I deserve it. He dashed for the door, close at my side, stopped, searched for the handle, breathing hard. And precisely then, with one movement, as I had been taught, I tore the knife from its sheath and flung it. It sped true, true, true, with a hiss. For the fraction of a second I saw it by the light of Horbury's cigar curve down and inwards and take him by the throat. I heard a horrible gurgle, a heavy fall of a heavy body upon the table, a jet like a fountain bursting, and a burning cigar described a circle in the air. But I had my own work to do. Devisher was dragging and scuffling at the door. He had forgotten, in his absence of more than six years, the height of the handle from the ground and whether the door opened inwards or outwards. I grappled with him, the blood surging in every vein. I was free from the old rogue with the lovely voice and the silky-smooth words and the cruelty of a cat.

" No, you don't ! " I cried. " You don't get away like that ! No, sir ! "

But I found the handle for him none the less, and tore open the door. He had shaken me off and flung himself through the doorway in a trice. I didn't make it very difficult for him. He was as panic-stricken as old dead Demosthenes Junior had been, but he kept his wits and, once he was out in the hall, he slammed the door hard and locked us all in. In the sudden silence, drop—drop—drop, measured like the drops from a medicine bottle, pattered on the floor. Olivia's voice rose in a scream.

" Lights ! Lights ! Lights ! "

Never did Hamlet's uncle call for them so eagerly. I turned the switch and the room sprang to light.

Preedy stooped, picked up a burning cigar from the mat and tossed it into the fire. So far as I remember, that was the third movement he had made during that evening.

Chapter 32

COUNTERPLOTS

OLIVIA was near to the centre of the room when the lights were turned on. Horbury's gross body had fallen forward over the blotting-book and the table, but in his panic he had drawn its legs so tightly to him as a defence that he was wedged in his chair. His head was turned towards me, so that she could not see the wound at his throat. But the pool of blood upon the floor and the blue-handled knife amongst it could have left her in no doubt of his death. She did not touch him but she covered her face with her hands, and then, taking them away, said in a pitiful quiet voice :

" Daniel ! Oh, Daniel ! "

I was hurt by her appeal. You may think that unimportant, but I was. It sounded as if a child were complaining of some injustice and asking for it to be explained to her ; and explained by the one man who would never explain anything any more—not even to an assembly of shareholders in the Cannon Street Hotel who wanted to know where their dividends had gone to. Did I utter some sort of cry? I don't know, but I felt that her face turned suddenly towards me. In a fluster I rattled the handle of the door.

"He has locked us in."

As I spoke I heard the whirr of an engine starting. And a car turned to the left out of the courtyard and raced down to the Turnpike Road, the noise of the engine dwindling as it went.

"He has locked us all in together," she said, and it seemed to me that a cruel, bitter little smile quivered for a second on her lips. "There has been murder done. We must ring up the police."

She was walking back towards the telephone on the long table close to the corner in which she had been sitting, when once more Preedy took charge.

"Wait, please, Mrs. Horbury!"

Olivia stopped and turned.

"Why? There has been murder done."

Again she looked straight at me. Did she know? Yes, but by nothing she had seen or heard. Perhaps her soul had claimed the truth from me and mine had been forced to answer. My secret was hers, too, I felt quite sure, and fortunately Preedy was there to stand between us.

"Murder, if you will," he said clearly. "He has stolen one of our cars, Crottle's or mine." There was a look of bewilderment in Olivia's eyes. "This man, Devisher, Bryan Devisher," Preedy explained. "But he can't get far. If you telephone now, he may very likely be caught within the hour. And then, of course, nothing could save him. He had suffered damnably—I am sorry to say it here and now—at Horbury's hands. If ever a man had a motive to take the law into his hands, Bryan Devisher had."

"Bryan Devisher?" she repeated thoughtfully.

" He has come straight from South America. I suppose that he had planned somehow to arrive a day before his time. He waits in the garden of a house he knew, no doubt well, in olden days, until he thinks the coast is clear. He uses a South American way of adjusting his wrongs and, as you said, locks us all in together and bolts."

" Bryan Devisher ? " Olivia repeated. When she used the name before she had been bewildered. Now she was realising how exactly he fitted the niche which was being built for him—Bryan Devisher. Murderer.

" Yes, no doubt he can be caught, tried, hanged. It is as you will."

Olivia looked at Preedy. She transferred her thoughts to him. He was now the antagonist, not I.

" You see," he went on, speaking reasonably, " Crottle and I are here. We are the witnesses. We saw Horbury in a panic. We saw Devisher come into the room with the moonlight behind him. We heard the swish of the knife, the struggle of George Crottle to arrest him, the slamming of the door, and the key turned in the lock."

How could she fight all this evidence ? But she stood where she was, giving no ground.

" But why were we here ? " he resumed. " George Crottle and Preedy, his lawyer. What were we doing at White Barn on this night ? We shall be asked. And we shall have to answer."

" What will you answer ? "

The question was stubborn and resentful. It matched her white, still face, the upright defiance of her stance.

" The truth," answered Preedy. " We were blackmailed. The wickedest crime in the Calendar of Justice. Worse than murder, judges say. More cruel, more "— and his voice dropped a little out of consideration for her, but lost none of its determination—" more mean."

Her head flashed up in revolt against the word and dropped again.

" If it's not murder, then, what is it ? " she asked.

" Suicide."

It was a hard choice and Preedy left it so. The decision must be hers. She stood and shifted a foot, following the pattern of the carpet whilst she made it. She might accuse me, of course. I could see the thought in her mind as she lifted a rebellious face towards me. But, if I had planned murder, should I have brought my lawyer with me to see it done ? Devisher was so much the more obvious criminal and usually the obvious criminal is the right criminal. Moreover, she wouldn't want the wrong man to go to the scaffold and she wouldn't want to listen to a true story of blackmail by Daniel and the judge's comments upon it. She suddenly sat down upon a chair as though her knees failed her.

" He was very good to me," she said in a whisper, her head bowed, her hands clasped together. And the battle was over.

" We must have the door unlocked," said Preedy briskly. " Perhaps Mrs. Horbury will do it, since you have a key."

Olivia looked blank until Preedy pointed out that she would have to go round by the garden and let herself in at the front door.

" Oh, yes."

She fetched her handbag from the chair in the corner and took from it a bunch of keys. She thrust the curtain aside and the moonlit garden seemed to be waiting for her.

" There was once a tree spoiling all the prospect," she said with a little break in her voice. " Oh, not a beech tree, but just a negligible Scotch fir, and I had it cut down, so that the eyes travel without fatigue across the lawn to a sunk fence and beyond that over the long meadow to the Turnpike Road. I had a curious sense of freedom when the tree had gone."

She stood looking out and behind her the blood from Horbury's throat which had splashed upon the table began again to slip from its polished surface. Again it fell slowly and horribly, one and one and one. The sound seemed to hush all the world so that it might be heard the better. Olivia's face was twisted with pain. She turned and flung the words at Preedy.

"Do you hear? You with the quick ears? Doesn't each drop cry aloud for vengeance?"

"I'm thinking of the cost of vengeance," he replied, "to all of us. To you. And even to him."

Olivia turned back to the window. I think that she saw Horbury alive and in the dock, sentenced. For she whispered, more to herself than to either of us: "Day after endless day. The vision—this——" and she reached out her hand towards the meadows and the trees, "narrowing with each year until it vanished."

She spoke as if you could punish a dead body. Then she did the last thing I wanted her to do. She took the key of the door from the small ring of keys which she held. She offered it, shining in the palm of her hand, to Preedy.

"One of you. I stay with my man."

There was a gleam of admiration of her in Preedy's eyes, and when he bowed to her, as he did, it was, I think, as much to conceal a little smile of defeat as to acknowledge her words with respect.

"You, George," he said to me, and Olivia turned her hand above an occasional table. As she walked away from it towards her dead husband's side, the key tinkled on the mahogany surface.

I took it, went out by the garden door and round by a little path to the front of the house. I noticed that it was my small car, the one nearest to the front door, which Devisher had taken. Then I let myself in. But I didn't immediately return to the garden-room. One Yale latch-key is like another, and I had in my pocket one which fitted the drawer of my desk. I compared the pair by the hall lamp, but it would not do to exchange them. Olivia's key was marked by three deep scratches at intervals, mine had no clues to ownership at all. I put my own key back in my pocket. The cupboard door stood open. My hat hung on a peg next to Horbury's coat. I took the sheath of the knife from my coat breast pocket and, after wiping it clean, put it into the pocket of Horbury's coat. On unlocking the door of the garden-room I saw Preedy busily polishing the furniture frames and the tables.

" You sat at the corner of that divan all the time," he said to me. " Yes."

He began to enumerate the places where fingerprints might have been found of others besides Horbury and Olivia—the garden-door and the door into the hall for instance.

" There's the outside of the door into the hall," he said. " Devisher will have left the palm of his hand upon the panels."

" Yes."

I had a picture of Devisher slamming the door and locking us in. I turned towards it, and Olivia said :

" You will leave my key, please."

I dropped her latchkey on the same table which she had used. Polishing the outer panels with the door half open, I saw her identify her key and replace it on its ring. I drew a breath of relief that I had not tried to substitute a key of my own for hers.

" There, I think that will do. Now it remains—a

rather gruesome business, I am afraid—to make a tableau which the police can reconstruct in the morning."

Olivia drew back with a shiver.

" Oh, no ! "

" Must ! " cried Preedy, and for the first time roughly. " It's getting late. We can't go on advancing and retreating. We are not dancing the Lancers." .

He approached her impatiently, almost threateningly. I suppose that from the other side I closed in upon her. For she looked at me sharply and then back again at the set and quiet features of Preedy. Quiet they were, but there was now a menace in the room, a chill.

" There have been pacts, haven't there ? " said Preedy.

" Pacts ? "

She was really bewildered.

" Don't ask me to take you for a fool. You understand well enough. Pacts. The coroners' courts are full of them."

Her eyes opened wide. She looked at Preedy. She looked at me. I think that we must both by now have been standing quite close to her.

" Suicide pacts," she said with a little falter in her voice. But she didn't move, not a foot, not a hand. I don't think it would have been lucky for her if she had. We were all three as motionless as effigies. All three might move as sedately or as violently as the plot demanded, but not one alone. No, indeed. But I believed, I still believe, that if she had been absolutely certain that I and not the innocent Devisher would be convicted of the murder, she would have taken her risks of us and let Horbury's blackmailing be exposed. But she had no such certainty. Whatever she might say, the evidence pointed to Devisher and not to me.

" Then that's settled," said Preedy. " We all three have the same secret to hide. Will you bring the little table—yes, the one from which you took your key, and set it between the corner of the divan and—well, here ? "

He pointed to Horbury.

" Now, please sit on the divan, your hand perhaps on the end so as to leave your prints."

He then asked her where the champagne, the famous Pommery '06, was kept. He left us together, and I can't remember a period more embarrassing. But, in truth, he worked quickly. He came back with two goblets of thin glass which Horbury affected. One was half full, and that he placed on the occasional table by Olivia. The other he set on the table over which Horbury lay. There was just room for it. He had a cloth in his hand and he wiped away from the glasses all traces of his own handling of them.

" Will you touch that with your fingers and your lips," he said, pointing to the half-filled glass in front of her. But she nodded to the glass on Horbury's table.

" That one first."

Preedy handed it to her and she drank it with a little nod and a small wistful smile towards the horror sprawled over the table. She drank it to the last drop, partly as a tribute to a good many pleasant hours spent with her ogre at White Barn, partly because she was as near exhaustion as a woman well could be. A little colour rose into her face as she handed back the empty glass to him. Preedy balanced it once more on the table, and then with a push toppled it off on to the ground, where the thin glass smashed into splinters.

" We were sitting here ? " she asked.

" Yes."

" Just the pair of us ? "

" Yes. Then you left him and went up to bed."

" And fell asleep ? "

" Yes. You heard nothing until your servant screamed in the morning."

" And I waked," she said sardonically, and so paused and shivered, " to find the door unlocked ? "

She thought upon the endless hours of darkness during which she must lie and listen, and perhaps hear that dead man struggling to rise from the table. Where she had shivered, she now shuddered so that her teeth rattled.

" What if the vigil—for that it must be—persuaded no one ? " she asked.

Preedy set out his argument. Men like Horbury had always troubles which were secret. He had weathered storms, no doubt, but men lose heart at the last. " And so, sitting up here alone at night, and, if things were well with him, perhaps thinking that he was, after all, doing his best for you, he sought this way out. There is one more thing to be done, alas ! "

On the floor, amidst the congealing blood, lay the long, thin-bladed knife with its gay blue handle. Preedy knelt, took his handkerchief from his pocket, and stooped.

" No ! "

The cry broke from Olivia Horbury passionately. Her eyes were ablaze, her arm stretched out with a pointing finger as steady as justice itself. Preedy sat back on his heels.

" His fingers held that knife ! "

That one fact swept all the arguments for our decision out of her mind.

" Yes," answered Preedy.

" His fingers were the last to hold it."

" Yes."

" The murderer's."

Proof was there lying in that red pool—proof which would hang.

" Yes."

I expostulated. Who knew but that some unlucky chance might send us a visitor who would know us again—a stranger asking his way, a motorist who had run short of petrol, a neighbour with sickness in the house whose telephone was under repair. Preedy waited with his eyes on Olivia.

"There must be other ways by which guilt comes home," she said. "Let me, please, do what must be done."

She knelt in Preedy's place. He handed her a clean handkerchief and, taking up the heavy knife by its blade delicately from the congealing blood in which it lay, she wiped the handle. Then, lifting it to Horbury's out-thrown hand, she placed it in his palm and closed his fingers about it. She opened them again. It needed now some effort, but she made it and, still holding it by the blade under the handkerchief, she replaced it exactly where it had lain.

"That is all?"

"Yes. We can go."

"Wait!"

She rose to her feet and with such a look of horror upon her face as neither of us had ever seen. She tore the curtain aside from the glass door and passed into the garden. Heaven knows what her thoughts were, but they did not hold her long. Long enough, however, to give me the chance of which I had begun to despair. A steel chain ran from Horbury's waist into his trouser pocket and the pocket gaped. At the end of the chain a ring of keys hung by a spring hook. I had the time to release the ring from the spring hook, replace the chain and thrust the keys into my pocket, when the garden door was slammed fast and locked. Olivia came back into the room and drew the curtains again so carefully that not a fold was disarranged, not a thread of light shone out upon the lawn.

I took up the ebony board with the chart pinned upon it. Preedy was looking about the room, touching a chair here and there with his handkerchief.

"We ought to have left the prints of the woman who cleans the room," he said, "but we couldn't." He turned to me. "You turned on the lights."

"Yes."

He dusted the switch with the white handkerchief and I noticed that a faint blue stain had been left upon the cambric by the handle of the knife.

"You will leave the lights on, of course," he said to Olivia who was following us. In the hall she latched the door and locked it. Preedy stopped at once.

"I am afraid not," he said gently. "In the morning the door must be found unlocked."

Olivia bowed her head and unlocked it. Then she held open the front door of the house. A small breath of wind was rustling amongst the boughs of the trees.

"There was much that was sordid—worse, if you will —in my husband's life," said Olivia. "You were right. I would not wish his story to be known to the world, just so that a man called Devisher might be hanged. No!" and she added, after a pause, "there would have to be a much better reason than that." Though her voice was low, her eyes were fierce, her face quite haggard and all its beauty gone. "Yes, a much stronger reason."

And upon the two men who listened to her a sense of new danger rolled like a tide.

Chapter 33

GEORGE RETURNS

WE rolled Preedy's car out on to the road, although there was really no reason for such secrecy. Preedy was in an excellent mood, one moment whistling a tune, another assuring me in answer to some anxious question, that it was all Sir Garnet. Certainly he was correct in one particular. The problem of Devisher was solved.

We found my car outside the gardens of Pevensey Crescent and Devisher inside it. He knew the truth and, at the same time, his own danger. He wanted no trouble any more. He had already endured his lifetime's share and, knowing as much as he did, he applied with some confidence for the opportunity of an easy life in some quiet corner of the world. This took place over a whisky-and-soda in my parlour.

" What about Cairo ? " I asked a little too promptly to please Preedy.

" All that has got to stop," he said. " I am going up to the Caledonian Market myself to see about it."

" But there are cargoes arranged and some on the way."

" They will be the last," said Preedy, and he looked at Devisher. " Well, for the moment, Cairo. Then what about Ceylon, where every prospect pleases ? They tell me that as you approach that island a delightful aroma of spices floats out to you across the sea."

" Either place will be A.1 for me," Devisher agreed with relief.

It was arranged there and then. I was not expected

at the office the next morning. I was to start in my car with Devisher at half-past eight. There would be traffic already on the roads and I must never exceed the speed limit or in any way attract attention. I was to drive to Southampton through Camberley and Hartley Row. At Basingstoke and Winchester I was to buy some ready-made clothes, shirts, flannels, underclothes and shoes. Devisher would have his new passport. Since I was well-known to the dock officials, there would be no trouble at the gates. I was to make him out a ticket in the Southampton office of the Line and see him off with the ship. I had the resident staff part of the Line under my control and could arrange by a telegram for his arrival at Port Said to be expected. Then Preedy took him away for the night.

Preedy was equally confident that I should have no trouble with Olivia. She wouldn't move for her dead husband's sake. But, although I had not argued, I had not agreed. The *amitié amoureuse*, which was all I was going to allow her with Daniel, would in time wear off. And then ? I could not but remember the bitterness of her last words. They had frightened Preedy.

I had, however, already taken Horbury's keys from his pocket and I meant to use them that night. I remembered that whenever Horbury had risen from his chair, he had kept a solid hand upon his blotting-book, and that when he had written in it the name of the ship *Sheriff*, he had lifted the stiff cover only just enough to use a corner of the blotting-paper. That precious letter to Septimus was between the covers of buhl and mother-of-pearl. Horbury had brought it to White Barn, had meant to hand it over, but I suppose lost his confidence in us at the last minute. I meant to get it before the police did. I don't think that Preedy had noticed me lifting Horbury's keys. He had been too busy polishing away fingerprints and I hadn't consulted him. This, the last achievement of the night, I proposed to carry out alone.

Instead of backing the car into the little garage at the side of my house, I drove it away to Battersea Bridge. I would keep within the speed-limit all the way to Southampton, but there was no reason why I should follow that good advice to-night. Night, I say, but it was half-past two in the morning when I left the car under the trees at the side of the road. A risk? Yes, but I had to take it. The choice lay between driving into the courtyard and very likely arousing Olivia's attention, or leaving the car beyond the reach of her ears. The chances of a policeman discovering it were about fifty-fifty.

There was no one whom I could see or hear. The moon was still bright and the world asleep. I crept up to the house and let myself in with Horbury's key, taking the bunch with me as soon as the hall door was open. I fixed up the latch so that I could get away quickly if it became necessary and I stood still for a few moments in the black hall, listening, until the silence itself began to roar in my ears. I moved like a ghost to the garden-room door and noiselessly turned the handle with my fingers wrapped in my handkerchief. The lights were burning. Horbury was sprawled across his table ; but there was a change in the room since last I had seen it—a change which caught me by the heart and stopped the blood in my veins. The blotting-book was on its edges on the floor now instead of lying flat under the weight of Horbury's body.

As soon as I recovered my breath, I crossed the room on tiptoe and stooped over it. It stood half-open, the back uppermost. There was no letter under it, none between the leaves. No danger from the woman upstairs ! Oh, wasn't there ? She had come back to this room when she was alone. She had pushed the blotting-book from under Horbury's body. I could hear the buttons of his waistcoat scratching across the metal cover. She had taken the letter to Septimus out of it and then she had toppled it on to the edge of the congealing blood on the floor. What a damnable woman ! I was wondering what I should do when the telephone rang on the long table against the wall. It wasn't possible ! I stood up stiff as a tombstone. No, it wasn't possible ! Who should be ringing up White Barn at half-past two in the morning ? The Love-Nest ? No ! But there the bell was, one, two, pause, one, two, pause. It had got to be stopped. It wasn't until I lifted the receiver from its cradle that I realised that I had acknowledged the call. Someone was in the house then, more, was in the room where a man had committed suicide three to four hours before and where he still lay sprawled across the table. I heard a voice calling Horbury. It seemed to come out of my hand. I looked down and saw that my hand was bare. I was not going to answer the call—not I ! The noise of ringing had ceased—that was one good thing. I took my handkerchief from my breast-pocket with my left hand and carefully wiped the handle between the ear and the mouthpiece. Then I replaced it on its cradle. The sound was not renewed at all events. The caller had ceased to call.

I rubbed the sweat off my forehead. I was streaming with it. I was thinking that, whatever happened, never in all my life could I be so startled again. And the next moment the thought was disproved. The last horror of that night capped all. Somewhere, above my head, a key was turned in a lock and someone fell. I didn't stay after that. I tossed Horbury's ring of keys on to the table by the instrument. Then I fled. Oh, yes, even in my panic, I pulled to the door of the garden-room and opened the front-door of the house with my handkerchief about my hand. I did it without reflecting, for I was incapable of reflection. I ran down the lane. It was still deserted. To put the proper finish on the night, I should have found that some thief had run away with my car. But, beyond expectation, it was there where I had left it. I drove back to London. My word, the lighted streets! I eased the car very gently into its garage and went to bed.

Mistakes, of course, were made. Preedy made one on this night. He cleaned the garden-room of fingerprints so thoroughly that the absence of them became suspicious. I don't see how that could have been helped, however, and I don't count that as his mistake. Where he really went wrong was in the matter of a bottle of Pommery '06. He opened it in the pantry without leaving marks on it, but, having filled two glasses, he stoppered the bottle again and put it back amongst the others. There is not very much to be said for Daniel Horbury, but he never opened a bottle of Pommery '06 without making sure that the very last drop was going to be squeezed out of it.

I, however, erred more completely. I should never have taken Horbury's keys from his pocket and returned to White Barn. I should never have taken up the telephone receiver from its cradle. I should have snapped Daniel's ring of keys once more upon his spring lock. But all these errors are nothing compared with the folly I was guilty of in letting myself go when old Septimus broke down over the captivity of the young Dauphin. It is said that I sighed! I let out a great big 'O' of delight. For the first time I had found a weak spot in the chain-mail of the old boy's authority. My hide-out became a prison. The Barnishes wouldn't be sorry to have Captain Septimus under their charge for a little. Captain Septimus had sacked Fred Barnish at five minutes' notice. A few weeks of Arkwright's Farm for

Septimus and I saw myself Chairman and Managing-Director of the Dagger Line. And then all's spoilt because a copper walks into the farm because he suspects that Barnish is keeping a dog without having a dog licence ! Well, I ask you !

However, even so, I might perhaps have got through but for the idiot Ricardo and the preposterous Nosey-Parker from Paris.

* * * *

Maltby was caught off his guard by the final sentence. He had meant to leave it out altogether, but discovered himself floundering amongst the opening words. He was then forced to read it without the omission of a word. Mr. Ricardo flushed with shame, but Hanaud jabbed him in the ribs with his elbow.

" Without Mr. Ricardo," he cried, " where should I be ? Like the good George, I ask you. I should still be driving over the Bridge of Battersea amongst the seagulls. As for mistakes, it is possible that once or twice in my life I make one," he said dreamily. " I do not know."

Chapter 34

THE LAST

AT luncheon the conversation was desultory, but a few additions were made, chiefly by Maltby, to complete the pattern of the story. For instance, certain changes were taking place in the staff of a foreign Embassy and a barber's shop on the edge of the Caledonian Market had been closed down. The presence of Mordaunt, as an officer in the Egyptian Coastguard Service, had caused one more upheaval to the unfortunate Bryan Devisher. He had been moved on, overnight, as it were, to Delagoa Bay, where a small trade had been carried on by the Dagger Line. He was now dismissed from that service altogether and was working as book-keeper in a Portuguese store. It would be for the Egyptian Government to ask for his extradition if it thought it worth while, but it probably would not.

" And now," said Maltby, " there is one question which we all wish to ask, Monsieur Hanaud."

Luncheon was over. Coffee smoked upon the table and a cigar, a pipe, a cigarette smoked in the air, dimming the bright aspect of the Thames.

Monsieur Hanaud beamed.

" Ask ! " he answered with simplicity.

" Where was the Crottle letter hidden ? "

" And how did you find out ? "

The questions were fired at him from right and left.

" It was not so difficult to find out, but it was amusing all the same. Maltby, with Bryan Devisher and the Dagger Line and the Caledonian Market all on his shoulders at once, he leaves that little problem to me. Listen ! The letter was in the blotting-book. Horbury had come to make a bargain. It was not in nature that he should not have with him his evidence that there was a bargain to be made. That was clear the next day when in the secret drawer in Horbury's office the letter was no longer to be found. But I was sure of it in the morning. I could not see how, in falling forward, Horbury had pushed that book with its heavy cover off the table. It seemed to me to have been worked from under him by someone else. The book was empty.` Who, then, had the letter ? Someone had come back for it. Someone who heard the telephone ring hours after Horbury was dead ? Had he found it ? I thought not. I thought that the lady who faced us in the dining-room would have had the courage to secure that weapon for herself as soon as she was left alone. Well, then, where was it ? The police went through the house with a toothbrush. . . ."

" Comb," said Mr. Ricardo.

" As I said," Hanaud continued imperturbably, " and they did not find it. Therefore it was not in the house. But it was near."

" In Olivia Horbury's handbag," Ricardo suggested.

" Not safe enough," replied Maltby.

" And too bulky for her dress," Hanaud corroborated. " So I smoke a cigarette and I reflect. The garden ?— with a gardener one day a week, that's what it looked like. Yes ? "

" Yes," said Ricardo ; and Maltby, looking out on his own patch of carefully tended flowers, nodded vigorously.

" But there was a fine thing in that garden which was tended with all the loving care it merited."

" The holly hedge," cried Maltby.

" Yes. It stood twenty feet high. It was clipped. It was smooth as a yew hedge. I wondered. Then, when I called on that kind lady for the money for my patient Gravot of the Place Vendôme, I praise the fine hedge and her face lights up. Always in the old days, when they were poor, she had clipped it on a ladder and looked after it herself, and still trusted it to no one. Then, a little quickly, she adds that it required little attention now. ' Once a year. I clipped it in the autumn,' and, rather red in the face, she wished me good morning. So I have it ! Carefully wrapped in waterproof rubber, it is, when it is advisable to hide it, hidden in the hedge. Then I make pictures. It will be high, yes. We will need the ladder. It will not be at the end near the road. No, no. Then I get from Maltby a description of her bedroom. There are two windows opening on to meadows and one window opposite the holly hedge. I do not need to seek more. On a level with the window, whence it could just be seen, thrust into the hedge out of reach."

At this moment, Monsieur Hanaud looked at his watch and leaped to his feet.

" My dear friends, I have to fly. I have promised to say good-bye to a young lady at the boat train on the Victoria Station at five o'clock."

" Oh, you Frenchmen ! Ha ! ha ! " roared Maltby, shaking with delight.

" No, no ! " replied Hanaud, catching up his hat and his gloves and his stick. " The days of the wink and the gay twinkle in the eyes are past for me. I say good-bye in all respect to a lady who returns to her duties in Cairo as the secretary of a famous archæologist."

" Oh ! " cried Ricardo, to whom this announcement was news. " Mrs. Rosalind Leete."

" Mrs. Leete," Hanaud agreed with a smile. " It is pleasant to see the young so devoted to such serious topics as Neferti and the mummies of dead kings. But I do not think that her duties will be prolonged."

" And how is that ? " asked Maltby, who had no liking for allusions.

" I gather from a word dropped here and there that the excellent Mordaunt will be on the quay at Port Said."

Mordaunt and Rosalind ! Yes, you have got to have it, you know. . . . Well, perhaps you needn't. We can more suitably complete the pattern of this story with the few words which passed between the two unlikely friends the next morning at the corner house and Hanaud's departure for the Continent.

For the end of the holiday so often postponed had really come. At two o'clock in the afternoon, Hanaud was to take the train to Folkestone. Meanwhile, over his cigarette after breakfast, he looked backwards to the morning at the end of August when, with seagulls swooping over the river, he had driven with Ricardo across Battersea Bridge.

" Until you told me the story of Devisher's rescue, I was ready to accept the theory of Horbury's suicide. But that made a difference, eh ? Here was a man, free as any stranger in London, with as black a score against Horbury as a man could have. Also he knew White Barn as Horbury's home. Someone was at White Barn unexpectedly that night. Otherwise all the usual, natural fingerprints wouldn't have been removed. Someone was too anxious. But, if Devisher had broken in and exacted his revenge, what was he doing in the house three and a half to four hours after he had committed his murder ? And why did Olivia Horbury protect him ? "

Ricardo nodded his head very wisely.

" So I began to wonder whether there was not, besides Devisher, someone else in the garden-room. And I was puzzled by that word ' *Sheriff* ' written on the corner of the blotting-pad. Yes, I was very puzzled. Could there perhaps be something else which explained Mrs. Horbury's silence, the lifting of the telephone receiver, the locked door, the *Sheriff*, everything ? "

" That afternoon Septimus Crottle swung into the picture," said Ricardo.

" The name of Crottle brought Maltby to help us. Why was it that this man without money, without friends, Bryan Devisher, could not be found ? Because, on Friday afternoon, the steamship *Sheriff* of the Dagger Line sailed with a last-minute passenger whom George Crottle had motored that morning to Southampton. The beautiful routine work, my friend, of the British police ! "

Hanaud and Mr. Ricardo said good-bye a few hours

later on the platform at Victoria Station, Mr. Ricardo all friendship and regret, Monsieur Hanaud a little lost, as though he had forgotten something important to remember. But, as the whistle blew and the train started, his face cleared. He stood in the doorway of the coach, beaming.

" You are quite yourself, eh ? " cried the anxious Ricardo.

Hanaud nodded. He had remembered. He laughed. He answered :

" I am all Sir Garnet."